HOLD ME

BY ANNA SAVAS

New England School of Ballet

Hold Me
Stay Here
Shine Bright
Move On

NEW ENGLAND SCHOOL OF BALLET

hold me

A NOVEL

ANNA SAVAS

TRANSLATED BY
KATE NORTHROP

LYX

An imprint of Authors Equity

Authors Equity
1123 Broadway, Suite 1008
New York, New York 10010

Cover design © Vivien Summer
Cover art from Shutterstock (© Maria Hamaniuk; © T-Shirt Empire; © MHD NUR AZIS; © SarraMagdalina; © EVKA; © Kaimen) and iStock (© SongSpeckels)
Book design by Scribe Inc.

First published in Germany in 2023 by LYX, an imprint of Bastei Lübbe AG
First published in the United States in 2026 by LYX, an imprint of Authors Equity

Library of Congress Control Number: 2025948389
Print ISBN 9798893311266
Ebook ISBN 9798893311273

Printed in Canada
First printing

www.lyxbooks.com
www.authorsequity.com

This book contains potentially triggering content. For that reason, you will find a trigger warning on page 437.

Disclaimer: The content warning includes spoilers for the entire book!

We wish you the best possible reading experience.

Love,
Anna & LYX

For Katharina
Thanks for everything

PLAYLIST

I Didn't Ask for This—Beth Crowley
Ghost of You—5 Seconds of Summer
IN THREES—As It Is, Set It Off, and JordyPurp
Without You—7ru7h and Promoting Sounds
I Need You to Hate Me (Piano Version)—JC Stewart
Safe & Sound—Hayd
Trauma—NF
Wrecked—Imagine Dragons
Chaos—Stateside
Pieces of You—Nothing, Nowhere
@ my worst—blackbear
I GUESS I'M IN LOVE—Clinton Kane
don't fall—44phantom
HALF HEARTED—We Three
Like That—Bea Miller
Let It Go—Chandler Leighton
When You Say My Name—Chandler Leighton
You and I—PVRIS
dying on the inside (stripped)—Nessa Barrett
twin flame—mgk
Take My Hand—5 Seconds of Summer
Brother (Acoustic)—Kodaline
The Last Time—Taylor Swift and Gary Lightbody

PROLOGUE
Zoe

It all starts with a game. I'm with my friends at our high school spring formal, and at first it's the perfect evening.

That is, until my best friend Charlotte sweeps into the ballroom two hours late with a radiant smile on her face. She looks drop-dead gorgeous, but then, she *always* does. She's absolutely perfect.

"Hey, I have to tell you guys something!" she squeals, reaching first for my hand, then Amber's, and pulling us onto the dance floor. I'm too surprised to pull away. I just let it happen.

Scarlett is watching us, rolling her eyes. She's the quietest of our group. It's not that she's shy; she just doesn't have a very high opinion of most people. Sometimes I think she's only hanging out with us because of Amber. The two of them have been best friends since kindergarten. They've known each other for as long as Charlotte and I have.

"What's going on?" I ask, trying to ignore the queasy feeling that's growing fast in my stomach. Charlotte is never late. Not without a reason. And she always tells us everything immediately. The fact that she just arrived and didn't text any of us about her news ahead of time can't be a sign of anything good.

Her smile grows even wider as she dramatically tosses her shiny black hair, which falls over her shoulders like a silky curtain. "My mom went out to dinner with Monsieur Duval tonight, and guess what? I get to dance the role of Aurora in *The Sleeping Beauty*!" She squeals again, the sound shrill enough to be easily heard over the music. I want to cover my ears, but I can't move. I'd give anything at this moment to be able to block out the sound of her voice.

I get to dance the role of Aurora.

My stomach turns. This can't be true. It can't.

"Oh my God, that's awesome!" Amber's eyes go wide, and she throws her arms around Charlotte.

I, on the other hand, stand frozen and watch in disbelief as Scarlett also hugs Charlotte, smiling. I can see their lips moving, but I don't understand what they're saying. I try desperately to hold back the bitter tears threatening to overflow.

That was my role. The role I've been working toward for years. Ever since I started ballet, I've dreamed of playing Aurora.

And I got it. Up until a few hours ago, I *was* Aurora. Monsieur Duval gave the part to me. He told me last week that I was going to dance the lead in *The Sleeping Beauty*.

How could this happen?

I know there's a simple answer: Charlotte's mother is involved. She would never go out to dinner with our ballet teacher if there weren't something to be gained for Charlotte. Ever since Charlotte's dad became the mayor of Boston, she and her older sister, Adaline, have gotten whatever they wanted.

A rush of sharp disappointment floods my brain. I never would have believed that Monsieur Duval could be manipulated like that. Not after he constantly drilled into us how important talent, discipline, and sacrifice are for our careers.

"Zoe?" Charlotte reaches for my hand, and it's only when her fingers wrap around mine, warm and a little too tightly, that I realize I'm cold as ice.

I look up to see her smiling, a flash of sympathy in her blue eyes.

Not real.

Nothing about Charlotte is real. Not her sympathy, not her smile, not her friendship. This is the first time I've been completely aware of that, though there have been signs for a long time. I've just ignored them, stubbornly repressing what my intuition told me. I didn't want to know. But now, ignoring them has become impossible. I can see it all.

"You're not mad at me, are you? I know you wanted the role too. But we both know that you're not ready yet, don't we?" She blinks at me innocently, and I have a strong urge to slap the faux-pitying expression off her face and shred her pale blue dress that matches her eyes so perfectly. I didn't just *want* the role. I already *had* it. I was chosen. Not her.

She stole it from me.

Because she couldn't stand not being in the spotlight. Because she can never stand anyone being better than her.

Her betrayal hurts. It hurts so much that it's hard to breathe. For a moment, I'm gasping for air and get the feeling that I'm about to lose my composure and just start screaming at her. And maybe I should. Just let it all out.

"Come on, Zoe, tell me you're not mad at me," Charlotte pleads. She begins to pout.

I know what I should do. I should tell her to stick the role up her ass, and our friendship with it. I know that I should man up and tell her what I think of her.

But of course, I don't. I've known Charlotte my whole life,

and she, Amber, and Scarlett are my only friends. It's crystal clear to me what will happen if I don't say what she wants to hear from me right now.

I'll become an outcast, ending this school year and starting the next one without any friends. Finding new ones as a senior will be impossible, and Charlotte will make my life hell. As opposed to now, when she at least pretends that we're friends. In her eyes, maybe we *are* friends—as long as she gets what she wants, and I stay safely where I belong. In her shadow.

"I'm not mad," I say, almost choking on the lie. Something inside me breaks. Maybe my heart. Or my dream of making it to the big stage. I feel it and hear the shattering sound so clearly that I wonder why no one else does. "You deserve it."

If you can't imagine any other way to get the role than to have your mother buy it for you, maybe you really do *deserve it.*

"I really do, don't I?" Charlotte says, beaming at me. My eyes burn with unshed tears. She continues her chatter, but I don't understand a word: My ears are blocked by an awful buzzing sensation. My heart races, and my breathing becomes too fast and shallow.

I have to get out of here. I murmur an excuse, something about going to the ladies' room, but my friends don't react at all. Amber and Scarlett are totally focused on Charlotte. I can suddenly see so clearly how our world revolves around her. It's enough to make me sick.

I walk away on shaky legs, staggering across the dance floor in my high heels and looking around hectically for my brother. I've got to find him so I can get out of here. Go home, where no one can watch me fall apart.

But I don't see Caleb anywhere, even though I know he's still here. He would never leave without telling me and making sure I had a way home.

At some point, I stop caring and give up on trying to find him. Tears pour down my face as I lurch out of the ballroom and rush outside. I'm greeted by a wall of pouring rain, but the last thing I want to do is go back in there and get my coat. It would be just my luck to run into Charlotte again.

No thanks, I can really do without that.

I angrily scrub the tears off my cheeks. They feel too hot on my cold skin and mix with the heavy raindrops that are falling from the dark sky as I hurry home.

It's not far, only fifteen minutes. But I'm soaked to the skin anyway when I finally reach the wrought-iron gate to our yard, which opens with a soft squeak. The houses on Beacon Hill may be big, but the yards are almost nonexistent. Ours is just big enough for my mother's beloved terrace and a small patch of grass where two beech trees are growing. Dad built a treehouse for Caleb and me in those trees years ago. I've always loved it, even more so since Caleb decided he was too cool for it.

Since then, the treehouse has been mine alone. It's my own personal haven, my hiding place.

A light is still on in the living room, and I slip out of my high heels and tiptoe as silently as I can through the garden. While it's unlikely that my parents will hear me, I don't want them to catch me climbing the ladder to the treehouse instead of going inside to bed. Then they would want to know what happened, and I don't want to talk about it.

I'm shivering when I finally crawl inside, my dress sopping wet.

It's no wonder, since I did just run through the March rain without a coat, like a living cliché.

Swearing quietly, I feel for the switch of the battery-powered fairy lights, and a moment later the warm light of countless tiny bulbs floods the treehouse. I pull the sticky, wet dress off my cold skin and reach for the old Harvard sweatshirt that I keep up here. It belonged to my dad; I rescued it months ago from the Goodwill box. Mom tends to get rid of anything that we can't save in time.

I sigh with relief as I cuddle up in the cozy hoodie, which is so big it reaches my knees. The material is soft, and it's coming apart at the seams, but that doesn't bother me. I collapse onto the cushions that almost completely cover the floor, pull two wool blankets over my legs, and reach for my notebook.

My racing pulse finally slows as I open it and gaze at the empty pages. Pages just waiting to be filled with my thoughts and pain. As I set pen to paper, I hear a familiar voice that makes me start with shock.

"What are you doing here, Pixie? Aren't you supposed to be at the dance?" Jase is standing at the door to the treehouse and doesn't seem to care one bit that he's just as wet as I am. Rain drips from his messy blond hair onto his shoulders, and for the thousandth time, I notice how beautiful he is.

More beautiful than an eighteen-year-old should be. Plenty of boys his age could be described as cute, maybe hot. Not beautiful. But with Jase, *beautiful* is the only word for it.

"How many times do I have to tell you not to call me that?" I say sharply, without answering his question. I hope he doesn't notice my face turning red, or that I've clearly been crying.

He grins. "Until I fall down dead someday from your constant complaining." He leans casually against the doorframe. The door hasn't closed properly behind him, and I can hear the rain, but I don't tell him to shut it. The sound is peaceful, different somehow from the sound of the drops that rattle on the roof.

"Then I should probably try a little harder," I tease, only just managing to hold back a smile. He thinks that I hate the nickname he gave me, and at the beginning I might have. Over the last four years, though, it's grown on me. Not that I would ever admit it. Jase is Caleb's best friend, and they spend so much time together that sometimes it feels like he's moved in with us.

He laughs softly, and my heart skips a beat. Jase doesn't laugh often, and it's nice to hear it.

"Maybe," he replies with a grin as he steps into the treehouse. The door closes behind him with a barely audible click, and all at once the room feels too small. He takes another step and kneels down in front of me on the floor so I'm looking directly into his eyes. They're much too green. "So what are you doing here?"

"It doesn't matter," I say with a sigh, plucking a wet strand of hair off my forehead as my thoughts wander back to Charlotte. For a few seconds, I almost forgot I left the party because of her.

Jase just tilts his head and looks at me. He's staring so intently that it makes my skin tingle. Then he takes the notebook and pen out of my hand, tears out a page, and puts it on the floor. He sits down with one leg stretched out in front of him, the other bent.

"What are you doing?" I ask suspiciously as the pen scratches across the paper.

Without saying a word, he hands me the piece of paper.

What happened?

I raise my eyebrows. "What are you doing?" I repeat, my question still unanswered.

He smiles and shrugs, holding the pen out to me. "Answer the question."

Part of me wants to push him out of the treehouse, crumple the paper up into a ball, and throw it out after him. But there's another part that's curious about where this all will lead. So I take the pen out of his hand and do what he asked. I answer the question.

Charlotte stole the leading role in The Sleeping Beauty from me, and I hate her for it. I really hate her. But I know that tomorrow I'll pretend I don't care. That makes me hate myself even more.

I really don't know why I trust him. Maybe I just want to find out if he's making fun of me. Maybe it doesn't matter anyway.

He reads what I wrote, folds up the note, and puts it in the inside pocket of his jacket. But before I can ask him what he's doing again, he points to the notebook. "It's your turn."

I hesitate for a moment and then put aside my doubts. The paper rustles softly as I tear my own sheet out of the notebook, write down my question, and hand it to him. He scans the question, then scribbles a quick answer on the paper and gives it back to me.

Why are you here?

I was bored.

I stare at his answer incredulously. He's here because he was *bored*? I'm about to ask him more, but I bite back the question and follow his example. I fold the note and stick it under the pillow I'm sitting on. Then I give him one of my blankets.

"Here. So you don't catch your death."

"You know you're just giving me the chance to keep calling you Pixie for years, don't you?"

I roll my eyes, but I have to smile. "If you don't want it . . ." I start to pull the blanket back, but Jase is faster.

He grabs the thick wool, slips out of his wet jacket, and wraps the blanket around his shoulders. Then he holds out his hand for the notebook. I don't hesitate to give it to him.

Questions are followed by answers. We don't speak another word to each other that night, making a silent pact that an answer must not lead to deeper questions on the same subject.

Two days later, I find a crumpled piece of paper in the treehouse. The handwriting is messy and already familiar.

Tell me your secrets and I'll tell you mine.
—J

That's how our game begins.

We play by rules that neither of us ever talks about, and we each play our own way.

I leave notes in the treehouse whenever something is on my mind. It doesn't matter what it's about. If I need to get it off my chest, I write it down. Jase, on the other hand, needs to be asked questions. I don't know why, and I never press him about it. But I learn quickly that if I don't ask him questions, nothing comes back. No note, no secrets, nothing at all.

It's like he wants to confide in me, but at the same time something is holding him back. Like maybe without my questions, he would lock everything up inside.

Jase keeps my secrets, and I keep his. Until I change the rules three months later.

Kiss me tonight.
—P

PART 1

Entrée

Phase One of the Pas de Deux

CHAPTER 1
Zoe

Why do you get along with your parents so well?

Because they let me be who I am. It's not that they let me get away with everything, but they let me make my own mistakes. And I know that they're always there for me, no matter what.
—P

"Zoe! Where the heck are you?" Caleb shouts through the house. In my mind's eye, I can almost see him standing on the first step of the stairs with an annoyed expression on his face, glancing every two seconds at his phone to check the time.

"I'm coming!"

"You do realize this is your first day of college, don't you?"

"Right," I say, rolling my eyes. It's my first day—not at college, but at the New England School of Ballet. But those are just details that Caleb is apparently not interested in. Whatever; there's still no reason for him to stress me out.

"You're going to be late!"

"Caleb, stop shouting!" I yell back, pushing a strand of auburn hair off my forehead. Rushing me has never made me ready to leave any faster. Usually, it makes me take longer. "I'll be right there!"

His loud groan makes me smile. I look around my room one last time, taking in the white furniture, the cream-colored bed linens, and the fluffy carpet. My desk was already moved during the summer, along with all my schoolbooks. Everything else, including my clothes, ballet gear, and all the odds and ends I need for my new room, was packed in four huge suitcases a few days ago.

I started packing a week ago, accompanied by the constant feeling that I would surely forget something if I didn't start soon enough. Now I know I shouldn't have worried about it. I've packed almost everything I own.

An entire life in four suitcases.

I pick up my backpack and leave my room. I stop again in the doorway and run my hand over the numbers that Mom scratched into the wood to mark my height whenever I had a growth spurt. A wave of homesickness hits me, even though I haven't left yet. It feels like a goodbye, even though it's only a short one. I can always come home. After all, I'm not even leaving the city. I'm just moving to the next neighborhood over. It's only about a twenty-minute drive. But I still have a lump in my throat, and my eyes start to burn.

Before I can get too sentimental, Caleb calls me again.

"I'm coming!" I shout for the third time. I walk into the hall and down the stairs.

My parents and brother are waiting by the front door for me. Caleb is sitting on one of my suitcases, holding his phone as usual. His dark hair, which is like Dad's, falls in messy curls over his forehead. He looks up when he hears me coming and sighs dramatically.

"Finally!"

"Caleb, leave her alone," Mom scolds. But her smile reveals that she's not very serious about it.

"Yeah, Caleb, leave me alone," I say with a provoking grin. "You don't have to come if it's taking too long for you."

Caleb stands up, and the suitcase he was just sitting on tips over and lands with a thud on the floor. I wince and bite my lip. I hope it isn't the suitcase the fairy lights are in.

"But then I would miss the chance to yell at you, and I can't pass that up." He grabs me and messes up my hair. I try to get away, but he's faster.

"God, Caleb, how old are you?" I pull out the hairband and make a new braid.

"Older than you, anyway," he says, laughing. "Let's go." He grabs the first suitcase. Dad, who's been watching the scene with a look of amusement, takes suitcases numbers two and three and follows my brother to the door.

Mom pushes me gently toward the door as she picks up the last suitcase.

A few minutes later, everything is in the back of Dad's oversized SUV, and Caleb and I slide into the back seat while Mom and Dad get into the front.

"You really don't all have to come," I assure them in a futile attempt to talk them out of it. I'm probably going to be the only student there with her entire family.

"Yes, we do," Mom and Dad say in unison.

Mom turns in her seat to look at me, and her green eyes have the telltale gleam of tears in them.

"We're just so proud of you."

I feel the heat of embarrassment rising in my cheeks and open my mouth to say something, but Caleb grabs my hand and squeezes it. "Leave it," he whispers. "Her baby is moving out today."

I want to tell him that it's nonsense, but I know what he means. I see the proud look in Mom's eyes, and I close my mouth.

"Who would have thought that you'd come so far?" She smiles broadly, and the corners of her eyes crinkle.

"Me!" Dad interjects without taking his eyes off the road.

"Thanks, Dad."

He winks at me conspiratorially in the rearview mirror. His eyes are just as warm and brown as Caleb's.

"That's not how I meant it," Mom protests. "I always believed in you, dear, you know that. But I'll always remember when I brought you to your first ballet lesson. You were so small and awkward, and now you're so . . . you're so beautiful and talented, and now you're going to one of the best ballet schools in the country. It's just so—" Mom stops and wipes a tear off her cheek. The last time I saw her this moved was when Caleb graduated from high school.

"Oh, Mom, don't cry." I lean forward and put a hand on her shoulder.

"Yeah, Mom, you aren't wearing waterproof mascara today," Caleb says, and I give him a look that could kill.

"Not helpful," I hiss at him, but Mom laughs, and Caleb grins triumphantly.

"I'm always helpful."

"Above all, you're always annoying," I retort, even though we both know that I'm not serious. Caleb is my big brother, and sometimes he really is annoying, but mostly he's my best friend.

"Love you too, little sis." Caleb tugs gently on my braid, and I resign myself to the fact that, apparently, tidy hair isn't an option today.

Sighing, I pull the hairband out. I don't make another attempt to tame my locks. Instead, I reach for my backpack to make sure I really packed everything, just to be safe. But before I can peek inside, Caleb grabs it and stuffs it onto the floor next to his feet, ignoring my protests.

"You packed everything," he says. "You don't need to check a thousand times. You already did that this morning after breakfast."

"Let me look anyway," I beg him, because I really need to convince myself that everything's there. I reach for the backpack, but Caleb shoves it out of my reach with his foot. "Come on, Caleb! Please. What if I forgot something important?"

"You're the biggest perfectionist I know. You didn't forget anything."

He's probably right, but what if I did?

"Besides, even if you did forget something, one of us could bring it to you, or you can come get it yourself," he says, unmoved, as though he can read my mind.

"At least check if I packed my ring binder. All the papers I need are in there."

Caleb gives in with a sigh. He opens the backpack and closes it again a second later, assuring me he sees the gray ring binder I received along with my acceptance letter a few weeks ago. I sigh with relief and sink back into the seat.

It still feels strange to realize that I was actually accepted. Unreal. Like a dream.

Like *my* dream.

And it came true.

I've been dreaming of going to the New England School of Ballet since it first occurred to me that dancing could be more than a hobby. Ballet is everything for me. I want to go all the way to the top. I want to be on the big stage. With my acceptance, I got a giant step closer.

* * *

Caleb whistles, impressed, as Dad parks the car in the lot right in front of the campus.

"Are you sure we're in the right place? This doesn't look like a ballet school."

"Crazy, right?" My heart leaps with excitement. I don't need Caleb's confirmation. It *is* crazy.

Caleb and Dad lift my suitcases out of the back, and then we cross the parking lot and walk toward the wrought-iron gate that's set in the high sandstone walls surrounding the campus.

A huge smile spreads over my face as we pass under the archway, where the name of the school is emblazoned in unadorned letters.

It's so beautiful here. Right in front of us, in the middle of the campus, is the centerpiece: the theater, with broad, inviting stairs, reminiscent of the ones in front of the Metropolitan Museum of Art in New York. Smaller, but no less impressive. The other buildings are centered around the theater. The little administration building is right behind the theater, between the classroom building where the theory courses are taught and the dance studio complex, where there are not only more than a dozen studios but also a gym, a swimming pool, and a sauna. Two dormitories sit on either side of the theater: one for the young students who are finishing their high school diplomas and the other for the older students. All the buildings are made of sandstone in the Victorian style that the posh Back Bay neighborhood is famous for. Behind the buildings, a wide green lawn stretches all the way to the wall.

All over the campus, crowds of students greet one another cheerfully after the summer vacation. Some of them are accompanied by their parents, especially the younger ones. But most of them are on their own.

"Where do we have to go?" Dad asks, looking over his shoulder at me questioningly. I point to the administration building.

"I have to get my room key," I say.

When I was accepted to the New England School of Ballet, I got a package that contained a gray sweatshirt with the school's coat of arms and the gray ring binder. In the binder was all the information I needed to get settled: my schedule; my program for the first week, including appointments with a physical therapist and a nutritionist; a map of the campus; and a list of all the rules, especially about drugs and alcohol. There was a short section about dress code and a much longer one about eating disorders.

The whole first day is planned out in detail. Between ten and three, new students can register, pick up their keys, and move into their rooms. At four, the principal will hold a welcome speech in the theater, and then there's a community dinner for everyone to get to know one another.

"Zoe, we'll wait outside for you. Is that okay?" Dad's voice shakes me out of my reverie, startling me. He, Mom, and Caleb stop in front of the administration building as I start to climb the stone steps.

"Sure. See you in a minute." I don't wait for them to answer; I just go up the steps and slip into the entryway.

Inside, it's surprisingly cool and quiet. All I can hear in the huge room with the high ceiling is the quiet murmuring of voices. I walk straight toward a reception desk. In front of the giant windows, through which I can see the back of the theater building, there's a cozy lounge area with two sofas, round tables, and a few armchairs. Warm sunlight casts shadows on the dark parquet floor and the high walls and on paintings of dancers in various poses.

Boys and girls are standing in separate groups, some with their parents and others without. Most of them look to be around my age. A few of them are glued to their phones, and others are talking to each other.

I get in line for the reception desk behind two girls, and ten minutes later I leave the building with my key.

"Did everything work?" Mom asks, shielding her eyes from the sun with her hand as I walk up to her.

"We have to go over there." I point to the dormitory before I fall in next to Caleb, who's busy with his phone, as usual.

I wait until Mom and Dad are a few steps ahead before I point at his phone with a meaningful grin. "You know, somehow I don't think you came along just to embarrass me. You're trying to distract yourself. Whose message are you waiting for so eagerly?"

Caleb's face turns red, and it's almost cute how he squirms with embarrassment. "Parker's."

"You're not serious!" I cry enthusiastically. "When did you two start texting?"

"A few weeks ago." His blush deepens.

"And you're only telling me this now?" I glare at him in mock indignation.

"There's nothing to tell. We text each other, that's it."

"But you've had a crush on him for months! The fact that you're texting now is really a big deal."

"I know, but—" he breaks off, and his expression turns uncertain. An insecurity that somehow doesn't fit with his personality.

My brother is the most self-confident person I know. He's over a foot taller than me and has the stature of a quarterback, because he is one. He plays on the Harvard football team, where he's a sophomore, and has big plans. He graduated from high school with honors, and after he finishes college he wants to go to Harvard Business School, get his master's degree, and then join my mother at her cosmetics company. He's an impressive guy, and he knows it. Except when it comes to Parker. Then he loses his self-assurance. And every time I see that insecure flicker in his eyes, my heart bleeds for him.

"What are you scared of?" I ask, poking him gently.

"That he doesn't like me?"

"That sounds like a question."

"Zoe—"

"He likes you," I say, interrupting him. "Definitely. It's impossible not to like you."

"No, it's not," Caleb murmurs and nervously runs both hands through his dark hair.

"But he does," I say, glaring at him again. Caleb makes a face at me, but he still doesn't look very convinced. I'm going to have to work on him.

"Hmm," he says.

"Trust me about this!"

"I trust you. But I don't trust myself."

"Then it's time to change that."

"Yeah, I get it. But today is about you, so let's focus on that, okay?"

I'm about to protest until I realize we've arrived at the dormitory. Dad holds the door for us as Caleb shoves me inside.

A tingle of excitement goes through me as I enter the building where I'll be living for the next four years, and at this moment it hits me that it's actually happening. I'm really here, in this long sandstone building with bright walls and dark, scuffed floorboards. There are four floors but no elevator. The dining room is on the first floor, and all the other floors have their own common rooms and bedrooms.

My room is on the top floor, the second-to-last toward the end of the hall. When I reach the door and take the key out of my pocket, I catch a glimpse of the adjoining common room.

I have to smile. And then my smile gets wider as I walk into *my* room. The dark wooden floor contrasts strongly with the white walls decorated with plaster moldings. A small entrance area, just big enough for a wardrobe, leads into a spacious room with high windows and a broad window seat. The bed is smaller than the one I have at home, as is the wardrobe, but I still have more space than I expected. There's a desk and a chair, and another door right next to the room leads to my bathroom. It's tiny, but I have a shower, a sink, and a toilet for myself. Thanks to the white walls and high windows, the room looks bright and friendly despite the dark parquet floor. Although it's practically empty aside from the few pieces of furniture, it's very charming.

"Your room is definitely nicer than the ones we have at Harvard." Caleb drops the suitcase noisily, and I have to laugh.

"You don't even live on campus."

Caleb's been at Harvard for a year, but he only went into the dormitory once before he decided that the alternative was much nicer. He lives with his best friends in a penthouse apartment in the West End. No dorm room in the world can compete with that.

"Well, I've seen the dorms. And this one is much nicer."

"It's true, it is," I say, happy to agree with him.

"Do you need help unpacking?" Mom asks, but I shake my head.

"Thanks, but I can manage alone."

"You just don't want anyone to mess up your perfect organization," Caleb says, teasing.

"So what?" I say, wrinkling my nose in annoyance.

I like my sense of order. It's the only thing I got from Dad. Mom and Caleb tend to be chaotic, and I don't have the slightest idea how they ever find anything they're looking for. For me, every little thing has its fixed place. That's why I have to unpack my bags myself.

"Then it looks like it's time to say goodbye," Dad says and gives me a big hug. "Have fun, dear."

"Thanks, Dad," I whisper. I suddenly have a big lump in my throat. *Oh God, don't cry, not now.* If I start crying, Mom will never leave.

"Call me if you need me. Or if you don't. You can always call me." Mom hugs me and kisses my forehead. Her eyes are glittering with tears again. She clears her throat and strokes my hair. "I'm so proud of you."

"Go get 'em." Caleb wraps both arms around me from behind and lifts me up so my feet leave the floor.

"This is about ballet, not football," I remind him, kicking his shins with my heels until he puts me down. Caleb always used to carry me around like a doll until I was old enough to defend myself.

"It doesn't matter. Go get 'em anyway. And never forget how good you are. And how strong." He puts me down, turns me toward him, and holds up his little finger to me. He looks serious, and I know exactly what he's thinking about.

I feel completely calm inside, and for a moment I can only hear the rushing of blood in my ears. I catch his little finger with mine and nod. "I promise."

BEFORE
Zoe

One year earlier
June 25, 6:32 AM

I sneak down the stairs as quietly as I can, past the kitchen, through the living room, to the back door. I hear Dad singing out of tune along with some song from the eighties and hope he hasn't noticed me. He hasn't noticed me much in the last few months.

Since Jase and I started to leave notes for each other in my tree-house, I sneak out of the house every morning to check if there's a new secret waiting for me.

My family knows nothing about it. Not even Caleb. *Especially* not him. I've considered telling him about it more than once; after all, Jase is his best friend. But probably for that exact reason, I couldn't get the words out.

Jase is his best friend. And I've fallen in love with him. Not head over heels, but slowly and gradually. I'm in love with him and his secrets. His vulnerability. His openness.

He showed me a side of himself that he usually hides from every-one. I know that because I've known him for years. And the Jase he pretends to be is not the same person who confides his secrets to me.

In exchange, he stole my heart.

The back door squeaks almost inaudibly as I open it and step out onto the terrace. The sun still hasn't made it over the rooftops, but the sky is clear and blue and promises a hot summer day.

The perfect last day of school. Starting tomorrow, nothing else counts for a few weeks, only ballet. I have a whole summer of extra lessons so I can prepare for my ballet school audition.

But today is Caleb's day. For him, it really is the last day of high school ever. He graduates today at noon.

I start to feel sentimental. It will be strange to go back to school in the autumn without my brother. Without his friends. Without Jase.

I shake off the thought, because for today, they're all still here. They're getting their diplomas this morning, and later we're going to celebrate their graduation, all together.

And then . . . who knows what the summer will bring?

Anything is possible.

Barefoot, I walk across the dry grass in our little garden. It tickles the bottoms of my feet, and the rungs of the treehouse ladder feel rough as I climb up and push open the door. I've spent more time here in the last few months than I usually do.

I can't just hide my secrets up here for Jase to find. I have to be here when I write them down too. Anything else would feel wrong. Incomplete.

I see the note immediately. It's sitting on the wooden crate that I brought up here a few weeks ago to store the wool blankets in for the summer. In their place, two light linen bedspreads are now folded neatly on the cushions that cover the floor.

The note is the only thing that doesn't look tidy in my little refuge, even though I folded it nicely before I left it here for him two days ago. He crumpled the paper into a little ball, and I have to laugh, because I know very well that he did it on purpose. He does it because he knows that, every time, I will meticulously smooth out the note I get from him and refold it perfectly before he gets it back.

He messes up my order, and I organize his chaos. There's a twisted kind of poetry in that.

My heart skips a beat as I reach for the ball of paper. I pause for a second, my hands trembling, tempted for a moment just to ignore the note. To not read his reply but throw the message away and never give him or his secrets another thought.

How could I ask him that question? What the hell has gotten into me?

But I know the answer already. I didn't think about it, and at the same time I thought about it far too much. He stole my heart, and I want to know if he's giving me at least a little piece of his. Just a tiny one.

Snap out of it and read the note already!

The voice in my head is bossy and loud, and it's right. I have to read the note. I can't just ignore it. I don't want to do that.

My pulse races as I smooth out the paper and see Jase's messy handwriting. It's much too familiar now.

My breath catches as I read the words that are written there.

What do you see when you look at me?

Freckles. Seven of them on your nose. Eleven on the right cheek. Fifteen on the left cheek.
—J

CHAPTER 2

Zoe

Sometimes I wish I were more like Caleb. Then I wouldn't worry about what other people think. I would make decisions for myself and not constantly wonder if I were being fair to everyone. Why can't I be more like him and less like me?

—P

Three hours after my arrival, my suitcases are empty, and I make a mental note to ask Dad if he can come get them as soon as possible, because my room is definitely too small to hold them all. My clothes are stowed in the wardrobe; my leotards, tights, and ballet skirts are in the top drawer of the dresser; and my ballet slippers, toe caps, and pointe shoes are in the bottom drawer. My resistance bands for stretching, exercise mats, and foam rollers are in a large wooden crate next to my desk, and my hair bands and clips are neatly tucked inside a little box on the dresser, under the mirror.

The books I need for theory lessons are lined up in a neat row on the dresser, sorted by size. My notebook and iPad sit on my desk, alongside my laptop. In the middle of the desktop, the gray ring binder is lying open, showing the appointments that I have scheduled for today.

Everything is exactly as I want it. Aside from the fairy lights, which I am currently holding in my hands. I want to hang them up over the bed, because I have a penchant not only for order but also for subdued lighting.

Unfortunately, I did forget something at home. I don't have anything to fasten the lights to the wall with. Sighing, I put them in the drawer of my bedside table. I'm about to reach for my phone to send Dad a message when I hear a crashing sound in the hall. Someone swears. That doesn't sound good. I leave the drawer ajar and rush to the door. I throw it open and gasp in surprise.

A girl is sitting on the floor in front of my room. One of her suitcases has burst open, and her clothes are all over the place.

"I told Mom that the suitcase wouldn't survive the trip!" she says to herself, carelessly pushing aside her backpack as she begins to pick up her stuff.

I clear my throat to get her attention. "Do you need help?"

She whirls around to look at me, a hand on her chest. Her dark green eyes are wide with shock. "God, don't scare me like that!" she blurts out.

"I'm sorry. I didn't mean to."

She smiles at me. "That's okay. It's not your fault. My day started off like shit, and it was clear that it was going to go on that way." She blows a strand of red hair away from her mouth. Her hair is darker than mine, not copper but mahogany, almost raspberry, with a violet tinge that fits perfectly with her olive skin tone.

"That bad?" I lean against my door with my arms crossed and can't stop an amused grin from spreading across my face.

"My sister has food poisoning and threw up all over the house this morning. That's why Mom couldn't bring me to the airport. I almost missed the flight, and now, with only a few feet more, this stupid suitcase couldn't even wait until I make it to my room before breaking." She grabs two bras off the floor.

"So it's *really* bad," I confirm, bending down to help her collect her things.

She smiles at me gratefully. "Thanks. That's really nice of you. My name is Mae, by the way."

"Zoe," I say. "Where's your room?"

She points to the door to the left of mine. "Looks like we're neighbors."

* * *

"Do you believe in fate?" Mae twists her hair into a messy bun, and her eyes flash with excitement. She's sitting cross-legged on the floor and picks up the last armful of leotards and ballet skirts, stuffing them carelessly in the bottom drawer of the dresser next to her bed. With difficulty, I hold back a sigh. My fingers are tingling with the urge to organize her things.

"Not necessarily," I reply slowly. Where is she going with this?

Mae laughs. "I do. It must be fate that I got the room next to yours, of all rooms. After all, I know nothing about Boston, and you were born and raised here. You can show me around."

"That might just be a coincidence," I say, but I still have to smile.

We've been sitting in her room for two hours and have talked the entire time about everything and nothing. I like Mae. She's easy to talk to, open and friendly, and she smiles all the time. She's so different from my high school friends that a part of me feels almost insecure because of how shockingly new that is for me. The other part of me is just relieved.

"No coincidence." Mae shakes her head. "Fate made sure that I got a neighbor who knows her way around Boston. And not only that, but you're also nice. A coincidence could have just as easily sent me someone I don't like. Fate made sure that we found each other."

"You've only known me for two hours. You can't know if you like me or not."

"Yes, I can. The first impression always matters to me. And I knew after exactly seven minutes that I liked you."

The corners of my mouth twitch. "Did you stop the clock?"

"Sure. I have a built-in stopwatch in my brain."

"Speaking of which, we should get going soon." I point at the alarm clock on Mae's nightstand. It's a quarter to four.

"We should. We don't want to sit all the way in the back at Mr. Pearson's talk." Mae jumps up and offers her hand to pull me off the bed.

Dozens of students come out of the dormitories, laughing and chatting as they walk across the wide lawns. The sun is already low on the horizon, and the buildings cast long shadows on the broad paths, but it's still pleasantly warm.

I look around curiously. In comparison to Harvard, Boston College, and MIT, the ballet school is tiny. There are four classes for the high school students and four for those of us studying dance as part of our bachelor of fine arts. No class has more than twenty students. Still, when we all walk into the theater at the same time, it feels like there are many more of us.

A group of giggling girls passes us quickly. They can't be older than about fifteen. Maybe it's their first day too.

"Are you nervous?" Mae asks quietly as we walk up the wide steps. The theater rises impressively in front of us. The bright sandstone looks like it's glowing in the late afternoon sunlight. There are pillars on either side of the wide door, above which a sign hangs:

New England Theater.

This is where the careers of the best dancers in the country begin. This is where dreams come true. My body begins to tingle. Now *I'm* here. This is *my* dream. I nod and hold my breath for a moment as we enter through the wide doorway and step into the theater. "I'm about to die of excitement!"

"That makes two of us." Mae laughs breathlessly and looks around with wide eyes as we both try and fail to get an impression of the entire inside of the theater.

It's beautiful, and we're not even in the auditorium yet, just the foyer. The plush red carpet absorbs any sounds made by our feet. My gaze lingers on the white walls. Here, the plaster moldings are covered in gold leaf, and they glow warmly as the rays of sunlight reach them through the arched floor-to-ceiling windows. The coat-check room is tucked away so discreetly in a corner that it's not even noticeable at first. There's a bar on the opposite side of the foyer, and spread throughout the area are small, round gold tables and armchairs upholstered in red velvet. But the centerpiece of the foyer is the huge door that leads into the theater. To either side, wide spiral staircases give access to the upper tiers. The voices around us hush as they enter, as though no one would dare to disturb the awe-inspiring silence in these sacred halls.

I let myself be carried by the stream of students and follow Mae into the auditorium. I get goose bumps as soon as I see the stage. The plush red curtains are raised, and although it may look like a totally normal stage, at the same time, it's not.

It's the stage upon which all our fates will be decided.

"Look, there are two seats free at the front." Mae touches my arm and draws my attention away from the stage. She points at two seats next to the aisle. I follow her down the narrow steps between the left and center sections, and again, I don't know what to look at first.

The parterre is divided into three parts, and it's even larger than I expected—eight seats to the right, eight to the left, and sixteen in the middle. I don't have time to count the rows, but together with the upper tiers, there must be at least enough seats for not only the two hundred students but also their families when there are performances. The seats are upholstered with the same red velvet as the chairs in the foyer, and the walls are also white and decorated with similar gold-leaf-covered plaster moldings.

"You look like you've just landed in your own personal wonderland," Mae observes, sinking into one of the seats.

Relieved that she left the place on the aisle free for me so I don't have to squeeze past anyone, I sit down next to her. I'm just about to answer when all at once, the whole room goes quiet, and all eyes turn to the stage.

Principal Pearson steps into the spotlight. He's a tall, thin man in his forties, and he moves with a grace that clearly betrays his years as a dancer. His dark hair, which is shot through with silver, is combed back smoothly. He's wearing a gray blazer and dark blue trousers. The smile on his face is both friendly and authoritative.

He's one of those people whose personality immediately fills a room, no matter how large it is.

Now he steps to the edge of the stage, his hands resting casually in the pockets of his trousers. He is just about to start his speech when I hear quick steps walking into the room and then a burst of nervous laughter. Almost simultaneously, everyone turns around to look. A boy and a girl are trying to sneak into the last row as quietly as possible, but they freeze abruptly as they notice that everyone is staring at them.

The girl turns to look at the stage, an innocent expression on her face. Her long, dark hair flows softly over her shoulders. She's tall, taller than me but just as delicately built. She's beautiful. She moves like a fairy.

I recognize the boy who walked in with her just as Pearson says his name.

"Jase! Skye! Why don't you sit here in the front, since you're already late?" It's a rhetorical question, and a mischievous murmur spreads through the room.

I don't understand a word. I can only stare at *him* as he turns around. He exchanges a brief, incomprehensible glance with Skye and then walks toward the front of the auditorium.

Jase.

CHAPTER 3
Zoe

Have you ever been in love?

~~I'm not sure. I mean, how does it feel to be in love? How do you even know if you are?~~

Yes.

—P

It feels like someone just punched me hard in the middle of my chest and knocked the wind out of me. I can't breathe. My heart skips a beat and then starts racing much too fast. I feel the blood draining out of my face. A cold sweat breaks out on the back of my neck, and my hands begin to shake. *No no no.*

I knew he was going to be here. I knew it, but I had successfully suppressed the knowledge. Now I realize there's a big difference between knowing something and actually being confronted with it.

It was over, everything with him and me. I ended it. Because anything else would have been too much.

I left it all behind me. I left *him* behind because I had to. I didn't have any other choice. I didn't see him again after that night. I refused to allow myself to think about him because it hurt. I shut him out.

But now it's all coming back. The notes, the secrets, the way one short glance from him could make me feel. Everything inside of me tells me to turn away, lower my head, and pray he didn't notice me. But I can't. I can't look away, and at this moment, I can see nothing but him. At the same time, my brain is unable to comprehend him in his entirety.

I blink.

Moss-green eyes under thick brows. Black eyelashes that are much too long.

I blink again.

High cheekbones. Straight nose. A jawline that looks as though it's been chiseled from stone.

Again.

Lips that are almost too full, smiling knowingly.

He's incomparable.

He always was, but now somehow he's even more so.

I feel myself blushing. The blood pounds in my ears, and silver stars are dancing in front of my eyes until I remember how to breathe again.

Breathe, Zoe. Breathe.

Jase walks past me without a glance and sits down in an open seat diagonally in front of me. Skye sits down next to him, and he puts his arm on the back of her seat, leans over, and whispers something in her ear.

My stomach cramps, and I feel sick.

"Wonderful. Thank you very much," Pearson says sarcastically, reminding me where I am and why.

The theater on campus. Our principal's welcome speech.

Jase is here, but it doesn't matter. Not anymore. I force myself to stop looking at the back of his head and focus on the stage.

It doesn't matter. It's over. You can't change the past. You can only move on.

"Now that everyone is here, I'd like to welcome you to a new school year at the New England School of Ballet." Pearson spreads his arms in a welcoming gesture and continues, his deep, resonant voice filling the auditorium. "I give the same speech every year, and some of you probably know my words by heart now, but I don't think it will hurt you to hear them again." Soft laughter spreads through the rows before he continues. "You're all here for a specific reason. You love ballet, and you have talent. But you also have foresight. At many public and private ballet schools, the focus is entirely on dance and preparing the students' bodies for the stage. We have the same goal here, and yet we expect much more. Experience has shown us that only a tiny fraction of all trained ballet dancers ever make it to the professional stage." The kind smile that now appears on Pearson's face takes some of the sting out of his words. "But the world of dance is so much more than just the stage, and that's why you're here. To prepare yourselves and find out what you were born to do. You are here to learn. But you should also have fun, make friends, and . . ."

A movement in front of me diverts my attention to a familiar head of blond hair. I can't help it; it's like an inner compulsion. I have to look away in order to continue listening, but the rest of Pearson's speech barely reaches me, as hard as I try to concentrate on his words.

Why did Jase, of all people, have to sit in front of me? Maybe he senses that I'm staring at him because suddenly he turns around, and his eyes meet mine. Direct. Hard. Cold.

My pulse races, and adrenaline shoots through my veins like poison. He stares at me so intensely that for a few seconds, it feels as though we're totally alone. Everything else blurs, and the sounds around me become undefined white noise.

I can't interpret the look in his eyes. I'm not sure if it's anger or indifference or something else entirely. Actually, I don't even want to know. Because whatever it is, it hurts like hell. My throat suddenly feels constricted. I blink as pressure builds up dangerously behind my eyes.

Don't cry. There's no way you're going to start now, do you understand? There's absolutely no reason for it!

I fight back the tears and breathe a sigh of relief as Jase turns away again, breaking eye contact as if he were cutting the connection between us.

Except I already did that.

* * *

After Pearson's speech, which I only caught half of, the whole student body walks into the foyer of the theater. While Pearson was talking about discipline, passion, heart, and soul, a buffet was being set up there. They want us to get to know each other. At one of the standing tables, I shift uncomfortably from one foot to the other and try to follow the conversation that Mae is having with two girls who are also new to the school, Kaya and Jessica. They're nice, but I can hardly focus on the conversation, no matter how hard I try.

My eyes are glued to Jase again. I can't manage *not* to look at him. He's standing next to Skye at a table on the other side of the room, and he seems so indifferent that I wonder if he'd even be here if it weren't a mandatory event. Probably not.

It's ridiculous that it upsets me so much to see him. The last time we saw each other was over a year ago. To react to him like this after everything that happened is totally irrational.

So what? Since when are feelings rational?

I ignore the voice in my head. It has no right to talk. At least not about him.

"Do you want something to drink?" Mae's question brings me back to reality.

I shake my head. "No, thanks."

"Okay, I'll be right back." She walks off, and it's only after she disappears toward the bar that I realize that Kaya and Jessica are gone too.

I look for Jase again, but he's gone.

Relief floods through me. *Good.* That's really good.

We go to the same school again, but that doesn't mean we're going to keep running into each other. He's a year ahead of me. At most, we might bump into each other in the corridor.

We don't have to talk to each other. We can just walk past each other. It's as simple as that. No big deal.

Taking a deep breath, I smooth back my hair and put any thoughts about Jase to the back of my mind. I reach for the water bottle on the table in front of me, which I haven't touched yet.

"Hey." Someone appears next to me, and I flinch so badly that I almost drop the bottle. Because of my frantic movement, water sloshes out the top and leaves a clearly visible wet mark on the tablecloth. I blush. *Shit.*

"I'm sorry, I didn't mean to scare you. Are you okay?" The voice, which is soft and melodic, sounds worried.

I look up and see a pair of unnerving green eyes that seem strangely familiar. With golden-blond hair that falls down her back in waves, a cute button nose, and finely formed features, the girl looks like a Disney princess. She's more than just pretty.

"It's fine, I'm good. It's only water," I say.

"All right, then." She smiles at me. "I'm Lia."

"Zoe," I say, wiping my hand inconspicuously on my dress.

"Nice to meet you. You're one of the new ones."

It's an observation, not a question. That's not surprising. There are only eighty students living on campus altogether. As a newcomer, you can't hide here. We stand out.

"Right."

Her smile widens, and that also seems strangely familiar, even though I have no idea why. "Then you can come with me."

"Where to?" I frown, unable to quell the wave of skepticism I feel.

"Just go with it. We're getting all the newbies together. But don't worry, it's not for sorority hazing or anything like that," she adds when she notices the apprehensive look on my face. "It'll be great. I promise."

She puts a hand on my shoulder and turns me gently but firmly toward the exit, where a small crowd is gradually forming. I'm too surprised to protest, and I let Lia guide me toward the others. I spot Mae with Kaya and Jessica. There are two other girls with them. They look older than us, just like Lia.

"Have we got them all?" Lia asks when we reach them.

One of the girls, her dark hair in two thick braids, nods a hello to me. Lia introduces her as Katie.

"Susannah is gathering the last few. Then we can go."

"You're really not going to tell us where we're going?" Mae says, looking curious.

"Then it wouldn't be a surprise anymore," Lia replies enigmatically.

"Let's go," says an excited voice behind us. We all turn at once to see a girl with hair so pale it's almost white. Her blue eyes shine just as brightly. Everything about her seems to glow. "I've spoken to Pearson too. We're officially excused."

Lia nods with satisfaction. "Thanks for sorting that out, Suzie."

"Sure. Pearson *loooves* me," she says so sarcastically that we all have to laugh.

Katie groans. "Oh, stop. It sounds like you have a thing with him. Please tell her not to do that, Lia. Especially in front of the newbies."

"That's nonsense. Besides, he's too old for me anyway," Susannah says dismissively. "Now get your sweet butts in gear. Follow me!"

Katie looks like she's about to say something else, but then sighs and shoos us out of the theater.

The sun is now low in the sky, about to set at any minute. Little clouds drift across the darkening sky, the air is clear and fresh, and I shiver in my thin dress. I should have brought a jacket.

Lia and the others lead us back to the dormitory. We walk up the stairs to the fourth floor, past Mae's room first and then mine, and climb the three steps that lead to the common room.

Four sofas and three armchairs are grouped around a low

round table in the spacious room. Light gray curtains hang at the windows, and there are portraits of various dancers on the walls. Between the sofas are little side tables that hold vases of fresh flowers.

Then we step over a wide windowsill onto a roof terrace.

"Wow," Mae says, her eyes wide. "Amazing."

I can only nod in agreement as I look around in surprise. Sofas made of wooden pallets with thick, colorful cushions on them have been set up. It's the perfect place to spend a warm summer evening. A net of fairy lights hangs over the terrace, and lush green ivy twines around the railings.

"Surprise!" Lia says with a wide smile, and all at once I freeze, realizing why her smile is familiar. I remember now where I've heard her name before. Or rather, read it.

Jase's secrets. His notes. His blond hair. His smile. Lia is his older sister.

I don't know much about her. Actually, I don't know anything except that she and Jase don't get along so well, even though they seem to be so similar. Even though they're both here to dance.

"It's a tradition that we all meet here on the first evening and get to know each other better, without being watched by Pearson and the other teachers the whole time," Lia says.

"And because there's booze," Susannah adds with a smile, tossing her blond hair over her shoulders.

Lia rolls her eyes. "Strictly speaking, it's not allowed here at all because most of us aren't twenty-one yet. But on the first evening, they turn a blind eye as long as we don't overdo it. And as long as the younger ones don't notice." She nods in the direction of the other dorm on the opposite side of the theater, where the high school students live.

"Oh, he shouldn't make such a fuss about it. Most of us are much too well-behaved. In the summer, sometimes we put up a screen and have movie nights up here," Katie says proudly, guiding us toward a group of girls who are already sitting on one of the pallets with their feet up, talking and laughing. We sit down with them, and even though they each introduce themselves, I forget their names almost immediately.

A group of boys brings cans of beer and a box of wine, and the terrace slowly fills up.

"I'm going to get a sweater," I whisper to Mae, because it's not only getting dark, but it's also quite cool.

"Good idea, me too." She gets up, and together we weave our way through the crowd and back through the open window in the common room.

We enter the hall just as the door of the last room, the one next to mine, opens. Skye steps out, and I'm just about to greet her when I spot Jase behind her and freeze, rooted to the spot. He leans against the doorframe and doesn't even look at me.

Great.

The back of my neck prickles uncomfortably, and I feel the urge to turn and run away, but I can't move. Either Mae hasn't noticed the strange atmosphere between us or she's ignoring it. She takes a step toward Jase and Skye and gives them a friendly smile. "Hi, I'm Mae. Looks like we're neighbors. My room is right over there, and Zoe's is next to yours."

"Hi, nice to—Hey Jase, wait a sec!" Skye laughs in confusion as

Jase pushes past her and disappears without a word. Skye gives us an apologetic shrug and follows him.

"What was that about?" Mae asks indignantly, staring after them in disbelief.

I answer before I can stop myself. "That was Jase."

And he obviously lives right next door to me.

Shit.

CHAPTER 4
Jase

Why are you telling me all your secrets?

Because you're real. And somehow, you're able to make me feel something.
—J

Fuck. This.

Seeing Zoe felt like having a bulldozer drive across my chest, breaking my ribs one by one. Like splinters of bone drilling into my heart, which for a moment must have forgotten that it's more than the muscle that's supposed to be keeping me alive.

What the hell is she doing here, of all places? She knew I would be here. I told her about it. That was the only note where I didn't need any of her questions to tell her one of my secrets.

She could have gone to any other school. Practically the whole world is open to Zoe. Instead, she stayed in Boston. Why couldn't she have chosen another ballet academy?

The answer to that question is very simple: There was no reason for her to. She wanted to go to one of the best schools in the country, and she doesn't give a shit whether I'm here or not. It doesn't matter. Not to her.

For me, on the other hand, it matters very much. I don't want her anywhere near me. Not now or ever again. Fuck. I wish she would disappear.

"Jase." Skye nudges me and snaps me out of my thoughts. I look up and meet her worried gaze. Skye has the darkest eyes I've ever seen. Brown, almost black. Abysses from which you can't be rescued if you fall.

I've already fallen. Not for her. But she pulled me out of my own personal abyss, and I still don't understand why. She simply decided I needed a friend and that she would take on the job. She constantly ignores the fact that I didn't ask to have her in my life.

Skye believes that everyone needs someone, and she's definitely right about that. But I've fallen flat on my face far too often when I try to let others get close to me. She doesn't care much about that either.

She's here, and she's staying. And if I listen very, very closely to my inner voice, there might even be a tiny part of me that's happy about that.

"Huh?" I say, taking a swig from the can I'm holding. The beer tastes stale, and I make a face. Whoever organized the drinks this year did a rotten job.

"Are you ever going to talk to me about it?" she asks gently, and I immediately tense up. I've never heard her use that tone of voice with anyone else. Only with me, and I deserve it the least. She may have decided that she wants to be my friend, but I'm totally incapable of giving anything back.

The concept of friendship has lost some of its appeal over the past year, after all my friends dropped me from their lives without a single word. At the thought of Caleb, Reed, Tristan, and Nick, my chest tightens painfully, and the back of my neck gets hot.

One awful night was enough to lose everyone who had made me feel like I wasn't alone in this world over the last few years. Because I made a mistake. Just one single fucking mistake. But it was obviously enough.

"Come on, Jase. Talk to me," Skye pleads, this time more insistently. The ugly memories that were rearing their heads slip back into the cave where they belong.

"About what?" I take another swallow, because even the worst beer is better than having to talk.

"About the little redhead who has obviously moved in next door. You know each other." She doesn't even ask. She says it firmly, as if she knows. As if it were an indisputable fact that I must know Zoe.

"Who are you talking about?"

I play dumb, but Skye just rolls her eyes and doesn't let herself be put off. She could see through me from the very beginning, although I refused to talk to her about my problems. But she knows that I have some. They're hard to miss.

She points at someone behind me. "Her." I know who's standing there long before I turn around. I don't want to do that. I don't want to see her, but I can't help it, because Zoe is Zoe, and that was always enough.

In the theater, I endured exactly seven seconds of staring back at her when I turned to see why it felt like someone was staring at the back of my head.

It only took seven seconds to realize that she was still the same person she was before. The girl with the copper hair, which she likes to wear in two thick braids, and those big hazel eyes that shine like amber, depending on the light. She is still beautiful, still tiny, almost too small for a dancer. She's petite with long, lean muscles and cute freckles on her nose and cheeks that are so pale that you can only see them if you stand right in front of her.

Now Zoe is standing in a group with four other girls. She's wearing the gray school sweatshirt that everyone gets at the beginning of the first year over a short floral dress, and I look at her legs for a second too long.

The warm glow of the fairy lights makes her bare skin shimmer golden, and I can't look away. My gaze drifts from her legs to the dress and sweatshirt to the ends of her red hair. Tonight it's loose, falling in soft waves down her back.

She laughs, and even though the music echoes over the roof terrace and a couple of guys near me are shouting a conversation at each other that I couldn't care less about, I can hear her laugh. Bright and melodic, and much too Zoe-like.

"See, that's exactly what I mean." Skye leans toward me until we're almost touching. "You know her, don't you? Otherwise, you wouldn't look at her like that."

I don't answer, because even if I don't want to tell her the truth, I'm not a liar either.

She sighs, giving in. "That's okay, you don't have to talk to me. But you know that you can if you want to, don't you?" Her eyes narrow.

"If I ever want to talk to anyone, it will be you," I promise her, completely seriously. If I needed to confide in someone, it would be Skye.

However, I realize that will never happen. The last time I opened up, everything blew up in my face. I won't make that mistake again.

Skye nods, apparently mollified. "That's what I wanted to hear."

"I know." I force myself to smile and pray that she'll finally let it go.

She's just about to reply when the music suddenly stops. Emily, Chris, Ruby, and all the seniors step into the center of the roof terrace, and I groan.

Shit, I totally forgot about this.

"This party isn't our only tradition," Chris announces with a grin, and someone cheers. Someone who knows what's coming next. "Pearson and the selection committee have seen every single one of us dance before. But I'd say it's time *we* had a look at who's going to follow in our footsteps."

The students cheer again, more of them this time. They play this stupid game every year. The new ones are shoved into the middle and are encouraged to improvise, like we're in the most clichéd teen dance movie you can think of.

I haven't figured out yet whether it's an attempt to unnerve or humiliate them or if the rest of the group is really just curious. Probably a bit of everything.

"Who wants to go first?" Emily, the star of the senior class, puts on an encouraging smile. She will be dancing the lead role in this year's Christmas performance, as sure as death and taxes, even though we don't know yet which piece is planned. She already has an offer from the New York City Ballet, and when she graduates next year, she will be one of the few who don't have to struggle to get auditions. She made it, and she makes it look almost easy.

"Come on, go for it. We don't bite. Everyone is going to get a turn tonight," Ruby says, pushing a lock of hair behind her ear.

Someone steps forward. A girl with copper hair and freckles that I once counted. Fuck.

"Great, we have the first volunteer. What's your name?" Ruby asks.

"Zoe." The sound of her voice sends a painful shiver down my back. Even after a year, she's still far too familiar. How the hell is this happening?

She stops a short distance from Emily, her eyes darting back and forth and then meeting mine for a split second. They go wide, and my entire body tingles as she bites her lower lip uncertainly and draws my attention to her mouth.

Inside me, hot anger collides with stabbing pain. Memories flood me. I suddenly taste peaches on my tongue, and my stomach turns. I push back the memories, just like the anger and pain and everything that has to do with her, because they don't matter anymore. We're over. We never even really started.

"I'm leaving," I say to Skye, not waiting for her to answer. I simply turn and walk away.

I'm not watching Zoe dance. Not a chance.

CHAPTER 5
Zoe

What does friendship mean to you?

I don't know . . . being there for each other? Telling each other all your secrets without fear of being betrayed? Being honest without worrying about being rejected? I think it's friendship when you have someone with you who helps you to be less afraid.
—P

Yawning, I stir my coffee and watch as the dark liquid mixes with the frothy milk. My avocado sandwich is lying on the plate in front of me, untouched. I've been staring at it for ten minutes. I know I have to eat something, but I can't bring myself to take a bite.

"Aren't you hungry?" Mae asks. She's sitting next to me, eating her yogurt.

We're sitting in the dining hall on the ground floor. It doesn't feel that much like a dorm because the Victorian style of the building is also reflected in its interior design. It's much fancier than the average student residence.

The first rays of sunlight are shining through the high arched windows, bathing everything in soft, warm light and casting shadows on the wooden floor. Sixteen round tables are scattered around the large room, with five chairs around each one. The dark green, velvet-covered seats look more like easy chairs and are far too comfortable when one is completely exhausted.

"I'm wiped out," I say.

"Had a bad night?" She frowns sympathetically.

"I couldn't fall asleep."

It's not a lie. I was totally restless because I couldn't stop thinking about Jase. The expression in his eyes and the bitter frown that I'd never seen before. Not to mention the fact that he was sleeping in his bed just a few yards away from me with nothing but a wall between us, even though it felt like the whole universe was separating us.

Which is good.

Because what I had with Jase is part of my past, and I need to look ahead. I've got to focus on my dream. My future. And he's not a part of it anymore.

"I'm so sorry. I slept like a log. Honestly, if it weren't so loud this morning in the hall, I would have totally overslept. I didn't even hear my alarm clock. But it was definitely worth it." Mae laughs. She laughs a lot. I noticed that last night, and a part of me envies the ease with which she's made her fresh start, while I . . . well, haven't.

"It was worth it," I confirm. We danced with the others on the terrace until almost midnight. No choreography, no pressure. Just having fun.

I tried not to dwell on the moment when Jase left right before I started my improvisation.

"I would definitely have woken you up if you hadn't shown up on your own," I add a little belatedly.

"You would have had to notice that I was missing first."

"I would have noticed that. There are only nineteen of us, so if one of us is missing, it's obvious."

"Probably. Speaking of which, which classes are you taking?" She rummages in her backpack and pulls out a very rumpled timetable, spreading it out on the table in front of her. The sight of the tattered paper irks me a little. I follow her lead and take my Bullet Journal out of my bag and open it. It's pink. It may be a total cliché, but I don't care; I love pink.

I've written my schedule tidily on one of the first pages. This new beginning was also an occasion for a new Bullet Journal.

Mae sighs, and I look up at her. There's a wistful expression on her face.

"What?"

She sighs again. "You're one of *those*."

"One of what?" My eyebrows go up.

"I have a theory about dancers: We're either absolute perfectionists or totally chaotic."

"Doesn't that apply to everyone?" I ask with a smile.

"Basically, yes, but in ballet, one tends to be a perfectionist anyway. You either transfer that to the rest of your life, or you go completely in the opposite direction. I bet you always got good grades in school."

I sense the blood rushing to my cheeks and feel like I've been caught red-handed. "Okay, that's true. I do tend to be a perfectionist. In everything."

Mae points her spoon at me triumphantly. "That's what I

thought. Come on, show it to me." She reaches out her free hand for my Bullet Journal. I hand it to her. She glances quickly at my timetable and breaks into a wide smile. "Looks like we have all our classes together."

"Really?" I reach for her schedule and have to smile too. She's right. Every morning, we begin with classical ballet, followed by pointe. On Mondays, Wednesdays, and Fridays, we have pas de deux up next, and on Tuesdays and Thursdays, contemporary dance and lyrical jazz. After lunch, we have the theory classes: music theory, art of performing, choreography, and two other subjects.

"Looks like you're stuck with me," Mae says with a grin.

"Or you're stuck with *me*," I say. All at once, I'm grateful that Mae's suitcase gave up the ghost yesterday.

"I think it's going to be pretty cool. Katie told me yesterday that all the technique classes are mixed with students from other years, aside from classical ballet and pointe. Maybe we'll even have some classes with her, Susannah, and Lia."

"Yes, maybe. That would be—" I stop abruptly as another thought occurs to me. If the technique classes are for all levels together, then . . . there's a chance that I might end up in a class with Jase. My palms start to sweat.

"What?" Mae asks, looking at me curiously.

I shake my head and actively repress every thought of Jase. I've already spent far too much time thinking about him over the last twenty-four hours. "Nothing. I think we should get going, shouldn't we? We still have to warm up before the first lesson."

"Exactly. But at least take a bite of your sandwich first." She firmly pushes the plate in my direction. "You can't dance on an empty stomach."

I sigh and do it for her. She's right; I have to eat something. I manage to get down two or three bites before I give up, and we clear the table.

We've brought our bags with us so we can go directly from breakfast to the practice building. We fall into a crowd of dozens of students on their way to the studios, just like us. The high school students are headed to the classrooms instead. Apparently, they've got theory lessons first. A tall boy with thick, dark hair smiles and holds the door open for us as we reach our destination.

There are ballet studios on all three floors of the building, separated from the corridor by glass walls. A few have curtains drawn across, but this morning, most of them are open. We go up to the second floor to the last studio on the right, where most of the other first-semester students are already standing at the barres or sitting on the floor, warming up.

In comparison to the others, our class is relatively small. Nine girls and ten boys, none of us older than nineteen. Five of them—Raffael, Lucien, Georgia, Kelly, and Julie—have been here for four years already and got their high school diplomas before the summer. The others are just as new as us. Kaya just recently moved here from Japan, and Anthony and Jessica are from Boston, like me. The other ten have come from all over the country to be here.

We take off our sneakers in the corridor because we're not allowed to walk on the studio floors with street shoes. Then we throw our bags in a corner and start to prepare for the first lesson. My hips crack in protest as I start my warm-up, and Mae sits on the floor, getting her ballet slippers ready.

Just before nine, Mr. Conrad enters the room with a slender middle-aged woman. According to the timetable, her name is

Deborah, and she's going to accompany our lessons on the piano. After nodding briefly in our direction, she sits down at the grand piano near the door, while Mr. Conrad stands in front of the large mirror. He's tall, handsome, and surprisingly young, perhaps in his late twenties.

"Good morning." He smiles warmly. "My name is Mr. Conrad, and I'll be your teacher this year. We're going to start with the basics today so I can get an idea of what you specifically need to work on in your first year. Let's start from the beginning. Pliés in five positions."

I step up to one of the barres in front of the window overlooking campus. All at once, I get goose bumps. I really made it! I'm here, in a studio at the New England School of Ballet. I get to dance and learn and improve. I'm here so I can reach for the stars. Even though not long ago I was convinced that I'd never make it.

But I'm here now. Nothing else counts.

"First position. Focus. This is about precision. I don't want to see any sloppiness." Mr. Conrad's voice fills the room as we follow his instructions in synchronized motion.

As soon as my hand relaxes on the barre, my heels touch, and my feet point outward in a straight line, everything else fades into the background. I take a deep breath, bend my legs slowly and precisely to the rhythm of the music, and stretch them out again. Bending and stretching with a straight back, knees turned outward. Every muscle in my body is working.

The third time, my heels lift in a grand plié. I lower my arm smoothly, move it forward and back to the side.

"Keep your arms steady. Shoulders back," Mr. Conrad says as he paces up and down the room. He's walking along the barres, checking our posture. Out of the corner of my eye, I see him occasionally correcting the others. Meanwhile, we switch from pliés to the *battements tendus*.

Right leg forward, diagonal, point the foot, half point, point, draw the right foot across the floor in a fluid motion. Pause. Keep your hips straight, stretch backward, half point, heels touching. Knees locked the whole time.

I breathe a sigh of relief when he gives me an approving nod, and Mae gets one too. He walks past us without comment. Mae gives me a conspiratorial glance over her shoulder, and I have to smile.

True to his word, Mr. Conrad only focuses on the basics in this first lesson, even when we move from the barre to the center of the floor. With every moment that passes, I feel more like myself. I've been doing these exercises almost every day for most of my life. They've become second nature to me. They are part of me, and last year they were my salvation. They're my anchor, something that always stays the same no matter how much else changes.

CHAPTER 6
Jase

I was accepted at the New England School of Ballet! Dad is going to kill me just for going to the audition. But I couldn't care less. I was accepted. How crazy is that?
—J

My muscles ache. Everything hurts. I'm feeling the lack of lessons during summer vacation in a very unpleasant way. Everyone who stayed here during the break, like Skye and me, technically had the opportunity to use the studios and gym whenever we wanted. But it turns out it's harder to be responsible for your own workout plan without the structure of daily classes.

"Get a move on, Jase. Francesca will kill us if we're late." Ches, the only guy from our class who's halfway tolerable, kicks my bag and turns toward the corridor while I heave myself off the floor with a dramatic groan. I grab my things and follow him. I'm tired, and for the first time, I wish that our teachers would go a bit easier on us the first day after vacation. Then again, it's not their fault I could hardly sleep last night. I only have myself to blame for that.

The pas de deux class is one floor up, in the same studio as last year. Skye and a few other girls are already there when we enter. They're sitting in little groups on the floor and talking quietly.

I throw my bag in the corner with the others, and I'm just about to go over to Skye when I hear a familiar laugh. A few seconds later, Zoe enters the room with two other freshmen, whom I haven't met yet.

At the sight of her, the muscles in my chest react with a warning twitch. My hands clench into fists all by themselves.

Fuck.

I force my pulse to slow down, consciously stretching every finger as I watch her sit down on the floor and take her ballet slippers out of her bag. I knew that we would have this class together because freshmen and sophomores always have pas de deux together. But I refused to think about what that meant, even for a second, because that would mean that I cared. And I don't.

So we have one stupid class together. That doesn't mean we have to talk to each other. I don't want to, and she clearly doesn't either; otherwise, she would have answered my damn notes last semester.

And that settles the issue.

Somehow, I manage to turn away before Zoe spots me. I walk over to Ches and the others, pretending to join their conversation but barely listening to what they're saying. I don't say a word while I wait for Francesca to show up so we can get this bullshit over with.

She arrives punctually as usual, not a minute late. Francesca was our teacher last year too. She's a petite, slender woman with an angular face and a low voice that has just a trace of an Italian accent. Everything about her is severe, except for a few dark curls that play around her face, as though they're trying to soften her up.

"Good morning," she says, stepping into the middle of the room. She introduces herself briefly and gets straight to the point. "I have big plans for you this year, and I expect you all to do your best. Do you understand?" Francesca doesn't mince words. Her explanations are just as concise as her praise and criticism. Precise and harsh, but always honest. "The pas de deux is all about trust and working together. It's about creating a connection with one another. That's why you will be divided into permanent pairs at the end of the week. After that, there will be no more changes for the rest of the semester," she explains. "Over the next few hours, I will decide who is suitable for whom. Is that clear?" She looks at us with her eyebrows raised. We murmur in agreement, and she nods.

"Skye, you will dance with Raffael, and Julie with Ben." Francesca goes through the names one by one, and the fewer of us that are left, the more my body tenses up. I know who Francesca is going to assign to me even before she says it.

"Zoe and Jase."

My pulse goes haywire, and I only realize that my hands are clenched again when I feel my fingernails digging painfully into my palms. *Great.* As if I didn't already have enough shit to deal with. Now I'm stuck with Zoe.

You're a coward.

The voice in my head is familiar, and it still hurts.

Shut up, Sam.

I turn toward Zoe to escape his voice, which is a joke because he's not there and he's not talking to me. It's all in my head, and I can't get away from myself. Believe me, I've tried.

Zoe is white as a sheet, looking as though she can't imagine anything worse than dancing with me. My nails dig even deeper into my skin.

She doesn't move a damn inch in my direction while Francesca assigns the last pairs, just stares at me, her eyes wide. I return her gaze coolly, and a hurt expression flits over her face. It's easy to see what's going on inside her. She's realizing I'm not the same person I was back then. I'm not the one who kept her secrets. I'm *different* now.

Well, guess whose fault that is, Pixie.

My mouth twists into a condescending smile. I can't help it. It's pure self-defense.

Her gaze wavers, and she blushes. Thanks to her fair skin, I can see the heat rise up her neck and into her cheeks.

I don't move, so she takes a step toward me with her shoulders hunched. Her insecurity is palpable, and in the past, I might have asked her what was wrong.

"Jase," she says softly. The sound of my name on her lips makes my shoulders tense. When she says my name, it sounds different than when anyone else says it. That alone is reason enough for me to never want to hear her say it.

"Very good, then. Everyone has found their partners." Francesca saves me from having to acknowledge Zoe. But then she claps her hands encouragingly. "Okay, let's go."

Francesca briefly explains the sequence of our first routine, but I'm barely listening. It's the same as last year, and I already know what to do. I step behind Zoe, just as Ches and the others step behind their partners. We're so close now that the familiar scent of her shampoo washes over me. She smells just like she used to. Like lavender, and something indefinable that is simply Zoe. My heart skips a beat, and my hands find their way to her waist all by themselves. She flinches as I touch her and place my fingers on her flat stomach.

Believe me, I don't like it either.

In the mirror, her eyes meet mine, and her pupils are so dilated that her eyes look almost black. My grip on her waist tightens instinctively, and her eyes widen even more in response. I can feel the heat radiating from her skin, through the thin fabric of her leotard.

We start moving at exactly the same moment, in perfect harmony. Her gaze in the mirror meets mine again and again, and there's something in her eyes that I can't make sense of.

But it's difficult to think about that now because my fingers are wrapped around hers, and my body remembers other things. Her fingers on my face, my hands in her hair. I grit my teeth so hard it hurts and push the memories back, concentrating on the steps and nothing else.

We follow Francesca's instructions, going into spins and bending forward. It's easy, far too easy, to dance with her. It shouldn't be this damn easy, not after everything that's happened.

I try as hard as I can to imagine the girl I'm dancing with is someone else, anyone but Zoe. She's just another dancer. And somehow it works. I ignore her gaze, even as it keeps shifting to my face. I ignore the fact that her skin is getting warmer and warmer under my hands. I ignore the lavender scent of her hair. She no longer exists.

And then all at once, nothing is easy anymore.

I lead Zoe into a pirouette, holding her just like before, but this time she loses her balance, stumbles, and doesn't regain it. Not even when she stands up again, her face scarlet, and puts her hand back in mine.

"Sorry," she mumbles. Her voice sounds thin and fragile. The hair stands up on the back of my neck.

"Let's just get on with it. Get this over with," I say gruffly, and she flinches again. I ignore it.

We carry on, but it's like a switch has been flipped inside her, and her movements are suddenly choppy and out of time, not flowing like they were a moment ago. She is stiff and can't be guided. She's either too fast or too slow. Nothing works anymore, and I feel Francesca's skeptical gaze on us more than once.

Zoe suddenly tears herself away from me and steps backward. Her breathing becomes frantic, and tears shimmer in her eyes. Is she fucking serious? Is she going to start crying now?

You're acting like a total jerk, Sam's voice says.

I roll my eyes, and I'm about to comment, but I don't get the chance. She whirls around and flees the room like she's being chased by a demon.

Stunned, I watch her run away and just leave me standing here. Again.

CHAPTER 7

Zoe

I dreamed about you last night. No, it's not what you're thinking right now! We danced together, and it was kind of strange and . . . beautiful. I have no clue why I'm telling you this. But sometimes I get the feeling that you need to know someone is thinking about you.
—P

My heart is racing. I'm dizzy. I feel sick.

Shit. Shit. Shit.

I can't breathe. My chest feels too small for my lungs.

I can still feel Jase's hands on my waist. On my fingers. On my leg. His touch branded my skin, and it burns and burns.

Tears blur my vision, and I run away. I run, and I know it's a mistake; I know I should have stayed. But everything feels unsafe, and my heart is about to burst. Not in a positive way. It beats too fast, trips, and stumbles around in my chest. I feel so hot. I'm burning up inside.

Part of me wants to stop and just curl up into a ball and cry until it's over. But I can't do that. Not here. If someone sees, then . . .

I lose my balance and just about manage to catch myself. I have to get away. I have to go somewhere no one will find me. I'm so nauseated that I'm afraid I'll throw up at any moment.

I'm falling apart; I can feel it. The first crack, and then the second. I know this feeling all too well. It shouldn't be here anymore—it was gone. I was stronger than the panic.

I push open the door to the girls' bathroom near the stairs so hard that it bangs loudly against the wall, but I don't care. It slams shut behind me as I rush to the sink, turn on the faucet, and let cold water fill my hands. I splash it on my face and hair. I have to take a shower. I have to wash it all off.

The dirt. The shame. The panic.

I only notice I'm crying when I choke on my own sobs. More water. More. More. Until I'm completely soaked and shivering all over. My reflection stares back at me, my eyes wide with panic, my cheeks pale, and my lips blue.

Finally, my pulse is slowing again. The panic subsides. My legs give way underneath me, and I sink to the floor. I pull in my knees and hug them to my chest.

It's okay.

Everything is okay.

It's okay.

It's okay.

But nothing is okay. I thought I had it under control, the panic that rose up whenever someone touched me. It's the only reason I made it this far.

Putting up with being touched was the minimum requirement that my parents and Dr. Somers set for me to be allowed to apply here in the first place. And I overcame my panic. It was just touching. Just normal touches.

But this was different. It was Jase's hands on my body, his fingers on my skin. Those were his eyes that met mine in the mirror, so cold and hard and filled with anger that something broke inside of me. He was standing behind me, but simultaneously, he was there, back then, on that night. And then he was gone, and everything fell apart. Suddenly, everything was too much, and nothing was right.

But there was something else beneath the panic: a sense of longing for him. Words ready on my tongue, an apology that would mean nothing without an accompanying explanation. A tingling on my skin, a single beat that my heart skipped. A brief moment, and then I lost control. I lost control over my feelings and myself, and the panic crashed over me like a wave, ready to pull me down and drown me. It stole my breath until nothing was left.

I forgot what it was like to fight it. I felt too safe, too sure that I had overcome it. I mercilessly overestimated myself. With my whole body shaking, I close my eyes, trying to pull myself together because I must. I must not fail, not on the first day, like this.

This is my dream. This school. Ballet. If I lose this . . . then everything will have been for nothing.

* * *

Somehow, I manage to sneak back to my room unnoticed. I'll have to throw away my ballet slippers after walking across campus in them, but I don't care. I need to shower and change. And then I have to come up with a solution.

I have to talk to Francesca and give her an explanation that has nothing to do with the truth. I have to rescue what I can.

I switch to autopilot, checking off one item after another on my imaginary to-do list.

Take a shower.

Don't lose your nerve.

Get dressed.

Don't think about Jase.

Blow-dry your hair.

Don't panic again.

A loud knock on my door makes me jump up in horror. *Please don't be Jase.* I don't want to see him, don't want him to look at me that way again. Even if I deserve it. I open the door anyway because I can't help it. But it's not Jase standing there in the hall outside my room. It's Mae. Of course it is.

Why would Jase come? There's no reason for it. I took every reason away from him.

But still, I taste bitter disappointment on my tongue before swallowing it down. I may have convinced myself that Jase was a part of my past, not my future, but the fact is, I will see him. It doesn't matter if Francesca makes him my partner or not; I'll still be forced to see him at least three times a week for an hour. I can't ignore him and just pretend that nothing happened.

I could never do that with Jase.

"Zoe? Hey!" Mae snaps her fingers in front of my face, snapping me out of my thoughts. I flinch and feel the blood rush to my face. The look of worry on her face deepens.

"Are you all right?"

"Yes, I . . . I'm sick," I reply, and it's not even a lie. Not really. "I think I should have eaten more this morning." Relief floods through me. That's a good excuse. Believable.

"You really should have." The slight sound of reproach in Mae's voice confirms it. She believes me. "You should talk to Francesca. She's worried. We couldn't find you anywhere after you left." Now her eyes are accusing, but she still seems concerned, and I realize that she doesn't want to upset me.

"I'm sorry, that was dumb. I just . . ." I manage a weak smile. "I didn't want to throw up in front of everyone on the first day."

"I can understand that." Mae begins to smile, but she immediately becomes serious again. "Did you eat something now?"

I nod. "I had a protein bar," I say, lying. Just the thought of eating anything makes my stomach turn.

"That's good. Then . . . would you like me to come with you when you go to Francesca?" Mae looks at me expectantly. At first, I'm tempted to take her up on her offer, but then I shake my head. I don't know how Francesca will react to my totally unprofessional behavior, and I don't want to have any witnesses.

"That's really sweet, but you don't have to. It's lunchtime now. I'll go over alone, and then I'll see you in class."

"Good. Are you sure you're okay?"

"Yes. I'm fine." I force myself to smile again, but my heart is already out of rhythm. Nothing is fine. Absolutely nothing.

CHAPTER 8

Jase

Have you ever felt lonely?

Always.
—J

"So, after that little drama, you really have to tell me what happened between you and Zoe," Skye demands in a tone that has no patience for an objection.

I object anyway. "Nothing happened between us."

Skye snorts indignantly. "Come on, Jase, I wasn't born yesterday. No one just runs out of class on the first day unless something completely tragic happened. How and when did you break her heart?" She sighs theatrically and clutches at her chest.

Furious, I grind my teeth. "Why do you just assume that *I* broke *her* heart?"

As if Zoe ran off without a word because I hurt her fucking feelings, either now or then. Skye's eyes widen in surprise, and I immediately wish I could take my words back. "Does that mean that she broke *your* heart?"

Fuck.

"I don't have one," I remind her tonelessly, although the muscle in my chest twitches in protest, insisting that it does, in fact, exist.

"Of course not. You're the only person in the world who doesn't have one. Self-deception is dangerous, Jase." She gets up and musses my hair.

I make a face involuntarily and refrain from answering, because I don't know what to say.

"Will I see you at lunch? I want to talk to Francesca for a minute." Skye raises her eyebrows questioningly as she walks backward toward our teacher. Francesca ended the lesson just a few minutes ago. Most of the class is still there getting their things together, though I notice the girl with the auburn hair who lives in the room next to Zoe has already left. Probably to find out if she's okay.

"Sure."

"Okay, see you soon. But then you have to tell me everything." She grins with satisfaction and turns on her heel.

"There's nothing to tell," I grumble indignantly, but either she didn't hear me or she's ignoring me. More likely the latter.

I get up, pack my things, and leave the studio in a rush because I want to stop at my room and change before lunch. But I don't get far. I'm almost to the stairs when I see a movement out of the corner of my eye.

A girl is alone in one of the ballet studios, practicing pirouettes in front of the mirror. Every movement is controlled perfection. She's brilliant, and she knows it with every fiber of her tense, controlled body.

Little Miss Perfect.

Ophelia Winslow.

My sister.

My stomach tightens. I didn't see her yesterday on the roof terrace, probably because I was busy dodging all the other people up there who I usually avoid like the plague. I should keep walking: The last few hours have been absolute shit, and watching Lia dance so well makes everything much worse. But suddenly, I can't move. I'm not only good at self-deception; I also have a knack for torturing myself.

As if sensing my gaze, Lia stops mid-turn and looks at me. Her face is expressionless, her green eyes as familiar as my own. We looked alike as children, with our blond hair, green eyes, and full lips. My sister's face is more finely formed than mine, but the resemblance is still uncanny.

Lia raises her eyebrows, a silent question. *Is something wrong?*

I imitate her expression because I know she hates it when I do that. Needless to say, we don't have a particularly affectionate relationship.

She rolls her eyes and turns away. I do the same. It wasn't always this way between us. It was never simple, sure, but it wasn't like this. Cold. Angry. Full of jealousy and hatred.

I started dancing because of her. A little boy who fell in love with ballet because he saw his big sister dancing. It wasn't even her grace that impressed me but her control over her body, over every tiny movement, coupled with the burning passion that it requires to captivate an audience.

That's exactly what I wanted. That power. The absolute mastery, the passion. *A dream.*

There was a time when I hoped that dancing would bring us closer together.

That time is long past.

My heart twitches a warning, and I push any thoughts of Lia to the back of my mind, because every time I look at her, or even think about her, I can't help but think of Sam.

And when I think of Sam, the indifference with which I suppress every other feeling cracks open, and that's the last thing I need right now. Or ever.

I've just reached my room when someone calls my name.

"Jase!" At the sound of the stern voice, I turn and see Camille, Mr. Pearson's assistant, walking toward me. As usual, her face is tense and pinched. She always looks like she's disapproving of something.

"Mr. Pearson would like to talk to you." She looks even more serious than usual, and my stomach sinks.

"Do you know what about?" I ask nervously.

She shakes her head. "Only that it's urgent. Come with me."

I hesitate, but I don't really have another choice, so I follow her. In silence, Camille leads me to the administration building and up to Pearson's office. With every minute that passes, my palms sweat and my stomach drops.

What the hell does Pearson want from me?

Students walk past us on their way to the cafeteria. I'm met by curious glances, and my shoulders tense again. Everyone knows that being seen with Camille is not a good thing. You're usually in a lot of trouble if you're escorted by her. But fuck, it's only the first day. And it's only lunchtime. I haven't even had time to do anything that might not suit Pearson.

The administration building is eerily quiet as we enter and walk through the corridor before finally reaching Pearson's office. Camille knocks on the door, and the sound echoes in the empty hallway. She doesn't wait for an answer, just opens the door and waves me in. I enter the room without looking at her again and let the door close carelessly behind me.

Pearson looks up from his laptop and points to one of the two armchairs in front of his desk, which are usually reserved for parents who are worried about their children or students who have gotten themselves into some kind of mess.

"Have a seat," he says.

In spite of the silver-gray strands in his dark hair, he seems younger than he actually is. I know his birthday, and not just because we get cake every year for it (as an exception—here, we're taught that refined sugar is practically poison). I knew him long before I was accepted here as a student.

"Have a seat, Jase," he repeats when I make no move to comply. I seem to have forgotten how to move. All at once, my body feels strangely numb. "We have something to talk about." The look in his dark eyes is serious.

I suppress the urge to turn around and walk away, but I sit down in the chair anyway. Whatever he has to say, there's no point in putting it off.

"What's up?" I act bored, as though I don't care at all about why he called me here. But my heart races, and I feel nauseated. My body can't deal with these damn feelings. Insecurity and fear. I can't do anything about them.

"I tried to reach your parents, both today and yesterday, but without success. That's why you're here now," he begins.

The mere mention of my parents makes me sick to my stomach. Fuck. This can't be good.

"So?"

"Their payment for the current school year has been withdrawn. Do you know anything about that?"

His words hit me like a punch in the solar plexus, hard and relentless, squeezing the last bit of oxygen out of my lungs.

"What?" I say, barely audibly. I stare at him, stunned. I blink, trying to understand what he just said.

"Your tuition fee has been withdrawn," he repeats, as if I hadn't heard him. But I did. I understood him far too well.

It's totally clear what it means. I'm screwed.

BEFORE

Jase

One year earlier
June 25, 12:43 PM

My parents didn't come to my graduation. Neither did my sister, my grandparents, or anyone from my family. Although part of me isn't surprised, the disappointment burns.

I watch as Caleb and my friends are embraced by their families while I stand off to the side. My throat tightens when I see Caleb's dad tousling his hair with a proud smile, and I quickly look away.

My gaze lands automatically on Zoe, who's standing between Tristan and Reed. Reed has an arm around her shoulders and is tugging on a strand of her copper hair. Zoe laughs, and something inside of me tenses at the bright sound.

"Jase, where are your parents?" I flinch at the sound of Ceara's voice. There's an expression on her face that's hard to interpret. A mixture of disapproval and sympathy.

I shrug and try to look indifferent. "They had an emergency patient. A high-risk pregnancy or something. There were complications during the birth." That's probably not even a lie. My parents are often called to emergencies. I guess that's what it's like when you run one of the most famous maternity clinics in the country.

But that doesn't explain why no one let me know. Or why Lia and my grandparents didn't come either.

The truth creeps closer to the surface, but I firmly push it back. I don't want to think about the possible reasons, because every single one of them hurts like hell.

A crease forms between Ceara's eyebrows, and she presses her lips together so firmly that I can easily guess what she's thinking, even if I hadn't seen her almost every day for the past four years. In some ways, she acts more like a mother to me than my own mom.

"We're about to take Caleb out to lunch. Would you like to join us?" She means well, but the kindness in her voice makes my shoulders tense nervously. I don't want her pity.

"No, that's all right. My grandparents wanted to come, but their flight was delayed. I should be at home when they arrive." Another lie. I force myself to smile. "But thanks anyway."

Ceara hugs me, and I stiffen before returning her embrace for a brief, weak moment.

"You don't have to thank me, Jase. You're family." She pulls away from me and musses my hair with a smile, just like Ethan did with Caleb a moment ago.

You're family.

I glance over at Zoe involuntarily and wonder if she sees it the same way. She turns around as if she feels me looking at her. Reed's arm slides down her back, and he says something to her I can't hear. Zoe answers him but keeps looking at me. Then she hugs him, Tristan, and Nick goodbye and finally walks over to her mom and me, her steps light and delicate.

She stands close to me, and the scent of her shampoo envelops me, but she isn't close enough to touch me. She makes no attempt to hug me as she did the others. Instead, a beaming smile spreads over her face.

"Congrats on graduating," she says.

"Thanks," I reply, not knowing what else to say. Ever since Zoe and I started sharing our secrets on little pieces of paper, it's become difficult to talk to her in person. Or even to be close to her. Because I suddenly want too many things that I shouldn't want from my best friend's little sister.

"I just asked Jase if he'd join us for lunch. His parents are stuck at the clinic. But I couldn't talk him into it. You try. Maybe he'll listen to you." Ceara gives Zoe a look that I can't interpret, but she obviously sees through the lie about my grandparents. Ceara kisses her daughter's cheek and leaves us alone.

"Don't you want to come?" Zoe tilts her head inquisitively, and her long hair cascades over her shoulder like a curtain. She doesn't ask why, and I suppress a sigh of relief.

"No, I have to go home. I should get going now. I'll see you later at Adaline's party, all right?"

"Sure. Jase—"

"See you later, Pixie." I cut her off and have to grin as she wrinkles her nose in exasperation. She always acts like she hates that nickname, but I know better. She secretly likes it.

I don't give her a chance to reply as I walk out and make my way home without even saying goodbye to my friends. We'll see each other again in a few hours anyway.

I'm met with complete silence in the house as the door slams shut behind me, and whatever little spark of hope I had left is extinguished. They really aren't here. When Lia graduated last year, it was a celebration: Mom and Dad were both home. Grandma and

Grandpa came all the way from LA. Grandma did the cooking. Meanwhile, my graduation is ignored completely.

I laugh bitterly, throw my cap and gown into a careless heap on the floor in the hallway, and go upstairs to my room. Maybe that will remind them that today is an important day.

My room is tidy, as usual, even though it only takes me about three seconds to create total chaos. Margaret, our housekeeper, is always tidying up no matter how often I tell her she doesn't need to. But since Margaret has made order of my chaos, I see the letter lying on my desk the second I enter the room. I immediately recognize the Harvard coat of arms on the envelope and freeze.

It's more than a reminder of what I'm supposed to do. It's an order. I already know what the letter says before I open it. My fingers are like ice as I pull it out of the envelope.

ACCEPTED.

It's a goddamn acceptance letter from Harvard University. Anyone else would probably flip at the possibility of going there. But I wouldn't, because I didn't even apply to the damn school. I drop the piece of paper as if it burned me.

Downstairs, the front door opens, and I hear Mom's voice followed by a deeper one: Dad. So they came home after all.

My legs move of their own accord as hope washes over me—stupid, irrational hope. But when I walk into the dining room, I see two boxes from the little Italian place they sometimes go to when Mom doesn't feel like cooking. Two, not three. They came home for their lunch break and didn't bring me anything. They didn't even ask me if I was at home or if I wanted something to eat.

Neither of them notices me as they talk about some bullshit

from the clinic. I have as little interest in what they're saying as they probably do in me.

Congratulations on your graduation, Jase.

Anger boils over inside me. They could spend at least one fucking day trying to pretend we're a normal family and that I mean something to them. A few hours, even.

I turn around without a word and go back to my room. I pick up the letter from the floor and go back to where they're eating. Dad only notices me when I drop the letter on his lasagna.

"What the hell is this?" I make no effort to conceal how pissed off I am.

Dad removes the letter from his food with such dispassionate composure that it makes me want to scream. "Looks like your acceptance letter to Harvard," he replies coolly.

I laugh involuntarily in disbelief. "I didn't even apply."

"Of course you did." Dad continues eating without even looking at me. "You wrote your application essay. Don't you remember?"

Yes, I remember writing that stupid essay that they require for the application. I also remember that I never sent it. Which can only mean one thing.

"Are you kidding me? You applied for me. You made sure I got in. I don't know which fucking contacts you used, but I certainly didn't apply to Harvard," I blurt out. Mom sighs.

"Jase, watch your language."

"I don't give a shit about my language right now! Dad, you know I don't want to go to Harvard. I've been accepted to the New England School of Ballet, and that's where I'm going." It's not like I haven't been making this clear to him for weeks.

"It's not."

"Dad!" We've had this conversation a thousand times. "I don't want to go to Harvard. I want to dance. Why can't you finally accept that?"

"Because you're not going to waste your high school diploma on a ridiculous dance school. You're a Winslow. Act like one."

I snort. As if it means something that I'm a Winslow. In his world, it does: It means wealth and a bunch of medical success stories. To me, it means nothing.

"If Sam were here—"

"Sam *isn't* here!" I shout, interrupting him. My heart is hammering, and my entire body is shaking. My voice too. "If he were here, you'd have come to my graduation. Which was today, by the way." I glance at Mom. A guilty expression appears on her pale face. She actually forgot. "But *I'm* here. Sorry if I'm not good enough for—"

"That's enough," Dad says definitively, finally looking at me. The expression in his green eyes—the same eyes as mine, damn it—is cold and merciless. "You're going to Harvard. Otherwise, you'll have to think about how you're going to finance your education yourself. And where you're going to live."

I freeze. "Are you seriously throwing me out?"

"Apparently, you want to make your own decisions, so you can live with the consequences. I guarantee you that I'm not going to fund a totally pointless dance education."

"But Lia is doing it. Why is she allowed to dance and I'm not?" I look at Mom pleadingly, but she refuses to meet my gaze and stares blankly at her salad.

I want to tell her how much ballet means to me and why I want to dance. That it's the only thing I can do well. That it's the only thing in my life that makes me feel like I can achieve something. That it helps stop me from going crazy and gives me an outlet for my feelings. I want to tell her that I feel more alive when I dance than when I do anything else and, above all, that it makes me happy. But I've tried more than once to express to them how important dance is to me, and they aren't interested. They refuse to listen. I don't even try anymore.

"You're not Lia. And I don't want to talk about it anymore. Make up your mind, and live with the consequences." Dad turns back to his lasagna.

Stunned, I stare at him.

Fuck you. The words are on the tip of my tongue, but I can't bring myself to say them. Instead, I turn away without a word and leave the house.

CHAPTER 9

Jase

Who do you hate most?

Sam. My dad. ~~Sometimes~~ myself.

—J

"We need the money in four weeks at the latest. Otherwise, you'll have to leave, Jase."

Pearson's words are still ringing in my head, on repeat in a continuous, toxic loop. I hear them again and again as I hurry to the parking lot to call an Uber. How could this happen? How could everything go so wrong?

Fuck fuck fuck!

It takes far too long for the damn Uber to finally appear. I slide into the back seat to avoid talking to the driver. My thoughts race as the car makes its way with agonizing slowness through the Boston traffic, across Back Bay to the West End. Half an eternity passes before it finally pulls up by the glass-fronted building complex where my parents have their clinic.

My parents are fertility experts and specialists in gynecology, and if they put half as much energy into their own son as they do into the unborn children of their patients, we'd probably all be doing a lot better.

The clinic takes up three floors of the building, with its own laboratory and several delivery rooms. My parents spend more or less every moment of their time here, unless they're called to one of the nearby hospitals to help with a cesarean section. My parents are brilliant, and medicine is their whole purpose in life.

It used to be different, back when we were still a family. But the old days are long gone.

My mother's office is on the first floor. I don't bother stopping at the reception desk to announce myself. Her assistant is sitting behind the desk, talking to a very pregnant woman, and doesn't even notice me.

Dark wood floors, bright walls, warm colors. The atmosphere is friendly and inviting, a place designed to make you feel safe and at ease.

Hypocrites.

The welcoming feel of the practice is totally different from our family home. The reception area is full of photos of families that Mom and Dad have helped over the years, beaming children with big, dewy eyes. But I know there isn't a single damn photo of their own family in the entire place.

No one notices me as I walk through the wide hallway and head to Mom's office. The door is open. I hear her voice, soft and warm and soothing. A tone that she only uses in the clinic, never at home. A pang of longing hits me. That used to be different too.

I pause in the doorway. Mom is alone and talking on the phone, probably to a patient. Locks of blond hair frame her delicate face, falling in perfect curls to her collarbone. Victoria Winslow is a beautiful woman, and I don't just think so because she's my mother and, at least at one time, my only ally.

I clear my throat, and she turns to look. A sharp crease appears between her finely arched eyebrows; she doesn't look particularly glad to see me.

I wish I hadn't had to come here either, Mom.

"Jase," she says coolly after quickly ending her phone call. "What are you doing here?"

I step into her office and close the door.

"We need to talk."

She stands up and smooths the skirt of her wrinkle-free dress. "You can't just come here without telling me first. I have appointments."

I bite back a snide remark and flop into one of the chairs in front of her desk without waiting to be invited. "I don't plan to stay long. The payments for my tuition have been withdrawn. Do you know anything about that?"

It would be better if she did, because there's only one other person who could have done it, and she doesn't want to argue with him any more than I do.

She goes pale. "What's that supposed to mean?"

So it *was* his decision. *Fuck.*

"I suppose that means that Dad found out that you paid my tuition," I say, unable to stop every muscle in my body from tensing. How the hell did he find out? Mom transferred the funds last year too, and he had absolutely no idea.

She stares at me silently, opens her mouth and closes it again, like a fish out of water. I wait for her to say something, to make things right.

Help me, Mom.

But she doesn't. She says nothing, just stares at me as she gets whiter by the second.

"What can we do now?" I ask, clinging to my pragmatism in this impossible situation.

"I . . . I . . ." Mom stops and goes a shade paler as the door flies open and Dad rushes into her office.

He barely looks at her, his piercing gaze focusing immediately on me. "I was wondering when you'd show up."

I grin at him, a stupid reflex and my own personal defense, because I know exactly how much it drives him up the wall. "Nice to see you too, Dad."

"Stop playing games, Jase. What are you doing here?" He steps behind Mom's desk and stands next to her chair, turning her office into his battleground.

"I thought you were expecting me. Then you should know why I'm here." I pick at a loose thread on the seam of my jeans. It's just my luck that I showed up at probably the only time today he wasn't busy with a patient. There's a reason I didn't go to him directly.

His nostrils flare, but I know he won't lose control. Not here. Never in the clinic. "I assume you're here because I found out your mother is paying tuition for your ridiculous dance school."

The thread breaks with a barely audible snap.

"Yup, looks like it," I reply, though inside I'm asking myself what I actually am doing here. What do I expect to gain from this? After all, I know exactly where this conversation is leading.

"What do you expect to gain from this?" he asks, like he read my mind. He taps his toe impatiently, clearly ready to be rid of me.

I cross my legs in an attempt to make myself more comfortable while my heart beats out of time. Suddenly, it's pounding far too fast, begging me with every beat to just disappear and spare myself the inevitable. But I can't leave. Not without at least trying.

"Actually, I wanted to ask Mom to transfer the money again." I ignore Dad's condescending stare and instead look Mom directly in the eyes, trying to remind her that I'm still here and that I'm her son. The one she used to love.

"Forget it," he replies, putting words in her mouth. They sound fast and hard, like shots from a pistol. They hit me right where it hurts, but I refuse to flinch. If I show weakness, I've lost.

"Dad, may I remind you that Mom can do whatever she wants with her own money?" My smile is more like a grimace.

"Not if it comes from our joint account." His mask of control is slowly but surely crumbling. But he's holding out longer than I expected.

I turn to Mom again. *Seriously?* She transferred my tuition fee from their *joint account*? It's no wonder Dad noticed it.

"You have exactly two options, Jase," he continues. He only needs a few seconds to regain his composure. "Either you come live at home and go to Harvard, with our full financial support, or you decide against Harvard and your family and deal with the consequences by yourself."

"Rufus—" Mom says, but Dad silences her with a sweeping gesture.

"We'll talk later, Victoria."

I get up and shove my hands in my pockets as Mom gives me an apologetic glance. I look at Dad like I don't care, but actually, I'm sick to my stomach. "Then I guess I'll live with the consequences."

Dad's mask shatters like glass. His face goes bright red. "Don't be a fool!"

A harsh laugh escapes me, but my eyes are burning. "I'm not the one acting like a fool here, Dad. You're determined to get your way? Fine by me. Then cut off the money if it makes you feel better! I'll be fine."

That's a lie, and we both know it, but I'm not going to back down. I can't. It's not about Harvard; it never was. It's about me not being who he wants me to be. And yes, I came here for money, but deep down, I know there's another reason. On shaky legs, I head for the door.

"Jason Alexander Winslow, you're not going to leave now." Dad's voice has become ominously quiet, but I don't stop.

I'm not afraid of him. Because no matter how angry he can get, he'd never hurt me. Or Mom, or Lia. My dad is a doctor, heart and soul. He doesn't hurt people; he saves them. He just couldn't save the one person who meant more to him than anything else in the world.

My heart is racing as I walk out of Mom's office and then the clinic. Did I really think I could fix the whole thing so easily? Ask Mom for money and everything would be fine?

Obviously, I was wrong. I'm not going to get the money, and that means I'm totally screwed.

CHAPTER 10
Zoe

Which parts of the world do you want to see most?

London. Verona. Edinburgh. Paris. Rome. Barcelona. Lisbon. After graduation, I would love to travel around Europe all summer and see every theater.
—P

I spend the rest of the day hiding behind a fake smile, even though I'm constantly nauseated and feel like I'm going to lose it at any moment.

The conversation with Francesca was difficult mainly because I had to lie, and I've never been a good liar. She wasn't thrilled with my behavior, but because it was my first day and nerves are normal at the beginning—her words, not mine—she let me get away with it. However, she also made it clear that she won't tolerate any more scenes like that. I have to get a grip on myself.

Somehow, I manage to get through lunch break with Mae. Kaya, Jessica, and two other girls from our class sit down with us, but I only register a fraction of their conversation. The afternoon goes only marginally better. I take notes during theory lessons, writing down the dates of exams, when we're going to cover which topics, and which books we're supposed to buy, even though most of them are already on my desk. I'm present and functioning, but I'm not really *here*. I can't think of anything but Jase and that damn pas de deux class. I keep feeling his hands on my skin and the panic that hit me totally out of the blue.

I don't understand where it came from. My last panic attack was months ago. I went on dates and danced with other boys to prepare for the entrance exam. I really thought I had myself under control. Obviously, I was wrong.

I should probably talk to someone. My parents. Caleb. Dr. Somers. But if I did, they'd make a bigger deal out of it than necessary. They'd jump to conclusions, and in the worst case, they'd pressure me to leave school again because they're worried. They're always worried.

I'm so tired of it. I'm tired of the worry and the panic. It's over, and that's how it's going to stay. Today was an isolated incident. A tiny, insignificant loss of control because I had to dance with Jase, of all people. Nothing more. It won't happen again.

For two days, I manage to convince myself of it. For two days, I manage not to go crazy, even though Mr. Conrad and our other teachers touch me several times to correct my posture. Until the next pas de deux lesson on Wednesday, when Francesca assigns me a new partner. Ches is nice. He's taller than Jase, and thinner, with a friendly smile and a warm look in his brown eyes.

But the second he puts his hands on my waist—hands that feel so different from Jase's—I realize I've been lying to myself over the last forty-eight hours. I didn't panic because the hands on my body belonged to Jase.

It was because they were large and masculine, with a grip that was firm and confident. My chest tightens again. I can feel my heart beating out of rhythm. I hear Francesca's instructions like I've got cotton balls in my ears, but I can do this. I must. If I fail, my dream will be over, and I can't allow that.

Pull yourself together, Zoe.

Just get a damn grip on yourself. It's not that bad.

You've got it under control. You are stronger than this.

But I'm not stronger, and what Ches and I are trying to do for the next half hour is anything but ballet. It's a disaster of epic proportions, and I want to cry and scream, but the panic chokes me. Everything, simply everything, is awful.

After forty-five minutes, Francesca assigns me a new partner, but things aren't any better with Theo either. The fear is still there, all the time, and I hate, hate, hate that I can't just shake it off. I feel sick again, but I can't fall apart now. Not again.

Keep your eye on the goal. That's all that matters.

I keep reminding myself of this, because it's what saved me over the past few months. I had a goal, and I did everything I could to attain it. That goal was getting into this school, and now that I'm here, I'm losing my grip because every other goal is too far away. There's nothing left within reach, nothing I can cling to and fight for. That's why I'm failing.

Again and again.

Francesca ends the lesson with a worried crease between her eyebrows, her gaze lingering on me for a moment too long. I rush out of the room before she can call me back and ask what my damn problem is. Because it's pretty obvious that my strange behavior this time wasn't due to excitement or the fact that I didn't eat enough.

I can't hide from Mae, though. She asks me what's going on. She does it in a sweet, caring way, but I can't bear to tell her the truth. We've only known each other for three days. Instead, I avoid her. She's understanding, but I can tell she's worried. I would be too, if I were her, but that doesn't change anything.

And then it's Friday. My first week at the ballet school is coming to a close faster than I expected. I should be happy about the weekend, like everyone else. Two free days that most of us will spend in the ballet studios anyway, but they're two days when we can do whatever we want and not be judged. We can practice on our own.

Unfortunately, there are still a few hours left before the weekend, and I have to dance with a partner for two of them. Or try to, at least. I can't panic again.

But I can feel the fear the entire time. It's lurking there beneath the surface long before I even enter the dance studio. I feel nauseated, and I am sweating even though it's not warm. I'm nervous, and part of me wants to run away, but I've got to face the inevitable. Somehow, I'll get through it. I've done it before, and I'll do it again. I have to.

I'm stretching the backs of my legs, eyes fixed on my feet, when Francesca rushes into the room like a whirlwind. She doesn't waste time with a greeting but points first at Mae and then Jase, assigning every girl a partner. She hesitates for a split second before saying my name and then tells me to dance with Devon.

He groans with annoyance, and I blush. Of course he noticed

how badly things went with Ches and Theo. My legs tremble as I stand next to him.

"Can you try not to do the all-bad thing again today?" he says not very quietly, with his arms crossed over his chest.

Kelly, who is standing just a few steps away from us with Ches, giggles, and Ches shoots Devon a dirty look.

I stare at him, speechless, too shocked to reply. His mouth twists into something like a condescending smile, which, despite his best effort, doesn't cover up the fact that he's giving me side-eye. He checks out my pale tights and form-fitting leotard with the narrow straps, and his eyes stay a little too long on my breasts. The panic eats its way through to the surface, and all I want is to run away.

"Concentrate!" Francesca orders. She didn't hear what Devon said to me or see how he looked at me, and while I wish she had, I don't say anything, because I hate being a snitch.

"We'll begin where we left off on Wednesday. Chester, Kelly, you start. We'll continue in order. Zoe, Devon, you're next."

* * *

"No, it's not going to work like this." Francesca rubs her temples and stares at me with such desperation that one would think I'm causing her physical pain.

I can't blame her. I'm in pain too. It's twice as bad with Devon as it was with Ches and Theo. My body is rebelling against being touched by him with all its power. Every muscle is stiff and cramped. There's no grace or control. I lose it as soon as he puts his hands on my body, on the thin fabric of my leotard. I feel naked, and it's all wrong. I feel like I'm about to burst into tears.

"Zoe, I really don't know why you're making such a big issue about dancing with a partner. But whatever the reason, you'll have to get it under control. Otherwise . . ." Francesca sighs, as if that says it all. And somehow, it does.

My heart falters. *No, no, no!* If I can't get a grip on myself, I'll be kicked out of school. For flunking a course. In the first week of the semester. I'm such a failure. Tears burn in my eyes, and I blink them away. I try with all my might to swallow the hard lump in my throat and almost choke on it.

"It would be better for all of us if she just ran away again," I hear Devon murmur.

I haven't even made it through a week, and it looks like I might have to give up my dream because my body can't deal with it. Because it's not doing what I ask it to. Because it's fighting me.

"Fine. Let's try something else." Francesca carefully evaluates one boy after another. "Jase, I want to see you with Zoe again."

No. Please, no. Please, please.

The words strain to come out, hoarse and pleading, but I can't bring myself to say them. I can't move. I can't manage to walk toward him. It's impossible. Why can't she see that?

"Zoe?" Francesca says, but my body is paralyzed, and I suddenly feel terribly cold.

Jase looks at me again. His empty expression is so unlike the boy I used to know that this time, my heart doesn't clench in fear.

"Come on, Jase. We don't have all day," Francesca says. I can see he wants to protest, but then he moves toward me with lithe steps. He doesn't look at me but past me. His eyes are fixed on a point behind me, and his face is a mask of complete indifference. As though he doesn't care one bit that he has to dance with me now.

Every hair on my body stands up when Jase steps behind me. He's not close enough to touch me, but he's near enough that I can detect his unmistakable scent, sweet and musky all at once. My skin starts to tingle, and my breath catches in my throat.

"Another reminder: The pas de deux is about passion. About love and pain. Think about Florine and the Blue Bird from *The Sleeping Beauty*. Think of Odile and the prince from *Swan Lake* and *Giselle*. You don't have to like your partner for your dancing to be effective. But the better you harmonize with one another, and the more you *feel*, the better you will be," Francesca says. I can't shake the feeling that her words are aimed directly at me. "Now, please try again, and keep that in mind."

Jase and I don't say a thing to each other, even when he comes to face me and offers his hand. He's still refusing to look at me, and I want to say something, anything. But my mouth has gone completely dry, and my mind is suddenly blank. There's nothing to say. It's too late for an explanation and way too late for an apology.

My fingers tremble, but I force myself to raise my arm and put my hand in his. When I feel his skin under my fingertips, my treacherous heart stops for a moment.

Time dilates, slows down, slower and slower until it seems to run backward, and my stomach begins to clench frantically. My breathing is suddenly far too fast and shallow. My body feels like it's burning.

The panic hits me again.

I twitch and start to pull back, but Jase holds my hands tightly, giving me no chance to pull away from him.

"Forget it. You're not running away again," he says. His sharp tone of voice sends a shiver down my back.

I didn't run away because of you, I want to say, but my vocal chords have other plans. I can only stare at him with wide eyes as a tingling numbness begins to spread from the back of my neck.

"I—" I say, but he interrupts me.

"I'm not interested. Just concentrate." He gives me a look that could kill as we take our position in the second row. I open my mouth and then close it again, because I don't know what to say. Instead, I do what he wants because I have no other choice, even though everything inside of me is resisting. I concentrate on Francesca's words, and my feet follow her instructions. Fifth position. The pain flares in each muscle, in my legs, arms, below my ribs, and in my back. The pain that has accompanied me for years. I have permanent tension in my whole body, which I owe to countless hours of practice every single day.

But I can't stop my muscles from trying to lock in place and my heart from threatening to jump out of my chest. If I could, I would have done it a long time ago.

Shaking, I exhale slowly and raise my head so I can look in the mirror. A pair of green eyes gazes back, unmoved. I blink. I hate that he's looking at me that way.

Francesca is still speaking, explaining which positions we should practice next, but I only understand half of what she's saying. Pirouette, attitude, and arabesque. The rest blends into an indistinct murmur that reaches my ears but doesn't register in my brain.

My hand is in Jase's, and the urge to run away again is overwhelming. At the same time, there's a part of me that wishes he would hold my hand tighter. A burning desire to throw myself against his chest and let him take me in his arms while I tell him all the terrible secrets I've kept from him comes out of nowhere.

I almost have to laugh. It's a sad, desperate feeling. It makes no sense. Jase is the last person I want to tell what happened to me, and I'm sure he's the last person who wants to hear about it.

Jase snaps me out of my thoughts by tugging roughly on my hand. I stumble and almost fall, but he catches me and sets me safely back on my feet. The muscles in my back tense as he puts his hands on my waist, and his touch burns like fire. Once again, the trembling creeps up inside of me. It starts in my hands, an involuntary tensing and relaxing of muscles.

Not now. Not again.

Francesca gives us a signal, and my knees go into a plié all by themselves. I listen to her instructions because it's the only thing I'm capable of doing right now. I push off the floor, relevé on top, stretch my right leg to the front, bring it to the side, bend it back to the left knee, and turn, my gaze fixed on Jase's far-too-perfect face in the mirror for as long as possible.

At this moment, he's my fixed point, and his gaze is responsible for ensuring that I don't lose my balance or get dizzy. And for that one moment, everything is easy. For a moment, the fear subsides.

He stands beside me, strong and unwavering, and my pirouette is . . . not perfect, but for the first time, not an absolute disaster either.

I almost weep with relief, but the feeling quickly fades when Jase looks at me from the mirror, his brow furrowed.

"That wasn't *complete* shit," he says.

The shame makes me blush. Is he serious? I stare at him uncomprehendingly, trying to find a clever answer and coming up with nothing. I'm at a loss for words.

Francesca appears next to us. "That was better, but not good enough yet. One more time from the beginning."

We take position again, and I'm so humiliated that I wish I could sink into the floor.

Jase blows on the back of my neck, and I gasp involuntarily. "What's wrong, Pixie? Have I left you speechless?" he whispers in my ear so quietly that Francesca, who is still next to us, can't hear him.

My face is burning, and now I'm even more determined to show him that I can do it better. We keep going. But I can't.

* * *

"Raphael and Skye, Mae and Ches, Kaya and Ben, Zoe and Jase," Francesca announces at the end of the lesson. I can't hear the rest of her choices; cold sweat is breaking out on my forehead.

Jase is my partner. We are a couple. A *dancing* couple. One part of me is relieved, and the other part is so panicked that I begin trembling and my teeth chatter. Bile rises in my throat, but I swallow it down. I can't throw up. Not now.

A few more minutes. Hold on for a few more minutes. I sigh with relief when Francesca finally lets us go. But I don't even make it to my bag before she calls me back. With Jase, of course.

I walk over to them on shaky legs, praying that whatever she wants won't take long. I really need to get out of here.

"Zoe, I've spoken to your other teachers," Francesca says as I stop in front of her. My stomach drops with a jerk. "You seem to be doing much better in every course but the pas de deux. Otherwise, I would have recommended that you give up your place to another student. What I've seen from you so far doesn't even begin to match the level of the other girls here."

Her words hit me like a punch in the gut. Hard and unrelenting. All at once, my throat closes, and I start blinking frantically to force back the tears welling up in my eyes. They burn like acid.

"I'm not happy about giving you Jase as a partner, but of all the pairings we've tried, you work best together." Either she doesn't realize how much her words are hurting me or she doesn't care. Jase makes a sound that could mean anything or nothing, but I can't manage to look at him.

"I'm sorry. I . . . I—" I stammer, but Francesca silences me with a gesture of her hand.

"I'm not finished. I'm not happy with the decision I had to make, but you can prove to me over the next few months that I'm wrong. The pas de deux is all about collaboration. It's about connection and trust. So make sure you can trust each other and learn to work together. I don't care how you do it, but make sure you work as a pair. Otherwise, I may have to reconsider my decision. Is that clear?" She watches us closely and waits until we both nod. "Fine. You can go now."

She shoos us out of the room, and I rush to pick up my bag and pack my things before I run away again. Francesca's words haunt me; they blur and become meaningless white noise until only two remain.

Zoe and Jase.

Jase and me. Jase and me. Jase and me.

PART 2

Adagio

Phase Two of the Pas de Deux

CHAPTER 11
Jase

Who would you like to hug most right now?

Sam.
—J

My pulse began to pound in my head hours ago. At exactly the moment that Francesca assigned Zoe as my partner.

Zoe and me.

Fuck.

It was so obvious that it would happen. I already knew it on Wednesday when Zoe danced with Ches and Theo, and it became even clearer today when she was with Devon.

On Monday, she didn't freak out because of me. She didn't run away from me. Something is wrong with her, and it doesn't have anything to do with me. She panicked. I don't have the slightest idea why.

I've seen Zoe dance with partners before. She was good, really good. What we saw this week wasn't her.

What the hell happened to her last year?

I rub my temples and suppress a sigh of frustration. Zoe's

problems are none of my business anymore. Damn. A few hours ago, I didn't care about them either.

But before, she didn't look like she was about to collapse at any moment. I hadn't felt the trembling that runs through her body as soon as I touch her. I hadn't felt how fast her pulse races. I turn the corner and block any thoughts of Zoe. I can't deal with her right now. I have my own problem to solve.

Camille isn't sitting at her desk outside Pearson's office. I look around, but there's no trace of her, and I don't have the time or the patience to wait for her to give me permission to enter Pearson's office. We have an appointment already; that should be enough.

It still feels weird to knock on his door myself. A few seconds later, I hear him answer.

Everything will be fine. I can do this.

I take a deep breath and relax my shoulders before I open the door, walk into his office, and stop dead when I see a familiar figure sitting in the same chair I was sitting in last week.

Reed eyes me with annoyance, and his expression darkens when he realizes it's not just some student who's barged in but me.

In the year since I've been here, I haven't seen Reed once, even though he's Pearson's nephew. But he's not a dancer, and as far as I know, he and Pearson aren't particularly close. The fact that he's here today, of all days, is the icing on an absolutely shitty cake.

We were never really friends, not like he was with Caleb or Caleb was with me. Zoe's brother was our connection, and after Caleb banished me from his life, Reed, Tristan, and Nick never tried to keep the friendship with me going. They had accepted me before because I was important to Caleb. Now I wasn't anymore.

"Jase, come in. Sit down. Reed was just leaving."

Reed snorts. He doesn't seem like he was about to leave, but he gets up without arguing and pushes back a lock of his perfectly styled dark hair. "Thanks for your time. I suppose I'll see you on Sunday with Mom and Dad," he says, and Pearson nods.

"Hi, Reed," I say curtly, because we're adults and it would be ridiculous to ignore him. After all, we hung out together almost every day for four years.

Reed takes a step toward me and raises his hand as though he's about to give me the finger but then remembers we're in his uncle's office and adjusts the collar of his neatly pressed white shirt instead. He shoves past me without a word. *Jerk.*

The door slams shut behind him, and Pearson turns his attention to me.

"What can I do for you?" he asks.

I sit down in one of the chairs in front of his desk and hesitate. Everything inside of me, above all my pride, wants to resist telling him why I'm here. But my pride won't help me pay the tuition, so it'll have to shut up.

"My father doesn't want me to go to school here," I say. "That's why the tuition payment was withdrawn. My mother paid for the first year, but I don't think she'll do it again. I've always worked during vacation and saved money, but I'm sure it will never be enough to pay for everything. So either I'll have to leave, or you'll have to give me the chance to apply for a scholarship so I don't have to spend my life as a doctor or a lawyer helping strangers instead of doing what I live for. Dancing." Those are the cold, hard facts. Pretty awful facts, to be honest.

Pearson's eyebrows have been rising as we talk, and now they almost disappear under his hair. The room is completely silent for a few seconds, so silent that for the first time, I hear the ticking of the clock on the wall behind me.

"Scholarships are always awarded at the beginning of a new semester," he says, his voice calm and emotionless.

"What does that mean?" I know exactly what it means, but I need to hear him say it, because I don't want to accept the simple truth that I might lose an entire semester. I can't. I just can't.

"You're a talented dancer, Jase." Pearson ignores my question. "But I can't just pull a scholarship out of a magic hat for you."

I wait, because even if it sounds like a no, it doesn't feel like one. Hope surges through my veins. It's a hope I can't justify, but I can't deny it.

"You can apply for a scholarship next semester like everyone else. I will ask Camille to provide you with the necessary paperwork."

My whole body tenses. That's not enough. Where the hell am I supposed to go if I have to take a semester off? I can't possibly go to my parents. I don't have money to rent an apartment either. What I've earned from the ballet lessons I've given the past couple summers can keep me afloat for a few months, but that's about it. I could ask East if I could live with him again, but he saved me once already, and I don't want to ask him again.

"What about this semester—" I stop when my voice threatens to break. I hate myself for the weakness. It feels like I'm standing at the edge of a cliff right now. It won't take much to make me fall, and I can't do anything to stop myself.

Pearson sighs. "This semester . . ." he hesitates. It makes me want to scream. My nerves are totally shot. "I'll have to speak to the finance department and the board to see if we can make an exception for this semester so you can pay the fees in installments. Without interest."

There's a twinkle in his eyes, and it takes me a moment to realize what he said. If I were standing, my legs would probably collapse with relief. "Thank you," I say, with a lump in my throat. "That would really help."

Pearson smiles empathetically. "I'm sorry your parents don't believe in your dream."

I don't reply, because there's nothing I can say about that.

"There's one more thing. If you want to qualify for a scholarship, I expect you to perform your best in all your courses. Especially the practical ones. Do you understand?"

"Of course."

His smile gets wider. "Very good. Then I'll take care of the rest, and Camille will be in touch with you."

He dismisses me with a firm handshake, and only after I leave his office do a couple of things make sense to me. First, I have been given a chance to follow my dream. Second, I can't perform my best in all my courses if I have a partner who can't manage the most basic moves in the pas de deux.

That means my entire future depends on Zoe.

Fuck.

Now I'll have to deal with her problem. Because both of our problems have just been irrevocably bound together.

CHAPTER 12
Zoe

The thought of the next school year scares me. When Caleb is gone, and so are Tristan, Nick, and Reed. And you. If you're gone, who can I talk to when everything gets too much for me with Charlotte again? I don't want to go back to school without you.

—P

CALEB:

I'm fucked. I think I have a hardcore crush on Parker. That's not normal! It really isn't!

I have to smile when I read Caleb's text. He sounds happier than he's been in ages. He spent the last half hour telling me about his date with Parker in minute detail. It's almost sweet. But only almost.

ZOE:

Yes, that's normal! And it's good! It really is! I'm so happy for you. But tell him that if he breaks your heart, I'll beat him up.

CALEB:

Hahaha, sure. I should tell him that if worse comes to worst, my little sister will defend my honor.

ZOE:

Even small fists can hurt.

CALEB:

I know, especially yours. How are you? How was the first week?

My smile fades. My thumbs hover over the screen, but I can't manage to answer. I can't possibly tell him the truth. Not now. Caleb is finally happy again.

There's no way I can tell him that Jase is my dance partner. And it would be even worse to tell him that the panic is back. And that it's jeopardizing my place at the school, my studies, my dream. He would worry, and I don't want that. I want him to enjoy his evening and his weekend.

He should be allowed to wear those rose-colored crush glasses a little longer. The last year has been all about me and my problems. He deserves for it to finally be about him again.

CALEB:

Zoe, are you still there?

ZOE:

Yes, sorry. My neighbor just knocked on the door. I'm fine. It's been a busy week, but everything's good.

CALEB:

Did vacation get you out of shape?

ZOE:

Maybe a little. I have to go now. We're going to see a movie. Have a nice evening, and remember to warn Parker for me.

CALEB:

I already passed it on. Have fun!

I throw my phone onto my mattress, roll onto my stomach, and bury my face in the pillow. The pillowcase is soft and familiar, and it still smells of Mom's laundry soap. All at once, my eyes fill with tears again because I feel so lonely. But I don't want to talk to anyone.

It's impossible. When I start to talk about it, everything gets worse. But I miss closeness and hugs and someone whispering that it's going to be okay. I miss Mom's reassurance that everything is getting better and that I'll make it. Right now, it doesn't feel that way. Everything feels extremely hopeless.

Tears burn in my eyes, and I can't stop them. I'm about to scream, and I try to hold it back. I try to swallow everything. To suppress it. To get it under control. But control is slipping away from me. Suppressing the feelings doesn't work anymore. And then I scream, wild and raw, in infinite pain. I scream and scream into the pillow because life is unfair, and I hate this weakness. I hate it, hate it, hate it.

Before I know it, I've started to cry. Hot tears run down my cheeks and soak into the soft pillowcase. I twist my fingers into the sheets and sob until my throat is dry and everything hurts. There's only anger and pain inside me. There's no room for anything else. I'm so angry, it's devouring me. Every little part of me that's left.

At some point, crying isn't enough anymore. My voice fails, and I can't scream. I punch the pillow with my fist. A tortured sound escapes my throat and cracks, because nothing is enough. Because I'm a failure. I've lost myself before, and now I'm doing it again.

Shit shit shit shit.

The pillow flies out of my hands. I didn't intend to throw it; it just happened. It hits the vase of dried flowers on my desk and knocks it over. There's a loud crash, and a thousand shards fly. I sob, because all at once, it feels as though I'm the one lying down there on the floor. I'm in pieces. Pieces that I stick together again. Apparently, I didn't make enough effort to do it properly the first time; otherwise, it would hold. Otherwise, I wouldn't break so easily again.

My bedside lamp lands on the floor next. More crashing, more shards. I wait for the feeling of satisfaction that comes when you destroy something. That's what's supposed to happen, isn't it? In movies and books, things are always being destroyed. People hit each other and feel better because they've let out the chaos that's inside of them.

But I can't feel anything anymore. There's only emptiness inside of me, and that's worse than everything else.

The door of my room flies open—I must have forgotten to lock it. All at once, Jase is standing in front of me, a wild expression in his eyes. His lips are moving and he's talking to me, but I can't understand a word he's saying. My ears are ringing, and that's all I can hear.

Suddenly, he grabs my upper arms, my body jerks, and then I can hear his voice. Loud, and angry, and . . . worried.

"Shit, Zoe! What are you doing? Have you lost your mind?"

I burst out laughing hysterically. Yeah. That's what's happening. I'm really losing it.

He holds my arms tighter, and suddenly I'm cold as ice.

"Let go of me," I choke out. I feel nauseated again. Oh, God, this has to stop.

He immediately lets go, but I can still feel his touch, and for a moment, I want to take back what I said, because I want to feel his skin on mine. But it's not right. It's completely twisted. Everything is twisted, including me.

Jase backs away just a little, but he's looking at me the whole time. His gaze is hard, like it has been since I saw him last week. I hate it, because that's not *my* Jase.

He was never your *Jase*, the voice in my head reminds me. I want to tell it to shut up, but it's right. He was never mine.

"Zoe." My name sounds wrong when he says it. He never used to call me Zoe. Only Pixie.

He stands there with his arms crossed over his chest, leaning against my wardrobe. I can feel his worry and empathy beaming directly at me, even though I don't deserve it.

With trembling fingers, I wipe the tears off my face and look down, because I can't look him in the eye. He shouldn't have seen me this way. I'm so ashamed, and I wish he would leave. But I can't speak, and maybe a tiny, stupid part of me doesn't want him to leave.

"What's wrong?" he asks, and his voice sounds like it did then, that first night, after he followed me into the treehouse after the school dance.

It seems like history is repeating itself: I lose it, and Jase is there to talk to me. Except I'm not the girl I was back then, and he's not the boy who followed me anymore.

I could lie, but what good would it do me? It's pretty obvious something's wrong. A muscle in his jaw twitches. He's silent. Three, four, five seconds. "What happened?" he finally asks. He doesn't want to ask the questions; that's easy to see. He doesn't want to be here. I can tell, just like he can tell that I'm a hot mess. But he's here, and he's staying. He's asking me the same question that he wrote on the very first note.

It doesn't mean anything. He probably doesn't even remember. But I do. I remember every question and every answer.

"What are you doing?" I ask back, just like I did back then. My voice is as rough as sandpaper from sobbing and screaming.

His eyes flicker briefly, just for a moment, but enough for me to realize that he remembers too. Then the coldness is back. "It sounded like you were tearing your room apart."

"So? Why do you care?" The words burst out of me more sharply than I intended.

"You know what? Forget it." He grunts with frustration. He turns to the door, and I find myself both hoping he'll leave and wanting him to stay. I can't tell him, though. I can't say anything. The door closes behind him with a soft click. I sink back into my pillows, suddenly exhausted beyond belief. I want to pull the covers over my head and sleep for the rest of my life, because I don't know how I'm going to pull myself together. I don't know how to fix this. I don't even know if it's possible. I obviously did something wrong the last time.

I rub my face, and it feels hot and sore. Now I'm not even pretty anymore. The thought is so ridiculous that I burst out laughing. Then there are tears again. God, this is exhausting.

My door opens again, and I don't even look up. I'm beyond caring who comes in anymore. It's Jase. *Of course it's him*, I think, and another laugh escapes. But even I can hear how tragic it sounds.

I stay where I'm lying, because I don't have the strength to sit up anymore, and watch Jase come closer. There's a scowl on his face, his eyes are like storm clouds, and there's a crease between his brows. His lips are pressed together, and his jaw muscles stand out clearly. I know that expression, and I used to know how to make him smile at me. Now I don't even know who I am.

He reaches out a hand to me, and I want to flinch because he can't touch me now, not without making it worse. But then I see the note in his hand, and it feels like a thousand-ton weight is on my chest.

I take the paper because I can't do anything else. He folded it messily, and my heart jerks. Before I can even unfold it, he turns around and disappears. This time, he's not coming back; I know it. But he doesn't have to.

He wrote me a note.

I unfold the paper, and it's the same question again. His handwriting is still messy and still familiar.

What happened?

And just like that, our game starts all over again.

CHAPTER 13
Jase

What's your favorite place in the world?

~~I don't have one anymore.~~ Your treehouse.
—J

Her eyes follow me. I wish it were different, but it's my own damn fault. After all, no one forced me to go into her room. Certainly not twice.

Fuck.

I'm so screwed. But apparently, so is Zoe. She had hit her breaking point when I burst into her room for no reason. It just . . . happened, because I heard all that noise and thought—

Yeah, what was I thinking anyway?

Obviously, I wasn't. I just opened her door, and there she was with wild hair and puffy eyes. She was pale, with red streaks going down her face. That's why I went in a second time. That's why I gave her the note.

Fuck. The note. What the hell was I even thinking?

Surprise! Again, I wasn't thinking at all. I don't even know what I expected. That she'll tell me the truth? Actually tell me what happened? She has no reason to confide in me, and we both know it.

But when I went back into my room and saw the notepad on my desk, my hands took on a life of their own. I tore off a sheet and wrote down the same question I'd asked her back then in the treehouse. It was easy.

Easier than it should have been.

"Jase! Are you even listening to me?" Skye throws something at my head, which on closer inspection turns out to be a T-shirt.

I look up and see her accusing gaze. "Sorry, what did you say?"

"I said, you're going to have to talk to Zoe. If she knows that your scholarship depends on it, maybe she'll make more of an effort," she says, pulling the straightener through her hair with a practiced motion. She glances at the curl she's created with satisfaction.

"Isn't that thing supposed to straighten your hair?" I ignore her suggestion because I can't shake the feeling that pressure is the last thing that Zoe needs right now.

Are you getting soft or what?

"Basically, yes, but this is an exception." Skye reaches for the next strand of hair. "Don't try to change the subject. You have to get this scholarship. I want you to be my partner next year. It would really be stupid if you were thrown out of school before that happened."

I groan and throw the T-shirt back in her direction but miss her. "No kidding."

"Exactly. That's why you have to talk to her. Maybe you could squeeze in a few extra practice sessions too."

"Are you going to need much longer?" I ask instead of answering her. I don't want to think about Zoe right now. I can't. It's all gotten much too complicated. I take my phone out of my pocket and check my messages. There's only one new one because only two people ever text me anyway, and one of them is standing right in front of me.

East is the other one. We got to know each other last summer by dumb chance, and he was the one who kept me from ending up on the street. It turned out that Dad was actually serious about his threat to throw me out if I didn't go to Harvard. East saved my ass, and I practically owe him my life.

"You could have gone ahead on your own," Skye says, giving me an annoyed glance in the mirror.

"We've been through this. I'm not going to let you go alone," I reply as I'm texting a response to East, who wants to know when we're finally going to show up. It'll probably be a while if Skye doesn't get a move on.

She sighs theatrically. "Jase Winslow, my knight in shining armor."

I raise an eyebrow and try not to smile. "If you say so. Now hurry up. Otherwise, we can save ourselves the trip."

"Okay, I'll hurry, and you tell Zoe that she absolutely has to get better so you can stay in school. Deal?" She grins at me.

I look back at her apathetically. Not a chance.

"God, why are you always like this?" Rolling her eyes, she turns back to the mirror when I make no attempt at answering.

"It's all a matter of practice."

"Are there courses for that? How to be the world's biggest asshole?"

"Yeah, but you can't afford the tuition."

"You can't either," she shoots back, and I have to smile.

A few minutes later, she puts the straightening iron aside, puts on mascara and lipstick, and is finally ready.

"We can go now," she says, reaching for her jacket and a tiny bag that's only big enough for her phone. She holds out her hand to pull me up off her bed.

Outside, it's totally dark. The neatly paved paths are only sparsely lit by some of the old-fashioned gas lanterns that are all over Beacon Hill and Back Bay. But in an emergency, I could find my way around blindfolded. I know practically every inch of the wide square and the surrounding meadows, where I spent half the summer lazing around, reading, and killing time when I wasn't at work.

As opposed to the younger students in the dormitory across from us, we don't have to worry about being caught by security. As soon as you move from the small dorm to the big one, a lot changes. At least, that's what Skye told me. Especially when it comes to curfew. We don't have one.

Our Uber is just turning into the parking lot when we step through the main gate. The ride doesn't take long, and I'm glad that Skye is there to talk to the young woman behind the wheel. I'm even less comfortable with small talk today than I usually am.

The longer we drive, the denser the traffic becomes, even though it's already late. At least, it's late for the dignified citizens of Back Bay. The West End, on the other hand, is bursting with life, and the line in front of The Lighthouse is visible from a few blocks away.

I thank the driver and get out as soon as the car comes to a stop. Skye follows me, and we walk past all the people, who are mostly students at all the local colleges. Then we turn into a small alleyway.

The Lighthouse is slowly but surely turning into one of the hottest clubs in the city. Technically, Skye and I have no business being here. We're only nineteen, too young to be allowed in. But age doesn't matter if you know the right people.

We stride purposefully through the alley behind The Lighthouse, squeezing past a couple who are leaning up against the wall. They're putting on a show that looks like it belongs in a porn movie instead of a public street.

At last, we stop in front of a beat-up wooden door that looks like it's seen better days. I send Easton a short message.

JASE:

We don't have to wait more than a couple of minutes before the door opens a crack, letting us quickly slip into the dark hallway. The pounding bass makes the floor shake.

The guy who let us in disappears immediately without a word. His broad shoulders fade into the darkness. Skye and I follow him and step through a curtain that separates the backstage area of the club from the main room. Now we're on a little balcony with a perfect view over the crowd.

The room is overflowing, and sweaty bodies jostle each other, swaying in wave-like movements in time to the beat like a single entity. The whole place pulsates like a beating heart. The air is stuffy, saturated with sweat, deodorant, and the undeniable scent of sex. But nobody here cares about that. This isn't the Boston upper crust. People come here for one thing: to let go for a few hours and forget everything. There's a reason that I'm here too, even though I might get not only myself into trouble but also East and his buddies if any of the staff figure out that I'm not twenty-one. Not to mention Skye. But unless there's a police raid, the chances of getting caught are minimal. Identification is checked so thoroughly at the entrance that the majority of students are sent away as soon as they show their fake IDs.

I spot East and his friends at the other end of the balcony, where he's standing at the DJ booth and making sure that the crowd on the dance floor is losing all their inhibitions.

Heading his way, I push past a group of girls sitting on the floor. One is crying, two are trying to comfort her, and another looks like she's about to throw up at any moment.

"There you are," East says with a wide grin. He grabs my hand and puts an arm around my shoulder before letting go of me and giving Skye a hug. "I was wondering if you changed your mind."

"Nah." I shrug, and East hands me a bottle of beer. He's three years older than me, and because he's responsible for the music at The Lighthouse most nights, anything he wants is brought up here for him. I've never seen him or any of the other guys lining up for drinks at the bar downstairs.

"Sorry, that's my fault. Getting ready took me a little longer than I thought." Skye blows a dark curl off her forehead and looks around.

East gives me a meaningful glance and points to his friends, who are lounging on beanbags in the back corner of the balcony and talking. We can't hear them over the music.

"Jax is back there with the others," he says to Skye. She doesn't even blush. I'm not the only one who wants to forget something here. She winks at East, kissing him on the cheek and leaving a red lipstick print, and strides over to the boys, her hips swaying.

Colin, Jax, and Beck are almost always here when East is DJing. The four of them have known each other since kindergarten. They discovered their love of music together and eventually formed their own band.

They're sometimes allowed to do live shows here when the owner of The Lighthouse remembers that it's mainly thanks to East that his club is doing so well. The band may not have made it yet, but in the meantime, they've gotten so well-known here that certain girls sneak up to the balcony to at least create the illusion that they've spent the night with someone almost famous.

"Are you okay? Looks like something's going on." East crosses his arms over his chest and sizes me up a little too scrutinizingly.

"Zoe's at the ballet school," I say before my brain can stop me. What a dumb idea, to tell East, of all people. He's the only one who knows everything. Telling him was impossible to avoid, considering he saved my ass by taking me in last summer. I talked a lot in the first few weeks I lived with him. I still don't know why I told him so much, but I did.

"Oh, shit." He gives me a look of sympathy. "How are you dealing with that?"

I shrug. "I'm not interested," I say, lying. East's eyebrows rise skeptically. He doesn't believe a word I'm saying. I wouldn't believe me either, in his position. If I wasn't interested, I wouldn't have mentioned it, would I have?

"Jase—"

"Don't you have to work?" I say, pointing at the DJ board.

He hesitates for a moment, then drops it. "I'll see you later, okay?"

I nod noncommittally, chug the last of my beer, and go downstairs, shoving my way through all the bodies until I'm swallowed up by the crowd. I close my eyes, and my body moves all by itself in rhythm to the music, following the pounding bass. I let myself fall into the music and the night, into the forgetting.

I only open my eyes when a girl presses her butt against my crotch. She gives me a lazy look over her shoulder that promises everything, and when I make no move to resist, she turns around and wraps both arms around me. I let her put her lips on mine and hope it will work this time.

For more than a year, I've been trying to erase it, to make it unhappen—that one kiss that I can't forget. It never works. It's burned irrevocably into my system.

I realize immediately that it's not going to work today either. Everything feels wrong, and I back away. The girl frowns irritably, but I don't say a word. I want to slap myself, because it's ridiculous that I can't forget one damn kiss. Zoe still haunts me, and I can't help thinking about how she took the note from me.

I'm sure that when I come back later, the note will be slipped under my door. With an answer. And maybe also with a secret.

I make my way back to campus because it was a mistake to even come here today. It was clear that it wouldn't do me any good.

BEFORE

Zoe

One year earlier
June 25, 3:09 PM

I push one dress after another along the rail, but I'm not focused on what I'm doing. I'm still thinking about Caleb's graduation. Caleb, my parents, and Jase. Jase, whose parents didn't come to his graduation.

"Zoe, have you made up your mind yet?" Charlotte brings me rudely back to the present. I suppress a sigh, choose a dress blindly, and turn around to see the annoyed look on her face. She's impatiently tapping her toe on the floor.

"Yes, I have," I say, plastering a beaming smile on my face that feels completely fake.

"Great!" Her face brightens, and she twirls around in a graceful pirouette, always showing off that she's a ballerina, and dances over to Amber and Scarlett. I follow her, even though I actually just want to go home. This shopping trip was a terrible idea.

"So, are you ready?" Charlotte pushes a lock of black hair behind her ear and points at the changing rooms.

"Yes," Amber says, and Scarlett nods.

"Let's do it, then." Charlotte giggles enthusiastically and

disappears into one of the cubicles a second later. Amber and Scarlett take the next two, and I sigh as I enter the fourth.

The dress I took without thinking turns out to be a surprisingly good choice. The soft pink brings out the red of my hair, and the skirt swings smoothly around my legs and hits above my knees. I smile. *Not bad at all.*

"All right, time to show yourselves," Charlotte trills, and if I didn't already know that she'd drag me out of here herself if I refuse, I'd just stay where I am.

I step out from behind the curtain and almost choke on my own spit. She looks stunning. The wine-red satin dress clings to her body like a second skin.

"You look beautiful," I say honestly, and Charlotte beams at me.

"Yes, isn't it gorgeous?" She strokes the smooth fabric with both hands in awe. Then she eyes the dress I'm wearing and takes on a pitying expression. "Sweetie, that dress is really cute, but are you sure you want to wear it? You look pretty pale."

"Do you think so?" Unsure, I take a step toward the mirror. Yes, I look pale. Because I am. My mom's Irish ancestry has left its mark on me.

"Yes . . . well, you can still buy it, of course, but . . ." She lets the words trail off, but of course I know what she's trying to say. *I wouldn't do that.*

"Oh, Zoe, that dress is lovely!" Amber steps out of her cubicle and gives me a warm smile. "You look like a fairy." Apparently, she didn't hear my exchange with Charlotte; otherwise, she would never dare say such a thing. She never contradicts Charlotte.

Charlotte looks at her coldly. "I was just saying that Zoe looks a little too pale in that shade of pink." She shrugs her narrow shoulders and wedges herself between me and the mirror. She gazes at her reflection in a way that makes me feel envious. Charlotte is way too aware of her own beauty. She has no complexes about that, like the rest of us.

"I think it's about time I make a move on Jase, don't you think?" she says, tapping her full lips thoughtfully with one manicured finger.

"What?" I blurt out before I can stop myself. My heart is suddenly beating way too fast, and I can feel the blood draining from my face.

No. No no no! Please, not again.

Either Charlotte doesn't hear the horror in my voice or she ignores it. She turns around and admires her butt in the mirror. "I heard he's going to the New England School of Ballet next year, and . . . well, if I go too, we'd be the perfect couple, wouldn't we?"

"That's your definition of the perfect couple?" Scarlett scoffs as she steps out of her changing room in a tight black dress.

I don't hear Charlotte's reply. My ears are buzzing, and I just want to leave. It's silly, I know. But if she wants him, she'll get him. Because Charlotte gets everything she wants. Just the thought that his secrets could easily be hers in the future makes me sick to my stomach.

My heart hurts. Everything hurts, and I realize I'm going to have to do something about it. It's not about a game or secrets anymore. Now it's about my heart. And maybe it's about his too.

CHAPTER 14
Zoe

I'm scared that I'll be stuck in Charlotte's shadow forever. I know that sounds ridiculous, because someday we won't even go to the same school anymore, but I still can't shake the idea.
—P

Yawning, my limbs heavy, I sit on the floor in the ballet studio. I'm exhausted. I didn't sleep well all weekend, which is no wonder, but it still sucks. You'd think it wouldn't wear me out so much to lie in bed for two days, watching one show after another. Soon the episodes all blend together, and you don't even know what they're about anymore because your mind keeps wandering everywhere but the present. Mae tried to lure me out of my room twice, but I pretended I had a headache and holed up for a while. Yesterday evening, she just barged in with ice cream, chocolate, and a pot of tea and cuddled up on the bed with me. Then we started a new series, even though I was too distracted to follow it. She didn't ask me what was wrong. Maybe she knew that she wouldn't get an answer out of me anyway. But she stayed, in one day becoming a better friend to me than Charlotte was for almost fifteen years.

"Oh my God! Is that Charlotte Hammond?" Jessica asks breathlessly. She's sitting right next to me, and her words seem unnaturally loud. Did she read my mind?

She pokes me. "Zoe, look! That's Charlotte Hammond. In our class. Oh my God!"

All at once, I hear her voice, and my heart almost stops. The far too familiar, much too shrill voice that rings in my ears and doesn't belong in this ballet studio.

"Oooh, Zoe, there you are!"

Somehow, I manage to get to my feet and turn around just in time to see Charlotte walking toward me with a beaming smile on her face. She moves so fluidly, and her steps are so light that it almost looks like she's floating. She throws her arms around me, and I'm too shocked to avoid her—too shocked to react at all.

Charlotte is here. Why is she here?

My heart is racing, trying to escape from the cage of my ribs and run away. But it's trapped, just like me. There's a rushing sound in my ears. Charlotte lets go of me so she can look at me, but she's still holding my arms. It's terrible. It's all completely wrong. I want to pull away, but I can't move. My body is totally paralyzed. It's shock; I'm sure of it. I was caught completely by surprise by her sudden appearance. She shouldn't be here. Not in this course, not even in Boston. She's supposed to be in Paris, where she spent the last year. Thousands of miles, but also an entire ocean, are supposed to be between us.

Charlotte's lips are moving, but I can't understand what she's saying. Over her shoulder, I can see that everyone is staring at us.

"Surprise!" she says, and I wonder who she wanted to surprise, although it's pretty clear it's me. But I never want to be surprised by her ever again. Her surprises always hurt.

"So that was the news she mentioned in her last video," I hear someone whisper. I think it's Kaya. Her voice sounds scarily reverent. News? Video? What the hell is going on here?

"Well, did you miss me?" Charlotte asks when I don't answer. She's still holding my arms tightly. I want to slap her hands away, but I still can't move. The fascinated looks on the others' faces aren't helping at all. How do they know who Charlotte is? I have an unnerving feeling that I've missed something vitally important.

"I—" I start to say, not knowing how to reply. But Charlotte dismisses my effort with a wave of her hand.

"That's okay, you don't need to apologize," she says, and I don't understand anything anymore. "I don't hold it against you that you lied. It's all water under the bridge. Forgive and forget, right?" She gives me her most radiant smile, and I'm freezing cold when the pieces finally fall together.

She doesn't hold it against *me*? Forgive and forget?

I feel so sick that I might really throw up in front of everyone this time.

"What are you doing here?" I finally say. My voice comes out choked and far too quiet.

She ignores my tone of voice, and her smile widens. Her ice-blue eyes gleam. "Why else? To dance, silly. I know I missed the first week, but I had a performance in New York, and Pearson said it was okay if I started a few days later. With my kind of talent, a week is no great loss." She shrugs her delicate shoulders, and only now do I realize that she's lost weight. Her collar bone is clearly sticking out, her cheekbones and jawline are sharper. She looks older. More grown-up. And she's *here*.

I'm getting dizzy. This can't be true. This has to be a nightmare.

Don't I have enough problems already? Why does Charlotte, of all people, have to show up here?

"How nice for you," Mae responds, because I seem to have lost the ability to speak.

"Isn't it?" Charlotte turns to Mae with the same smile, but I know the expression in her eyes. She's not thrilled that Mae is joining our conversation.

"Totally! But I think—" Mae stops when Mr. Conrad enters the ballet studio and immediately notices Charlotte.

"Charlotte Hammond?" He looks at Charlotte in a way that I've never seen him look at a girl in our class before. As though she were something special.

"Yes. Hi. That's me." She takes a step toward him and engages him in conversation, eyelashes fluttering.

I sink to the ground as though I've been anesthetized. The day has only just started, and I already wish that it was over.

"You know Charlotte Hammond?" Kaya asks, and I look up. How long has she been sitting right next to me? And she's not the only one. A few moments ago, only Mae and Jessica were sitting on the floor with me, and now a whole crowd of girls are standing around us, staring at me curiously with wide eyes.

"We went to school together," I explain, my voice raspy. My mouth is dry, and I need something to drink. But for that, I would have to get up and get my bag. I don't know if my legs will hold me.

"That's amazing." Kaya's eyes get wider.

"Sorry that I don't share your enthusiasm, but can anyone tell me how you all know that girl?" Mae says and looks around curiously.

I send her a grateful glance because now I don't have to ask the question. Mae gives me an encouraging smile. Of course she realizes how much Charlotte's unexpected appearance has thrown me off balance.

"Don't you have TikTok?" Kaya asks.

Mae and I both shake our heads. I've avoided social media like the plague over the last few months.

"Okay, wait a sec." Kaya jumps up and comes back a moment later with her phone in her hand. She opens the app and shows us Charlotte's profile, @charlottehammond.ballerina. I shudder when I see how many followers she has. Almost seven hundred thousand.

"She's next level," Jessica says with a sigh, an almost dreamy expression on her face. "I mean, you can see that she's beautiful, but she's *so* talented and just seems super nice."

I flinch a little. Charlotte is many things, but she's certainly not nice. She's just a damn good actress. A beautiful girl with big doe eyes who can hypnotize the entire world. But behind the facade, behind the sweet smile and the charm, she's a monster. It's just that nobody looks closely enough to realize it.

* * *

Half of the students are in an uproar just because Charlotte is here. I can't understand it. I don't get what she's doing here or why everyone is fawning on her like she's Anna Pavlova. She's good. She's even very good, but she's also nothing special. At least when it comes to dancing.

Somehow, Charlotte managed to get into every single one of my classes. Her mother probably helped, because her daughter always gets what she wants. And if it wasn't her mother, it was her father, the mayor. At least she doesn't live in our dormitory. In the short break between classes, she explained to everyone that the rooms here are way too small, so her parents rented her an apartment nearby. The other girls hang on her every word as though she's sharing ancient wisdom. I want to wake them up and tell them that this version of Charlotte isn't real. I want to tell them that she's only playing with them, laying it on thick until they let down their guards so she can catch them unaware.

The problem with Charlotte is that she can make anyone believe whatever she says. She's just one of those people. Charismatic. Charming. She sparkles brightly, dazzling everyone.

Mae is the only one in our class who isn't clinging to Charlotte like a fangirl, and I don't know if it's because she noticed that I have a problem with Charlotte or because she just isn't interested in her. I hope it's both, but I can't ask her, because then I'll have to explain what my problem with Charlotte is, and I can't do that.

Luckily, my question is answered before the third lesson has even begun.

"God, she's unbearable! How did you stand her?" Mae whispers so that only I can hear her. We're sitting on the floor in the ballet studio, and she's reaching over her legs to stretch while I pull my knees to my chest and do my best not to fall apart.

Charlotte is standing with Kaya, Kelly, and a few others, still laying on the charm.

"You don't want to know," I murmur. I'm just about to explain when Charlotte squeals with delight. I look up just in time to see her throw her arms around Jase as he enters the studio with Skye.

His eyes widen in surprise, and then his gaze hardens. He grabs Charlotte by the arms and firmly pushes her away from him. Maybe that's why my heart skips a beat.

"Charlotte, what are you doing here?"

"What does it look like?" She laughs, a shrill, familiar sound that hurts my ears. "I'm here to dance."

"Good luck, then," he says gruffly, not sounding a bit like he means it. He tries to walk past her, but she blocks his path and puts a hand on his chest. I can see his jaw muscles clenching. I should look away because it's none of my business what Jase does, but this is Charlotte. It's like being a rubbernecker at an accident. I can't help looking.

"I'm really happy to see you again." Her voice takes on a deep, seductive tone that makes me want to puke.

Jase starts to answer but is interrupted by Francesca rushing gracefully into the room.

"Sorry I'm late, I had an important meeting. Your break is over. Take your places with your partners. We have a lot to do." She claps decisively, and I get up from the floor on wobbly legs to go over to Jase. I still haven't reached him when Charlotte takes a step forward.

"Excuse me, Miss, this is my first day, so I don't have a partner yet." She pouts a little, and I roll my eyes involuntarily.

Francesca frowns. "Yes, I already heard that there's another latecomer." She sizes Charlotte up. "I think—"

"I'll dance with Jase," Charlotte says, interrupting her.

"Jase is already dancing with Zoe." Francesca's tone is noticeably cooler. She's probably never been interrupted by a student before.

"Yeah, but Jase and I know each other. We're a good team, and I'm sure Zoe won't mind trading with me. Right, Zoe?" Charlotte turns to me with a fake smile.

For a second, all I can do is silently stare at her. Everything inside of me screams to say no. I want to slap her in the face for this ridiculous proposal, but I can't bring myself to do it.

"I don't give a damn if Zoe wouldn't mind trading with you, Charlotte. *I* mind."

I turn to look at Jase, too surprised to hide the expression of relief on my face. But he just mirrors back my gaze, completely unmoved. Then I realize his words aren't about me but about Charlotte, and my relief evaporates.

"Devon doesn't have a partner yet. You can dance with him," Francesca says, and Charlotte's face darkens.

She doesn't protest, but she isn't happy. And an unhappy Charlotte is unpredictable.

CHAPTER 15
Jase

What do your parents think about
you wanting to dance?

They hate it.
—J

Congratulations, you moron. You just blew your chance at a scholarship.

I could have said yes. Charlotte is a good dancer, and she can definitely do the pas de deux better than Zoe. Unfortunately, Charlotte is a total bitch, and my dislike of her far outweighs my dislike of having to dance with Zoe. I've never liked Charlotte. She's a nasty person who's just good at covering it up. So good that maybe she should be an actress instead of a dancer, but I could see through her relatively quickly when I first got to know her. She's selfish, manipulative, and mean.

Still, it might have been smarter to say yes. Zoe obviously has a problem, a pretty serious one, and I have no idea how we're going to fix it. And we have to, because otherwise I can forget my scholarship. That's not something I can live with.

The note that I gave her was a start, but I don't really believe it's the solution. Her answer was waiting for me on Friday night when I got back to my room. But her words didn't actually tell me much.

What happened?

I had a totally horrible year.
—Zoe

I want to ask her why, but that goes against the rules of the game that we silently agreed on over a year ago. I know if I ask that question, I won't get an answer. If she had wanted to tell me the truth, the whole truth, she would have done it already. The old Zoe always wrote down anything that was bothering her, no matter how small. I was the one whose answers were so short they barely counted.

The Zoe I know now is about as communicative as a rock. She looks like she hasn't slept properly all weekend. I don't want to make an issue out of it, but I can't help it. We're partners, and I need this damn scholarship.

I have to do something, whether she likes it or not. Unfortunately, I'm pretty sure I can do something that will help get Zoe out of her shell. I just don't like it very much.

"You've already found your partners. You're now a pair, a team," Francesca says, bringing me back to the present. "Use that to your advantage. Get accustomed to one another—build trust. And now: position!" She points to the middle of the floor, and we follow her instructions and take our places. Zoe looks at me in the mirror with a mixture of mistrust and skepticism.

Her hair is up in a tidy bun, as usual, and all at once, my fingers are tempted to pull out every single hairpin just to see how her red locks tumble over her shoulders. I clench my hands into fists before my body can act on its own and get me into trouble.

Zoe is still staring at me.

"What's wrong? What are you looking at, Pixie?" The nickname comes out of my mouth before I can stop it. She turns red, and I know that we're both thinking of the same thing. She signed her last note with her name. Not P, not Pixie. But Zoe. And now I just reminded her that she was always Pixie for me and still is, no matter what else has changed.

Fuck.

"Why don't you want to trade?" she asks, her chin jutting out defiantly. "With Charlotte, you'll definitely have it easier than with me. I totally suck."

"You don't *totally* suck," I object. But I save myself the trouble of pointing out that I never said that *she* sucked. Only her pirouettes.

"That makes me feel so much better." Her eyes narrow to slits. "So? Why didn't you change partners?"

"Because Charlotte is Charlotte," I reply resolutely, as though that explains everything. And in a way, it does.

Zoe bites her lower lip and nods, and I can't help but stare at her mouth. My mood darkens as I grasp her waist, turning her back toward the mirror and actively ignoring how small and light she feels between my hands.

What I can't ignore is the trembling that runs through her body. She goes pale, her eyes widen, and all at once, she's rigid.

"More dancing and less chat," Francesca says, popping up behind me, her reproachful gaze going from me to Zoe.

We nod simultaneously, and I repress the question that's burning on my tongue. Now is not the time for questions or secrets.

CHAPTER 16
Zoe

I know it sounds totally cheesy and cliché, but someday I want to dance with someone on a dark street at night when it's raining. I want a moment when everything is the way it should be. Without doubt, without thoughts, without yesterday or tomorrow.

—P

This lesson with Jase is even worse than the last, and it's no surprise why. Charlotte is here, and every move she makes is absolutely perfect. Flowing and bold. Magical.

She's looking at me; I can feel it. She watches my body and analyzes every step, every movement of my arms, and every angle of my torso. She's studying me intensely, and her thoughts are so loud she doesn't even have to speak for them to reach me.

You are so bad. You don't deserve to be Jase's partner. I should be his partner. You're a liar.

I can't concentrate; it's even worse than last week. She has to stop looking at me, and Jase has to stop touching me. They should both just leave me alone.

When Francesca finally ends the lesson, I get the feeling we've barely begun, and I'm already on the verge of losing it. I slip out of Jase's hands before Francesca has even finished what she's saying and hurry over to my bag. I quickly take off my ballet slippers, stuff them carelessly inside, and pull on my sweatpants and hoodie. I'm freezing cold, but I'm sweating, and the soft fabric sticks to my damp skin. I have to take a shower. I hate that I feel like this, but there's nothing I can do about it. With touch comes shame. The feeling of being dirty. I have to get rid of it right now because anything else is unbearable.

Normally, I wait for Mae after every class, or she waits for me, but today I can't wait. Charlotte is here, and I have to leave before she catches me. I just need a few minutes to pull myself together, because otherwise I'll fall apart again. But I'm not fast enough. I'm not even out the door when she catches up with me.

"Zoe, sweetie, wait for me. We have to talk about something." She takes my arm like it's the most natural thing in the world. I flinch. My whole body objects to her touch. My heart skips a beat and then restarts far too frantically.

I want to pull away from her, but she's clamped onto my arm like a vice. I can't get away from her, and the skin on the back of my neck begins to crawl. "Actually, I don't have time. I still have to—"

"But you have a few minutes for me, don't you?" she says, interrupting me. Her tone is sugar sweet, just like her smile, but there's a silent warning in her pale blue eyes, and I realize now that things have changed. Charlotte isn't pretending to be my friend anymore. On the one hand, I'm relieved, and on the other, it scares the shit out of me.

I'm about to tell her that I don't even have a few minutes for her, but someone beats me to it.

"She doesn't. We still have something to sort out." Jase strides toward us, hands shoved into the pockets of his sweats. He put on a hoodie over his T-shirt, and his hair is sticking up in all directions. The color of his eyes is so intense that it must be possible to see it from across the room.

It's unfair that he looks so good. And there must be something wrong with me for noticing it again at this very moment, while Charlotte is grabbing me and my pulse is shooting into a range that can't be healthy. I can feel it in my whole body, right down to my fingertips. My head is spinning, and I can't think properly. All I know is that Charlotte has to let me go and I've got to leave. I'm about to freak out, and she notices. I can see it in her eyes, and I hate her even more for it.

"We need to talk," Jase says when I don't answer. He nods in the direction of the corridor. He doesn't dignify Charlotte with a glance, and that sets off a warm tingling sensation in my stomach. It's gratitude for rescuing me from Charlotte.

"Then go ahead and talk," Charlotte says before I can even open my mouth.

Jase gives her a razor-sharp smile. "Then get lost."

She gasps indignantly. I almost burst into hysterical giggles. Jesus, it really can't go on like this.

"You know, Zoe and I have a lot to talk about; we haven't seen each other for a long time. If you want to talk to her alone, why don't you do it later?"

"I don't care how much you have to talk about. Since you haven't seen each other in so long, a few minutes won't matter. Now go away, Charlotte. Don't you have to shoot some TikToks?" Jase takes my upper arm and tugs me away from her.

He's too fast and she's too slow. She doesn't have time to react, and I don't react at all. I feel like a doll that two kids are fighting over. But if I'm honest, I'm almost okay with it because Jase is rescuing me, even if he doesn't know it. I'm sure it's not his intention.

Charlotte has gone white with anger, but her smile doesn't slip an inch. Maybe that's because we're not alone in the studio. Everyone else is still here, and Charlotte can't just drop the nice-girl mask. She opens her mouth, but Jase is faster again. He pulls me out of the room without waiting for her to answer, and I just let it happen.

We walk into the corridor, and Jase immediately lets go of me. He glances at me, and his jaw clenches, just briefly, but it's enough to let me know that he wants to say something. But then he doesn't. He's silent, and I'm grateful for the stillness because at least it gives me a few moments to pull myself together. Deep breath. My heart finally slows to a more normal rhythm. The panic fades, and I should be happy about that, but I know it will be back. This is just a short respite because my body can't keep it up any longer.

We leave the building, and the sky is an intense blue, the sun shining brightly. A breeze tugs at my hair, pulling individual strands out of my bun so they blow in my face.

"What did you want to talk about?" I ask as soon as I'm sure my voice will come out sounding reasonably calm and not like I'm going to burst into tears at any moment.

"We're crap. We're pretty much the worst pair in the whole class."

His words hit me where it hurts, even though I know he's only telling the truth.

"Thanks, I hadn't noticed," I say. Now my voice breaks, and I realize that I sound extremely weak.

"We should try to change that. I think it would be a good idea if we get together in our free time and practice the choreography so we don't fall even further behind. You have a problem, and it looks like you need all the help you can get."

I smile, bewildered. He's right, but Jase is the last person who can help me. And he's also the last person who wants to. At least, that's what I believed until now. It makes no sense that he wants to help me, not after I pushed him away last year.

"You want to help *me*?"

"Do you see anyone else here?" His voice is sarcastic. He rolls his eyes and looks like he wishes he had kept his mouth shut.

"Why? Why would you, of all people, want to help me?" I think that's a fair question, but he seems to see it a little differently.

"Maybe because I'm generous," Jase replies with a shrug.

"Yes, maybe. But that's not the truth, and we both know it."

Jase stops. His expression of apathy has changed to one of irritation. There's a deep crease between his eyebrows. "Let's just say this course is important to me."

"Why?" I can't help it; I have to know.

He groans. "Like you care."

"But I do," I say honestly.

"Oh, fuck." He tugs at his hair. "If you really want to know, I'm trying to get a scholarship, and my performance in this course plays an important role in it. Are you happy?"

I immediately have a thousand questions—mostly, why? Jase is the last person who needs a scholarship. His parents are rich. So why on earth would he apply for one?

"Then why didn't you trade partners?" I ask for the second time in a few hours. If he's trying to get a scholarship, I understand even less why he wouldn't want Charlotte as a partner.

"I already told you that. Because Charlotte is Charlotte," he growls. "So what's your answer? Yes or no? It's your call, Pixie." His voice softens as he says my nickname. He probably doesn't even realize he's doing it. But I can hear it, and a warm feeling spreads through me, because he sounds just like he used to.

I hesitate. More practice means more touching. More touching means more panic. But above all, it means more Jase. I don't know if I can do that—spend more time with him, let him get close to me. Get closer to him again. But I don't really have a choice, do I?

Not unless I want to lose my place here because I'm incapable of solving my problems. I take a step back and look at him. His gaze is unfathomable, his eyes burning into mine, and suddenly I find it hard to breathe. I wish I could read his mind. My skin starts to tingle again, but this time it's not panic. It's just the way he looks at me.

Yes or no? It's your call, Pixie.

I make up my mind. "Yes."

BEFORE

Jase

One year earlier
June 25, 6:32 PM

"Come on, Caleb; it's about time. This is your night! You're not seriously going to college holding on to the V-card, are you?" Nick throws one of the sofa pillows at him, but Caleb wasn't quarterback at Westview High for nothing. He neatly catches the offending object and spikes it back hard.

"Shut up, Nick."

But Nick doesn't shut up. He never does. "I've got a feeling tonight's your night. Don't argue with me. Adaline has had the hots for you for ages. She's spending the summer in Europe and then going to college in Rhode Island. It's your last chance!"

Caleb looks like he needs help. His cheeks are bright red.

"Nick, leave him alone. He can decide for himself." I toss my own pillow and hit Nick in the head, but I'm not really focused on what I'm doing. I've mulled over the conversation with my parents a thousand times, even though it's the last thing I want to think about. Especially today. This should be a good day. After all, I'm graduating. So far, though, it sucks.

Nick swears, and Reed and Tristan turn away from the TV for

the first time in an hour and laugh at him before concentrating on the screen again. They're playing some game; I don't know exactly what it is. I've never been into gaming.

"Yeah, sure." Nick rolls his eyes but isn't ready to give up. "Do you really want to go to college as an eighteen-year-old virgin? Even our little dancer here got himself laid." He grins at me, and I grit my teeth.

Yeah, the dancer got himself laid and wishes he hadn't.

Nick's actually a good guy, and he's smart, but unfortunately, he's about as sensitive as a block of wood. He's never able to read the room or figure out when he should just shut up.

"That's enough, Nicky." Reed punches Nick's shoulder without looking, and Nick, perched on the back of the sofa, falls over backward with a shout of protest.

"Fuck you, Reed."

"No, thanks. Tammy will probably take care of that today." Reed grins, and his smile gets wider as Tristan groans and drops the game controller onto the coffee table.

"Tammy desperately needs better taste." The contemptuous voice makes us all jump at the same time. Zoe is leaning in the doorframe, her ankles crossed casually, a white garment bag hanging over her arm. I can't help staring at her long legs and tight shorts. Her skin has taken on a golden glow in the last few weeks. I want to reach out and touch her. It's not the first time I've wondered if her skin is as soft as it looks and how her slender muscles would feel under my fingers. My mouth goes dry, and my cheeks turn hot. Fuck. Not good. Not good at all.

"Tammy's taste is excellent." Reed gets up and pushes past Zoe, probably to go to the bathroom. As he passes her, he musses her red hair, and somehow it bothers me that it's so easy for him to touch her. For all of them. I'm the only one who doesn't manage to greet her with a hug, mostly because my body goes crazy every time I do.

I know why it's happening. It's because of her secrets. The way she gazes at me with those hazel eyes. And her smile. That smile that makes me forget that she's my best friend's little sister and that what I feel for her is wrong, because I don't talk to Caleb about it.

"Sometimes I forget why I like you. Leave my hair alone," Zoe retorts, giving Reed a dirty look.

I repress the urge to add that he should leave her alone completely.

Reed just laughs and then leaves.

Zoe glances at Caleb and, for a second, at me too. "I just wanted to say that I'm going now. I'm getting ready at Charlotte's place. See you later."

"Sure. We're probably coming around nine. I guess." Caleb gets up and gives Zoe a hug. "Drive carefully."

She rolls her eyes. "I always do. Besides, it's only ten minutes away. See you." She waves to Nick and Tristan, and then her gaze lands on me again. Longer this time. Until her eyes shift to the big window that looks out directly into the garden. To the treehouse. I know what that means.

She left a new note.

My heart skips a beat as Zoe bites her lower lip and blushes.

"Okay, see you."

Why does she suddenly sound so breathless?

She turns on her heel before I can say anything.

I wait fifteen minutes—the longest quarter of an hour I've ever experienced—before I sneak out of the living room, through the kitchen, and out the back door. My friends are busy with their game and don't notice what I'm doing. My whole body tingles with excitement as I climb the ladder.

Since the night our game began, we've been hiding our secrets up here. This evening, she left one for me. The note is easy to find, there on the blankets, and my fingers tremble as I unfold it. I have no idea what I expect, but it's definitely not the words that I see written there in her tidy handwriting.

Kiss me tonight.
—P

CHAPTER 17
Jase

What do you miss about LA?

Everything.
—J

Fat raindrops splash against the window next to my bed. Outside it's dark, even though the sun hasn't set yet. The sky is full of thick storm clouds that swallow what's left of the daylight.

The song "In Threes" echoes from my headphones. I have no idea how long I've been sitting on my bed and staring out the window. I've been trying for almost twenty-four hours to figure out how the hell Zoe managed to break through my defenses enough that I would answer her questions honestly. But I did it, and maybe that's good, because otherwise she might not have agreed to meet me for practice. On the other hand, it sucks because I don't want her to know what's going on with me.

There's an insistent knock on my door, loud enough to hear over the music. I don't make the effort to go see who wants something from me. But whoever it is is persistent, and I finally give in, annoyed. I take off my headphones and get up.

I'm expecting Skye, but it's Mom at the door, the expression on her face a mixture of uncertainty and impatience.

"I thought you weren't here," she says instead of greeting me.

I don't answer. What does she expect me to say? *Yes, I'm here. I just didn't want to answer at first, and now I really wish I hadn't.* Yeah, that might have been a good idea, but Mom can rarely take the truth.

"What do you want?" I say instead.

"Can I come in?"

"I'd rather you didn't."

This room is my kingdom, the only home I have left. Mom would rather fly to the moon than set foot in my room. She rolls her eyes and brushes a strand of blond hair behind her ear. Despite the persistent rain outside, it's strangely dry. Only now do I notice that she's holding an oversized umbrella.

"Don't be silly, Jase. Let me in, please."

I snort. "Why should I?"

"Because it can't go on like this. You can't turn away from us like this. We're a family." She impatiently shifts from one foot to the other.

I laugh out loud, making a sound of surprise and disbelief. "Since when?"

"Jase, you're impossible. Let me in so we can talk." She takes a step forward, but I refuse to take even a single step back.

"You can just tell me what it is you have to say and then leave again," I suggest dispassionately.

Mom sighs. "I know you're angry, and you have every right to be. But your father and I only want what's best for you and—"

"Dad only wants to get his way. That has nothing to do with what's best for me," I say, interrupting her sharply.

"Your father wants a secure future for you. He wants you to finish an education that you can build your life on. That doesn't mean you have to study medicine. But even you have to admit that dancing won't give you the same security as a degree from Harvard."

"What about Lia?" The question bursts out of me before I can stop it. I've been asking myself the same thing for ages, and maybe it's about time that I get a goddamn answer. "She's allowed to dance. You're even paying her tuition. Why should it be any different for me?"

Mom sighs again and runs her hand over her beige trench coat to smooth out a nonexistent wrinkle. "Jase, can't we discuss this in your room?"

"No, we cannot."

"Your sister was four years old when she started ballet. Even then, she had exceptional talent; you know that."

Yes, I know that. I was there. But it's not an answer to my question. "I have talent too. Which you might know if you ever watched me."

"Besides, you also know that Lia's career won't last forever," Mom continues, as though I hadn't said a thing. "She's been with Archie so long that it can't be much longer until they get married. Then she'll have kids, and she can concentrate on being a mother. Just like she's always wanted."

There's so much wrong with those few sentences that I wonder if it's really my mother standing there or just a clone of the woman who raised me.

"Lia wants to dance," I finally reply. "And if anyone has shown us that it's possible to have kids and a career, it's you."

"My situation was completely different back then. And Lia is going to be a Goodwin. You know how important Archie's family is in Boston. She's going to have other responsibilities."

"You mean producing children and showing up at charity events, looking pretty and smiling nicely? That kind of thing?"

"Please don't be so cynical, Jase. Besides, this isn't about your sister and her future; it's about you. As I said, you don't have to study medicine if you don't want to, but we had hoped that one day you would take over the clinic."

"I'm not Sam," I say between clenched teeth. A stabbing pain pierces my heart. It's old and familiar, and it hasn't gone away after five years. "He wanted that. I never did! I'm sorry I'm such a disappointment to you."

"You're not," she replies, but we both know that it's not the truth. "But if I had known you would be so fixated on dancing, I never would have sent you to ballet lessons and . . ." she stops as she realizes she's gone too far this time.

I'm filled with a stoic sense of calm. "Then why did you pay the tuition for the first year even though Dad would have preferred it if I were out on the street? And why did you try to pay the second year, before Dad caught you?"

I don't add that if it weren't for East, I really would have been out on the street. Even though part of me wants her to know, a bigger part doesn't want to show weakness.

Mom barely flinches and quickly regains her composure. "Because I was hoping that you'd realize for yourself that this place isn't right for you. You don't belong here."

She's lying to me, I know that, but it doesn't matter. I can ask as many times as I want, but she'll never tell me the truth. Because then she'd have to turn against Dad.

"No, I belong at Harvard," I say, my voice dripping with irony. I'm still clinging to the doorknob so hard that it hurts. "You should leave."

"No, I won't go. I want us to be a family again."

"Then good luck fixing everything you've screwed up over the last few years." I'm about to slam the door in her face, but Mom is quicker. She slides her foot into the doorframe and stops me.

"Jase, please." There's a sound of desperation in her voice that I've never heard before. She's about to say something else, but someone interrupts her.

"Mom? What are you doing here?"

We both turn at the same time. Lia is standing at the other end of the corridor in front of her room door. She's soaked to the skin, and her hair is plastered to her head and neck.

"Lia, darling, what happened?" Mom gasps, horrified.

A deeply hurt expression briefly crosses Lia's face, but it disappears again immediately. Instead, she forces a smile. "We had an appointment to plan the party for your birthday, remember? I was at Le Chat Noir waiting for you, but you were obviously busy. The rain surprised me on the way home."

"Oh, Lia, I completely forgot about that. I'm so sorry." Mom moves toward Lia, and it's the perfect opportunity to finally close the door, but something stops me. Probably the final dissolution of our family, which is playing out right before my eyes. "Would you like to freshen up, and then we'll drive to the restaurant together? I'll come get you in a few minutes, okay? Jase and I have something to clear up."

Lia looks at me sharply, and if I didn't know any better, I'd think she was jealous.

"Go ahead, Mom. I guess we're done." I stretch and yawn, feigning boredom.

"We're not." She rubs her forehead. She's probably getting a headache again, like she always does when I do something that freaks her out. "What do I have to do to make you part of this family again?"

"Maybe just accept me for who I am," I suggest, my voice artificially cheerful.

"Jase—"

Now another voice interrupts her. The last one I wanted to hear. But hey, this whole situation has to get even worse somehow.

I turn and see Zoe. I didn't notice the door to her room opening, and if I'm unlucky, she's heard every word. The walls between our rooms are so thin that you can hear almost everything.

"Sorry, I don't want to interrupt you," she says, not dignifying my mother with a glance. "We need to go over the choreography again." She gives me a meaningful look, and it takes me a moment to realize what she's doing. She's trying to rescue me. We didn't have a practice scheduled, not today.

But instead of feeling gratitude like any normal person in this situation would, I start to get angry. Anyone else could have overheard this stupid conversation and I wouldn't have cared, but not Zoe. She already knows too much. If I'm unlucky and she's been listening, now she knows even more.

Still, I take her up on it. Anything is better than dealing with Mom and Lia any longer. I turn to Mom. "I have to leave."

She looks from me to Zoe in amazement. "But we're not finished yet."

"Yes, we are. Lia's waiting for you. Go plan your party. I've got things to do now." I turn around, grab my key, which is always on the coat hook, and pull the door shut behind me.

I ignore her as she calls my name, with Lia still standing soaking wet outside her room, staring at me in disbelief as I walk away. Zoe follows me, even when I leave the dorm and head to the practice studios. It's pouring, and we're soaked to the skin in seconds. I don't say a word, and neither does she.

We silently enter the building and walk up the stairs, then cross the hall on the fourth floor to reach another staircase. It's the one that goes up one more floor to the old studio under the roof that's too small for group lessons. The floor here is worn wood, not the gray linoleum in the lower studios. The old boards have some creaky spots. The round windows can't be opened—some kind of security measure to keep people from falling out. In summer, it's also roasting hot. Now it's just stuffy, and the smell of sweat hangs in the air.

"Jase, are you all—"

"Don't ask!" I say, interrupting her harshly. I feel the pressure building up inside. I have to pull myself together. I'm so furious I'm about to explode.

She wants to know if everything is okay, if I'm all right, and of course, after that scene in front of my room, anyone would ask. But it's not just anyone with me; it's Zoe. The girl who knows more about me than anyone else does, even Caleb. I didn't write any notes to him, after all.

Zoe gazes at me silently, and something in the way she looks almost makes me walk away. It's not pity but something else. I can't define it, but she looks at me and actually *sees* me, directly into my soul. She's always done that, and before, it made everything a little easier. Not today.

Her gaze sends a shiver up my spine, and I get goose bumps. Partly because I'm cold in my wet sweatshirt. Without thinking about whether it's a good idea, I pull it off over my head. When it lands on the floor with a splat, I look up and see suspicion in her eyes.

"What exactly are you planning?"

I roll my eyes as if it's not perfectly clear. "I'm cold."

"And it's warmer without a shirt?" she asks skeptically.

"It is. Which you'd notice if you took off your sweatshirt too. It's always pretty warm up here. But we can forget any extra practice if you get sick from walking around in wet clothes." I give her a meaningful look, but she just crosses her arms in front of her chest and narrows her eyes. Then she exhales with a sigh, as if she's made a decision.

She puts a hand to her shoulder, and it's only when the strap slides down her arm that I realize she was wearing a backpack. She opens the zipper and pulls out a dry sweatshirt and two towels. She tosses one of them to me. I catch it reflexively. My eyebrows go up. "You're prepared."

"Actually, I was just about to go to the gym," she says, shrugging. She pulls out her hairband and wraps the other towel around her head.

I follow her example, rubbing my hair dry and then the rest of my body as best I can. But my pants are wet and cold, and they're going to stay that way.

When I see Zoe reach for the hem of her sweater and pull it off over her head, I'm almost relieved. She's wearing a black leotard under her sweater that contrasts with her pale skin, and even though I've already seen her in leotards a thousand times back when Caleb and I were friends, this is different. The thin material is clinging to her slender body because of the rain. I don't want to look, but I can't help it, and then I remember why we're here. I remember why Zoe needs this extra practice, and I feel like the biggest asshole in the world.

I only look at her again when she clears her throat. Her wet clothes are lying a few steps away on the floor. Now she's wearing soft sweatpants and a cropped hoodie that would end at her navel, if she weren't still wearing the wet leotard underneath it.

It does something to me to see her that way. With messy hair and not anywhere near as tidy as she always is in class, when all the girls wear their white tights and black leotards and have their hair in smooth buns. Now there's no sign of her perfectionism.

I can't help the fact that all at once I'm not cold anymore, and my heart might be beating just a little bit faster.

"And now?" she says. Her voice sounds different than usual. "What kind of extra practice did you have in mind?"

Fair question. I have no fucking idea.

CHAPTER 18
Zoe

Thank you for following me after the prom. That really meant a lot to me, and I don't care that you're probably rolling your eyes now because you think it's cheesy and stupid. It's my secret, so shut up and don't complain.
—P

Jase stares at me silently, and I can only stare back, because my ability to think coherently went up in smoke as soon as he took off his wet sweatshirt. He's not wearing a T-shirt. It's a miracle that I could put together a single, more or less reasonable sentence in the last few minutes. Some part of my brain seems to be working after all. I'm not so sure about the rest of me.

Jase is slender and strong, like all dancers, with long muscles, a six-pack, and those V-shaped muscles on his hips that just beg to be touched. He's beautiful, but that's nothing new. What's new is getting to see him this way, and I get all warm and soft inside. There's nothing I can say in my defense. This whole situation is absurd.

We shouldn't be here. I don't know what got into me when I interrupted the conversation with his mother. It was totally rude of me, and I shouldn't have done it. I had been about to go to the gym because I neglected my weight training this week. Then I heard their voices and heard what they were talking about. They were practically standing in front of my door, after all. I could hear every word, and I couldn't just stop listening, turn away, and pretend I hadn't heard anything.

It was the tone of Jase's voice that made me want to help him. I heard the anger and pain that his mother didn't seem to register. It was his voice that made me forget to bring my jacket and an umbrella. I was too distracted. I still am. Because now we're in this tiny studio, and he's not even wearing a damn T-shirt.

"Since you're the one who has a problem, I thought you might have a plan," he says sharply, reminding me that I asked.

I blush and pull the sleeves of my sweatshirt down over my hands. "I . . . um . . . No. I don't have a plan. I'm pretty disorganized." God, what am I saying?

"I guess that figures." He sighs and runs a hand through his damp blond hair, and once again, all I can do is stare and watch the movement of his muscles.

My stomach begins to flutter, and I don't know why. Nerves? Excitement? Fear? No clue. It's all wrong. I shouldn't look at him this way. I shouldn't be alone with him here in the first place. But I am, and I can't help staring either.

"Okay," he says, taking a step toward me. "I would suggest that we go through Francesca's routine again, but I'm not sure that will make any difference."

I just nod, because he's right. It will make no difference at all. His brow creases, and I want to reach out and smooth it. What the hell is going on with me?

"You have a hard time being touched, right?" he asks carefully, and I'm glad that he says it and I don't have to.

"Yeah," I whisper, hoping he doesn't ask why. With our notes, the rules are clear, but this is totally different. Obviously.

"Only when you're dancing, or also . . . like this?" He takes another step closer, and my stomach cramps. My body is always working against me.

"Always." I can barely get the words out. I don't want to admit it, but there's no other way we're going to make progress.

His eyes widen in surprise, and I think I see worry shining in them. But the expression disappears immediately. I must have been mistaken. "Always?"

I nod. It doesn't matter that everything was different two weeks ago. Then, at least, I felt halfway normal. I should probably hang out with Caleb or go see my parents, find out if I have the same reaction with them too. But every time Mom has called me in the last few days, trying to convince me to go out to eat with her, I tell her I'm too busy with classes. The thought that my body might betray me even with my own family scares me. As long as I don't see them, as long as no one tries to hug me, I can at least pretend that my problem isn't as huge as I'm afraid it is.

"Then basically, it's easy. We don't have to practice dancing—just touching."

I have to laugh, but it's not a happy one. Jase's suggestion might sound easy, but actually doing it . . . It will be anything but easy.

"How exactly do you plan to do that?" I've barely finished asking when he reaches out a hand to me.

"At first, just like this."

I want to raise my arm and give him my hand, but all at once, I'm paralyzed. My body is no longer my own. I can't move.

Jase's eyes narrow. "Come on, Pixie."

What are you afraid of?

I can almost hear the words. I know exactly what he's thinking and that he wants an answer. But he's not going to get one.

He sighs in frustration and then takes a step back. He murmurs something to himself that I can't understand. Instead, I stare at him again. His broad shoulders, his muscular back, and . . . *what the hell is wrong with me?*

He whirls around to face me again so fast that I flinch with shock. Great, as though I'm not weird enough yet.

"Come here," he says, beckoning me forward. I hesitate. What does he have in mind? This is completely pointless. It won't help. I open my mouth to tell him that, but I can't get a word out. Instead, I just walk toward him. I pull my fingers into the sleeves of my sweatshirt. I stop next to him, right in front of the mirror.

"Wait a sec." He goes over to the little Bluetooth speaker in the corner, pulls his phone out of his pocket, and connects it before coming back to me.

I know the song as soon as the first few notes echo through the studio. It's "Take My Hand" by 5 Seconds of Summer. I freeze, my pulse races, and my eyes start to burn. I frantically blink away the tears before he notices them. He remembers.

He remembers my answer from back when he asked me what my favorite song was. The realization hits me straight in the heart. Why does he remember that?

For the same reason you remember every single one of his answers too.

Jase stops close behind me. He doesn't touch me, but I can feel the heat coming from his body. I would love to lean back, directly on his chest, and feel his skin.

"Look in the mirror." His voice sends a shiver up my spine, and I do as he suggests. My reflection looks back, and for a moment, I can only think that my hair is a damp mess and I look tiny next to Jase.

He's tall and handsome and is waiting calmly for my eyes to meet his in the mirror. He only reaches out a hand after I look at him, and I realize what's happening with the mirror. I can see what he's doing, but I don't have to look at him directly. Not really. I look at him in the mirror, and it's our reflections that are touching, not us. Even though, of course we are.

I take a deep breath and finally manage to put my hand in his. His skin is warm and smooth, and mine begins to tingle immediately. In the mirror, I see how his lips press together. I'm concentrating on him so intently that at first, I don't notice how his fingers interlace with mine. They move of their own accord, as if it were the most natural thing in the world. My pulse is already out of the normal range again.

I don't know if Jase can feel how fast my heart is suddenly beating, but he can see it in the mirror. The artery in my throat is pulsing.

"How do you like the school?" He asks casually, and at first I'm annoyed. Does he really want to make small talk? But then I feel his fingertips on my other hand. He's trying to distract me.

His fingers stroke the back of my hand. It's the lightest possible touch. My breath catches, but this time there's no panic or fear closing off my throat. It's just Jase.

It takes me a few seconds too long before I find my voice again. "I like it a lot. How about you?"

He can't suppress the smile that appears on his face, even though he's trying to. "Me too," he answers just as simply. His smile gets a little wider. I see little creases form around his eyes, and I return his smile automatically.

"What do you like about it?" Now he interlaces the fingers of his other hand with mine. He squeezes gently, and heat shoots through my body.

For a second, I can't tell which way is up, or where we even are, and then I remember.

"I . . . . Our rooms are great," I respond, since I can't think of anything better to say. My mind is blank, my entire essence focused on the feeling of his hands on my skin.

It's all so strange. *I* am strange. And so is he. We're acting weird. We don't even know how to talk to each other. When Jase was at our house, Caleb was always there. Yes, I hung around with my brother and his friends a lot, but Jase and I never talked. Not like this. Because we were never really alone, aside from that night in the treehouse. And the night of Adaline's party. On the night that it all started, and then again on the night that it ended.

I start to get cold, but before the memories catch up with me, before the panic can flame up again, Jase lets my hands go. The images fade as his fingers stroke the backs of my hands and wander up my arms, lightly enough that I can barely feel it through the thick material of the sweatshirt. I still get goose bumps all over my body, my breathing speeds up, and my heart skips a couple of beats again. Whatever this feeling is that's taking me over, it's not fear, and it drives the cold away.

His hands rest for a moment on my shoulders, heavy and calm, and I instinctively lean back against him. His skin is warm on my back; I can feel his muscles and his heart underneath them, and I feel totally calm.

I want to turn my head to look at him, really look at him, but his gaze in the mirror has me captivated.

"How does that feel?" Jase whispers. His voice is low and hoarse. It seems like it's been ages since he spoke, when only a few minutes have actually passed.

I answer without thinking. "It feels like you."

CHAPTER 19
Zoe

What would you do if you couldn't dance?

That's a mean question. I have no idea. I really don't. I've always danced, my whole life. I can't even imagine life without ballet. I know that I should have a plan B just in case, but I don't.
—P

I can't stop thinking about Jase. This is crazy. I didn't think about him for an entire year. But now I think of almost nothing else.

Since his hands were on my shoulders in the attic studio a couple of days ago, I can't stop thinking about how it felt to be touched by him. It was different than in class. It felt natural. We didn't dance, we just stood there, and his hands touched my arms. Inch by inch.

The memory makes me warm. Why did it feel so good? The answer is quite simple. Because it was Jase who was standing behind me, and those were his hands moving up my arms.

How does that feel?

It feels like you.

The fact is that I can always tell him the truth, and at the same time, I'm hiding far too much from him. Maybe I should tell him everything, just let it out. Somehow I want to, but somehow I don't. Why is everything always so complicated?

Why can't I just tell him?

I sigh quietly. Too much has happened, and Jase has changed too, just like me. We aren't the same as we were before.

I reach for the little box on my nightstand. It's been there for a few days, since Jase gave me the first note. In the meantime, he's received two secrets from me, and I've gotten one from him. I try not to think about the notes that I've written to him over the last year that are still lying in the treehouse in my parents' yard, waiting for him to read them.

My heart clenches as I take out the crumpled ball of paper. I smooth it out and read his secret for the thousandth time in the last thirty-six hours.

Why do you need a scholarship?

My parents cut off my funds.
—Jase

I trace his untidy writing with my finger. I hate his parents. What they're doing is totally unfair. I want to help him, but I know he would never accept my help. I want to ask more. I want to ask him everything. I want to know who Sam is and why his parents refuse to support his dream. I want to know how he feels, and above all, I want to know if he hates me or if he just doesn't care about me. I want to know if I was the only one who felt something when we were standing there in front of the mirror.

I'm startled by a soft knock on my door. I quickly fold the note and put it back in the box. On the way to the door, I kick aside the new pointe shoes lying on the floor of my room. I bought them today during the lunch break, and I still need to sew the satin ribbons on and break them in. My last pair was used up, and it's time for me to prepare the new ones.

Normally, preparing my pointe shoes is almost meditative, a routine I've had for years that helps me stop overthinking for a while. But today, my mind didn't calm down at all until I finally read Jase's note again. And even that didn't fully work either.

"Just a minute," I say when the knock repeats. Mae is standing by the door and is regarding me with a worried look.

"Hey," she says. "Can I come in?"

I silently take a step aside, and she walks into my room.

"You can just throw me out again if I'm too pushy, but the curiosity is killing me. That's why I had to come. Besides, I'm worried about you." In the middle of the room, she turns halfway back to the door and waits in case I really do want to throw her out.

I collapse onto the bed and tell her to sit down.

"Thank God," she says with relief as she sits down on the mattress with me and pulls up her knees.

"You don't have to worry about me," I say.

"I know. But I do anyway. You've been acting totally strange for days. Sure, we haven't known each other very long, and basically, I don't know if you're acting strange, but I have the feeling that something's bothering you."

If you only knew.

I start to braid my hair, giving my hands something to do while I decide what to say to her.

"Is it because of Charlotte?"

I look at her in surprise. I haven't spared a thought for Charlotte since the last lesson, if only because I've suppressed anything that comes up. We've hardly spoken to each other since the first day she showed up, and I should be worried because she's definitely planning something. But I have more than enough problems. It's amazing that Charlotte, of all people, is the least of them.

"Or is it Jase? Because the two of you are giving off some weird vibes."

The corners of my mouth lift in a barely perceptible smile. "Weird vibes?"

"Yeah. You know." She makes a gesture that's supposed to mean something to me, and eventually I figure it out.

"We've known each other for a while," I say, finally, with a sigh. "He was my brother's best friend."

"Oh, my God." Mae's eyes go wide, with an enthusiastic glitter in them. "Were you a thing? Oh, please tell me you were. Your brother's best friend. That's so hot."

A mirthless laugh escapes from my lips, and a familiar feeling of tension starts building behind my eyes. "No, it wasn't like that. Well, sort of, but not . . . really. A lot went wrong."

"Oh man, I'm really sorry. That was stupid of me! I didn't want to . . . we don't have to talk about it," Mae says, backpedaling.

I don't say anything because I can't.

"Okay, what if we do something fun tonight? If we stop talking about Charlotte and Jase, do you want to go out? That is, if you want to spend any more time with an insensitive bitch."

I have to smile. "You're not insensitive, and you're definitely not a bitch. Actually, I'm meeting my brother. But if you want, you can come with me. I'm sure he'd love to meet you."

Mae gives me a mischievous grin. "Is he cute?"

"I can't answer that because he's my brother. But you're not his type anyway."

* * *

I sit in the lounger with my legs up, watching Mae argue with Tristan, Nick, and my brother about which of the *Star Wars* trilogies is the best. I can't contribute much to the discussion because I've never seen the movies. Science fiction just isn't my thing. Still, there's something comforting about listening to them talk, seeing Mae laugh, and watching the boys banter with her like she's been here a thousand times.

But someone is missing, and I don't mean Reed, whose absence doesn't particularly affect me. It's Jase who's missing. I always miss him when we're all together, and I wonder if I'm the only one who notices his absence.

I get up and sneak out of the spacious living room without the others noticing. They're too caught up in their conversation. I open the door to the roof terrace and step outside. It's chilly and windy, and I briefly consider going back inside to get my jacket but decide against it. Someone would probably notice me going out, and I need a moment alone.

I lean against the glass railing that surrounds the terrace while the wind tousles my hair. Boston's skyline stretches out in front of me. From up here, you can see as far as the Charles River, and on good days when the wind is blowing in the right direction, you can smell the sea. The light of the setting sun refracts off the glass facades of the skyscrapers. Boston's West End is beautiful. It's different from Back Bay and Beacon Hill, much more elegant and modern but no less stunning.

"What are you doing out here?" I turn to look when I hear Caleb. He comes over carrying one of his jackets, which he puts around my shoulders. I give him a grateful look.

"Just thinking."

"Are you okay?" He stands next to me, gently bumping his shoulder against mine.

I breathe a sigh of relief as my pulse remains steady. No tingling, no panic. *Thank goodness.*

"Charlotte is back."

"What?" Caleb sounds so horrified that I almost laugh.

"She's here. We have a few classes together."

"I thought she was in Paris."

"That's what I thought too." I clutch the railing so tightly that my knuckles turn white.

"Is it bad?"

"It's Charlotte," I reply, and that's enough to answer his question. "But she's been leaving me alone. For now, at least. Who knows when that will change."

He sighs and rubs his eyes. "Is there anything I can do to help?"

I shake my head. "That's nice of you, but you're already doing enough."

"I'm not doing anything."

"You're here."

"It feels like I'm not doing anything."

"Caleb—"

"It's all right," he says, interrupting me. "I know what you're going to say now. That I'm talking shit and I should stop." He rolls his eyes, and I take a deep breath, because I don't really want to talk about Jase to Caleb. But I should.

"There's something else . . ." I say slowly, giving myself a chance to gather my courage, and then I spit it out. It doesn't matter; he has to know. "Jase is my dance partner."

Caleb freezes next to me. His face is blank, but I can see something in his eyes. He's trying not to let me notice that he cares, but I know my brother.

"Caleb?" I tap his shoulder carefully.

He shakes his head and then comes back to himself. "Sorry, that was unexpected. How do you feel about it?"

I shrug and bite my lower lip. I might as well spit it out while I'm at it. "In the first class, everything went wrong. I panicked, and since then . . ." I stop and shrug again, but then it all comes out. About the first pas de deux class, and the second and third, until the moment that Jase suggested we practice together outside of class. And that our practice wasn't ballet but touching.

A deep crease of worry forms between his eyebrows. "Have you talked to Dr. Somers about it?"

"No. If she knows, she'll tell me to stop, and I can't do that. I'll figure this out, I promise."

Caleb sighs. "You don't have to promise me. This isn't about me."

"Well, yes, it kind of is," I remind him. And hate myself for it, but I can't just ignore it. "He was your best friend."

"And then he wasn't. For me, it's over."

"Are you sure?"

He nods, but I don't believe him. I know that he misses Jase.

"Caleb—"

"Let it go. So Jase is your dance partner. You're practicing touching. What does your heart say about it?"

My heart . . . all at once, my heart hops around in my chest, like it was waiting for this question. Involuntarily, my thoughts wander back to Jase's fingers interlaced with mine and his gaze meeting mine in the mirror.

"My heart has nothing to do with it."

"Zoe, come on."

I make a face and sigh. "Honestly, it's not like that."

"But it could be again." Caleb looks at me searchingly, and I squirm uncomfortably because I know exactly what he's getting at. He knows what Jase meant to me. But I put the thought out of my mind because it feels much too likely that it could happen again. Much too fast. And then I wonder if it ever really stopped or if all the chaos of the last year just covered it up.

I shake my head. "It can't. We rejected him, Caleb. Both of us. And he has no idea why."

"Are you going to talk to him about it?"

"No," I say. And at the same time, I'm thinking *yes*.

"Liar."

"What if it changes everything?"

Caleb puts an arm around my shoulder and pulls me close. "Yeah, what if it changes everything?"

He means it differently than I do, and I want to tell him that what he's thinking isn't possible. But I remain silent, because part of me wants exactly that.

For everything to change.

CHAPTER 20
Jase

What are your parents like?

Workaholics. Control freaks. They worry too much about what other people think. Emotionally unavailable. Not there.
—J

"This has to be a bad joke," I mutter as I flip through the forms that Camille has just given me, like maybe doing so would make the monthly sum I have to pay smaller.

I knew the tuition was high, but somehow, I seem to have repressed the fact that it's almost thirteen thousand dollars for a semester.

I'm screwed.

I don't have that kind of money. Not even close. What I saved from my vacation jobs teaching at my old ballet school isn't even half of what I need. Even if I could pay the fee in installments, my account would be empty in three months at the latest.

"Is everything okay, Jase? Do you have any questions?" Camille peers at me over the edge of her glasses.

Just one. Where the hell am I supposed to get all that money?

I've forgotten a few not entirely unimportant details. I desperately need new clothes and practice gear, and I have to pay my phone bill. I don't need much, but I won't have enough for even the most basic things if I don't manage to get more money from somewhere.

The most obvious solution would be to get a job, but that's not easy for a lot of reasons.

1. I have no professional experience other than teaching children the basic steps of ballet.
2. A job at a ballet school would be the obvious choice, but there's no way in hell that I'll earn enough with that.
3. Studying is practically a full-time job. I practice six hours a day and then have two theory courses. Thanks to Zoe, I now have additional practice in the evenings.
4. At nineteen, I'm too young for any job I might have time for after this workload during the day. If I were older, I could ask East to get me a job at The Lighthouse. But I'm not, so that's the end of it.

"Jase? Do you need anything else?" Camille repeats. She sounds a little more annoyed than before. She wants to get rid of me; it's obvious. And for a change, I have no problem granting her wish.

"No, I have everything."

"No questions?" Her eyebrows go up, and she looks at me skeptically. As if I were too stupid to understand what the documents said.

"Nope, I get it."

I understand completely that I'm screwed. Thank you for asking.

"Good. Then you can fill out the forms and give them back to me next Wednesday."

"I will." I stuff the papers back into the envelope that Camile gave me and leave her office, immediately colliding with a petite figure.

At first, I'm expecting Zoe, because let's be honest, my karma is crappy enough that it must be her. Especially since I've been trying to avoid her outside of class as much as possible since our first practice session.

But the girl in front of me is blond, not a redhead. Lia.

Super.

I try to walk around her and disappear, because I have nothing to say to my sister. Honestly, I have no idea when we last had a real conversation with each other. But I'm stopped by a guilty expression on her face and an embarrassed blush.

It's not difficult to put two and two together. The door to Camille's office was open the whole time. I didn't worry about whether someone would find out what we were talking about because it didn't matter to me if anyone knew.

Except it matters to me that it's Lia who heard everything.

"Are you happy now?" The question slips out before I can stop myself.

"Jase—" She stops as I push past her and continue down the corridor. "Why are you acting like this?" She calls after me, her voice sounding so desolate that I turn back and stare at her.

"What are you talking about?" I return her gaze in disbelief. Her green eyes glitter tellingly. Lia is the last person who has the right to cry right now.

"You could have it all. Some people would kill to have the chance to go to Harvard. Why can't you just do what Mom and Dad want?"

I stare at her, unable to comprehend what I'm hearing.

"You're making a huge drama out of nothing."

I laugh, stunned. "You're kidding me, right? Would you do it? Give up your dream because Mom and Dad want you to?"

She hesitates for a second. "This isn't about me, Jase."

"That's not an answer. Would you?"

She shrugs, and I want to shout at her, but I know it wouldn't get me anywhere. "You're not interested in my answer anyway. You don't care about anyone but yourself."

"And you're so incredibly selfless, are you?" I say disparagingly.

"I never said that." She sighs and brushes a strand of hair behind her ear. "But unlike you, I care about our family."

"Give it a few years. Mom and Dad will probably manage to cure you of that."

"You know what? Forget it! I can't talk to you."

She turns on her heel before I can reply and stomps away down the corridor.

I stare after her blankly. I could tell her that I do care about our family, just not in the way she thinks. But that would lead to a complicated conversation full of questions and accusations, and we don't have conversations like that in this family.

* * *

Two days later, I'm walking out of a shiny glass building feeling angry and powerless. It's the third bank I've visited today.

I'm sorry, Jase, there's nothing I can do for you. Your father . . . blah, blah, blah. Bullshit and more bullshit.

I'm on the verge of lashing out, even though I know it won't help me.

Christopher Shaw is my godfather. He just threw me out of his office with a sympathetic look on his face and a huge ass-kicking. He's a finance guy who works in a bank, and about seventeen minutes ago, I more or less begged him to give me a student loan. Maybe it would have been smarter to go to him directly instead of trying two other banks first and being turned down by them in a friendly but consequent manner. Not even my name got me anywhere, even though half the city knows my parents and how wealthy they are.

But that's exactly the problem. It's my parents who are wealthy. I, on the other hand, am totally broke.

Applying for a student loan was one of the last of my almost nonexistent options. Chris was my last chance, and that's probably why I put off going to see him. I knew he would probably email Dad the second I left his office.

I just didn't realize that Dad was a few steps ahead of me and had already talked to Chris.

No loan, no scholarship, no job. That went well.

I pull my phone out of my pocket and check my messages in the faint hope that my old ballet teacher, Miss Plum, has answered and can create a job out of thin air for me. She hasn't.

I hesitate for a moment, then I text East.

JASE:

Do you have time to talk?

His answer comes a few minutes later:

EASTON:

I'm at home. The guys are here, but come over if you want.

I write a quick reply and call an Uber, which pulls up a few minutes later. A good fifteen minutes later, my ride spits me out in Southie in front of the tiny house where East lives with his sister, Willow.

I can already tell from a distance that Jax, Beck, and Colin are there. The music from the house is deafening. I don't bother knocking on the front door, because no one would hear me over the noise, but instead walk around the house and through the microscopic yard to the back door, which is usually open when the band is rehearsing.

I go into the kitchen, which is also ridiculously small, and find Willow standing in front of the fridge wearing oversized noise-canceling headphones. I try to alert her to my presence without startling her. No luck.

She shrieks as she closes the fridge door and notices me.

"Jeez, Jase! Don't scare me like that!" she cries, pulling off her headphones with one hand and holding the other to her chest.

"Sorry," I say, then point at the back door. "Maybe you should lock the door if you're going to walk around with headphones."

She sighs and rubs her eyes. She looks tired. "I know. East and the others are in the living room. As you can hear." Willow is a few years older than me and dances for the Boston City Ballet, though she seems to be on an involuntary hiatus, judging from the thick bandage around her ankle.

"Is it bad?" I ask over the music, giving her a sympathetic look. Injuries can end badly for dancers, not least with regard to their careers.

Willow turns pale and avoids my gaze. As though her brother realized something was happening, the music stops. An oppressive silence falls in the small kitchen. "I'll be fine," she says softly. Her voice trembles. "A few weeks of rest, then I'll be back to my old self."

I just nod, because nothing I say could make the situation any better for her.

"I'm going back upstairs. If you can convince the guys to call it quits for the day, I'd be grateful." She gives me a weak smile, but tears are shining in her eyes.

"I'll do my best," I promise her.

She nods and disappears, limping down the narrow hallway.

I go over to the living room, the biggest room in the house, where East and the others are now sitting on an old swayback sofa, bent over a tattered notebook. East looks up as I enter.

"Jason Alexander Winslow, to what do I owe the pleasure?" He laughs.

I roll my eyes. Aside from my father, East is the only person who ever uses my full name. I have no idea why he does that.

"You can skip the formalities," I say, slapping the other guys' hands.

"Nope. I like your name."

"If you want, I'll give it to you." Along with all the obnoxious problems that I have at the moment.

"Hmm, I'll think about it. What are you doing here, Jase? You didn't come just to hang around with us, did you?" East eyes me skeptically. Jax, Colin, and Beck look curious. East is right; I wouldn't just pop by, even though I lived with him and Willow for almost three months last year when I had no idea where to go and East took pity on me. I still hate the fact that it was necessary.

I cross my arms and lean against the wall. "I need a job."

Colin's pierced eyebrows go up. "*You* need a job?"

"My parents cut me off. So yeah. I need a job, and a little help wouldn't suck."

* * *

East promised me he'd ask around, but he didn't sound very optimistic. After spending the last two hours searching for jobs online, I'm not either. Every job I find, either I'm not qualified enough for, the work hours interfere with my classes, or the job is so badly paid that I'd end up having to spend the entire paycheck on the commute.

My mood is at an all-time low when I return to the dorm. Then I see Zoe standing at my door, just about to knock, and the words "all-time low" take on a completely new meaning. I want to turn around and disappear before she notices me, but of course it's too late.

A shy smile appears on her face when she sees me, and my body tenses. *Fuck.*

There are reasons why I've been avoiding her for the last few days. They have a lot to do with her smile. And the way her hands felt in mine. And the way she leaned against me. How fast her heart was beating, not because she was scared, but . . . Yeah. I don't know why, and I really don't want to know.

Liar.

"What do you want?" I ask before she can open her mouth and say something I don't want to hear.

"Can we talk?"

"No, I don't have time."

She takes a step back, and the muscle in my chest complains, but I can't pay any attention to that.

"Only for a minute. I want—"

"I don't care what you want, Zoe," I say, bluffing. "I'm not interested in what you have to say. Is that clear?"

She goes pale, and I hate myself for it, but I really don't want to hear what she has to tell me. When she asks if we can talk, especially in that tone of voice, insecure and hopeful at the same time, I can tell it's not going to be about ballet. It's about us. But there's no such thing as "us," and it can damn well stay that way.

How does that feel?

It feels like you.

Her words have been haunting me all week, just like the feeling of my fingers on her skin and the way my body reacted. Not the way it should have.

"Are you serious?" Her expression hardens, her nails dig into her palms, and she shudders. I hate everything about this, but at the same time, it's exactly what I need.

"Do I look like I'm joking?"

"You look like you're acting like a jerk."

I laugh. "Not my problem. Get used to it, or don't bother."

She shakes her head in disbelief, opens her mouth, and closes it again.

I push past her and open the door.

"What about our practice session? Is that out too? Or don't you care about the scholarship anymore?"

I turn around. She has her arms crossed over her chest, and her eyes flash with anger. Anger is good. I can deal with anger. Better than the damn closeness that she's trying to build up. Unfortunately, she's right. I can't cancel the extra practice session, even though I'd love to. We need to improve. *She* needs to improve, and there's no other way.

"We can do it tomorrow," I say, because I don't have the nerves for it today. I don't wait for her to answer, just slam the door firmly behind me. What a fucking awful day.

CHAPTER 21

Zoe

Do you know that feeling when you feel nothing and everything at the same time? I'm a mess at the moment, and I have no idea why or what I can do about it.

—P

I'm such an idiot. How did I ever think it would be a good idea to try to talk to Jase? Because things went reasonably well between us one time? Because I didn't panic the last time he touched me? Because I feel guilty? That's so stupid.

I know that I screwed up, and so did Caleb. Jase is right to be angry, but if he can't even give me the chance to talk about it . . . I guess there's nothing I can do about it.

Maybe his reaction was a sign that I shouldn't tell him anything. The thought of telling him the truth was crazy anyway. What did I imagine would happen? Why should he even have to know? Whatever happened between us is in the past, and telling him what happened on that terrible night isn't going to help us get it back.

Worst-case scenario, he'll pity me, and that's the last thing I want.

"Why are you so pissed off?" Mae's voice snaps me out of my thoughts. We're on the way to the theater, just like on our first day. Mr. Pearson has summoned the entire student body, but we still don't know why. The older students are acting like they have an idea, but they're keeping their mouths shut.

"I'm not pissed off," I lie, but Mae just snorts.

"Sure. Of course you aren't. There's such an aura of anger around you that I can almost see it. Even your walk sounds pissed off."

I automatically adjust my steps, realizing she's right. "Oh, it's just . . . Jase is acting like a jerk." The answer sounds so childish that I'm embarrassed. Jeez, I really need to get a grip.

"Okay, somehow that doesn't surprise me."

"Doesn't surprise me either," I say, which is a big fat lie.

"I thought the extra practice went well." She looks at me doubtfully.

"It did, at least the one time that we did it. But afterward, he avoided me, and now he won't talk to me anymore. It's really frustrating." I grimace, thinking about what an idiot I am.

I told Mae about the extra practice, but not that it consisted of Jase holding my hand rather than doing the actual exercises.

We enter the New England Theater and follow the other students into the auditorium.

"Maybe it went too well."

I lose my train of thought for a moment as the beauty of the theater almost overwhelms me again, the sight of the stage filling me with yearning. Then I register what Mae said.

"What do you mean?"

"Well . . . I don't know, maybe he still likes you, and the closeness is too much for him . . ." She stops and shakes her head with a soft laugh. "Oh, don't listen to me. I'm a hopeless romantic. I read too much."

I have to laugh in spite of everything. "I'm pretty sure that's not the reason."

"It would be nice if it was, though." Mae sighs theatrically, then grins at me. "But hey, at least you don't seem angry anymore."

I smile wanly. "At least there's that."

We sit down in two empty seats next to Katie and Susannah, and I have to stop myself from looking around for Jase. We'd be in our next practice session right now if Pearson hadn't called us in, and I'm secretly relieved that it was canceled. I have to sort out this mess in my head first.

I've been too busy with Jase in the last few weeks. I should concentrate on myself and my own problems. I already have enough on my plate without having Jase in my head all the time.

Our dancing is awful. I still panic when he touches me in class. If I don't get it under control, I can forget my dream of being on stage, and then everything will be for nothing.

I just want to be normal again, to have a normal life.

I look up as Principal Pearson steps onto the stage, smiling just like he was on our first day almost three weeks ago. Three weeks. It feels like a lot more time has passed since I've been here.

"Thanks for coming," he says, his gaze wandering around the audience, as though he's counting to see if all eighty students are really here. "Most of you already know that the seniors get a chance to shine on this stage every winter." He makes a sweeping gesture that includes all of us. If everything goes well, I'll be on this stage in three years' time. I want it so much that it hurts.

"Of course, the senior class has a special role to play in this performance, but it's still important for you all to be involved. You're here to learn and surpass yourselves, yes. But there's much more to it than that. You're a team, a family, as long as you're at this school together. That's why you will each be given a job. Some of you will help with preparations. An event like this requires not only dancers but also costumes and stage sets. I know, I know," he says, interrupting himself as a soft murmur is audible in the room. "You're not here to paint and sew, but you will be part of this performance, and I want you to make an effort. I want you to be proud of what you have achieved when the ballet we've chosen for this year is performed. Mr. Conrad will divide you into groups and give you your assignments. Any questions before we continue?"

"Which ballet will it be this year?" a girl in the next row asks.

Mr. Pearson smiles. "*The Sleeping Beauty*."

My heart accelerates. I've always loved that ballet. It's been ages since the last time it was performed in Boston. Of course, not counting last year's performance at my old ballet school, when Charlotte stole the part of Aurora from me.

A quiet murmuring spreads through the room, and you can literally see the excitement leap from one person to the next.

"If you have no other questions, I'll hand you over to Mr. Conrad now," Pearson says as Conrad comes on stage. But I can barely focus on who he is assigning to each task.

All I can think about is the performance. It hurts a little to know that I won't be on stage dancing. But at the same time, I'm looking forward to helping to prepare the show and then watching it without being envious, without fighting back tears. I want this performance of *The Sleeping Beauty* to erase the last one from my memory.

Then Mr. Conrad assigns me to the group for set design. With Mae, Skye, a few others . . . and Jase and Charlotte. This can't be real.

* * *

Francesca is helping us with the set, and Mae being in my group is the only positive part of the whole thing. Seeing Jase and Charlotte in class every day is more than enough for me without spending time with them on weekends too.

"We meet on Saturdays from eleven to two," Francesca announces, and a tortured groan goes around the room. "Don't be like that. You've got plenty of time to sleep in. We'll start tomorrow, and I expect you to be on time. Do you understand?"

Everyone nods. She dismisses us, and we make our way back to the dorm. Mae is talking to Katie and Susannah, but my mind is somewhere else. It's only when we're standing in front of our rooms and I fish for the key in my jacket pocket that I realize it's not there.

"Shit," I say. That's all I need.

"What's wrong?" Mae pauses in the doorway to her room.

"The key must have fallen out of my pocket. Probably in the theater."

"That's annoying."

"I'm going back to look for it. I'll meet you later for dinner, okay?"

"No worries, I'll come with you," Mae offers, but I decline.

"Thanks, that's really nice, but you don't need to."

"Are you sure?"

"Yup. See you later."

There's no one in the theater but me when I arrive. Everything seems deserted, and an excited tingle goes through me because it feels so different to be here alone. Fortunately, the door to the auditorium is still open, so I don't have to ask anyone to let me in. My key is probably under the seat I was sitting in. Once I have it, maybe I can sneak onto the stage . . .

I stop abruptly when I hear familiar voices. I recognize them immediately. Jase. And Charlotte. My feet stop moving of their own accord. I dart into the auditorium and stop right next to the door when I spot them. They're just a few yards away from me, so focused on one another that they don't even notice I'm there. I should go, I know, but then I hear my name, and my heart suddenly starts beating fast.

"We both know that Zoe is a total catastrophe," Charlotte says, in her simultaneously condescending and sickly sweet voice. It sends an unpleasant shiver down my spine.

"So what? What does that have to do with me?"

"You're in another league, and we both know that."

I gasp indignantly and curse myself the next second, but they don't seem to have noticed.

"Stop wasting my time. Get to the point. What does that have to do with me?" Jase growls.

"I want you to talk to Francesca. You should be my partner. You were always the best. We belong together."

The corners of Jase's mouth twitch with amusement, and he crosses his arms over his chest. "Do we? You seem to be doing fine with Devon."

"So what?" Charlotte shrugs, and I start to feel angry. She's trying to steal my dance partner, and all at once, it doesn't matter how things are between Jase and me. If she gets away with this, I'll have to dance with Devon, and I can't do that.

"I don't like you, and you know it. And I guess you're not my biggest fan either. So why would I want to do that?"

She lifts her hand, strokes his shoulder, and smiles, and something inside me reacts with a furious stab of jealousy. "You don't have to like me. We can be great together in all kinds of ways without you liking me."

I clench my teeth. I'm about to explode, but I force myself to remain calm.

Jase takes a demonstrative step away from her, and Charlotte's hand slips off his shoulder. "I'll repeat myself. Why would I want to do that?" He sounds bored, but his shoulders are tense, and he looks annoyed.

Charlotte sighs. "Okay, fine. If that's how you want to play the game, that's all right by me. I know your parents refused to pay your tuition. I also know you need a scholarship. But those are only given out at the beginning of a new semester. Which brings us to the question of how you're going to finance *this* semester. And no, I'm not expecting an answer, because I already know. You're not. You have no money, Jase. You're broke. And you can't get a credit card because your daddy very carefully blocked all your options."

I wait for him to deny it, because it can't be that bad, can it? His parents won't pay his tuition, but he must be able to get a loan. He's Jase Winslow, and half the city knows his family. But Jase doesn't say a word. His teeth are grinding, and the look of annoyance on his face transforms into murderous fury.

"And that brings us to the offer that I can make you," Charlotte says, casually tossing her shiny black hair over her shoulders. "My parents will pay your fees for this semester. Plus, my mother can help you get a scholarship. She knows a few people on the board and can put in a good word. The only thing you have to do is be my partner. That's all."

I make my presence known by clearing my throat before Jase can answer. I don't want to hear what he's going to say. If he really wants to trade partners, I'm screwed.

Charlotte and Jase both turn in my direction. Charlotte's eyes flash with anger, but Jase looks almost amused.

"Where were you?" I ask him, ignoring Charlotte as much as I can. "We had an appointment, remember?"

He shakes his head and gives Charlotte a regretful smile, which I don't buy for a second. "Sorry, I have to go."

Her smile is just as fake. "Think about it. My offer stands."

Jase doesn't answer. I find my key, and together we leave the auditorium, then the theater building.

"Eavesdropping is rude," he says once we're outside.

I repress the excuse that's on the tip of my tongue, because he's right. But I'm not sorry. So I shrug. We enter the practice studios and silently climb the stairs to the little studio under the roof, not saying a word.

This time, I'm the one to break the ice between us. "Are you thinking about accepting Charlotte's offer?" I ask. I have to know. I hope his answer will be no. But I can't be sure.

CHAPTER 22

Jase

What's most important to you?

Ballet. And your family. And telling you my secrets.
—J

Part of me wants to answer Zoe's question with a yes, because it would make everything easier if I took Charlotte up on her offer. Aside from the fact that I'd have to deal with Charlotte. But otherwise . . . My problems would disappear in a snap and dissolve into thin air. Still, I can't do that, and I think Zoe knows it just as well as I do.

"No."

She looks at me skeptically. "Why not?"

"Because I don't like to be blackmailed," I say, leaving out the whole truth, which I won't admit, not even to myself. Charlotte is the most manipulative bitch I've ever met. She may always get what she wants, but I'm not some designer handbag she can buy with her parents' money.

"Your life would be a lot easier if you did."

"I know."

"Then why didn't you say yes? You need money, and she offered it to you." Zoe looks at me as though she really can't understand. But what is she expecting me to say?

"Do you want to get rid of me?"

She shakes her head. "I want to understand you."

This time I won't ask her why. I don't answer at all, instead opening the door to the little attic studio and kicking off my shoes. Zoe follows me in, tossing her jacket in the corner and stepping in front of the mirror without being told. I stand behind her.

"No music today?" she asks, and her voice carries a slightly sarcastic undertone that I don't recognize at all. I roll my eyes but pull my phone out of my pocket and connect it to the Bluetooth speaker. "Any requests?"

"You can choose."

I hesitate for a moment before searching for Harry Styles on Spotify and randomly clicking on a song. I know Zoe loves them all. She needs to relax, and music helps with that, doesn't it?

When I turn around, she's staring at me, eyes wide.

"Since when do you listen to Harry Styles?" She sounds so confounded that I almost have to laugh.

"For a while," I answer curtly, because there's no way I can admit that I chose the song for her. That would mean that I was thinking about her, and . . . No. Just no.

I stand behind her and decide to focus on the original problem. I pluck at the hem of her sweater. "Are you wearing anything underneath?"

Zoe stiffens, and when her eyes go wide this time, it's not because I've confused her. "Why?" she asks. Her voice goes up an octave.

"Because in class you're never wearing a thick sweatshirt. Doesn't it feel different through all that material?"

She hesitates and then nods and pulls the sweatshirt off over her head. Underneath, she's wearing a fitted black T-shirt with short sleeves that's a lot like a ballet leotard.

"Ready?" I ask her, and also myself, because this isn't a great idea. I've known that for days, and nothing has changed.

Instead of answering, she puts her hand in mine. It feels like a jolt of electricity is shooting up my arm from my palm. It goes straight into my chest and that damn muscle that's not supposed to feel anything. It seems to constantly forget that when I'm around her.

I take a deep breath, trying to remember how it felt last year when Zoe stopped answering my notes and Caleb didn't call me back anymore. All at once, I no longer had a second home that felt more like a real home than anywhere I'd been in years. Ceara stopped making me eat more, and Ethan stopped asking me how I was doing and if everything was okay.

Every muscle in my body tenses, and Zoe stiffens with me and pulls back her hands.

"Relax," I say to both of us.

"You relax," she retorts, and my mind goes quiet as she puts her hands in mine again. They're small, much smaller than mine. It's not the first time I've noticed that. I noticed it a long time ago, back when I held her hand properly for the first time. The fact that I'm noticing it again now is . . . yeah, well, it probably means something.

I continue like the last time. I slip my fingers between hers, even though that's technically unnecessary, because we don't need to touch that way when we're dancing. But apparently, my hands want to know how her fingers feel between mine again.

Familiar. Strange. Painful. Yearning.

My hands move of their own accord, gliding up her arms and over her shoulders. She holds still, but I can tell my touch is doing something to her. I can feel her heart beating faster. Just like mine. Damn traitor.

My fingertips slide over her back. After all, I have to touch it when we dance. Her hips, her waist. Everything makes sense. It feels right, I think. Or I don't think. I'm not really sure anymore what's going on in my head. My hands come to rest on her stomach. I don't do it deliberately; it just happens. And it just happens that Zoe leans back against me again. Just like last time.

She's on fire. Her skin gives off an incredible amount of heat, even through her T-shirt. I automatically pull her closer until we're pressed together lengthwise, just slightly, but it's enough to make me feel just as warm. Adrenaline rushes through my veins, along with something else, when I notice Zoe's breath speeding up.

Her chest rises and falls, faster than it did a moment ago. My eyes are automatically drawn to her breasts. It's wrong, but I can't look away, and all the blood goes from my head to my dick, and I know I have a problem. An even worse one than I thought.

"How does that feel?" Zoe asks, even though it's me who should be asking that question. But her voice is strangely hoarse, and this definitely feels like my downfall.

I give her a different answer. Because I'm an idiot. "It feels like you."

BEFORE
Zoe

One year earlier
June 25, 10:17 PM

Charlotte and Adaline's house is practically bursting at the seams. I don't know how they managed to persuade their parents to let them invite so many people. It's not only the entire graduating class of Westview High but also most of my class, along with some kids I've never seen before. A few of the guys look older, probably college students.

My friends have disappeared into the crowd and are looking for something to drink. I'm standing alone in a corner trying not to freak out.

In the living room, all the furniture has been shoved aside to make space for a dance floor. Caleb is standing on the edge of it with Reed and Nick. I just saw Tristan on the way to the kitchen, and Jase . . . I haven't seen him anywhere.

My stomach is fluttering nervously, my heart is beating too fast, and there's a quiet, unsure voice inside me that's wondering if I made a mistake by writing that last note to Jase.

What if it was a dumb idea? What if I chose the wrong moment? Would it have been better to talk to him than to write him a note? Why don't I just do it instead? Kiss him, I mean. But what if he doesn't even want to kiss me? What if he doesn't feel the same way about me as I do about him? What if I ruined everything with that note and everything that was happening between us is over now just because I wrote those three words on a piece of paper? Because I couldn't stand the thought that Charlotte might be the one he kisses.

I want to be the girl he kisses. I've wanted it for weeks. And now . . . I notice a familiar head of blond hair moving through the crowd. A moment later, Jase's eyes meet mine.

My heart skips a beat and then picks up where it left off, even faster. Blood rises into my cheeks. He's here.

He's smiling at me, and my heart is ready to break out of my chest. My skin begins to tingle as his smile gets wider. His eyes are shining, and all at once, I have no idea if I'm nervous or excited. I don't know anything anymore. Only that I can't stop looking at him.

He holds up his hand, and at first I don't understand, until I see he's holding something white. It's my note, I know it, without him having to say so or show me.

The fluttering in my stomach gets a thousand times stronger as I approach him.

"Hi," he says softly when I get there. So softly that I can barely hear him over the loud music. But I can read his lips.

"Hi." My voice is just as soft. I have to crane my neck to see him properly. His hand strokes mine, a tender touch that hits me right in the heart. I can't breathe anymore; I can only look at him. His fingers interlace with mine. It feels like it should have always been like this.

"Are you coming with me?" he tugs at my hand, and my feet move of their own accord. I let him lead me through the crowd at the edge of the dance floor until we reach the wide patio door.

It's quieter in the Hammonds' yard; the music isn't nearly as loud out here. It's still warm even though it's late and the sun went down a long time ago. I breathe in the smell of freshly mowed grass and summer.

Jase guides me away from the door, and our footsteps echo too loudly on the wood of the deck but go silent as we step onto the lawn and walk farther into the yard. The whole time, he's holding my hand and doesn't let go until we're standing between two tall trees. Someone hung a string of lights around the tree trunks, and the world around us is bathed in a warm glow. It's absolutely perfect.

Jase turns to look at me, and his eyes have an expression that I've never seen before. There's a gentle, almost shy smile on his lips. Locks of blond hair fall over his forehead, and I want to push them back and caress and kiss him. He's so beautiful that it almost hurts.

"I found your note."

I can't look at him anymore, because everything inside me is urging me to touch him. But I can't look away either, just because he's too much Jase and I'm too much Zoe.

"Did you?"

He grins. "Yeah, I did."

My mind is suddenly blank. I want to give him a response that means something, but every single word escapes me.

Jase takes a step closer, and now the entire lengths of our bodies are touching. His legs are touching mine, his chest, his arms—everything. And he's still holding my hand.

"Why do you want me to kiss you, Pixie?" His voice is soft and warm, and I never want to hear anything else.

I swallow hard. "You know why."

"Say it anyway." His thumb strokes mine, gently and carefully. I gasp.

Because we've trusted each other with every one of our secrets for the last three months, I will do it again this time.

"Because you're you, and I'm me. And I believe that together, we can be everything."

He lets go of my hand and strokes my bare arm, my shoulder, and I feel the touch in every nerve of my body. My skin glows as if he has set it on fire.

"We really can, can't we?" he whispers. "Be everything, I mean." His hand rests on my cheek, firm and sure. His gaze wanders from my eyes to my lips, and he pauses.

"Yes, we can." My voice doesn't sound like me. It's far too hoarse and far too excited. I hold my breath. *Kiss me*, I beg silently. Maybe I said it out loud. Either way, it doesn't matter, because Jase closes the last inch between us, and his lips meet mine.

My eyelids flutter closed, and my heart is ready to leap out of my chest, straight to him—not only because I want to give it to him, but because it's already been his for a long time.

The kiss is gentle, careful and unsure, and somehow everything at once. Just like us.

PART 3
Variations of Her
Phase Three of the Pas de Deux

CHAPTER 23
Zoe

I lost myself last year, and now I'm frantically trying to find myself again. But it feels like I'm constantly chasing after something I can never reach.
—Zoe

The next three weeks pass so quickly that I can hardly keep up. The grace period is over, and our teachers pick up the pace in all our subjects. Mr. Conrad and Miss Chelsea, who teach us pointe, are almost as relentless as Francesca.

I know Francesca isn't happy with our performance, but she hasn't warned me again about the consequences. I take that as a good sign. At least, I *hope* it's a good sign and not just the calm before the storm. But even though I don't panic every time I dance with Jase anymore, it's still not going very well, and I don't understand why.

We've spent a lot of time together in the past few weeks. The more time we spend alone in the little attic studio, the safer I feel with him. With his hands on my body. His body behind mine, his breath on my skin as he gets a little closer to me every time.

Something has changed between us, but I can't put my finger on it.

The morning after our second touch practice session, I found a note in my room. Messily folded, as usual, slipped under my door. A secret. Without a question. It felt different from the last time. Then, when he asked me what had happened, I gave him an honest answer. But I didn't trust him with the truth. This time, he was confiding in me, and I gave him something back.

If you tell me your secrets, I'll tell you mine.

Our game has changed, just like *we* have changed. And I have no idea where that's leading.

Now it's Saturday, and we're meeting in the theater with the group that's responsible for the *Sleeping Beauty* sets. I'm a nervous wreck, even though there's no reason to be. But I slept badly and had strange dreams that made no sense but felt totally real at the same time. I dreamed about Jase, and that threw me so far off balance that I couldn't eat a thing in the morning.

"Here, you look like you could use some caffeine." I turn my head at the sound of Mae's far too cheerful, awake voice. She holds out a takeout cup, from which the heavenly smell of coffee and pumpkin pie wafts.

"You brought me a pumpkin spice latte?"

She puts the cup in my hand and drops into the chair next to me. "If I'd only gotten one for myself, you would have died with envy, and I didn't want to be responsible for that."

"I think I love you," I say, taking a sip. I immediately feel better. It's later than usual because Francesca has an important private meeting today, so we're left to our own devices. But I'm still just as tired as I was this morning when I woke up from my confused dreams and couldn't get back to sleep.

Mae tosses her auburn hair over her shoulders and sighs dramatically. "It's impossible not to love me," she says.

I roll my eyes, laughing, but she's right. It's impossible not to love her. I think Mae is the nicest person I've ever met. We've spent so much time together since the semester began that it almost feels as though we've known each other forever. In comparison, my high school friendships with Charlotte, Amber, and Scarlett feel like a bad joke. They never treated me like Mae does, never showed real interest in me or listened to me properly. They never gave me the space that Mae does, like when she realizes that I'm not doing well and I don't want to talk about it.

"Where's the rest of our group?" She looks around. There are only a few of us in the auditorium: two boys from the junior class and a group of sophomore girls. But most of the group is missing.

I check the time on my phone, and I see a text from Caleb.

CALEB:

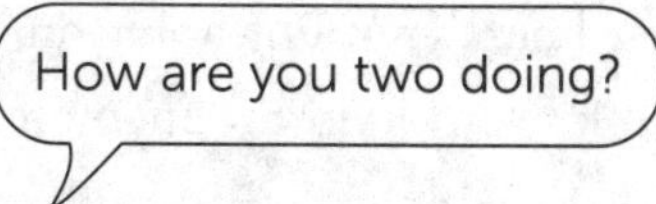

I turn red because I know exactly who he means by "you two." Nothing has changed since the last time he asked me three days ago.

"You're blushing," Mae says unhelpfully, and my cheeks get even hotter. "Why?"

"Caleb is making comments that are uncalled for," I say, putting the phone into my backpack again.

"About what?" She peers at me curiously.

"How is it going with Tristan, anyway?" I ask to change the

subject. Since Mae and Tristan got to know each other that evening at Caleb's place, they've had a few dates, and I'm really hoping it will grow into something more. I'm also hoping that she'll forget about Caleb's message. But I should have known that changing the subject wouldn't help.

"Pretty good. We're meeting tonight. So, what kind of uncalled-for comments is Caleb making?" she says with a wide grin.

I'm spared having to answer because the door opens and the rest of the group finally arrives. I automatically look for Jase. His gaze meets mine, and a small smile appears on his face. My heart jumps. Every little smile from Jase, no matter how small, is a victory for me.

"Why, exactly, is nothing going on between you?" May whispers, drawing my attention away from Jase and back to her. Her eyes gleam, and I blush again. This really needs to stop.

"Because there's no chemistry."

"Uh-huh. Your look says otherwise."

"You've got to stop assuming things. There's nothing going on." Except there is, and I'm starting to think I can't ignore it anymore. Or suppress it. But regardless, it's all too complicated to explain right now.

"You know, you can lie to yourself all you want, but I see what I see, and there's definitely something happening." Mae nods decisively.

"Maybe you should get your eyes checked," I suggest dryly. She's about to retort when Charlotte walks to the front of the room. I tense automatically, but I'm not surprised that she's trying to take charge. She always has to be the center of attention, and if she's not on stage, she'll find another way.

For the last few weeks, she's basically ignored me, which only makes me more nervous. I have a feeling she's planning something. Maybe I'm just paranoid. After Jase told her off the other day, she left me alone. Maybe I'm just taking myself too seriously right now, but it all feels off. She wants Jase as her dance partner, and Charlotte always gets what she wants. But she doesn't seem to be doing anything about it, and the longer I wait for her to react, the more nervous I get.

"We should—" she starts, then stops again. The door opens, and Katie hurries down the stairs.

"Sorry I'm late, I was just talking to Francesca." She grins. "I get to torture you today. So come on, let's get started. The fairy-tale forest won't paint itself."

* * *

Despite what Pearson said at his assembly, we don't actually have that much to do with the stage design. The concept was developed long before the semester began by a set designer and the director of the ballet. A large part of the work is done by trained craftsmen because, as Pearson rightly pointed out, we are dancers and not visual artists. If we were allowed to create the whole set on our own, it would probably be kind of mediocre.

So in the end, we're responsible for the details. But even little things need to be done properly, and after a while, my fingers are cramped from holding the brushes, and the effect of the pumpkin spice latte doesn't last very long. My body craves more caffeine and exercise. I feel stiff and awkward, but there's nothing I can do about it right now.

"Zoe! Mae!" I stop working and look up after Katie's sharp whisper. She's standing a few yards away and beckons us over, looking excited.

I glance at Mae in surprise, who shrugs. I put my brush down in the drip tray so no paint gets on the floor and stand up.

Mae has already gotten up and dances toward Katie with graceful steps. "What's going on?" she asks.

"Come on." Katie peers around to make sure no one is looking and then grabs Mae by the wrist. But none of the others are paying any attention to us. Everyone is absorbed in their work except for Charlotte, who doesn't want to get her hands dirty and has talked her way out of it by offering to document the process on video. Katie tried to convince her that no one wants to see a video of us painting parts of the set in a less-than-professional way, but Charlotte insisted. At some point, Katie gave up. She probably realized there's no point in arguing with Charlotte.

Katie leads us backstage, past the changing rooms and the back door and around a corner, until we're finally standing by the emergency exit.

"Tadaaa!" She lets go of Mae and spreads her arms wide.

"Katie, not to kill the vibe, but that's a door. Why the excitement?"

Katie rolls her eyes. "Mae, you have to trust me. That's not just any door."

"No, it's the emergency exit," I add, and Katie wrinkles her nose in annoyance.

"If you keep making stupid comments, I won't tell you the secret."

"What secret?" May says, and Katie finally looks satisfied.

"First of all, if you tell anyone about this or tattle to a teacher or Pearson, the next few months will be hell for you. Is that clear?" She smiles at us, but it's clear she means it. I get goose bumps, but at the same time, my heart accelerates with excitement.

"We won't say a word," I promise.

"Won't tell a soul," Mae adds, nodding.

"That's what I wanted to hear." Katie reaches for the door handle and pushes it down. It swings open completely silently. "The lock is broken," she explains. "It has been for years. No one's noticed it yet, or at least, it hasn't been fixed, and the door can be opened from the outside."

"What's that supposed to mean?" Mae's voice sounds a little skeptical, but Katie grins.

"What else? We all want to be able to dance on this stage without waiting until we're seniors. You don't know how magical it can be until you sneak into the theater at least once at night and dance here all by yourself."

* * *

Katie's words stay with me all day. Even when she finally kicks us out of the theater because we've done enough for today. Even as I help Mae pick an outfit for her date with Tristan. And even as I'm lying in bed later, tossing and turning, unable to sleep even though I've been dead tired all day. Now I'm wide awake.

I almost never break the rules, and the few times I've done so can be counted on one hand. My pens are sorted by color, as are my ballet leotards and all the books I own. I like everything to be in order, and deliberately breaking rules isn't compatible with my perfectionism.

Still, I've been thinking for hours now about breaking the rules, sneaking into the theater, and dancing on that stage.

Be courageous. Trust yourself.

It's not a conscious decision, but shortly after midnight, my legs swing over the edge of my bed, and I quickly dress and hurry out of my room. There are voices coming from the common room; I hear laughter. It's Saturday night, and I'm probably the only one who's been in bed.

I don't see anyone on the stairs, but music echoes from a few of the rooms. When I push open the door and step outside, I see no one but me. It's dark and surprisingly cold. It's October now, and winter is coming fast.

My breath makes little clouds in the air, and I snuggle deeper into my down jacket.

It feels forbidden to walk into the theater in the middle of the night, which is probably because it is. Adrenaline is rushing through my veins, and my brain wants me to turn around and go back to bed, but I ignore it.

I can only think about the stage and the fact that I haven't danced just for myself in ages. Without being criticized by teachers, without Mae and the other girls I meet at the end of the week for practice, which is always fun but never gives me the feeling of peace I only feel when I'm alone. It takes me a few minutes to find the door. I hesitate as I grab the handle.

This is crazy. I don't do things like this. But my stomach is fluttering nervously, and the stage is calling me. I shake off the rising sense of doubt and push down the handle, and the door opens. I cast one last glance over my shoulder, but the campus is a ghost town. I can see the administration building, a dark warning behind me. If I get caught, I'll probably get into a lot of trouble, but the urge to do this one forbidden thing is simply overwhelming.

I slip inside, and the door closes behind me with a soft click. Darkness surrounds me. I fish my phone out of my pocket and turn on the flashlight, and suddenly I'm where I've always wanted to be. I carelessly drop my shoes and jacket on the floor and start my warm-up exercises before I finally put on my pointe shoes and my little Bluetooth earbuds, because it feels wrong to dance on this stage without music.

I have a weakness for pop songs that morph into classical music. Somehow, this makes every song sound even better.

My eyes have long since adapted to the darkness as I enter the stage, my heart beating wildly. There's nobody here but me, and no one can see me, but at the same time, it's everything to me. Suddenly, it doesn't matter whether I'm allowed to be here or not. I *want* to be here, I've always wanted to be here, and right now, this is exactly where I belong.

The stage floor creaks softly. I take a few steps, pause, and all at once find it difficult to breathe when I see the theater stretching out in front of me. The rows of seats that descend toward the stage. The fancy box seats. It's completely dark, but it doesn't matter. I can see enough. Red velvet and absolute emptiness. Music fills my ears, and I move of my own accord.

I improvise, not following any choreography. I feel the music, I feel free, and for a moment I forget everything. The chaos that is my life, Charlotte making mysterious plans, my family, Jase telling me his secrets again.

Now my mind goes silent. I only feel my heart beating, my breathing getting a little stronger, and my muscles working. I gaze out into the theater, and my steps turn into Aurora's. Then I dance *The Sleeping Beauty*, the role I practiced so many times that I can do every step in my sleep.

I dance it because it was the first ballet I ever watched with my parents after I fell madly in love with the Disney movie. I can't remember why I loved the movie so much, but I loved the ballet even more. I fell in love with Aurora and even more in love with the music. I was captivated by the story and the feelings that the story created inside of me. Longing, tingling excitement, hope. Everything about this ballet is full of magic and dreams that sneak into my heart. *Sleeping Beauty* is a fairy tale, and somehow it has become *my* fairy tale. I fell in love with the lightness and grace of the dancer who had played Aurora in that production. I was mesmerized by her beauty and her ability to make me feel the character's emotions with her dancing.

Now I dance the role myself, gliding over the dark stage with my body feeling more under control than it's been for ages. Adrenaline rushes through my veins, my skin tingles, and I feel so infinitely alive as I push off into a pirouette, spinning around and around on my axis, not once losing my balance.

The music in my earbuds doesn't fit with the steps or the story, but it *feels* right. For a moment, I'm weightless and simply happy.

I had forgotten how that feels.

To be happy.

Tears flood my eyes, but I let them come, because it's time to let them go. And then I just *feel*. I feel everything.

CHAPTER 24
Jase

The whole last year of my life felt like someone pressed the pause button. Somehow everything kept on going, but it didn't feel like my life. Not the way it was supposed to be after graduating. Because suddenly everything was different, but in the wrong way.
—Jase

I should have left as soon as I heard someone come into the theater. Those are the rules. As soon as someone wants to use the stage, no one else has any business being here. Anyone who comes and realizes that someone is already there leaves, and anyone who has finished packs up their things and gets out as quickly as possible.

Sneaking into the theater at night and dancing isn't a group thing. Everyone who comes does it for themselves, to have the chance to dance the lead role for once in their lives. It doesn't matter that there's no audience. It's just about being on that stage and being free to do what we were all born for.

My time has been up for a while now, since I jumped off the stage and sat down in one of the back rows, killing time to avoid going back to my room. My room, which is right next to Zoe's. I stayed here to stop myself from doing something stupid.

But as it turns out, it was just as stupid to stay. Because it's not just anyone sneaking into the theater tonight. It's Zoe.

Of course it is. Who else would I expect? She's everywhere, and I can't escape her. How can I, when we see each other three times a week at pas de deux class and meet on other days to get her panic under control?

It's gotten better, much better, even if the pas de deux still doesn't work the way it should. We're still ridiculously far behind the others, but we're making progress. Especially when we're not dancing, and that's a problem because my idiotic brain turns off completely whenever she puts her hands in mine or leans against me. All I can do is feel, and there's far too much soft, warm skin, too much heat, and too múch Zoe. My damn body is getting me in trouble, because every time she touches me, it forgets what happened, and the last thing I want is to let Zoe get close to me again.

But somewhere deep inside, I know that it's too late. I'm already writing notes again. Notes that I actually give to her, not just hide for her like I did all of last year. I'm telling her my secrets even though I don't really want to. But I can't stop. I started, and now I'm lost. Completely and irrevocably. If I fall again, this time there will only be the abyss below me. No safety net. Only a bottomless pit.

I've been standing at the edge for a long time now, but tonight there are only a few inches left as Zoe steps onto the stage and begins to dance to music that I can't hear. It's pitch dark in the theater, but I've been sitting here long enough that my eyes have adapted to the darkness, and I can see every one of her movements. I see *her*.

Zoe has always had her own special way of dancing. Every movement is perfect, her muscles taut with flexibility and grace. You can tell that Zoe loves ballet because she feels it. Everything. The music, the pain, the tension in every muscle. She makes it look easy. We all do, but somehow there's a special aura around her. Or maybe I'm the only one who sees it.

Either way, I know I'm screwed as I watch her dance when I should be leaving. I stay where I am until she finally sinks down into a deep *révérence*. I can't see her smile, but I can feel it, and the muscle in my chest twitches, and my legs act of their own accord. I stand up and go to the stage, not thinking about what a stupid idea it is. I just do it.

CHAPTER 25
Zoe

Sometimes I wish that I had never
stopped writing you notes.
—Zoe

My heart races, and my chest is moving at an alarming rate from breathing so fast. There's a smile on my face as I straighten up, and then I almost freak out as I see someone just a few steps away.

Jase.

"God, don't scare me like that!" I shout and take out the earbuds while my heart pounds hard against my ribs.

His gaze is serious, and something in his eyes triggers a frantic fluttering in my stomach. "I'm sorry, I thought you heard me."

I shake my head. I didn't hear anything. Just the music. "What are you doing here?"

"Same as you, I guess." He takes a step toward me, then stops right in front of me and just stares.

"You've been watching me," I say. Maybe, probably, certainly the thought should worry me, but it's Jase that's standing here in front of me.

He shrugs, but there's no apology in his eyes. "I couldn't look away."

His words hit me right where it hurts. Right in the heart.

"Why?"

A sound that's something between incredulous laughter and a frustrated sigh escapes him. "Because you're you, Zoe."

"What's that supposed to mean?" I ask, and my voice is soft and all at once a little hoarse. It doesn't sound like me at all. But he's so damn close to me and is saying things he shouldn't, and I want to hear all of it. Whispered secrets that are even more intense than written secrets on crumpled pieces of paper.

"If I knew that, I'd have one less problem." His voice resonates with a tone of desperation, and my heart tightens.

"So now I'm a problem for you?" It's a rhetorical question; I know it's true. I'm a miserable dance partner, but Jase is making it sound like it's more than that. And if it's not that, then what?

Jase shakes his head so firmly that a few strands of hair fall over his forehead. I want to brush them away, to know how they feel between my fingers. I bite my bottom lip, because this is all wrong. I can't feel this way. Not for Jase, and not at all. I shouldn't. Am I even allowed to?

But then he stares at my lips, and even though the whole room is dark, I can see his pupils dilate. His eyes look darker, and the fluttering in my stomach turns into something different, warmer, more urgent.

"You cause problems, Pixie, but you're not a problem yourself. Because you're you." He moves a little closer, and all at once I can't breathe. My throat is getting tight, and my heart is beating way too fast.

His fingertips graze my hand, and an electrifying tingling runs up my arm to my chest, a warm flicker that becomes too strong, too fast.

Why do you want me to kiss you, Pixie?

Because you're you, and I'm me. And I believe that together, we can be everything.

All at once, I can hear our voices, what we said over a year ago. The questions and secrets, the goose bumps all over my body. And then the kiss. A single, short kiss that was simultaneously everything and nothing. Too much and too little.

"I can't stop thinking about that kiss."

At first, I think it's me who's spoken, because the memory of Jase's lips on mine feels very real right now. But it's his voice, huskier than it was before, and I grow warm as his fingers interlace with mine, all by themselves. He tugs gently at my hand, almost carefully, and I let it happen. There's no way I could stop myself even if I wanted to. And I don't want to. Definitely not.

"Why not?" I ask, waiting for him to repeat my words from back then.

"Because I want to do it again," he says softly instead. This answer is almost better, because I want him to do it again too.

I've wanted it from the first time that we stood in front of the mirror together and he ran his hands over my arms and shoulders. I've wanted it since he asked me the first time how it felt to be touched by him, and my answer was far too simple.

"Then do it." The words slip out before I can stop them. Before I realize that it's a terrible idea, because I don't know if my body will behave or if I'll panic. Jase is the first and only boy I've ever kissed, but maybe that's why it's exactly the right thing to do. Maybe I just need to be brave.

His hand tightens a little on mine. He looks like he's about to shake his head, and he looks so torn, which is exactly how I feel. He looks into my eyes and then at my mouth, and then I'm the one who decides. I close the space between us and put my lips on his.

In the first second, he doesn't react, and I panic. It's a different kind of panic, not as bad, but a panic that maybe I shouldn't have done it at all. *He said he wanted to, but maybe he didn't really mean it, and—* My thoughts stop in their tracks when he lets go of my hand and strokes my face. His skin is soft and warm, like his lips. He kisses me gently and carefully. But that's not what I want. I want all of him.

Molten heat surges through me. I open my lips, and Jase accepts the invitation without hesitating. He groans a little as our tongues touch, and a tremor runs through his body. Then all at once, nothing is gentle or careful anymore.

It's just us, his lips on mine, his tongue in my mouth, his hands on my face, my neck, my fingers in his hair. Soft moans. Jase pulls me closer, and I press myself against him, soaking up his warmth, the kiss, his breath. His erection presses against my stomach, and it's all too much and nowhere near enough.

My pulse is racing. I can feel it in my whole body—my fingertips, my stomach, even my toes and between my legs. It throbs and throbs. There's nothing but pure desire, and I feel like crying because I didn't know it was still possible for me to feel this way.

But it is, and I want more.

As I lean against him, Jase abruptly backs away. His face has become an expressionless mask, and all at once, I'm freezing cold.

"Jase—" I say, but he turns on his heel without a word and leaves me standing there.

* * *

I'm confused when I finally crawl into my bed. Confused, tired, and hurt. Even if I would never admit it. I'm hurt because he just left. He made me feel things that I haven't felt for far too long. And then he just stopped. It feels like he's taken something away from me.

Once more, I can't fall asleep, even though it's almost four AM. I desperately need to sleep, but I can't. Despite Jase's rejection, I can't stop thinking about the kiss, and when I think about the kiss, my whole body starts to tingle. I can feel his lips on mine again. I can feel him moaning in my mouth . . .

My eyelids flutter shut.

His body pressed against mine, his hardness against my stomach. His hands on my skin. I heat up, my heart starts to race, and my fingers take off on their own, wandering under my pajama shorts and into my underwear. I don't think about what I'm doing. I just do it, let it happen, because I want to know if I can. If it still works. I want to be able to feel my body again. I want my control back.

I imagine that they're his hands, despite everything. Because it can only be his fingers touching me. I sigh softly as I realize how wet I am.

His fingers, my fingers. Everything throbs, pushes, wants more, and then . . . everything inside me tenses up. I go cold, and my body fights me. I can't hold on to the feeling, and the ghost of his lips disappears. Tears fill my eyes because I'm broken and nothing, absolutely nothing, works the way it should. Because Jase wants to kiss me, but he doesn't want me, and I don't even *know* if I want him at all. But of course I'm lying to myself again.

I pull the covers up over my head and cry until I eventually fall asleep.

BEFORE

Zoe

One year earlier
June 25, 10:32 PM

Jase's lips are indescribably soft. He moans, a soft, barely audible sound, and my heart staggers out of rhythm. I instinctively nestle against him, his body presses against mine, and we fit perfectly. It's a slow, gentle kiss, new but somehow familiar.

I never want this to stop.

The thought pops into my head so unexpectedly that I lose my balance for a second. Jase catches me and lets me go, and I see a mixture of hope and pain in his eyes. I want to ask him what's wrong, but as soon as I open my mouth to speak, he kisses me again, and all thinking stops.

"What the hell?" A familiar voice startles us, and we jump apart. Caleb is a few feet away, staring at us in shock. It takes me a few seconds to recognize the anger in his eyes, and my stomach tightens.

Shit, shit, shit!

I should have told him about Jase, about the notes, and everything else.

"Caleb—" Jase says, but my brother silences him with a cutting gesture.

"My little sister? Are you serious?" His voice rings with annoyance, and I want to explain, but there's nothing I can say.

Caleb turns away and stomps toward the house. I can't help it; I have to follow him.

Jase grabs my wrist, stopping me. When I look into his eyes this time, all the hope has disappeared, and there's nothing but fear there.

"I have to talk to him!" I say, trying to get away from him. His grasp tightens almost imperceptibly before he finally lets me go and nods.

"Let me . . ." His voice breaks, and he clears his throat, and my heart breaks a little for him. "Let me talk to him."

I shake my head. "No, he wouldn't listen to you. Trust me."

Jase hesitates and then gives in. "Do you want to meet later in the treehouse?"

I nod quickly and run after my brother. I want to explain everything so he understands what's going on between me and Jase.

As I walk into the house to look for Caleb, the music blares in my ears. But I don't see him anywhere. I find Reed and Tristan playing beer pong at the dining room table.

"Have you seen Caleb?" I ask.

Tristan shakes his head, but Reed grins at me. "He just went upstairs. I think he was looking for the bathroom."

"Thanks!" I blow him a kiss and push my way through the crowd to the stairs and past a couple who are making out on the bottom steps. Most of the doors are locked, but I know exactly which bathroom Caleb is in, and I'm pretty sure he didn't go in there to use the toilet. It's the last door on the left, the guest suite where I always sleep when I spend the night at Charlotte's.

When I open the door, Caleb is there on the bed, his elbows resting on his knees, his hands buried in his dark hair.

He looks up when he hears me, and I gasp in surprise as I realize that my brother is crying.

"Caleb? What—" the rest of the question sticks in my throat.

"I'm such an idiot," he says desperately, wiping the tears off his face.

"Why? What's wrong?" I close the door behind me and walk over to him. An uneasy feeling hits my stomach.

"What's going on with you and Jase?" His voice breaks as he says Jase's name, and the uneasy feeling turns into a dark foreboding.

No, no, please not this.

"I . . . We . . ." I fall silent, and he laughs. It sounds infinitely sad.

"Are you in love with him?"

There's no point in denying it. I can't lie to Caleb. "Yes. But you don't have to worry. Honestly. This is . . . different. You—"

"I'm not worried," he says, interrupting me. And now angry tears pour down his face again, and I understand what he wants to tell me but can't say.

"So you are too," I whisper. This has to be a bad joke. There's no way Caleb and I could have both fallen in love with the same boy. With his best friend.

Caleb nods, and my heart breaks.

He already told me weeks ago that he's gay, and I know he only told Mom and Dad about it a few days ago. I also know he hasn't come out to Jase and his other friends yet. He says he wants to wait because high school sucks and teenagers can be cruel.

But he didn't tell me that he was in love, and I didn't ask because I was sure that he would tell me if he was. I didn't want to push him.

I don't care who he falls in love with as long as it's someone who treats him well and makes him happy.

Now I wish I'd asked him.

"Shit, I'm sorry, Zoe. I should just shut up. Forget what I said—I'm drunk!" he blurts out when I don't answer. My mind has gone completely blank. Ten minutes ago, everything was fine. Ten minutes ago, I was the only one who was in love with Jase. I kissed him. He kissed me. It was perfect.

And now . . . how could so much go wrong so fast?

Caleb covers his face with his hands again. "How could I be so stupid? I knew that he wasn't into me. I *knew* it. Why couldn't I just keep my mouth shut? Why did I have to fall in love with him?" His shoulders begin to shake, and he's crying again. My heart breaks along with his, a little bit more.

"I—" I stop. Words start to form in my mind, but I can't say them.

Because it's much too easy to fall in love with Jase. I want to be with him. I want to do everything with him.

But *everything* just got a lot more complicated. Caleb is in love with Jase, and clearly it's not just a crush. This is the kind of love that really hurts when it's not returned.

I'm still at a loss for words, and there's nothing I can say that would make him feel any better. Instead, I put my arms around my brother and let him cry. I cry with him because everything sucks, and I hate it. I hate that he's hurting, I hate that he's sad, and I hate that I would hurt him even more if I kissed Jase again. If we were really a couple.

I never thought Caleb and I would break each other's hearts. But here we are, both crying over the same boy. At some point, after we've calmed down enough that it at least doesn't hurt to breathe anymore, we leave the guest room and return to the party. Our eyes are red from crying.

My friends and Caleb's are waiting for us in the kitchen, looking worried. They only have to look at our tearstained faces to know that something has gone seriously wrong.

Tristan hands Caleb a drink, and Amber gives one to me. We look each other in the eyes, clink our glasses, and swallow them down. I ignore the fact that Jase is waiting for me in the treehouse and will be worried when I don't show up. I know I should talk to him, but I have no idea what I'd say. I can't be with him without hurting Caleb.

Caleb is my brother and my best friend. I can't be so egotistical.

That's the last clear memory I have of the evening. Then . . . everything falls apart.

My life. My body. All that's left of my heart.

Everything that makes me who I am.

CHAPTER 26
Jase

It felt like a piece of me was missing when I couldn't write to you anymore. You were the remedy for the chaos in my mind, and it was terrible when you weren't there.
—Jase

Five years ago, I was happy. I had a functional family, a stable circle of friends, a dream, and every chance in the world to fulfill it. I had everything I wanted.

And then that bubble of childish innocence and cluelessness just popped. Since then, my life has been in a fucking downward spiral. Broken family, no friends, and a future that could dissolve into thin air at any second.

And then there's Zoe.

The girl who kissed me, then rejected me.

The girl who stopped answering my notes.

The girl who obviously doesn't want me.

Except the damn kiss last night didn't feel like she didn't want me. It felt like something completely different, and I don't understand it. I don't understand *her*.

It's not like I don't have enough problems that I have to deal with. Like the scholarship that I'm busting my butt for and might not get anyway. Like the tuition fee for this semester that I can't afford, even with the movie theater job East got me two weeks ago. But it won't be enough, not even close. I might be able to cover another two months, but that's it. Then it will be over, and I'll be out on the street. There are only so many hours in a week, and I've used them all up.

I'm completely screwed. My problems are piling up all around me, but I can't stop thinking about that kiss.

I can't stop thinking about her lips on mine, her fingers in my hair, the soft sigh that gave me goose bumps all over my body. Her tongue in my mouth. She still tastes like peaches.

I don't want to think about it. Not about the kiss, and not about the money. I don't want to think at all. But I can't stop, damn it. I shouldn't be thinking about her, shouldn't let her get close to me, shouldn't let her kiss me. But it's too late. I'm not standing on the edge anymore. I've fallen.

I want to talk to her. I want to run my hands through her hair. I want to feel her skin on mine, feel her heartbeat. It's all so wrong, but at the same time, it feels like the only thing that's right.

Zoe once asked me why I trust her with my secrets. I told her it's because she's real. Because she can make me feel something.

That hasn't changed. I don't want these damn feelings; they get me absolutely nowhere. But I can't just turn them off either. The wall I'm hiding behind hasn't just begun to crumble; Zoe completely decimated it with a single kiss.

Now it's all back. The pain, the anger, missing her, and the fucking hope that I've tried to squash. The feeling of being completely alone in the world, even though I know I'm not.

My body can't cope with it. It fights back. My heart beats too fast every time I think about Zoe. I'm restless. And I'm angry—at Zoe and Caleb, at my parents and Lia, and at the whole fucking world. Most of all at myself, because I simply can't stay away from her.

A knock on my door snaps me out of my thoughts, and I think—I hope—that it's Zoe. I rush to open it, but it's just my sister. Her blond hair is in a neat braid, and there's a serious expression in her green eyes.

"We need to talk, Jase."

* * *

My sister isn't usually able to catch me off guard. To be honest, I can't ever remember her doing it. Maybe when she didn't come to my graduation, but even that wasn't really surprising. It was more of a confirmation of what I already knew.

But today she manages to throw me off balance.

"Are you fucking kidding me?" I say for the third time, still struggling to believe what she's saying.

Lia stares daggers at me. "Can't you put a sentence together without swearing?"

"I can, but not in this case."

"You're acting childish," she says, groaning in annoyance.

"Good thing I'm your little brother, because that's basically my job." I'm frustrating the hell out of her, and considering the offer she just made me, I probably shouldn't be. But I can't help it. I've forgotten how to deal with Lia in a normal way.

She glares at me. "So? Do you want the money or not?"

Her perfectly manicured fingernails tap impatiently on the tabletop. We've been sitting in a little hipster café for about fifteen minutes. It's just a few blocks from campus. Lia avoids my room like the plague, and I refused to go to hers.

But neither of us wanted an audience for this conversation, so rather than going to the hall or the cafeteria, we ended up here. Over a cup of the most disgusting coffee I've ever had, Lia offered to give me the tuition fee for this semester.

The offer is so absurd that I think my question is completely justified.

"Where did you get that kind of money anyway?" I lean back on my chair and cross my arms over my chest. Lia avoids my gaze, her hands cramping around her coffee cup.

"Lia," I say sharply, "why do you have so much money that you can just give me thirteen thousand dollars?"

Her face is an expressionless mask that is painfully familiar to me. For a moment, it feels like I'm looking in the mirror.

"Grandma and Grandpa set up a college fund for each of us. Not for the tuition—they knew Mom and Dad had that covered—but just to make our college experiences . . . a little more comfortable." She's clearly reluctant to tell me about this, and as soon as my brain computes what she's said, I almost wish she hadn't.

I stare at her, nonplussed. "Grandma and Grandpa set up a college fund for *each* of us?"

She nods.

"Why don't I know anything about it?"

The answer is so simple, so goddamn obvious that I know the answer as soon as the question is out of my mouth. My parents aren't the only ones who cut off my funds. I never thought of asking my grandparents for help, but apparently, it wouldn't have worked anyway.

Lia sighs. "You know why. Don't force me to say it. Just take the money. It belongs to me; it's my account. Dad won't find out."

It would be so easy just to say yes. It would be so stupid not to. But my pride sees things differently.

"Why do you want to help me?"

"You're my brother," she says, as though that would explain everything. In our case, it definitely doesn't.

"So? You didn't care about that in the last few years."

She flinches almost imperceptibly, and a pained expression crosses her face but disappears again quickly. "You asked me if I would have given up my dream just because Mom and Dad wanted me to. I . . . well, let's just say, I don't want you to have to give up your dream."

It's been three weeks since I said that to her. Three damn weeks. Why is she only getting to it now? My eyes narrow to slits. Part of me wants to believe her, but another part knows better. "So you want to give me thirteen thousand dollars. Just like that. Without asking for anything in return?"

Lia blushes, and my shoulders tense up. "Yes . . . well . . . can't you just try to smooth things out with Mom and Dad?"

I snort. That was so obvious. "So you'll only give me the money if I make nice with Mom and Dad? Are you fucking kidding me?"

"I just want you to try not to act like a complete asshole. They'd do anything for you, and you're totally ungrateful!"

"I'm *ungrateful*?" I snap and jump up. I bump the table as I move, and my cup falls over with a clatter. At least I don't have to drink the stupid coffee now.

I notice the irritated glances of the other guests, but I couldn't care less.

"Yes, you are!" Lia stands up too, and her eyes gleam with tears. "Mom and Dad would really do anything for you, and you don't even notice!"

"They don't accept or respect what I want or who I am, but sure, they'd do anything for me."

"Jesus, Jase, they're worried about you! You're just not listening."

"That's total bullshit. Dad just wants to get his way, but I'm not Sam!" I shout. I lose control. The pain that I thought I'd buried is coming back up to the surface, and my heart clenches. Suddenly, everything hurts.

"No, you're not Sam," Lia says calmly. It's clear what she's thinking. *It would make everything easier if you were.*

"Fuck off," I say flatly.

She crosses her arms over her chest, and her shoulders begin to shake. "None of this is any fun for me either, you know. I just want us to be a family again, so get it together and take the money." She grabs her handbag and leaves the café before I can answer.

I wouldn't have known what to say anyway.

CHAPTER 27
Jase

I always envied your relationship with Caleb. Lia and I never got along. I think she hates me, and I think I hate her too. Sometimes. Or always. I'm not sure anymore. And I hate that even more.
—Jase

I hate that Lia is putting me in this position. I don't want her damn money, but I need it. There's no way to sugarcoat it: If I don't take it, I'm screwed. But if I do take it, I am too. I can't just crawl back to my parents and pretend to be part of a happy family. I wouldn't do that for all the money in the world.

As I return to the dorm, I feel numb. Empty. Exhausted. But I can feel the anger, disappointment, and frustration poised to take over. Waiting for the right moment to pounce on me when I lose control again.

That moment comes too soon, just as I unlock my door and hear another door opening as someone comes into the hallway. I can tell it's Zoe without even looking. My shoulders tense before she says a word.

"Jase, can we talk?"

No, we can't. If I talk more right now, I'll say things that I'll regret later. I ignore her, open my door, and am about to slam it behind me, but Zoe is faster. She blocks the door and slips into my room before I can stop her. And now I can't avoid looking at her. The first things I notice are the dark circles under her eyes. She slept badly, just like me. Then I see sparks of anger in her eyes.

"Are you serious? You're just going to ignore me? After that kiss? After everything you said?" She comes closer, and there it is again, her damn lavender scent. I don't want to breathe it in. I don't want to breathe *her* in, but I do anyway. I try to resist, but I can't help it.

"You ignored *me* for a year after we kissed the first time. After you told me things that you shouldn't have if you weren't serious. So deal with it."

She flinches and goes pale. My stupid heart reacts with reproachful hammering against my ribs, but I couldn't care less now. The wall is shattered, and there's nothing but the abyss. I was wrong: I didn't fall. I threw myself over the edge intentionally. I'm so furious that it feels like I'm being torn apart from the inside. Blood rushes in my ears, and my hands are shaking so violently that I have to clench them into fists so she can't see.

But that's unnecessary. Of course she looks at my hands and notices. She sees everything.

"Jase . . ." she says. I know what she wants to say. That she's sorry. But I'm not interested in her apology. She can't give me back what I lost.

"What did you expect, Zoe?" I snap.

She reaches out her hand, and I want to take it, to feel her skin on mine, and that makes me even angrier. At myself.

"I wasn't expecting anything. I want to talk to you," she says. Her voice is gentle and soft, and I never want to hear anything else. At the same time, every cell of my body is fighting against hearing what she has to say. "About the kiss. What that means. You just left yesterday, and—"

"You just left too!" I say sharply, interrupting her. "After our last kiss! You ran away and were supposed to come to the treehouse later, but you never showed up. Do you remember?" I can't stop myself, even though I don't want to talk about it. I can't hold the words back. "I still wonder how I could have been so stupid. How could I have believed for even a second that the worst day of my life might not turn out to be so terrible because you wanted to kiss me?"

"What do you mean?" Zoe asks softly. I can hear the worry and alarm in her voice. She's not angry, and I can't deal with that. I want her to be angry. I want to hurt her like she hurt me. But the look in her hazel eyes is so concerned that I can't do it.

I laugh, back away with my arms outstretched until I bump backward into the windowsill, and then I tell her the truth. I do it because I've always told her the truth, and because it's too late to go back now anyway.

"My parents kicked me out that day. First they didn't come to my graduation, and then they kicked me out because I didn't want to go to Harvard. Dad refused to pay for my *ridiculous* dance education." I almost choke on the words as my chest tightens more.

"No," she breathes, shaking her head as if she can't believe it.

"When you left me that fucking note in the treehouse, I had hope for one stupid moment. And then you disappeared after that kiss and wouldn't talk to me anymore. Caleb ignored me too, because apparently, I'm not good enough for his little sister. And then I was fucking homeless! I had absolutely nothing!" I shout. My voice breaks with fury. "I had nothing. I had no one to talk to or ask for help. Do you know how often I tried to reach you? I needed help because my father threw me out, and there was no one in my life who could help me. I was alone, and I lost *everything* in one day. My best friend, my home, and . . . you." I fall silent, breathing hard. My eyes are burning.

Fuck, no. I'm not going to start crying now. No way. But the tears won't stop, and the pain is unbearable. Everything hurts, and I want it to stop, but I'm not strong enough. I reach the bottom of the abyss and shatter into a thousand pieces.

CHAPTER 28

Zoe

Without Caleb, I think I would have lost my mind last year, and I'm so sorry that you had to lose him.
—Zoe

My heart breaks. I stare at Jase, unable to speak. Jase, who has been so cool and distant for the last few weeks, hiding behind a mask that now lies in shards on the floor between us. His eyes are full of unshed tears, and it breaks my heart a little more because I can tell he's fighting as hard as he can to keep from crying. His whole body is shaking, and I can't bear to see him like this. I hate myself and Caleb for being responsible for this whole mess. His parents threw him out, and we rejected him.

We . . . *I* hurt him. I hurt him so much. Even more than I thought I had. I was too occupied with my own problems to consider that he had problems too.

I open my mouth to say something, but an apology would mean nothing. I still can't explain it to him or tell him the truth. Besides, this isn't about me. I move closer to him before I can stop myself or even waste a thought on whether it's a good idea or a terrible one.

"Jase." His name comes out as a soft whisper. It's an apology and an explanation and a plea, all in one. I reach out and touch his face, and he lets me.

His breath comes in gasps. He avoids my gaze, staring at the floor, biting his lower lip. My heart isn't just broken now; it's bleeding. I stroke his damp cheeks, and he turns his head away. He doesn't want me to see him like this, but he can't avoid it. I hold his face in my hands.

"Jase," I whisper again, moving my hand to the back of his neck, caressing the sensitive skin there. He sighs. It's a tortured, broken sound that brings tears to my own eyes.

I wrap both arms around him, pull him close, and just hold him tightly. There's nothing else I can do now besides just being here.

His heart beats directly against my chest, fast and hectic. Mine adapts to his rhythm. He's warm, so warm, and totally tense. I kiss the sensitive skin below his ear. It happens naturally, without thinking. He sighs again, and then all at once he relaxes. He wraps his arms around my waist and hugs me so tightly that, for a moment, I can hardly breathe.

I don't know who makes the first move, but we come just close enough for our lips to touch, and suddenly we're kissing. It's our third kiss, but it feels different.

Like a first kiss. Our third first kiss.

I taste coffee and mint. My heart stumbles, beating unevenly. Jase lets go of my waist, and his hands move up my body to my head, burying themselves in my hair, tipping my face upward to him, gentle and demanding at the same time. The kiss deepens. My lips open of their own accord, our tongues touch, and Jase moans in a way that sends brilliant flashes of lightning through me.

My skin is tingling, my fingers, my whole body. I want more.

More of his lips, more of his taste in my mouth, more of his skin beneath my hands.

Every coherent thought disappears as he lets go of me, only to lift me up the next moment. My legs instinctively wrap around his hips, pulling him closer. My pelvis presses against his. I can feel his hardness, and I feel a strong pulsing between my legs.

Desire rushes through me, and I bite his lower lip very gently. He gives a throaty laugh that goes under my skin, deeper and deeper until I can feel it all through me.

He stops kissing me and pulls away, just a fraction of an inch. "Pixie," he whispers in my mouth. Just hearing him use my nickname again makes me absurdly happy.

I pull at his jacket, a silent request for him to take it off. It's not enough, I need more of the soft skin on the back of his neck. I need so much more. He carefully lowers me to the floor and lets me go, and I immediately miss the feeling of his hands on my body. And that's crazy, because it wasn't very long ago that I couldn't tolerate any touch from him at all. But right now, it feels like it's been a lifetime since then. A different Zoe, a different Jase.

Yet somehow we're still the same.

Zoe and Jase.

Jase and Zoe.

The jacket slips off his shoulders and lands on the floor behind him with a rustle. He hesitates for a moment. His gaze is dark and stormy, and a warm flutter spreads through my stomach. I reach out for him with both hands and pull him closer again. My fingers wander over his T-shirt, doing whatever they want. They trace his hard, defined muscles, and I feel goose bumps prickle on his skin as I gently stroke his chest with my fingernails.

"Jase." His name is on my tongue again. I can't say anything else, but no words are necessary because he understands. He understands because he knows me, and he knows me because I have told him almost all of my secrets.

He pulls his shirt off over his head, and I forget to breathe as my eyes roam over his chest, down his stomach to the V of his hips. I look up at him, and my heart skips a beat. His eyes are so infinitely green. His hair is messy from my fingers, and he's so *Jase* that it hurts. It not only takes my breath away—it actually hurts.

I want to take off my clothes. I *must*. But as I grab the hem of my sweater, he stops me, and all at once his hands are on mine. I look up uncertainly. If he rejects me now, I'm going to die, because my body won't be able to take it. The racing heart, the tingling, the desire, and the longing. God, I want to touch him so much. Really, really touch him.

But Jase has no intention of stopping me. He takes the soft fabric of my sweatshirt and rolls it upward as I lift my arms, so he can remove it. Now I'm just as naked as he is. I don't have a shirt on underneath, and I'm not wearing a bra.

I blush as his eyes wander over my body, and with his gaze alone, he sets me ablaze.

"Fuck," he murmurs. It's a breathless, admiring word. The fluttering in my stomach grows stronger, the throbbing between my legs more urgent. I want him. *Now. Now. Please.*

Somewhere deep inside, I know there's something I should be remembering. But I don't want to think; I just want to feel. I reach for the waistband of his jeans and slide my fingers between the fabric and his skin. I tug on the cloth, a silent invitation. His breath comes out in a hiss, and I have to smile because I realize he was holding it. Because of me.

His eyes burn into mine, and we both know where this is going.

"If you want to stop, all you have to do is say the word." His voice is husky and sends a pleasant shiver down my back.

"Don't stop," I say.

He pulls me close again, kisses me deep and hard, and I see stars. My head tips back as his lips wander down my neck, over my collarbone, and down my breasts. I can't breathe anymore when he takes a nipple in his mouth and sucks. His tongue is playing with it, and I almost can't take it anymore. I've never felt this way before. So complete and so vulnerable at the same time.

I moan, unable to repress the sound, and I feel Jase shiver under my hands. They're tangled in his hair again.

He murmurs words into my skin that I don't understand, but I don't need to. He guides me toward the bed. I bump into the mattress with the back of my knees and collapse backward, and then he's above me. He kisses me again before pulling away from me. Then his hands are on the waistband of my jeans, and he hesitates again.

"Keep going," I whisper hoarsely, because he obviously needs to hear it, and I don't want him to stop.

He unzips my jeans and pulls them down my legs along with my underwear in one fluid motion. Then I'm lying naked in front of him. Naked and vulnerable, and a voice inside me whispers that I should feel exposed, but I don't.

Jase takes a deep breath and swallows hard. My mouth goes dry. "Why are you so damn beautiful?" It's a rhetorical question, and I have no answer for it.

I can't see myself the way he sees me, but just like this, in his bed, right in front of him, I feel beautiful. Safe. Confident.

He swallows again. The desire in his eyes sends the heat flooding right to the center of my body. I sit up and reach for the waistband of his jeans and push my fingers into his boxer shorts. He groans as I squeeze his butt, then slide my hand to the front and grip his hardness. The skin is silky soft, and he twitches in my hand as I begin to move it a little. I'm surprised by how courageous I am.

"Are you trying to kill me?" Jase moans, but he's pushing toward me, not pulling away.

I have to smile at how good it feels to know I'm responsible for his excitement. "Not today."

My lips touch his, and then I lean back and pull his jeans and boxers down all in one motion. I stare at him in wonder, first gazing at every muscle and then tracing them with my fingers, and then my lips. I've never done this before. Not the way we're doing it now. Maybe I should tell him that, but I don't want to. I don't want to talk. Plus, I know that Jase is definitely not a virgin, and I don't want him to treat me like one either.

When I look up again, his gaze is both dark and promising at the same time, and my stomach tightens. He goes to the bedside table and opens the drawer, and I hear the soft crackle of plastic as he tears open the packet of a condom and slips it on.

I watch him, following every little movement. My heart is racing again, my breathing is shallow, and everything inside me feels hot and sensual. He *must* touch me now, because anything else would be pure agony.

Then he holds out a hand to me, waiting. He lets me make the decision again. He lets me be in control, and I take a shaky breath. He's doing all this, even though he has no idea what I've been through.

I put my hand in his, making my decision. I let him pull me back onto the bed and fall onto the mattress. My mind switches off, and I feel so damn safe that it's strange, but also completely right. The mattress is soft, the sheets smell like him, and I breathe him in, moaning softly as he leaves a trail of hot kisses from my collarbone across my breasts and down my stomach.

I spread my legs eagerly, and then his tongue is at the center of my desire. I gasp as my muscles tense in a delicious way. I lift my pelvis, and he keeps licking me, increasing the pressure. I didn't know anything could feel this good.

I moan loudly as he slides two fingers inside me and thrusts, gently at first, then faster as I start to squirm under him. I feel like I'm about to die. It's too much and not enough at the same time. If he goes on like this, I'll come in two seconds, and even if it's a complete miracle, I don't want it to be over so soon. Not yet.

"Wait," I gasp, and he stops immediately. He looks up at me, an unspoken question in his eyes, his lips glistening. Because of me. That knowledge is doing something to me.

"Come here."

I sit up, pulling him toward me, and he willingly does as I ask, allowing me to push him back on the mattress this time. I lower myself onto him with my legs spread wide and feel his erection throbbing against my wet warmth, and if there's any last remnant of sanity in me, now it disappears completely. I bend down to kiss him and taste myself in his mouth. And him. Us. Together.

His eyes smolder as I back up enough so we can look at each other. We're still staring into each other's eyes as I reach between us and guide him inside me, agonizingly slowly. We groan at the same moment, and he curses softly. I have to smile. I don't ever think I've felt so strong.

"Are you sure you're not trying to kill me?" he says through gritted teeth. The tendons in his neck are showing. He's struggling to control himself, and that makes me happy, because he's doing it for me. He's letting me take control.

"Pretty sure." I tilt my hips, and he makes a sound I've never heard before. "After all, we're not done yet."

I don't know what I'm doing when I start to move, but my body does, and I let myself go, moving my hips. His hands slide over my legs, but he doesn't hold on to me. Beads of sweat cover his skin, and I lean forward, kissing them off his face, tasting the salt on my tongue. A quick, teasing bite of his lower lip, and he loses control. I love it when he starts to move now too, no longer hesitant and gentle, but hard and deep. I moan, and all I want is more.

We move in unison, our hips crashing together. My muscles are burning, and every fiber of my body is electrified. He kisses me. God, I didn't know it was possible to be kissed this way! My hips thrust forward, and he slides a hand between us, finding the exact point that's throbbing with desire. I gasp, pushing myself toward him. It feels like an altered state of consciousness. All of it. Both of us.

My whole body begins to pulse in the best possible way. How is it possible to feel like this? How could *I* feel like this?

Heat explodes inside me. I come with a stifled scream, and then I understand why an orgasm is called "the little death" in French. It really does feel a bit like that. My muscles contract around him, and he comes too. All I can feel is our bodies pulsing together.

I sink onto his chest and can feel his racing heartbeat under my hands. Then there's nothing but deep satisfaction and peace.

Jase's lips brush my temple, and I lift my head. His lips are puffy, his cheeks are red, and his hair is disheveled. Because of me. I always want it to be that way.

He looks at me and *sees* me, and at that moment, we really are everything to each other.

CHAPTER 29

Jase

When my parents kicked me out, I didn't know where to go. I've never felt as lost as I did on that day when I couldn't go back home—to your house.
—Jase

I had sex with Zoe. That really, really shouldn't have happened. Unfortunately, it felt way too good. Not only the sex, but everything: switching off my mind, escaping from reality. For a moment that wasn't long enough. She knows. She knows everything. Well, almost everything. I, on the other hand, still have no fucking idea exactly what happened back then and why everything happened the way it did.

Right now, I'm not even sure if I want to know. As I come out of the bathroom after throwing away the condom, Zoe is sitting on my bed with her arms wrapped around her knees. Her tangled red hair is spread out over her shoulders. She's wearing her underwear and her sweater again. I'd prefer to take them off her again, but I can't do that.

I want her to stay, but I want her to leave even more. My mind is overflowing, and I have no idea what to do. I'm tired. Not physically, but mentally exhausted. I feel empty. I kind of am too. I let it all out when we had sex. We lost control. And now? Does it change anything?

"Jase," she says softly. Just my name, which she's said too many times today, sighing and moaning. Each time, there was a certain sound in her voice that's only there when she says my damn name.

I tense and avoid her eyes. I don't know what I should say or how I should react. Just a few minutes ago, everything was right. Me under her, her on top of me, skin on skin, and her mouth on mine. No thoughts, no words. Nothing and everything.

Now it all feels . . . not wrong, but also not right. It's some kind of fugue state that I absolutely can't deal with.

"Talk to me," she pleads.

I reach for my boxer shorts. "I did talk. What else do you want to hear?" I ask more sharply than I intend. But what the hell should I say? What should I do? I have no idea how any of this works.

All I know is that she ended whatever it was that we had back then in the blink of an eye. But I don't know why. I don't know what happened last year, and something *did* happen.

I'm not stupid. Something must have happened. Someone doesn't have a problem being touched without a reason.

You don't panic if there's not an explanation for it. And either I'm the reason, because yes, we were dancing the first time I saw her panic, or there's another reason. Either way, I don't understand. I don't understand *her*. She remains silent, so I'm the one who has to start talking. Fuck, I hate this.

"You rejected me. In the worst possible way. I can't pretend that it never happened. I can't pretend it's okay just because we . . . fucked. Nothing is okay, and I can't . . ." I gasp for breath and search for words. Then I just tell her the truth. What good would it do to lie? "I can't do that again. It was all a mistake. The notes, the sex. You and me. You're going to reject me again, sooner or later. And I'll never understand why. I just can't do it again. It doesn't work."

Zoe turns pale, and my heart cramps painfully because it wants something different from what my mind does. But apparently, my stupid heart has a terrible memory too.

It hurts to tell her the truth, but if I don't do it, it will only get worse. "You make me feel something, and I can't deal with that. Because it always hurts so fucking much. You hurt me, and I finally want that to stop. Now. That's why you should go."

But Zoe doesn't move, and shit, she has to leave now, otherwise I'll go totally crazy.

"Please," I say desperately. And finally, she stands up, reaches for her pants, and leaves. As the door closes behind her, I feel like the most egotistical asshole in the world. And also like I've made a huge mistake.

CHAPTER 30
Zoe

I think you only realize how much you've taken something for granted when you lose it. When I suddenly couldn't stand to be touched anymore, not even hugs, it was like not knowing who I was anymore. I've always needed hugs, and then all at once, I couldn't stand them. I think that was almost the worst part of it.

—Zoe

It's strange how torn you can feel all of a sudden. I mean, how can you be relieved and a little happy and totally disappointed and very sad all at once? I have no clue. But if anyone can explain it to me, I'd like to know.

I'm relieved and happy because I had sex with Jase and it was so good, so right. My body didn't rebel against me. I felt safe and strong with him. I felt like I was in control. And I didn't just feel that way; I *was* in control. I had control over him and myself and what we were doing. That made me happy. Really, truly happy. Because I finally felt more like myself again that way. At least a little.

Still, it hurts because Jase is right. I rejected him, and I can't demand that he pretend nothing happened without giving him an explanation. He deserves that much, especially after everything he went through.

Shit, his parents kicked him out on his last day of school. Just because he didn't want to go to Harvard. I knew that his parents weren't happy he was dancing, but I never thought it was that extreme. How could they kick out their own son just because he has a dream and wants to fight for it? I don't understand.

I don't understand anything. My mind races. Where did he go last summer? Who helped him? Someone must have. The thought that he had nowhere to go before he could move into the dorm hurts too. It's not a piercing pain but a terrible burning. Because I know we could have helped him then. Mom, Dad, Caleb, and I.

God, we let him down. *I* let him down. He trusted me, and I pushed him away. Right now, it doesn't matter that I couldn't help because I was too broken and devastated myself.

And somehow, I still am, but now I know he is too, and I understand why he wanted me to leave. He doesn't trust me anymore. He's protecting himself like I protected myself last year. History is repeating itself in a completely twisted way. Right now, I feel like the ball is in my court, because I don't want our story to be over. Not like this. We can't jump straight from the beginning to the end. There's too much missing in between. I don't want it to be that way. I want all of it, and I want him.

* * *

I was awake half the night, but still, I'm not that tired when my alarm goes off the next morning. I'm too nervous. It's Monday, and that means Jase can't avoid me. We have to dance together, and after that, we have to talk. I don't know what I'm going to say to him yet, but I have to do something.

Lost in thought, I get ready, and because I've been a terrible friend in the last few days, I knock on Mae's door to pick her up for breakfast and ask how her date with Tristan went.

She greets me with a beaming smile. "Good morning, Zoe," she says, her eyes glowing. She grabs my wrist and pulls me into her room. Her fingers on my skin are warm, but the brief touch isn't unpleasant. "Come in; I'm running late."

"And you're in a great mood," I say, smirking.

"I am." Grinning, she does a pirouette. Her red hair flies around her face. She pauses in front of the dresser across from the bed and looks in the mirror that's hanging over it. "Damn, I look awful."

I snort. "In which universe?"

"This one." She reaches for her brush and begins to smooth back her hair. She looks at me curiously in the mirror. "How can your hair always look so tidy?"

"Perfectionism," I remind her, and look around her room. There's a pile of leotards and tights next to her bed, and there are countless barrettes and all kinds of makeup lying on her dresser. I can't even begin to figure out the chaos on her desk.

Mae sighs. "Yeah, somehow I'll never be able to do that."

I sit down on her desk chair. "You don't have to. How was your date?"

This time, she sighs happily. "Wonderful. We were at the planetarium. It sounds a bit silly, but Tristan is really great. Otherwise, I wouldn't have only come back this morning."

"What?" My voice shoots up two octaves. "You spent two nights with him?"

She spins around, a wide smile on her face. "I did, and God, football players are good in bed. You know, he did this thing, and I—"

"Mae, I care about you, but I've known Tristan for twelve years," I say, interrupting her. "It's like hearing sex stories about my brother, and that's a no-go. Tell me everything, but leave out the gory details, okay?" I make a face at her, and she shrugs and laughs.

"Okay, fair enough. But I can tell you that he has amaaaaazing stamina, can't I?"

I nod and can't help but smile. "You may."

"Thank you." She grins and then sighs longingly. "It was so good with him. Not just the sex, but everything."

"So are the two of you an item?"

"We haven't talked about it yet, but I think so . . . Oh, Zoe, he's so sweet and kind, and I think I'm really falling for him." She blushes, and I squeal with delight as I jump up and hug her.

"That makes me so happy. Honestly, Mae, I think it's perfect. You two are good together."

She regards me skeptically for a second. "Really? You don't feel weird about me being with a friend of your brother's?"

I shake my head firmly and hug her a little tighter before letting her go again. "No, not at all. I think it's very, very nice. Tristan is one of the good guys, and you're my best friend. That's just lovely."

She breathes a sigh of relief. "Okay, good. That makes me feel better."

"Does he make you happy?"

"Yes."

"Then I'm satisfied."

She smiles broadly. "Me too. And how was your weekend?" She turns back to the mirror and concentrates on her makeup.

Unfortunately, she can still see me blushing. She looks at me with narrowed eyes as she applies her foundation.

"Zoe? How was your weekend?" she repeats her question, this time more emphatically, with a teasing undertone in her voice.

I'd like to lie, but I don't think that would help. Not when she looks at me like that. Embarrassed, I start to bite my nails. "That's a really good question," I say.

"I know. And I want an answer." Eyebrow pencil in her hand, she turns to me again.

"You'll get one. Just not today."

She makes a disappointed face. "Why not?"

"Because . . . it's all kind of complicated."

"It would be too easy if it weren't complicated, wouldn't it?"

"Probably." I rub my forehead in frustration and stare at my hands.

"Hey, Zoe." Mae's voice softens, and I look up. "It's going to be all right, okay? Whatever's going on between you and Jase, you'll work it out."

I bite my lower lip uncertainly, and then I realize why I went to see Mae this morning, as much as I don't want to admit it. It wasn't because I wanted to be a good friend but because *I* needed a friend.

"I hope so," I say quietly.

"I'm sure of it." Mae puts her makeup aside and grabs my hand. "Now come on, we've got to go or we'll be late."

* * *

Somehow, I manage to get through my first few classes without freaking out. I mainly have Mae to thank for that. In every moment that we're not concentrating on ballet, she helpfully distracts me with details about her weekend with Tristan. Even if part of me really doesn't want to hear the gory details, another part is happy that Mae ignored my complaint about it this morning.

But in the end, no distraction in the world does me any good. After all, the pas de deux class won't be canceled just because Jase and I have a problem.

Mae's voice fades into the background as we enter the studio, and my eyes dart around the room looking for Jase. He's not here, and my stomach cramps. He wouldn't skip class just to avoid me, would he? The room fills up, Francesca tells us to sit down, and Jase still hasn't shown up.

Feeling a little lost, I stand a few steps apart from the others and don't know where to go.

"Zoe, where's Jase?" Francesca raises her eyebrows. Yes, where is he? I'd like to be able to give her an answer, but I have no idea. I can't exactly tell her that he's probably trying to avoid me right now.

"I'm here. Sorry. Pearson called me to his office."

I feel a flood of relief when I hear Jase's familiar, slightly breathless voice. I turn around just in time to see him pull his sweater over his head. His T-shirt rides up at the same time, showing off his sculpted abs. My heart skips a beat again, and the blood goes to my face. Great. Absolutely super.

"All right," Francesca says with a nod, without questioning Jase's excuse. "Then please go to your partner. We have a lot to do today."

Jase nods, but I see his jaw tense. He hasn't looked at me yet, even though I've been staring at him since he entered the room. I can't stop, either, when he finally comes over to me. Not that it surprises me now, but still . . .

Look at me, I plead silently, and finally, he turns in my direction, and his green eyes focus on me. Have they always been this green? Probably. His gaze is darker, more withdrawn, and at the same time, I can read him a lot better than I could a few days ago. After all, he's told me a lot of secrets, while I'm still keeping mine to myself.

"Hey," I say quietly, cursing myself at the same time for not coming up with anything better. Also because my voice sounds like this. Just as breathless as his just did, even though I didn't just run across half of campus twice because the principal wanted to talk to me.

I stop. Pearson. What did he want from Jase? Was it about his tuition fees? Or his scholarship? I want to ask him all the questions that are going through my head, but Jase avoids my gaze again, and I can't get a word out. He takes his position, and his closeness does strange things to my body, not to mention my emotions.

I get warm as he takes my hand, and my heart beats out of rhythm again.

Pull yourself together, Zoe.

I take a deep breath. Francesca gives us instructions. We begin to move, and this time, I'm not the one who is tense, can't keep pace, and moves stiffly. Jase is.

"Jase, what's wrong with you today?" Francesca asks disapprovingly.

Jase tenses, and all at once his face is blank.

"Nothing."

She sighs. She doesn't believe him, I can tell, but she doesn't ask any more questions. "One more time, from the top," she says.

"Jase." I tug gently on his hand. He looks at me, and I give him an encouraging smile, which is immediately extinguished when his face darkens.

"Don't do that," he says, and I bite my tongue to keep myself from asking what he means: Don't smile or say his name? Probably both. The rest of the class is agony, and when Jase almost drops me during a lift, Francesca has had enough. She finishes the lesson and shoos us out of the studio. Jase is gone faster than I can take off my ballet slippers.

I quickly pack my things and don't even bother to put my pants on over my tights. I just pull on my cardigan and hurry after him.

We have to talk.

Unfortunately, Jase's legs are much longer than mine. I see him disappearing into the dorm just as I leave the practice building. It's cold out, and it's raining enough to make my cardigan damp and sticky on my skin by the time I finally reach the dorm myself.

I walk directly up to the fourth floor—Jase certainly won't be stopping at the cafeteria to get something to eat. The corridor is totally quiet, with everyone still leaving their classrooms and on their way to lunch.

I hope I'm not doing the wrong thing as I knock on his door. But it opens, and all at once my mind is totally blank.

"How much of *no* didn't you understand yesterday?" he asks sharply.

"I understood it all, and I know why, really. But please . . . can't we talk?"

"I really don't know what you want to talk about. I mean, what do you have to say, Zoe? Are you going to tell me what happened last year? Or why I suddenly became public enemy number one? I really don't care—don't you get it? I have enough problems, and

I can't deal with you too." Jase tries to slam the door in my face, but I block it.

I stop worrying about whether I'm doing this right or whether it feels right. I just know that I've considered telling him everything before, and sure, the timing absolutely sucks right now. But I think there's just no right time for the truth.

You always imagine it that way: a right moment and a right place with the right person to say the things that need to be said. Aside from Jase, nothing here is right, and maybe it's a mistake, but I've already made enough mistakes, and I can't keep this secret anymore.

"I didn't come to the treehouse that night because someone put roofies in my drink." My voice is monotone. I've practiced saying these words, the truth, in the hope that they'd lose some of their horror. So far, that hasn't happened.

AFTER

Zoe

One year earlier
June 26, 6:07 AM

Everything feels wrong when I come to. My head is pounding; my skin is sticky with cold sweat. My entire body hurts, and my stomach cramps. I have to throw up. I fall out of bed rather than get up, and when I do manage to get to my feet, my legs buckle under me.

Dizzy. I feel so terribly dizzy. My pulse is racing, too fast, too frantically.

Everything is wrong.

So wrong.

I feel numb. I try to sit up again but fail.

My body no longer belongs to me; it doesn't obey me. I feel so sick. Somewhere in my head, a voice tells me to get help.

Help.

I need help urgently, but no sound comes from my mouth. My voice doesn't obey me any more than the rest of my body.

Slowly, far too slowly, I manage to turn my head. I know where I am. It's Charlotte's guest room, familiar from all the times I've stayed here before. On the chair are the clothes I was wearing yesterday. My bag is next to it.

My phone. I left it in my pocket, didn't I? I can't remember.

I don't remember anything.

Nothing. My mind is completely blank. I'm so dizzy.

I whimper as I crawl to the chair and reach for my bag. My hands are shaking so badly that it takes a while before I can finally pick up my phone. The letters and numbers on the screen swim in front of me, but I find the right name, the right number.

"Zoe, have you looked at the clock? Do you know what time it is?" Caleb grumbles sleepily. I can only sob, a sob that contains a hint of relief and a lot of confusion.

"Caleb," I manage to say.

"What's going on? Are you okay?" Suddenly my brother sounds wide awake, and I want to cry and curl up and sleep.

"Something's wrong. I don't . . . feel good."

"Are you still at Charlotte's?"

I nod before remembering he can't see me. "Yes."

"Okay, I'll be right there." He doesn't hang up. I hear him getting dressed and saying something to someone, but I don't understand a word. Then he talks to me again, but my brain feels like it's wrapped in cotton balls. I'm so dizzy.

All I know is that Caleb takes seven minutes and forty-three seconds to reach me, and he doesn't finish the phone call until he's there in the room. The back door wasn't locked, so it was easy for him to get into the house.

I see his look of horror when he finds me cowering on the floor.

He begins to swear, reaches for my clothes, and helps me get dressed. I'm not wearing my underwear anymore, and I didn't even notice. I start to cry, because only now do I realize what must have happened. And at the same time, I understand nothing. Because things like this happen to other people, not to me. I was at a party with my friends. I knew almost everyone there.

"We have to take you to the hospital," Caleb says. He's pale as chalk. He seems totally overwhelmed, and I'm starting to feel guilty for having called him. "I have to call the police."

I shake my head. "No police. Please."

Caleb looks at me like I've lost my mind, and maybe I have.

"I don't want to . . . Please, I . . ." I can't tell him why; I don't even know myself. But everything inside me is protesting against calling anyone. "Just bring me home."

I just want to be in my own bed and bury myself under the blankets. Forget everything. I wish I had never woken up this morning, and everything is so, so wrong. Caleb helps me to my feet, then half-carries me downstairs. There's a car I don't recognize parked in front of the house, and Tristan is sitting in the driver's seat. Caleb says something I don't understand, the car starts moving, and I vomit my guts out.

After that, everything is a blur. They take me to the hospital, where the nurses take my blood and give me an IV. A doctor examines me and then confirms what I figured out too late.

I can't remember anything.

I only see black spots in front of my eyes, and I want to die.

My parents come. They also want to call the police, and I know it would be the right thing to do. It's what you're supposed to do in a situation like this. If you're thinking rationally, that is.

But I'm not rational anymore. I'm broken, and I don't know anything anymore.

It feels like drowning. I can't breathe.

It has to stop. Everything has to stop.

Please.

CHAPTER 31
Jase

It took Mom five weeks to get in touch with me after I was kicked out. Five fucking weeks. And even then, she didn't ask me to come home. She only said that she'd pay my tuition fee and that Dad could never find out about it. She didn't ask me where I had been living or how I was. Nothing.
—Jase

I'm in shock. I must be. There's no other way to explain why I'm so calm. Zoe is sitting on my bed. She's wearing one of my sweaters because her cardigan was soaked from the rain. It's way too big for her. She has her legs pulled up, arms around her knees, just like yesterday before I kicked her out. It all feels like a fucking dream.

Yesterday we lay in this bed, she was on top of me, moaning, and today she tells me that she was raped. At that party. After we kissed. After I went to the treehouse to wait for her, until the sun came up. She didn't show up, and I came to my own conclusions about her silence. And Caleb's. But I had no fucking idea what really happened.

I feel like I need to throw up, but I can't move. I lean back against my desk, arms crossed over my chest, and try to figure out how this could have happened. The problem is, there's nothing to understand. There's no good reason for something like this. There's only one bastard who made a decision. That's it.

"I'm so sorry," I say with difficulty. The words taste bitter and feel totally wrong. They don't even begin to express what I'm feeling. I hate what happened with every cell of my body. I'm so furious that I want to burn the whole world down. At the same time, I want to hold Zoe close and never let her go.

But I can't do that, not now.

A sad smile appears on her face. "You know what I don't understand? Why do people use the same words to apologize and to express empathy? Every time someone says *I'm sorry*, even though they never did anything wrong, I have the urge to ask them exactly what they're sorry for. And why. And then it occurs to me how difficult it is to answer those questions. That's why I don't say it anymore."

I can't ask her what happened afterward. How she felt. "I don't know what else to say," I finally admit helplessly.

"That's okay. What else *can* you say?" She bites her lower lip. She takes a deep breath. "My parents wanted me to go to the police," she says. Her voice is firm and determined, just like the expression on her face, but I can see her eyes gleaming with tears. She blinks, forcing herself not to cry. "But for me, just the thought of having to talk to someone I didn't know was unbearable. I couldn't . . . I still can't remember what happened. After a certain point in the evening, my memory just stops. It's completely blank. It's like I just fell asleep and woke up without even dreaming. Except that everything was different afterward. The feeling of waking up and—" she breaks off.

"You don't have to tell me about it," I say, because she really doesn't have to, even if part of me wants her to.

Zoe sighs and starts to pull the hairpins out of her bun. "I know. I don't have to do anything. Just what I feel comfortable with. My therapist has been telling me that for months. But I want to talk to you about it."

I nod. My heart leaps.

"You know, sometimes I think if Caleb hadn't brought me to the hospital and I hadn't been examined, maybe I never would have known what happened. Maybe it would be like waking up from a nightmare. Because I can't remember that night at all."

One hairpin after another drops onto the mattress until Zoe's hair falls over her shoulders. Then she starts weaving single strands into tiny braids, as if she needs something to do with her hands.

It's hard for me to breathe, and I clear my throat, because otherwise I wouldn't be able to say a word. "Then there were . . . traces?" The question sounds just as wrong as *I'm sorry* did before. But fuck, everything about this is wrong.

"Nothing helpful. They were able to detect the roofies in my blood and figure out that I . . . I was raped. But there was no trace of who . . . did it." Her hands are shaking, and all I want to do is take her in my arms and hold her. But I'm not sure if she wants that, and I can't ask her right now.

"Later, my parents talked to Charlotte's parents. They wanted to know how this could have happened in their house and who was at the party. I heard them arguing. Caleb and I were sitting together on the stairs, and our parents were downstairs. It was . . .

awful. Charlotte's parents said I was lying, that I made up the whole thing to create a scandal for her family and get revenge on Charlotte for taking my part in *The Sleeping Beauty*. Even though I had proof of what happened from the medical exam."

"What?" I almost shout in disbelief.

"Funny, huh?" Zoe looks up, her eyes glittering with tears. There's absolutely nothing funny about this. "Mom and Dad wanted me to go to the police and for everyone to be questioned. They wanted to find out who did this to me. But then . . . everyone would have known. And Charlotte . . . She said the same thing as her parents, that I was lying because I wanted attention. And besides, I . . . I couldn't do it. There were so many people there. Your whole graduating class. Almost all of mine. The college guys." Now she's talking faster, like she wants to get it over with. "I couldn't bear the thought of spending my last year of high school as the girl who said she was raped. And Charlotte's father is the mayor. He knows so many people. *Everyone* would have been judging me. I know it was wrong, but I . . ." tears roll down her cheeks, and now I can't hold back anymore. I sit next to her on the bed, but not close enough that we're touching.

"You didn't do anything wrong."

"We both know that's not true." She sniffs but doesn't dry her tears. "I pushed you away and ignored your notes. Your calls. Everything. Even though *you* had done absolutely nothing wrong. You didn't deserve that. But I couldn't . . . I was so ashamed. I felt dirty, and I was afraid. I was so fucking afraid of everything, and I didn't want you to know. I didn't want you to see me that way. As a girl who things like that happen to. Because there must be a reason it happened to me."

I want to tell her that there's no reason. Not her behavior or her outfit or anything. But she's already ahead of me.

"A few days later, the panic attacks started. Every time someone touched me. Mom, Dad, Caleb—it didn't matter who. It was terrible. I started therapy because I felt like there was no other choice, even though I'd refused at first. I hated losing control of myself, not having control over my body. Shit, I'm a dancer, and that's exactly what I'm supposed to be able to do!" A strangled sound escapes from her throat, and my fingers run over the back of her hand all by themselves. She doesn't flinch. But she doesn't look at me either. "Anyway, last year was pretty awful. But I've got it under control now. Don't ask me how. I was fine for a while. At least I could dance again. Even with a partner. Until—" she breaks off, but she doesn't have to complete the sentence. I know exactly what she's trying to say. Until she had to dance with me.

"Why—" I start to say, but she silences me with a wave of her hand.

"I have no idea. But it wasn't your fault," she says, and I really want to believe her. But a part of me refuses.

We're silent.

Zoe was raped. She doesn't know by whom, and that means the bastard is still walking around free instead of rotting in prison.

At some point, she sighs softly and picks up the hairpins she's dropped. I tense as she stands up. "I didn't tell you this so you would forgive me. It doesn't fix what happened or the hurt I caused you. What you've been through . . . I'm so sorry that I wasn't there for you and that I made it even worse."

I want to shake my head and deny it, but she's right. She gave me an explanation, and I understand it. I understand everything, and I wish that was enough. But it doesn't change what happened and how terrible I felt last year. How alone. How lost. How much I hated the whole world. How much I still hate a big part of it. It always works out in movies, doesn't it? The two main characters talk it out, forgive each other, and get their happy ending. What bullshit.

Reality doesn't work like that.

In my reality, I'm overwhelmed and have absolutely no idea what to do next.

* * *

"Jase! Are you deaf? Jesus." Skye's pissed off voice finally gets through to me, past the layers of fog wrapped around my brain. It could also have something to do with the headphones I'm wearing, turned up so loud that my ears are ringing. I'm hoping that they'll drown out my thoughts, but unfortunately, it isn't working. My thoughts are way too loud.

My muscles are burning with strain when I put aside the weights I've been lifting. Everything hurts, and I'm breathing heavily, but it's not enough. The pain is nothing in comparison to what's going on inside of me.

I look up. Skye is standing in front of me, her eyes flashing with anger, her hands on her hips.

"What?" I say rudely, even before I take off the headphones.

"You've got to stop." She points at the weights and then at my trembling legs.

"I don't have to do anything."

"Yes, you do. We lift weights to prevent injuries, not to cause them. You're overdoing it."

I shake my head, even though she's right. I've gone way over the top, and I'm trying to justify it with the fact that we have two hours of weight training built into our schedules on Tuesdays and Thursdays. It's supposed to make us less likely to be injured; protect our hips, knees, and ankles; and make lifts easier. Heavy weights, few repetitions. Every one of us has a workout plan.

But today is Monday. I skipped a theory class this afternoon, and I've been here far too long.

"Leave me alone."

She laughs in disbelief. "Forget it. What's wrong with you? You've never skipped class before, not once. And today—"

"Forget it, all right?" I say harshly, but Skye doesn't bat an eyelash.

"Stop messing with me. What did Pearson want anyway?"

I frown, irritated. It takes me a moment to remember what she's talking about. I was late to the pas de deux class because I had just been to the principal's office. Fuck. It was only a few hours ago, and I've already forgotten. Or rather, I repressed it.

Because at least one of my problems was just solved. Lia paid my tuition fee for the semester without waiting for my decision. I should probably be grateful to her. But actually, I'm just angry.

Angry at her, Mom and Dad, Caleb and Zoe. At myself. And the whole rest of the goddamn world.

"Are they throwing you out?" she asks when I don't answer. Her voice sounds worried.

I shake my head. "Not yet."

She breathes a sigh of relief. "What happened then?"

I shake my head again. I can't tell her what she wants to know.

"Is something going on with you and Zoe?"

I laugh without amusement. I open my mouth and close it again, because I don't have the damn words. I can't tell her what Zoe told me. It would be wrong and unfair. After all, it's not my story, even though somehow, I'm a part of it. The whole thing is just so fucked up! What the hell am I supposed to do now?

I don't answer and reach for the weights again. But Skye is faster than me. She grabs my wrists and firmly pushes me back. The fact that she manages to do it so easily should probably make me think twice, but I don't want to think at all anymore.

"Okay, fine. You don't have to talk to me. But you'd better stop now, or I'll go tell Francesca, or even go straight to Pearson, and let them know you're being irresponsible."

I narrow my eyes at her. "You'd really rat me out?"

"To keep you from destroying yourself? Absolutely." She smiles wanly.

"You're not my sister. You don't have to take care of me," I say. I'm acting like an asshole, and I hate it, but I can't stop. I shut down and lash out because I can't deal with the chaos in my head and in my fucking heart. Someone has to tell me what to do, because I really don't know.

You know what you have to do.

I flinch. Sam's voice is in my head. It's been weeks since the last time he chimed in.

You know where you want to go and who you need to see.

"Yeah, but somebody's got to do it," Skye retorts, unmoved, and it takes me a second to realize that she's reacting to my words, not those of the voice in my head. "You seem like you're headed directly for self-destruction, so sorry if I'm worried."

"You don't have to be."

"Someone has to."

I reach for my towel and wipe the sweat off my face. "Do what you want. I can't stop you."

"No, you can't." She punches my shoulder and gives me an encouraging smile. "If you ever do want to talk . . . I'm here, okay?"

I nod, even though we both realize that's not going to happen. There are only two people I want to talk to, and neither one of them is an option.

Not Zoe, not Caleb.

Why not?

Because I don't have a fucking clue what to say.

CHAPTER 32
Zoe

No secret in the world means a thing unless there's someone who believes it. Thank you for believing me.
—Zoe

Hot water streams down on my shoulders as I lean against the cold tiles with my eyes closed. Tears run down my face, stinging my eyes.

Jase knows.

He knows.

And he believes me.

He believed me without hesitation. Without doubt. Without questioning.

I sob. Everything hurts: my body, my heart, my soul.

But it's the kind of pain that means a wound is slowly healing. I hadn't realized that deep inside, I was afraid he wouldn't believe me.

Just like Charlotte's parents. *Nothing like that could possibly happen in our house.*

She'd been drinking. Her dress was too short. She was flirting. She wanted attention.

Is this her revenge for Charlotte getting the role of Aurora?

She's trying to create a scandal for our family because she got so drunk that she can't remember what happened.

Nothing happened.

It doesn't matter how long it's been since I overheard the conversation between Charlotte's parents and mine; I can still hear it. It's etched in my memory, and it will probably never fade away completely.

But today, for the first time, the voices are a little quieter. A little less threatening. They have less power over me.

Something inside me relaxes. Comes to rest. The pain is still there, just like the anger and the feeling of being lost. But the storm inside me has receded a little and become less violent.

I stay under the shower until my tears are cried out and I can barely feel the heat of the water. It's already dusk when I finally leave my little bathroom, with no makeup on and my hair still damp. Jase's hoodie is lying on my bed. He didn't ask for it back when I left.

I told him the truth. Almost the whole truth.

Oh, God.

I told him what happened. A tremor runs through my body, my pulse races, and for a moment, I can't breathe. My hands trembling, I reach for my phone and text Caleb.

ZOE:

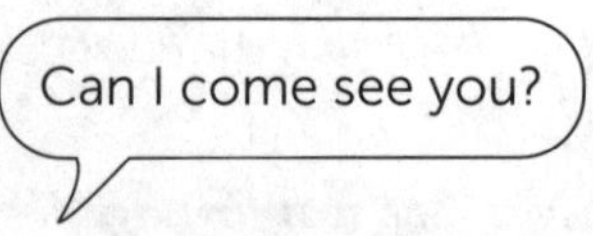

I throw the phone on my bed. It lands on Jase's sweatshirt as I quickly get dressed. Something feels strange. *I* feel strange.

My phone vibrates just as I finish dressing.

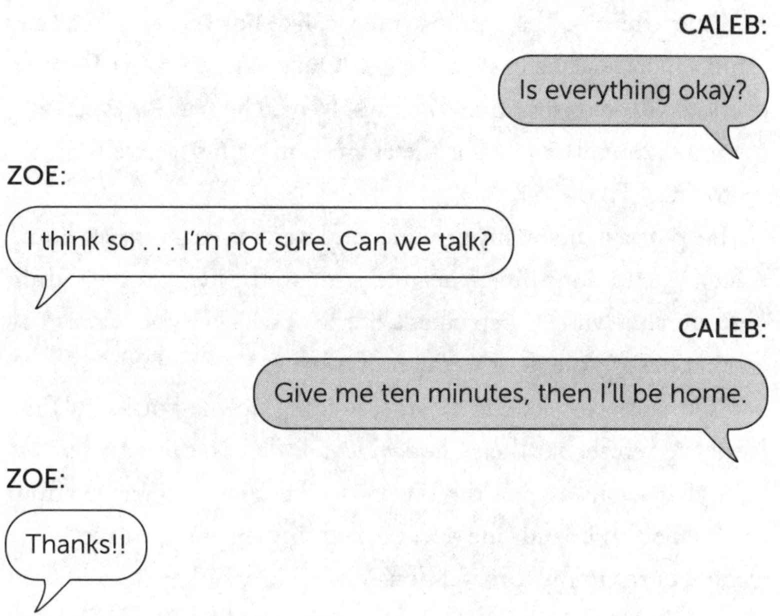

Relief floods through me. I quickly call an Uber and don't bother to blow-dry my hair. I just braid it and go.

The drive is a blur of flickering lights in the darkness. I'm warm and cold at the same time, even though I'm still wearing a coat over my sweater and it's hot in the elevator in Caleb's building. It feels like an eternity until I arrive at the penthouse Caleb shares with his friends.

I've barely knocked on the door when he opens it, with such a look of worry on his face that I immediately feel guilty.

"Are you okay?"

I nod and walk into the apartment.

"Yes. Everything's okay. I . . . think so. Are the other guys here?"

“No, they’re all out. What’s going on, Zoe?”

“We have to talk about Jase.” It’s no use putting it off.

Caleb freezes. His eyes get intense, like he’s trying to read my mind. Then he exhales with a sigh. “Okay. Phew, I think I need a drink for this conversation,” he says. Maybe he really was reading my mind. Something about the expression on his face tells me he knows why I’m here.

He puts a hand on my shoulder and waits a second to see how I react. When I don’t flinch, he guides me to the living room. I drop onto the sofa while Caleb takes a bottle of whiskey out of the glass cabinet next to the door to the roof terrace.

“Do you want some?” he asks, holding up the bottle. At first, I want to refuse, but then I nod. “Just a little.” To calm my nerves.

Caleb seems to feel the same way. He gets two glasses from the kitchen and hands me one. I take a tiny sip and grimace as the alcohol burns in my throat. I don’t really like whiskey or alcohol in general, but a pleasant warmth spreads through my stomach.

Caleb downs his whiskey in one go and regards me with a look that’s simultaneously anguished, worried, and curious. “Okay, I think I’m ready. Shoot.”

I hesitate and bite my lower lip. I don’t know where to start.

“What are you worried about?” he asks, because he’s my brother and knows me better than anyone else in the world.

“I don’t want to hurt you.” I’m honest. I have to be, because I already hurt him once, and I never, ever want to see him the way he was that night again.

Caleb swallows and then shrugs, grinning at me. “If you’re worried that I might still have feelings for Jase, I can put your mind at ease: I don’t. But you already know that.”

"Yes, I know."

Caleb has Parker, and he's totally infatuated. But that's not the only reason I was worried.

"Then spit it out." He pokes me encouragingly, and then I just say it.

"We argued. I mean, that's not quite right. Jase . . . he told me about a lot of things—things from last year that you and I didn't know. And somehow, it got out of hand."

Caleb stiffens, but I keep talking before he can get the wrong idea.

"We had sex, and—"

"Wait. What?" Stunned, he stares at me, but I'm not done yet.

"We slept together," I repeat, and his look becomes even more incredulous. I understand how he feels. Even I can barely believe it. "But then Jase told me to leave, and earlier today, I told him everything."

"You told him *everything*?" I hear shock in his voice, and it takes me a moment to understand his reaction. I shake my head vigorously.

"No, not *everything*. I didn't tell him anything about you. Just about me."

Caleb remains silent, reaches for the bottle, and fills his glass again.

"Caleb, I'm sorry. I know you don't want to hear this. I shouldn't have told you." I make an effort to get up, but my brother pushes me back onto the sofa.

"Stop apologizing. You have nothing to be sorry for. I want to hear everything. I just have a feeling that you've left out an essential part of the story. So let's start again. What did Jase tell you? And why?"

"It's about his parents. Did you know they kicked him out?"

Caleb goes pale, and his eyes widen in horror. "What?"

"They put him out on the street. Because he didn't want to go to Harvard."

Caleb begins to swear. "I knew his father was an asshole, but . . . what the hell? How could he? Fuck!"

"I know. It's awful."

"What else did he say?" Caleb's hands are wrapped around his glass so hard that his knuckles are white.

I hesitate for a moment, but then I tell him what Jase said. How he said it. How terrible it was to hear what he'd been through. Caleb grows paler with every word. He swears. A lot. And then he gets very quiet.

"He must hate me," he whispers. "I let him down."

"You didn't know. How were you supposed to know?"

"But that's exactly it! I ignored his messages and calls. Because seeing him kiss you broke my heart, even though it wasn't his fault. I knew he didn't feel anything for me. Fuck, he must really hate me."

I hate myself. He doesn't have to say it for me to know what he's thinking.

"Caleb, stop it."

He grimaces, and we go quiet. Caleb is the one who breaks the silence. He shakes his head like he's trying to clear it, then smiles painfully. "Go on," he says.

"Are you sure?"

"Very sure. How did you get from fighting to fucking?" His voice has a touch of humor. He's trying to salvage the situation, but I guess there's nothing left to save.

There are only things I need to say and that he needs to know.

My face is burning with embarrassment, and I'm glad I have my glass to hold so I don't start picking at my cuticles.

But the longer I talk, the more relaxed I get. Meanwhile, Caleb finishes his second drink.

"So?" he asks, stretching, when I'm finally finished. "How is that going?" He shrugs helplessly. "I'm sorry. I don't really know what to say. Or how to react." He breaks off, and I squeeze his hand.

"I know. I don't either. This is all so crazy. I have no idea. It could be that nothing else happens between us. But if it does, I don't want to keep it a secret from you. Because maybe—"

"Maybe your heart still wants him after all, and if he feels the same way, then you don't want me to feel weird. Right? Because my sister might get together with my former best friend, who I was in love with?" Caleb helps me out, looking about as overwhelmed as I feel.

I breathe a sigh of relief. "Yes. That's about it."

Caleb swallows hard. "Well, I'd be lying if I said it made me overjoyed. But it's okay. Honestly. As long as you're all right, I'm okay with it."

"Really?"

"I promise. Then . . . you're fine? With everything?"

"Yes, I'm fine. I feel good even. I feel . . ." I falter. My heart is beating too fast again. "Very good." I make a choked sound that's somewhere between a laugh and a sob. "It felt so . . . incredible."

All at once, tears well up in my eyes. Jase has given me something that I thought I could never have. A first time that I can remember—that I *want* to remember.

"Hey, Zoe." Caleb puts his glass down on the coffee table and scoots over to me. "Don't cry."

He hugs me so tightly that I can't breathe for a moment. I bury my face against his shoulder, and then I do cry. I can't stop, no matter how hard I try to pull myself together. My brother murmurs soothing words to me, but I don't understand a single one of them.

* * *

It's late when I get back to the dorm, and I'm exhausted. The day has worn me out in a way that demands a hot bath, a pot of herbal tea, and twelve hours of sleep. But my alarm clock is going to ring in less than seven hours, my eyes are swollen from crying, and my nose is blocked.

I have countless unread texts from Mae. She's probably worried because I skipped a theory lesson and she hasn't seen me since I followed Jase after the pas de deux class. But I don't have the energy to answer her now or go to her room.

I kick off my shoes as soon as I'm inside and slip into my nightshirt. I'm halfway to bed when there's a soft, hesitant knock at my door. My heart leaps, and I hurry to answer it, not thinking. I open it, and there he is. My legs go weak with relief. His hair is messy, and he looks tired, but his eyes are wide awake.

"Hi," I whisper.

"Hi." He rubs his nose, and the corners of his mouth twitch, almost a smile. "Can I come in?"

Nodding, I step aside, and then he's in my room. It feels strange, the air between us, full of unspoken words. I close the door and go back to my bed because I suddenly remember I'm not wearing any pants. I shouldn't care. After all, he's already seen me naked. But I feel more vulnerable right now.

"Why are you here?" I ask.

Jase stands at my desk and checks out the photos I have hanging above it. Mom, Dad, Caleb, me. He turns to me, burying his hands in his pants pockets, and rocks back and forth on his heels. "I don't know," he replies.

"You don't know?" God, I have to breathe. *Breathe, Zoe.*

He shakes his head, runs a hand through his hair, and groans with frustration. "No, I don't know. I shouldn't be here. I don't know . . . It really doesn't make sense. Or maybe it does. No clue."

I sit on my bed and pull up my knees. "Do you want to talk?" I ask carefully.

He shakes his head again. "I don't want to talk anymore. We did enough of that. My head is so full that I don't even know where to put all the damn thoughts. I . . . actually, I just want to sleep. I'm sorry. I shouldn't have come over, I—" He breaks off and turns to the door. He's just about to open it again when I stop him.

"Do you want to stay here?" The question escapes before I can hold it back.

Jase turns to face me. "Are you serious?"

"You don't have to. Only if you want," I say, backpedaling. "I just thought—"

"Yes," he says, and the relief in his voice pierces my heart.

I slide over on the mattress to make room for him, and he comes to bed. Only now do I realize he's not wearing any shoes. He came over in his socks. I don't know why, but that touches me. I slip under the covers, and Jase lies down next to me. We don't touch, but I can feel warmth radiating from his skin.

"Are you okay?" I ask, and he laughs softly.

"Shouldn't I be asking you that?"

"You can, once you've told me if you're okay."

He narrows his eyes. "No, not really. How about you?"

"Better," I say honestly, feeling under the quilt for his hand. My fingers brush his skin, a silent question, because I know everything is far from being okay between us again. But he's here, and maybe that's a start. "I'm glad you know what happened."

"And I'm glad you told me." His fingers interlace with mine, and we instinctively move closer together until I can feel his breath on my skin, and he can feel mine.

"Tell me your secrets, and I'll tell you mine," I whisper. His eyes gleam. I turn off the light, and darkness floods the room. Warm darkness that feels like an embrace. Jase kisses my forehead, and I close my eyes.

CHAPTER 33
Zoe

I have no idea why I panicked the first time we danced together. I really don't understand it. And I understand even less why it's gone now.
—Zoe

A merciless beeping sound tears me out of my sleep. I grunt and fumble for my phone, and I'm startled that my fingers don't hit the wood of my bedside table, but a firm, warm body next to me.

Jase.

He grumbles softly, a deep sound that comes from his chest. Blinking, he opens his eyes. His gaze is unfocused, his lashes a little sticky.

The alarm continues to ring, but I'm frozen in motion. Jase looks younger, so sleepy, with messier hair than usual. He smiles lazily. He's not quite awake yet, even though my phone is right next to his head, and the sound is truly awful.

Oh man, this isn't good. Except that somehow, it feels like it is.

"Hi, Pixie," Jase murmurs. His vision focuses on me at the same moment the alarm stops. We have three minutes before the snooze function kicks in again.

"Good morning." My voice sounds just as sleepy as his. "How did you sleep?"

Yawning, he rubs his eyes. "Like a rock."

I smile. "Sounds good."

"It was." Under the quilt, his hand wanders from my waist to my back. Gentle pressure. A question and an invitation at the same time. I move closer to him, his hand slides up my spine, and I snuggle up to him. My eyes close again all by themselves. Three minutes before the alarm rings again. That's a hundred and eighty seconds we still have next to each other in bed. My body feels warm and heavy as Jase caresses me, and my breathing deepens. If he keeps this up, I'll definitely fall asleep again. We lie close to each other, so close that my nose touches the hollow at the middle of his collarbone. I inhale his scent and sigh softly.

The sound makes him tremble; I can feel it. Can we please just lie here like this forever?

"You're about to fall asleep again," Jase whispers in my ear. His soft voice sends a delicious tingle through my body. I move a little away from him, just far enough that I can look at him. My breath catches, his eyes darken, and his touch changes almost imperceptibly.

His fingertips dance lightly on my skin. Warmth spreads through my middle. It's not even a real touch, but I can still feel it *everywhere*. I sigh again and snuggle closer. My hand slides under his sweatshirt. He holds his breath as I lightly caress his hips with my fingernails. His pelvis moves forward, just like mine. Then his erection presses against my middle, and I feel a throbbing between my legs. Our legs wrap around each other instinctively, and I feel a wave of heat overtake me.

Our movements are dreamy and slow, but my pulse quickens,

along with my breathing. We rub against each other, and he moans deeply. I've never heard a nicer sound. His desire makes me brave. I feel free and strong, and I want more . . .

The alarm rings again, and we start.

"Fuck, no!" Jase swears, and I have to laugh. Grumbling, he switches it off.

"I'm afraid we have to get up," I say, stretching with a yawn.

"We could just stay in bed." His look sets my whole body on fire, and I almost say yes. But only almost.

"We can't cut class again. You can't endanger your scholarship." I don't want to remind him of it, but it's better if I do.

He sighs with a deep disappointment that I share. "I know."

I sit up, and Jase slips out of the bed, holding out a hand to pull me to my feet. I follow him into my tiny bathroom. The drawer of the sink cabinet sticks slightly as I open it to get a new toothbrush for Jase so he doesn't have to go back to his own room yet. I want him to stay here with me.

"You're prepared," he says with amusement.

I hand him the toothbrush and reach for my own. "I'm just a neat freak. I have half a drugstore in this drawer," I say dryly. It's not a lie. I buy a reserve of everything: After all, you never know what the future will bring.

Jase shakes his head, grinning. "Why am I not surprised?"

"Because you know me."

* * *

"Very good, Zoe!" Miss Chelsea smiles with approval. "Now from the top, please."

Miss Chelsea is our pointe teacher. She's a tall, slender woman with a heart-shaped face and gentle charisma. She's the complete opposite of Francesca.

I stretch my arms and legs briefly before returning to position and going *en pointe* again, my supporting leg and raised leg turned out evenly. I remind myself to concentrate on my back and hips and not to forget my arms. I stretch my free leg far back, my arms *allongé*, palms down.

We're working on our arabesques, a position I've always loved. My body feels light, free, and weightless. My muscles are flowing in sync; my movements are soft and fluid. All is as it should be today. When I remember how I woke up this morning, my mouth curls into a smile all by itself.

I turn, making sure my upper body isn't too far forward and my shoulders are aligned. Endorphins flow through my veins, and my smile widens. I no longer feel the constant pain in my feet. The pointe shoes are now part of my body. They are an extension of me, and they help me to put all my weight on my toes.

"Very good," Miss Chelsea says again as I sink back onto my heels. My inner thigh muscles are still tense, something that was drilled into me as a child until all my muscles learned to keep the tension by themselves. I don't even have to think about it anymore.

"That was excellent." Mae, who's standing next to me, smiles. It's a broad, meaningful smile. "Did you know you're glowing? You're practically floating," she says casually. "And you skipped an afternoon class yesterday and didn't answer any of my twenty-seven messages. I'm very curious about why."

I silently curse my mother for passing on her genes that make me blush. I have no control over it.

I can't help looking over at Charlotte, who is standing a few yards away from us, hands on her hips as she corrects Jessica. When she notices me looking at her, she turns around and gives me one of her saccharine smiles, sending an unpleasant shudder down my spine.

I turn away quickly and concentrate on Mae again. I want to tell her everything, but I can't do it here, with Charlotte nearby.

"Can we talk about it later?"

"Mm-hmm." Mae narrows her eyes, peering back and forth between Charlotte and me. She understands. "Sure," she says. "But at least tell me if things are less complicated now."

I nod. It's not easy yet, and a lot still has to be cleared up. But everything is a little less complicated than it was yesterday.

"I'm really happy for you." Mae's gaze softens.

I'm about to say something else when Miss Chelsea turns her attention back to us. "Don't dawdle. Keep it up," she urges us. "We still have a lot to do today."

We nod at the same moment and return to position. But there's still something I urgently need to say.

"Hey, Mae?" I whisper.

"Hmm?" she raises her eyebrows questioningly.

"I'm glad your suitcase broke on the first day."

She grins. She understands what I'm trying to tell her.

Thank you for being my friend.

Thank you for never pushing me to tell you why I panicked so much at the beginning.

Thanks for just being here.

"Me too," she says.

* * *

Mae and I spend our lunch break in her room after getting something to eat in the cafeteria. Then I tell her everything. Well, not *everything*. I'm not quite ready for that. But I tell her enough, because I need to talk about it, and because Mae is the one I want to talk about it with. Just because she's herself.

I tell her about Jase and what happened back then, leaving out the reason why we didn't actually get together. And she doesn't ask because she can tell it's something I can't talk about. I tell her that we had sex and that he spent the night in my room. I tell her how strange it feels, because my whole life has revolved almost exclusively around ballet so far, and suddenly it's different.

When I tell her this, she smiles. "That's because we've been told all our lives that ballet is the most important thing in the world. And for us, it is. It's our whole lives. It defines who we are. What our future looks like. Where we come from and where we're going. But it's okay if you get a little distracted now."

I sigh. "Is it?"

"Yes. Do you know why?"

"I'm sure you're about to tell me."

"Of course. I can't keep my wisdom to myself." She grins, then quickly goes serious on me again. "This thing with you and Jase, it's not just a distraction. He's making you better. Think about what your first week was like and what it's like now. Okay, we can leave out yesterday's lesson because something obviously went wrong, but in the last few weeks, you've gotten better the closer you've become. And I'm not the only one who noticed it. Francesca did too. I don't think she meant that we should fall in love with our dance partners when she said we should build up trust. But hey, you can't have everything." She shrugs, giggling, and I want to tell her she's wrong. That I'm not in love with Jase. But the objection catches in my throat. Shit.

CHAPTER 34

Zoe

I feel safe with you. It's always been that way.
—Zoe

"What's up?" Jase is at my door. Recently, he's been here a lot. Not that I'm complaining. His eyes sparkle mischievously, and my heart jumps. I automatically think of what Mae said, but no, I'm not in love. It's just the damn hormones. His gaze makes my skin tingle, and I want him to touch me and explore my body with his mouth. I want to do the same to his.

You see? It's just the hormones. And a bit of lust because it's so new.

"I'm copying Mae's notes from yesterday." I let him in and point at my desk, where Mae's notebook is lying next to mine, with half a dozen highlighters next to it.

Jase makes a face, and I can tell he's thinking about his scholarship. "I have to do that too. I'll ask Skye if she took notes. She probably didn't."

"You're good friends with her, right?" The question jumps out of me before I can stop it.

Congratulations, Zoe. It's exactly the right moment for this. But maybe it is. I never asked him about Skye before. But all at once,

I remember Jase and Skye arriving late to Pearson's talk on my first day and how he put an arm around her shoulders. The image annoys me. Damn, why am I even thinking about this?

Because maybe Mae is right.

Jase raises his eyebrows, as if this is the last question he could imagine me asking, and I wish I could take it back.

"Right," he says honestly, seeming a little surprised, as though it just became clear to him why I asked. Then he answers the question that I don't dare to ask. "Skye likes to act like she's my big sister and I'm the little brother she has to take care of. Sometimes she's really annoying." A mischievous grin crosses his face. "The way siblings are, I guess." His smile slips, and I quickly change the subject because I don't want to talk about Caleb, and I'm sure he doesn't want to talk about Lia either. He's never talked to me about her.

"You didn't come to talk about the notes from the class we missed, did you?"

He shakes his head, and the gleam in his eyes is back. "Do you want to do something forbidden?"

"How forbidden?"

"Just a little." He reaches out a hand, and I give him mine without hesitation. At this moment, something becomes clear to me. Until yesterday, Jase had no idea what had happened to me. But from the beginning, from my first day at this school, he was the one who held out his hand to me. Waited for me. He was always waiting for me. In the ballet studio and outside of it.

His hand was always the question, and mine was the answer. Our fingers twine together as though they've never done anything else, and we leave my room. We walk across campus in the twilight, shuffling through the red and yellow leaves.

Jase leads me around the theater to the emergency exit, and after a cautious glance over his shoulder, he opens the door. We slip inside. He seems to have a plan, and I follow him although I have no idea what it is. Voices echo through the auditorium, and then the music begins. I recognize the piece immediately and stop dead.

"Jase," I whisper. "They're rehearsing *The Sleeping Beauty*."

He grins at me. "Exactly."

"We shouldn't be here."

Rehearsals for the senior ballet are off limits to underclassmen. Although Pearson wants us all to be part of it, only the seniors and a few juniors who were needed to fill out the cast are allowed to be at the rehearsals.

"I know. But if you don't come with me now, we'll get caught, and then it will all have been for nothing," Jase says. But he doesn't sound worried at all.

I hesitate for just a moment before following him. We slip out of the backstage area into the foyer and then into the upper balconies. From here, we won't be seen from below if we're careful.

My heart hammers as Jase bends down and pulls me into the front row. He gives me a warning look but can't hold back a smile. We sink into the soft cushions. It's dark up here, but we can still see everything. Emily is standing in the middle of the stage with Mr. Conrad. He's explaining something to her that we can't hear. Other dancers stand and sit at the edge of the stage, watching them and whispering to each other.

I lean forward, resting my forearms on the railing, and just watch. There's something magical about rehearsals, and not only when you're the one dancing.

Of course, they can't be compared to performances. At the premiere, everything is flawless. The costumes, makeup, hairstyles. Every step, every movement. Every smile. But you're also nervous. You're afraid of failing, even more than usual. Because everything has to be perfect. For the audience and for everyone who has put so much work into the production.

But the moment when you move from the practice studio to the stage for the first time, putting the steps you've learned over weeks of hard work into context, it's a totally different feeling. Everything is a little easier, with less pressure. The pain that accompanies us every day as we push our bodies to their limits fades into the background. It's pure adrenaline and euphoria. It's the last moment before everyone sees it. It's the one time you're dancing for your own pleasure.

Everything feels more real, but at the same time, it's like a dream. The space is bigger, it smells different than the practice studios, and the sound is better, deeper. The texture of the stage floor is different. Even the air feels changed.

On stage, and backstage, everything feels extra special. It feels like you're getting closer to your big dream. Everyone is more excited and calmer at the same time, out of respect for the stage, the audience, and the dream.

Emily nods, and Mr. Conrad steps aside, leaving the stage for her alone. He gives someone a sign, and the music rings through the theater.

My feet twitch of their own accord. I know the steps, and I want to be down there in Emily's place. I want to dance the part of Aurora, because it was always *my* role.

I only realize I'm on my feet when Jase steps behind me and

puts an arm around my waist. His breath caresses the sensitive skin behind my ear, and I get goose bumps.

"In three years, that will be you, Pixie," he whispers. He makes it sound like an indisputable fact.

I turn my head, just a tiny bit, so his lips meet my skin. "You can't know that."

"Yes, I can. You know why? Because I saw you dancing on Saturday night. And I saw you last year before Charlotte stole the part from you. Emily is good. Charlotte is kind of good, when she's not busy making people cry in bathrooms. But neither of them dances like you do. You're tougher than they are because you had to fight."

I turn in his arms to look at him, leaning back against the rail. He's looking directly into my soul. He's picking up the shards of my broken spirit and putting them back together piece by piece.

"You're stronger than they are. That's why you'll be down there in three years."

"Okay," I whisper, because I want to believe him. Then I kiss him, because he's so close to me that I simply have to.

This kiss is different. Slower, gentler, more careful. He holds my face between his hands, and then I lay my hand on his chest. I can feel his heart. It falters and beats just a little too fast. I have to smile, because mine is doing exactly the same thing.

My lips open. His tongue is in my mouth, and everything is different, but I can't tell why. We kiss while *The Sleeping Beauty* is being rehearsed right below us. Voices and music blend into an indistinct blur. All I can hear is Jase's breathing, which accelerates as I run my fingers through his hair and gnaw gently on his lower lip. His body reacts, rising against mine.

The kiss changes. It becomes deeper, more eager, more demanding. Heat shoots through me. We kiss endlessly, and I lose all sense of space and time. I can only feel. I feel him and myself and this desire for more. An intense pressure builds up that's almost unbearable in a bittersweet way.

I push myself against him, and there's too much clothing between us. I'm so hot. I want to feel his skin on mine and nothing else. His tongue plays with mine. The pulsing between my legs grows stronger, and I want to feel something else there.

Jase lets go of me and steps back, just far enough that he can see me. His lips are swollen from our kisses, and his eyes are shining. I'm sure I look exactly the same way. His gaze roams over my face and then focuses on my mouth. He swallows hard and then puts a hand on my lower back, turning us around together and lowering me gently into one of the seats behind me. The cushions are soft. My breath catches as Jase sinks to his knees in one fluid motion. He smiles, and his eyes flash with the same hunger that I feel.

Desire pulses through my veins, so strong that it makes me dizzy. I must be losing my mind a little, because I let Jase put his hands on my knees and spread my legs. Not just let him; I want it. His fingers wander up my thighs, inch by inch. Agonizingly slowly.

I have to bite my lower lip to stifle a moan as my head falls back. His fingers reach the waistband of my tights, and I thank myself for having chosen to wear a dress this morning. I close my eyes. He tugs at the thin fabric, and I raise my hips so he can pull off the tights and panties. They bunch up around my ankles, and I kick my shoes off so the ball of fabric falls at my feet.

There's a quiet voice in my head whispering that I shouldn't be doing this. And certainly not here when the rehearsal is going on below us. I look into Jase's eyes, and he returns my gaze. God, I'm so hot I'm melting. My whole body is pulsing, longing for more.

I ignore the voice. I should, and I want to.

Then Jase lowers his head between my legs.

CHAPTER 35
Jase

There's something I wanted to tell you
the whole time: I missed you.
—Jase

It's the wrong place and definitely the wrong time for this. We're in the theater, and we're not alone. But fuck. Nothing has ever felt more right than kneeling in front of Zoe, between her legs, inhaling the scent of her skin and hearing her breathing accelerate, because she's not just allowing this; she *wants* it.

In the meantime, my pants have gotten so tight that it hurts, but this isn't about me. It's about her. Fuck. It was always about her.

I caress the inside of her thigh with my lips, and I have to smile as her fingers twist in my hair and tug demandingly. I look up without taking my mouth off her. Her head is tilted back, exposing her long, slender neck. Her copper hair stands out against her pale skin.

She's so incredibly beautiful.

Kiss by kiss, I feel my way along her leg, closer and closer. Her grip on my hair gets stronger. She wants to pull me in, but I'm not going to let her rush me.

Not now. Not here.

She slides restlessly back and forth on the seat. She tries to push her pelvis forward, but I put my hands on her hips and keep her exactly where I want her.

My cock twitches, but I ignore the pressure building up inside.

"Jase." Her whisper is a soft, breathless plea for more, for me, and all the blood above my waistline is rapidly making its way downward.

Fuck, I think I'm dying.

I push her dress up around her hips, and then I lower my mouth to the center of her desire. When I taste her, I really think I die a little. She whimpers, and this time I can't hold her back as she pushes against me. My eyelids flutter shut, and I just feel, concentrating fully on her. Every twitch of her hips, every tug on my hair. I focus on her ever-accelerating breath, the soft gasps, making me almost come in my pants as I make circles with my tongue.

She raises her hips, wraps both legs around my shoulders, and pulls me even closer. Damn, why is it so hot in here?

As I slide two fingers inside her, Zoe suppresses a moan, and her muscles tighten around me. She's so wet, and now I'm really about to die. I move my fingers slowly, but that's not what she wants. Her hips leap forward, so fast that I have to be careful she doesn't fall off the seat.

"More, Jase, please . . ." As she whispers my name, her voice soft and trembling, I lose control. I push deeper inside her while using my tongue, and the taste of her is certainly going to be the end of me.

Her orgasm builds up like a wave. I can feel it, before it breaks in a series of powerful contractions. Her muscles pulse; everything throbs. She arches her back, her hips slide even farther forward, and she stifles a scream by biting her lip. Fuck, she really is killing me.

I want to hear her, every single sound that she makes, unrestrained and uncontrolled. I want everything from her, and I want to give her everything she wants from me.

* * *

I slept in Zoe's room that night too, as if it were the most natural thing in the world. And every other night this week. I should probably be worried about how easy everything suddenly is. How normal it seems.

And how safe I feel.

But I'm not worried. I'm also not worried about the fact that it can't be this simple. Not after all the shit we've already been through.

But I should have guessed it was too good to last.

The universe takes revenge for my carelessness on Friday, during the pas de deux class.

"Today we'll be working on our lifts. The last few times, I wasn't convinced of what I saw," Francesca says, giving the pianist a sign and sending us to our positions.

I wait for Zoe to give me her hand before I take her by the waist. My body reacts to her closeness with an unmistakable tingle as I start to think about how she moved under my hands in the theater. Her moan in my ear, her taste in my mouth.

"You're thinking dirty," Zoe whispers so quietly that no one can hear but me. In the mirror, I see a wide grin on her face.

I lean forward a little until my cheek is touching hers. "Do you want to know what I'm thinking about?"

Her lips open, and I want to kiss her, right now, but we don't have a chance to continue our conversation, or kiss. Francesca stops in front of us and raises her eyebrows disapprovingly.

"Concentrate," she orders.

Zoe and I nod at the same moment, but she's smiling.

"Later," I whisper to her as soon as Francesca has moved on to the next couple.

We do one lift after another, and it's so easy to dance with Zoe now. We react to each other; we understand each other intuitively.

Until I turn around. Zoe is sitting on my shoulder. I see a tall, familiar figure watching us from the hallway. I lose my balance, and Zoe lets out a startled cry as she slips off my shoulder. Somehow, I manage to catch her. It's pure instinct; I can't let her fall.

Francesca shouts something, but her words don't reach me. All I can hear is the sound of blood pounding in my ears. My heart is racing, and my whole body tenses. I look into Zoe's surprised eyes, yet all my attention is focused on the man watching me, his face expressionless.

Dad.

What the hell is he doing here?

"Jase, are you okay?" Zoe frees herself from my grip and gives me a worried look, even though I'm supposed to be the one asking. After all, I almost let her fall.

"Yes," I lie. "Are you okay? Are you hurt?"

She shakes her head and smiles at me reassuringly. "It's okay, I was just shocked."

"I'm sorry, I—"

"It's okay," she says again, nodding toward the glass wall. She's already noticed him. Of course she has. Her smile fades and her brow creases, as though she's wondering the same thing I am.

Francesca comes over to us to make sure neither of us is hurt and then has us start from the beginning. But I can't concentrate anymore, no matter how hard I try.

I can't ignore my father. He's here, watching me, judging me, evaluating me. He probably feels justified now that I don't belong here. And I'm not even in a position to prove him wrong.

When Francesca finally ends the lesson, I'm both relieved the torment is over for now and dreading what comes next. Dad is waiting for me, and I don't believe for one second that I can just ignore him.

I purposely take my time packing my things and putting on my sweatshirt, but I can't delay the inevitable much longer.

Zoe and Skye are the only ones who are still here when I look up. Everyone else has gone to lunch. Both girls give me worried looks. It's the first time I notice something they have in common.

I leave the studio alone, even though everything inside me wants to leave with Zoe and just ignore Dad. But that won't work. I know that from experience.

"What do you want?" I ask him without a greeting, because he doesn't deserve one. He hasn't been in touch with me for weeks, not since our conversation in Mom's office. Now he just shows up here like it's normal.

"We have to talk."

"We don't." I push my way past him and walk down the corridor. I have to get out of here. He follows me outside, and the cold air hits me like a slap in the face.

"Jase! Listen to me." Dad easily keeps pace with my long strides. I stop in the middle of campus, because I don't want him to follow me into the dorm, and I definitely don't want him in my room.

"Why should I? Do you want to take something else away from me? I don't have anything left, Dad."

"I'm not here to take anything away." He sounds annoyed, as though I'm acting like a defiant child.

"Then what do you want?" Anger flares up inside me, burning through my body like hot embers.

"This is about your mother," he replies reluctantly. "Her birthday party is tomorrow, and it's important that you be there."

His words leave me speechless for a moment. But then I laugh in disbelief. "Oh, you mean the party that I wasn't invited to?"

"You're our son. Of course you're invited."

I shake my head uncomprehendingly. Mom's birthday was two weeks ago. I went to my parents' place, and I have no idea why. It was stupid. But it was Mom's birthday, and some idiotic part of me just couldn't ignore that.

I was still sitting in the Uber when they walked out of the house. Mom, Dad, Lia, and her boyfriend. They didn't even notice me as they got in their car and drove away. Without me.

"I find that difficult to believe."

Dad rubs his forehead. His shoulders are tense. He's just about to lose his cool. "If our family still means something to you, you'll come to the party tomorrow."

My chin juts out in opposition. "And if I don't? What then?"

"Jesus. I don't want to hurt you. When are you going to figure that out?"

Never. Because you never accept me or my decisions about my own life.

"Do it for your mother. She's done a lot for you. Don't disappoint her," he says. And then he leaves. Just like that, without another word.

I stare after him. I'm boiling inside. *Don't disappoint her.* As if

I don't do that every single day of my life anyway. I hate myself for it, but I know that tomorrow I'll go to the fucking party. Her fiftieth. Tomorrow . . .

My heart skips a beat. *Tomorrow.*

My stomach turns. For a moment, I can't breathe. I'm dizzy. I stagger.

The pain is there again so suddenly, as though it never faded. As though I never learned to deal with it. It hits me full force, driving me to my knees, mixing fury and hatred in an uncontrollable hurricane inside. My eyes burn, and I want to scream, but the sound gets caught in my throat.

Mom's birthday was over two weeks ago.

Seventeen days after her birthday a few years ago, Sam died.

Tomorrow. Tomorrow he will have been dead for five years.

And she's celebrating her fucking birthday.

CHAPTER 36
Zoe

Last year, I was afraid. Every single day. Not because of what happened, but because of the consequences. I was afraid I'd never be able to dance again, and I don't think I would have been able to survive that.
—Zoe

Something is wrong. I want to believe that I'm exaggerating and have been trying to convince myself of it for hours. Unfortunately, I don't buy it.

Not after being an involuntary witness to the conversation between Jase and his father.

Skye and I didn't agree to stay after class; we just did it. Just like we both left the room together as soon as Jase and his dad disappeared. There's no way we could have known that they'd stop to argue in the middle of campus, or that the wind would carry their words in our direction. But we moved on, both realizing that Jase wouldn't want us to hear it.

Now I wish I'd stopped and waited for him, offered to talk. But I didn't, and now he's gone. He's not in his room and hasn't answered my calls or texts.

My phone beeps, and I collapse onto my bed. But the message that pops up on my screen isn't from Jase; it's from my brother.

CALEB:

I'm about to die of excitement. If you don't like Parker, we're going to have a problem!

I stifle a groan. Damn it. I totally forgot. Caleb asked me two days ago if I wanted to go out to eat with him and our parents so he could introduce us to Parker. I said yes because, at the time, there was no reason not to.

Hopefully, there's still no reason not to because Jase is doing okay.

But I'm worried, and spending the evening with my brother and his new boyfriend feels wrong right now, and that bothers me. Part of me wants to stay here and wait for Jase to get in touch. The other part knows very well that he won't show up today. That he won't sleep next to me in my bed and wake up next to me tomorrow. My chest tightens. He was with me the entire week. It's crazy how fast I got used to having him sleep with me. How strange it is that he's not lying on my bed right now, listening to music in his headphones and playing with my hair as I read.

A new message pops up on my phone. It's Caleb again.

CALEB:

Zoe? I can see that you read my message! Calm me down! Please!!!

I sigh and type a reply. Staying here won't do any good. Besides, I shouldn't spend the evening by myself right now. I would just overthink everything.

ZOE:

Stop worrying. I know I'm going to love Parker. Mom and Dad are probably already planning your wedding.

CALEB:

That's somehow not as comforting as you probably thought it would be . . .

ZOE:

Everything's going to be fine, I promise!

I send him a few hearts, throw my phone back onto my bed, and get ready. When I finally leave my room, I still haven't heard from Jase.

* * *

I'm the first one to arrive at the little Italian restaurant where we're meeting for dinner. It's Caleb's favorite. We've spent every one of his birthdays here, except for one year when he was in bed with a stomach flu; I ate his birthday cake almost all by myself. As a little sister, that was practically my job.

He saw things differently and returned the favor on my next

birthday. By then, however, I was too into dancing to even think about eating more than the two pieces I had allowed myself as a treat. Still, I would kill for a piece of that sticky-sweet chocolate cake with the liquid center, no matter how little it fits into my diet plan.

"Zoe!" I turn to look when I hear Caleb's excited voice. I'm already sitting at our usual table in the back left corner. I don't know how, but Caleb and my parents always manage to get the same table.

Allesandro's is small and cozy, with dark wooden floors, exposed brick walls, rustic furniture, and dark-green-and-white checkered tablecloths. The low-hanging lamps bathe everything in a soft, warm light.

Caleb walks up to me with a big smile, a dark-haired, absolutely gorgeous guy in tow. I get up as the two of them approach the table and hug my brother before Parker hugs me. A little surprised, I return his embrace.

"Mom and Dad are going to be a little late. Mom got stuck at the office. Maybe that's not a bad thing, so you two can get to know each other a little. Then we'll have an ally if Mom and Dad ask questions that they shouldn't," Caleb says. I have to smile. He's totally smitten.

"Don't worry, I'm always on your side. And I'm really happy we finally get to meet," I say to Parker after we sit down.

He looks stunning with his jet-black hair and fair skin. His eyes are an almost-unnatural blue, framed by long, thick lashes that I immediately envy. Everything about him looks British, from his clean-cut facial features and the shape of his lips to the burgundy-colored chunky knit sweater he's wearing.

"I'm happy too," he replies, and he even has a slight British accent. His smile is so sweet that I completely understand why Caleb is smitten. "Your brother tells me you're a ballet dancer?"

I sigh exaggeratedly and give Caleb a reproachful look. "Is that the only thing you can say about me?" I tease him.

"No, but I'm proud of you, so let me be." He taps my nose.

I have to laugh, but it doesn't feel entirely genuine. "That's not fair—I can't be mad at you that way."

"You're not supposed to be," Caleb says with a grin, reaching for Parker's hand. Their fingers intertwine, and my heart quickens as I think about Jase. He still hasn't reached out, and I'm really starting to worry.

"He also showed me videos of you, if that helps in any way to be mad at him." Parker winks, and I push my worries about Jase aside. He'll text soon. I'm sure he will.

"Unfortunately not." I sigh. "But thanks for your help." I'm pretty sure I know which videos he means. Mom and Dad have seen and taped every one of my performances, but my brother knows exactly which videos are allowed to be seen and which are not.

"It was worth a try," Parker says with a shrug, while Caleb looks from him to me, relieved.

He gives me a silent *thank you*, and I smile at him because Parker really is great.

* * *

"It was so nice to meet you all," Parker says with a warm smile as we say goodbye to each other outside the restaurant a few hours later.

"It was nice for us too," Mom says, hugging him. She's beaming. She's been doing that all evening, as have Dad and Caleb.

I can't help but feel like I wasn't quite present this evening, and I have a terribly guilty conscience about it.

"Everything okay?" Caleb whispers, so no one else can hear him. "You seem a little distant. Don't you like Parker?" A worried expression crosses his face, and I feel a stab of guilt.

"Of course I do! He's wonderful, honestly. You're perfect together."

"Then what's going on?"

"Nothing at all," I lie, because I can't tell him about Jase. Not today.

Caleb doesn't look convinced, but he gives in. "Okay."

I breathe a sigh of relief.

"Zoe, can we give you a ride back?" Mom puts a hand on my shoulder.

"That would be great, thank you."

"Of course. We're going in the same direction." She winks at me, smiling.

I hug Parker and Caleb and follow my parents to their car. The whole drive, they talk about Caleb and Parker, and while Dad isn't quite planning the wedding yet, the next family celebration will certainly be a vacation together. I only listen with half an ear, mumbling in agreement from time to time so they'll at least think I'm taking part in the conversation. But I'm checking my phone every few seconds.

But—surprise—Jase still hasn't texted.

"Zoe? Honey?"

I look up. Mom is looking at me questioningly. "What? I'm sorry, I was thinking about something."

"We're here. Is everything okay?"

"Yes," I say, lying again. I squeeze out a smile. "I'm just tired."

"Then off to bed with you."

"Good plan." I lean forward to kiss her, then Dad, and get out of the car.

I'm just about to go to the dorm when I realize there's still a light on in the practice studio. Upstairs, in the little studio where Jase and I usually meet for our extra practice. My heart leaps. I can't see him in the window from down here, but I'm pretty sure that he's up there. It must be him.

I start moving without thinking about whether or not he'll actually want to see me. I just want to find out if he's okay. Aside from me, there's no one out right now, and I've never been in the practice building so late. On the first day, we all got a chip card so we could practice any time of the day or night, but this is the first time I'm using it.

The building is dark, and something in me resists switching on the lights. Instead, I take my phone out of my pocket and turn on the flashlight. I hurry upstairs. It's a bit creepy to be here so late, especially alone. But I'm not really alone. Jase is up there. Or if he's not . . . well, who knows?

The steps to the little studio creak under my feet as I climb up. I can hear the music echoing through the room. It's angry, with a pulsing bass. I hesitate at the door. My pulse has already adjusted to the music, and my palms are sweating. I carefully open the door and peer in, and there he is.

He's dancing. And I can't help watching him. He's not wearing a T-shirt, just leggings. Sweat is shimmering on his skin; his hair is hanging damply on his forehead. There's an expression of unbridled rage on his face. And boundless pain. His movements reflect his feelings, powerful and strong. He is so damn beautiful. And so, so angry.

I should leave. I should leave him alone, but I can't take my eyes off him. I'm completely frozen. And then he notices me. His gaze meets mine in the mirror, and he pauses, breathing heavily. His eyes widen.

"Pixie." His voice is hard and just as angry as his gaze.

"Jase." I take a step forward into the room. The door slams shut behind me.

"What are you doing here?"

"I was looking for you. I was worried about you."

"Why?" His tone is dismissive, and everything inside me tenses. He's hurt, and I know it's not because of me, but I still can't help the fact that it stings.

"You know why. You didn't answer any of my calls or messages."

He runs a hand through his hair and swears softly. "I . . . I'm sorry."

"It's okay." I take a step toward him, hold out my hand, and lower it again. I want to ask him if he's all right, but that feels unnecessary when he's obviously not. "Do you want to talk about it? What's going on?" I ask gently. But Jase shakes his head.

"No, I . . . Oh, fuck!" He whirls around, and his fist hits the wall between the round windows so hard that he must be bleeding. I'm shocked for a split second, but then I'm next to him, holding his face between my hands and making him look at me so he'll talk. He does.

"Dad wants me to come to Mom's stupid party," he says through clenched teeth, "and they didn't even invite me properly. I'm just supposed to show up and pretend that everything's okay."

"You don't have to go."

He exhales loudly. "I know. But I do. I have to." I want to ask why, but something in his eyes stops me.

"Do you want me to come with you?" I say instead.

He shakes his head, laughing humorlessly. "You really don't have to put up with that shit."

"But do you *want* me to come with you?" I stroke his cheeks, and my thumb comes to rest on his lips.

He whirls us around until my back is against the wall behind me and props his hands next to my head. His gaze is dark and still angry, but it's now also full of desire. My heart skips a beat, heat shooting through my body as he stares at my mouth. A voice reminds me that I should be afraid because I don't have control right now. But still, I feel safe.

All I want is for him to answer me. My skin tingles, and my whole body throbs. For a second, all I can think about is how badly I want to explore every inch of his body with my mouth right now.

"Jase, do you want me to go with you?" I ask, a little hoarse and out of breath.

He leans his forehead against mine, and my hands slide automatically over his shoulders and down to his chest, pausing over his heart. It's racing.

"Yes," he whispers.

"Okay, then I will."

Instead of answering, he kisses me. Hungrily. Wildly. Desperately. I return his kiss without hesitation, even though I have a thousand questions. Even though I know so much about Jase, even though he's told me so many secrets, I can't shake the feeling that there's more to his anger than just this party. I pause.

"Jase," I whisper against his lips. "Why are you so angry?"

He pulls back to look at me. Anger is still flickering in his eyes. But beneath it, I can see his pain. "Please . . ." He swallows hard, "Please, Pixie, I can't talk about it right now."

"Okay." I nod, and he kisses me again, hard and deep. I taste his salty sweat on my tongue, and I realize that this is not the time for questions and secrets. Jase doesn't want to talk, and to be honest, I don't want to talk now either.

His hands slide under my jacket, pushing it off my shoulders. He finds the zipper of my dress, and a moment later, the fabric parts and slides down my chest to my waist. I'm only wearing a thin lace bra, and Jase hesitates for a second to make sure I'm okay with it. I want him, here and now. My body is begging for more. He pulls the thin straps down my arms. My eyelids close as his lips find my nipple, and then his tongue. A whimper escapes me, and I thrust my hips toward him. Jase's hands roam over my body and cup my butt. He lifts me up, and I instinctively wrap my legs around his hips. I can feel the throbbing of his own desire against my center, and I wish the thin fabric of my tights and underwear would just melt into thin air.

Jase backs away a little, and I feel his breath on my cheek. Goose bumps.

"I hate them," he says. "Mom, Dad, Lia, Sam. Everyone but you." His husky voice sends a shiver down my back.

"You can hate me. It's okay if you hate me a little bit."

He smiles grimly. "No, it's not."

"Yes, it is. Today you're allowed to for a moment. Really. I'm strong—you said it yourself. Let me catch you. Let it out. Please." I pull him close, and our lips collide. He groans and presses himself against me. I writhe under his touch until he lets go again, this time to take off his leggings and help me out of my clothes.

Then he's with me again, lifting me up and pressing me against the wall between the windows. The bricks feel cold against my naked skin, but the cold only intensifies the heat inside me. My body thrums; my skin glows. I scratch Jase's back with my fingernails, and he moans desperately into my mouth.

"Hate me," I breathe. I guess I'm losing my mind. But that's exactly what I want to do right now.

Jase loses control at my words. I can feel it. A tremor runs through his body; the muscles in his back tense. His hand slides between us, and then he enters me with a powerful thrust. I whimper again, and my back rubs against the cold, rough bricks every time Jase thrusts into me.

It's crazy and exciting at the same time, the slight pain on my skin, and the desire flooding my body. Strangely, it feels incredibly good. He's angry, and I absorb his anger, again and again and again, with every furious thrust, and each time his fingers touch my skin.

And then . . . he stops. He just stops. My whole body is throbbing in protest, because I need more. More of him. More of this.

"What—" I say, stopping as Jase backs away from me, panting, and my legs slide off his hips. I feel the wooden floor under my bare feet, cool and smooth, and I reel in confusion as Jase rests his forehead against mine.

"Fuck! I . . . can't. I can't hate you," he murmurs, his lips caressing mine. They trace my jawline, and I forget that I want to reply.

"You're the only one I can't hate." He backs away a little, turning me toward the mirror until I can see our reflections, with red cheeks and shining eyes. "You're the only one that gives my life any kind of sense." He slides behind me, tall and warm, until his chest touches my back. He still has one arm around my waist, and the other hand rests on my thigh, tracing lazy circles on my naked skin. My body reacts to his touch with a hot tingle, and my heart reacts to his gaze, his words.

Longing. Fierce. In love.

"Why do you make so much sense?" He kisses my neck, biting gently, just enough to make me whimper again. My head tips back. I close my eyes and press up against him, so close that I can feel his erection on my bottom. At the same time, I push my hips forward so his hand can slide deeper.

"Because you do," I reply hoarsely. I moan as his thumb circles the center of my desire, which almost hurts with longing, and I see stars.

"Open your eyes," he says, and I do, because I would do anything he tells me right now. "Look at yourself."

I blink until my vision clears. Until I can see us. But I can't look at myself. I can only see him. Jase, who's standing behind me, big and strong and beautiful. He commands the entire room with his dark gaze and the haze of anger that still surrounds him.

"Look at yourself," he repeats, more urgently this time. He increases the pressure between my legs, and I can't help it. I sigh yearningly, rub myself against his hand, and watch his eyes seeking mine. The girl looking back at me from the mirror is obviously me, but she seems strangely unfamiliar. And at the same time, I know her too well.

Red cheeks and swollen lips. Gleaming eyes, full of lust.

"Do you have any idea what you're doing to me?"

I shake my head, and finally, he slides a finger inside me. My muscles tighten around it of their own accord, my eyelids flutter, wanting to close again, but Jase's grip on my waist tightens.

"When I'm with you, I can forget all the shit for a few minutes. When I'm with you, I feel so damn alive that it scares me sometimes." His mouth moves over my neck, and my lips pulse with desire. I want to kiss him, taste him, but I don't get a chance to turn and face him. His grip on my waist is too tight. He wants me to watch what he's doing to me. And I want that too. The realization hits me hard. I want it desperately.

I move, writhing my hips, moaning as his finger slides out and back in hard. The girl in the mirror arches her back, pushing up against his hand. I tangle my fingers in his hair, tugging at the blond strands. Jase smiles. His thumb hits the place I want it to be again, where I *need* it to be. My whole body thrums with desire. He thrusts into me again. Faster, harder, more urgently. He presses me so close to his body now that there's no escaping.

I'm in free fall, all because of him. I come with a stifled cry, watching myself, and see how something in my gaze snaps.

Jase holds me tight as the muscles inside me contract again and again. My heart is racing, and my body feels too small to contain everything I'm feeling right now. For what he's made me feel.

He doesn't let go of me even when I slowly come to rest. He holds me very close and kisses my temple. I turn to him, because we're not finished yet. I'm intoxicated by him, and I want him to feel like I do right now. That's why I drop to my knees in front of him.

"Pixie, you don't have to—" Jase abruptly falls silent when I take him in my mouth and let my tongue glide over the tip of his hardness. He exhales with a hiss, and if I could, I would smile.

"Fuck, you don't have to—" He stops again as I suck on him. I always imagined this would feel different. Like I'm not in control. But I am, completely and utterly. And I want that. I want him to feel good. I want to give him an outlet for his anger and pain, because he did the same for my fear.

He buries his fingers in my hair, and then he loses the rest of his self-control and thrusts into my mouth. It's almost too much and not enough at the same time. Now he sees both of us in the mirror as I feel his yearning. For me.

"Pixie, I'm about to come, you don't—" He wants to pull back, and I know why, but I don't let him. He comes with a deep groan, and I swallow by pure instinct as he holds my hair more tightly.

I look up when he's done, and he strokes the corners of my mouth with his thumbs. His gaze is soft and apologetic.

"I'm sorry."

"You don't have to be sorry about anything. I wanted it. All of it," I reply, because I have the feeling he needs to hear it. I stand up.

He pulls me close and kisses me, and I taste him, and me, and us. Then we hold each other tightly, and we don't talk about his anger or pain or anything. We just hold each other in this little studio, in the middle of the night, in front of the mirror. And I'm hopeful. I don't know what I'm hoping for.

Maybe I'm hoping that tomorrow, everything will be all right.

But somehow, I don't believe it.

PART 4

Variations of Him

Phase Four of the
Pas de Deux

CHAPTER 37

Jase

Sometimes I wonder if my relationship with Dad would be better if I had actually gone to Harvard. But then I remember that it was already difficult before, because he just can't come to terms with who I am.
—Jase

I hate you, Mom. *I hate you*, Dad. *I hate you*, Lia. *I hate you*, Sam.

But above all, I hate this damn party. Everything about it is wrong. The white decorations, the guests, the fucking date.

Above all, the date.

Sam has been dead for five years. Today it hurts like it's only been a few days since it happened. I can't breathe. It's tearing me apart from the inside.

As one of the waiters walks past me with a tray in his hand, I reach for a glass of whiskey. I don't care whether the drink might actually be meant for someone else. I'll never survive the evening without it. I'm not sure anymore if I'll even survive it with it.

Zoe isn't here yet. She's coming with her parents, who are also on the guest list, because all the dresses that are appropriate for Victoria Winslow's event are hanging in her closet at home.

I wish I wasn't here yet either. Really, I wish I didn't have to be here at all. I should have just stayed away. I feel so out of place that it would almost be funny if it weren't so damn sad. I don't belong here, in this posh ballroom in one of the most expensive hotels in Boston. My parents are here somewhere, as are Lia and her boyfriend, but I'm staying as far away from my family as possible.

Dad wanted me to come, and I'm here. But that doesn't mean I have to talk to anyone.

The only person I want to talk to is Zoe.

I can still feel her body under my hands, her lips on my cock, and I wish I could go back to that moment yesterday. Back to her, and away from this fucking party.

The alcohol burns in my throat as I take a sip. I hate whiskey, but right now it's my only option. There's never beer at my family's parties; it's too "common." I wander through the room, trying to avoid everyone and hoping that Zoe will be here soon.

I find Lia standing next to Archie, her almost-fiancé. She turns to me when she feels my eyes on her back. There's a strange expression on her face, and for a moment, she looks like she'd rather be somewhere else. But that can't be true, because she's Lia, and Lia is perfect. She's wearing a floor-length pink evening gown, and her golden hair is properly pinned up. She looks like a damn Barbie doll.

I want to leave, but I'm too slow. Lia steps away from the group she's with and is next to me before I can get away.

"Are you for real?" she hisses, pointing at my glass.

"What does it look like?" Provokingly, I take another sip, and this time it burns a little less.

"Can't you behave for even one evening?" She moves to take my glass, but I'm faster and hold it out of her reach. I'm taller, even though she's wearing killer heels.

"I always behave," I say sardonically.

She rolls her eyes. "In which life?"

"What do you want from me, anyway? Go back to your Disney prince."

She laughs in disbelief. "Jesus, what made you into such an asshole?"

Sam dying. Dad. Mom. You.

I shrug noncommittally. I hate being this way. I don't feel like myself anymore. Not like the person I know I can be. Not when I'm around my fucking family.

"Maybe I shouldn't have given you the money after all."

I grimace. I had done my best to ignore the fact that Lia had, in fact, paid my tuition for this semester, even though I never agreed to her terms. Because if I had thought about it, I would have felt forced to talk to her. I would have had to go down on my knees and thank her for saving my dream, at least for the semester. But I couldn't manage to do it. I couldn't thank her. Even if that made me an even bigger asshole.

"You can take it back, just like Mom and Dad did. You're copying everything they do anyway. So go ahead. Don't feel obliged." *Shut up, you idiot.*

"God, Jase, why are you like this?" Lia asks, frustrated.

"Did you also not bother to remember that today is five years since Sam died?"

Lia goes pale. So they really forgot. Or they didn't care. I'm not sure which is worse.

"Jase—" Lia starts, but I push past her.

"Leave it, Ophelia." She flinches. She hates her name. "You're here to celebrate, so do it. Just leave me out of this shit."

"Then why are you here?" she calls after me. But I don't answer.

Yeah, why the hell am I here? I get another drink and chug it down at a standing table in the corner of the ballroom. I can't remember the last time I was drunk, but today feels like a good day for it. I stare into the golden liquid in my glass and think of Zoe's eyes. They're the same color. Where the hell is she? It scares me a little how much I want her here. How much I *need* her.

I pull my phone out of my pocket and am just about to text her when I hear someone come up next to my table.

"Hi, Jase." The annoying voice makes me look up, and I immediately wish I hadn't.

"Charlotte," I say in monotone.

"I want to introduce you to my parents," she trills, pointing to a couple behind her, who are looking at me with distant smiles.

I know Charlotte's parents. I never met them personally, but I know who the mayor of Boston is. And I also know that his wife gives her lovely daughters every damn thing they want.

"They want to talk to you about the scholarship," Charlotte continues, giving me a meaningful look when I don't answer.

The fucking scholarship. Charlotte's offer. She hasn't mentioned it in weeks, and I wonder why she's doing it now, of all times. But actually, I don't care.

"No need," I say, stepping away from the table. Time to leave.

I walk purposefully toward the bar, ignoring Mom, who is hanging on Dad's arm and wearing a white, figure-hugging dress with a bright smile on her face that's so fake I could puke.

I signal to the bartender, and a few seconds later, he hands me a full glass. But before I can take it, someone grabs my hand. I don't even have to look to know who it is. I know the touch intimately. I look up anyway, and Zoe is standing next to me, a worried expression on her face. Relief floods me, and I can't help it. I have to hold her close, inhale her lavender scent, and feel my fingers on her skin.

She looks surprised and returns my embrace. She kisses my cheek. It's crazy how much better I feel just because she's here.

"Hi," she says softly, taking a step back. She looks absolutely beautiful, wearing a calf-length dress in rust-colored silk that clings to her upper body like a second skin. The skirt falls softly and flows around her long legs, and I catch myself wondering if she's wearing anything underneath it.

"You're here."

"Of course I'm here." She smiles, and my heart beats out of time again. Fuck. Our fingers weave together all by themselves.

"How much does it suck?" She's sizing me up. I can't look her in the eye; otherwise, I'll end up saying things I shouldn't. If I tear down all the walls I've built around my heart to reach her right now, I'll fall apart.

So I shrug. My eyes wander automatically to my parents, who are talking to some people whom I don't know but are probably terribly important. Then my gaze shifts to the empty dance floor. I know Mom and Dad will have a big plan to kick off the dancing later this evening. Yes, it's kind of childish and a little mean, but I want to ruin the moment for them.

"Dance with me," I beg her, even though it's a totally stupid idea. But I'm not sober, and I'm not here to make sensible decisions.

"Okay," she says without hesitation, even though there's no one else on the dance floor and the music is playing softly and unobtrusively in the background. She pulls me toward the dance floor, and suddenly I have a problem. What I feel for her now is more than I've ever felt for anyone else.

I want her to be mine. Not just in the theater. Not just in the studio. Always. Everywhere.

CHAPTER 38

Zoe

All last year, I tried not to think about you.
But to be honest, I failed utterly.
—Zoe

Jase is drunk. At first I wasn't sure because he had himself completely under control, but he is. I can tell by the way his eyes are gleaming. He's still angry, still hurt, still filled with pain. Feelings like that don't disappear from one day to the next. Not even because of sex.

That's the reason we're on this dance floor, all by ourselves. Because of his feelings. Because he doesn't have them under control. Not yesterday, and not now.

"Are you ready?" he whispers. His gaze burns into mine, and even though I know he doesn't want to be here, a little smile sneaks across my face.

"Always."

He returns my smile for a split second, and then he starts moving with me in his arms. Despite the alcohol, Jase's steps are sure and smooth. He can dance. Of course he can, but this is something different. Most ballet dancers can manage a waltz, but we struggle with the other ballroom dances, especially the Latin ones.

It's totally different from ballet. A different tempo, a different kind of control, different steps. I have no idea exactly what kind of dance we're doing here, but in the end, it doesn't matter. Jase leads, and I let him, with every step, every turn, and every arch of my back.

"Where did you learn this?" I whisper as he pulls me up out of a bend, so close that our chests touch for a moment.

"My dad showed us," he replies curtly.

I don't press him for more information. He doesn't give me the impression that he would want to answer any of the questions running through my mind.

"Right now, he's probably wishing he hadn't."

I have his father directly in my line of sight, and he doesn't look happy. His features are schooled into an expressionless mask. He's staring at us along with everyone else. I'm trying not to think about it. Jase whirls me around, my dress flares around my legs, and I lose sight of Rufus Winslow.

"I guess he's wishing he hadn't asked me to come."

"Why did you come if you really didn't want to?" I tip my head back and look up at him. He lowers his eyes, and at that moment, we're completely alone. The pain in his gaze hits me straight in the heart. But there's something else there. Smoldering anger and even hatred. "My brother died exactly five years ago today. And my parents are having a fucking party."

The world stops and goes silent as everything finally makes sense. Every single note he ever wrote to me.

Sam was his brother. And he died.

I want to get him off the dance floor, talk to him, say something that will fix what happened. But there's nothing I can do. There are no words that will help. Jase doesn't stop for a second. He keeps dancing, and I follow him because it's the only thing I can do for him right now.

"Jase—"

"Don't," he says. "Don't say anything. Please." He looks at me imploringly. "I can't talk about it now. If I start, then . . ." He shakes his head, and I understand.

"Okay," I whisper, letting him guide me into the next spin, spotting my parents before he pulls me toward him with a flourish. Even though they aren't particularly close with Jase's parents, the guest list was apparently big enough for them to score an invite.

"Thank you for being here." His voice is soft and a little choked up. My heart aches for him.

"There's nowhere I'd rather be."

His eyes flicker. He opens his mouth, then closes it again, and I'd love to know what he wants to tell me, but whatever it is, he doesn't say it. Silence overtakes us, and suddenly the quiet conversations around us are very loud, and I become even more aware of how everyone is staring at us.

The guests. Jase's parents. They don't want their son to dance. They've stopped paying his tuition fees. And here he is, doing it anyway. He's dancing. He's not hiding it. He's not hiding, and his brother is dead, and everything about this evening is terrible.

It breaks my heart.

"Do you trust me?" he murmurs, his face suddenly so close to mine that I would only have to stretch a little to be able to kiss him.

I swallow hard, every inch of my body responding to the husky sound of his voice. "Yes."

His fingers glide lightly over my bare back. He spins me around, grabs my waist with both hands, and lifts me up. I react instinctively, tense every muscle, and stretch my arms wide upward. At that moment, I can fly, and Jase's hands are my wings.

It's over too quickly, and he lowers me back down to the floor, turns me to face him, and brushes a strand of hair that's come loose from my updo off my forehead.

"Thanks for the dance." His lips touch mine, and before I can reply, he takes my hand and guides me off the dance floor. We cross the room and step outside onto a wide terrace with a breathtaking view of Boston. No one's here but us. Everyone else is in the ballroom.

It's dark and quite cold.

"Let me get my coat," I say. I want to pull back my hand so I can wrap my arms around myself, but Jase holds me tight and guides me farther until we're swallowed by darkness. Then he lets me go and takes off his tux jacket. Silently, he lays it on my shoulders, and a tingle goes through my body as I feel his warmth and his familiar scent envelops me.

"Aren't you cold?"

"No," he says. Then he takes my face between his hands—and hesitates. We're so close that his nose is touching mine, and his warm breath caresses my skin. His gaze lands on my lips, and he looks tormented. "I hate this whole thing."

"I know."

"I don't want to be here."

"We can go."

He shakes his head. "I can't. Sam . . . Sam . . ." He stops, and a sad smile crosses his face. Then he kisses me.

I return his kiss, even though a distant voice in my head is telling me it's wrong. We're in public. Someone could come at any moment. It's his mother's birthday party. The anniversary of his brother's death.

But maybe it's not wrong at all. Maybe it's completely right. Because this isn't about me; it's about him.

My lips part, and I welcome his tongue. I can taste the whiskey that he drank, bitter and smoky at the same time. And I taste Jase. All of him. His hands move to the back of my head, plucking one hairpin after another out of my hair before sliding under the jacket and onto my waist. They glide over the bare skin of my back, and suddenly I'm not cold at all. I reach up and twine my fingers in his hair, and as I turn his smooth locks into a tousled mess, he smiles against my lips.

I can't help it—I back away a little because I want to see his smile. His smile, the smile that started everything last year, is so beautiful it hurts.

"Why does being with you make everything a little more bearable?" he whispers, so quietly I can barely hear him. I'm not sure if the words are even meant for me to hear.

I answer him anyway. "Because you make everything a little more bearable too."

His eyes widen, but he doesn't answer. Either he has nothing to say or too much. Instead, he pulls me close again, and I feel his breath against my skin, and then his mouth meets mine.

"Jase!" The deep voice makes us jump apart in surprise.

Shit.

Jase turns around and steps in front of me as if to protect me, while I wrap his jacket more tightly around myself.

"Haven't you ever heard of privacy, Dad?" Jase asks so calmly that I flinch.

I peer past him and see Rufus Winslow just a few yards away from us. His eyes are full of barely suppressed anger as he confronts his son. "What do you think you're doing here?"

Jase shrugs and moves a little more in front of me. It's like someone flipped a switch inside him. He talks differently than he did a moment ago. He moves differently. He *is* different. Harder. Colder. Not himself. "I think it's pretty obvious," he says.

"Why can't you behave, just for once?"

I can't see the expression on his father's face, but I see Jase's shoulders tense.

"I asked you to come so your mother wouldn't be disappointed. But—"

"Spit it out, Dad. Say it already," Jase says sharply. "Go ahead and say that I'm one big disappointment anyway. Say it. You wish I had died instead of Sam. Then your golden child would still be alive, and you wouldn't have to put up with me." He moves nearer to his father, until they're so close they're almost touching. "Say it already," he demands. "Then both of us will probably feel better."

"I don't want to discuss it with you right now, Jase," his father says, coolly and controlled. I flinch, and my heart falters. Did he really just say that?

"Fuck you!" Jase's voice rings with undeniable pain. And burning hatred.

His father doesn't deny the accusation. He just refuses to address it. Something shatters inside me. It might be my heart—again.

"You should go now. And if you ever speak to me that way again—"

Jase pushes back his hair, and a laugh escapes him—so broken it brings tears to my eyes. "Then what? Will I be dead to you?"

He doesn't wait for his father to answer before storming back into the ballroom. I'm frozen in my tracks, though everything inside me demands that I follow him. Instead, I wrap his jacket more tightly around me and look his father straight in the eye. "Maybe you should think about who's disappointing who here," I say, then follow the boy whose heart he just ripped out so easily. His son.

CHAPTER 39

Zoe

When you asked me if I'd ever been in love, I wanted to ask you the same question. But I was afraid of what the answer would be.
—Zoe

I get back inside just in time to see Jase slipping behind the bar while the bartender is busy flirting with a young woman in a tight gold dress. He doesn't notice Jase grabbing a bottle before quickly leaving the room, not bothering to look back.

Shit shit shit.

My heels clack too loudly on the parquet floor as I hurry after him. I'm still wearing his jacket, and I can feel the disapproving glances of the guests. I hear them whispering, but I somehow manage to block out the voices. They aren't important. I rush out of the ballroom and hurry down the stairs to the hotel lobby, but he's gone.

I'm overwhelmed by fear and sick with worry. Sure, he's an adult and can take care of himself. But he has that damn bottle with him, and his dad just more or less confirmed his suspicion that he would have preferred if Jase had died in Sam's place. Nobody should have to hear something like that from their father.

The whole situation is so damn unpredictable. Because even if he can take care of himself, he might not want to right now.

I ask the two receptionists if they saw a blond boy leave the hotel, but they just shake their heads without saying a word. I say a quick *thank you* before heading toward the exit. I've almost reached the door when a familiar voice stops me.

"Zoe, where are you going?" Startled, I whirl around and see my dad following me, looking worried. "Is everything okay?"

I can hear the concern in his voice, and I nod reassuringly. "I'm fine. It's Jase. His . . . His father—" I stop. I can't tell him what happened; it's not my place. "He's not well," I say, and it's not a lie. "I have to find him, and then . . . I don't know."

"Okay. Let's go. I'll come with you."

He puts a hand on my back reassuringly. He doesn't ask what's going on or why I'm wearing Jase's jacket over my dress. Instead, he leaves the hotel with me.

Cold wind hits us at the exit, and I immediately start to shiver. I look around desperately to find the guy in the white shirt whose hair I just messed up a few minutes ago.

"There he is." Dad points across the street, and my heart drops in relief.

Jase is walking along the street with his head lowered. His steps are slow and unsure. He's swaying a little. He still has the bottle in his hand.

Dad leads me across the street, making an apologetic gesture to the drivers who have to brake because of us, honking in annoyance.

"Jase!" He pauses at the sound of my voice, but only for a second. Then he keeps walking. I let go of Dad's hand, ignoring the fact that I'm wearing high heels, and run after him. "Stop," I say as soon as I reach him, grabbing him by the shoulder. He's freezing cold.

"Leave me alone." He breaks away from me, but I stand in front of him and stop him from moving forward.

"I'm certainly not letting you go like this!"

He shakes his head and turns around to walk in the other direction, but I stand in his way again.

"Just leave me alone." His voice breaks, and I see an unmistakable plea. Part of me wants to grant his wish, but I can't. He's falling apart, and I can't leave him alone.

"No," I say calmly. I take the bottle and work it out of his fingers. I put it carefully out of his reach and take his hands. They're cold as ice.

"*Please.*"

"Would you leave *me* alone if I were like this?"

His shoulders tense. I know that he wants to say yes, but he can't do it.

"No," he sighs.

"Then don't try to send me away. Let me be here for you," I say simply. I take off his jacket and put it awkwardly around his shoulders. I hold him tight, even though he's fighting my embrace. I can't leave him to his own devices like this, even if I wanted to.

Not him. Not this broken boy who doesn't want to be saved and has stolen my heart.

I can't save him, but maybe I can help him save himself. Just like he helped me.

CHAPTER 40
Jase

I dreamed about you a lot last year, even though I really just wanted to forget you. But in my dreams, everything was easy. It was all good.
—Jase

Zoe gets me into a car. I don't know where it came from, but when Ethan gets behind the wheel, I figure it belongs to her parents.

She slides into the back seat next to me, and then we're driving off into the dark night.

I should say something, do something, anything. But my mind is totally blank, and my body is numb. It's not because I'm cold; I hardly feel the temperature. I can't feel anything anymore. There's only emptiness.

Zoe says something to her father that I can't understand. The world around me is spinning. I'm drunk, and yet far too sober.

I don't want to discuss it with you now.

I don't want to discuss it with you now.

I don't want to discuss it with you now.

Dad's words replay in my head in an endless fucking loop. I hear them again and again, and I just can't turn them off, no matter how hard I try. It's not long before the car stops and Zoe gets out. I know where they've taken me even before I look out the window. We're at her parents' house. Her dad gets out too, but I stay where I am. I don't want to move. Maybe they'll just forget I'm here.

But a moment later, the door opens. I grimace as a wave of cold air hits me.

Ethan holds out a hand to me. "Come on, Jase. It's time for bed." He beckons to me, and for some reason, I do as he asks. Maybe because he's taken on the role of a father for me more often than my own dad has in the last five years. I heave myself up from the back seat with a groan and hit my head on the top of the doorframe as I get out, but I barely feel the pain. I turn toward the house, look around for Zoe, and start to move, but Ethan stops me.

"Jase."

I turn toward him slowly. My vision is blurred, and I have to blink until the double image clears.

His eyes are hard and cold. He's never seen me like this before. "She likes you. You know that, don't you? So if you ever do anything to hurt her, I'll break your neck. Is that clear?" His voice is firm and determined but completely calm. His presence isn't threatening to me, and he doesn't come any closer.

Still, the warning is clear. I nod. I would never do anything to hurt her.

"Then go sleep it off. I'll see you in the morning." He firmly pushes me toward the house, and I stumble up the steps. I stop at the door, turn around, and realize that Ethan is still standing next to the car, waiting for me to go inside.

I nod to him one last time and enter the hallway. Only after the door closes behind me and the warmth of the house envelops me do I realize how cold I actually am.

Zoe appears at the top of the landing, still wearing her dress, but she's gotten rid of the high heels.

"Come up," she says, and I do as she asks.

I climb the stairs slowly and carefully, then almost trip on the top step. I'm lucky that I don't fall backward. I know the Youngs' house well. Nothing has changed in the last year. The wall is still covered with family photos, pictures of Zoe and Caleb at all ages. The first room on the right is Caleb's, the second is Zoe's. On the left is Ceara's office, and then the large bathroom.

I hear the sound of the shower and pause uncertainly until Zoe sticks her head through the bathroom door. Her eyes are full of warmth, and she's got a tiny smile on her face.

"What took you so long? Come on in—I'm cold." She holds out a hand to me, and I take it. Her skin is freezing to the touch, and my guilty conscience hits me like a blow. She gave me my jacket back.

Steam wafts through the bathroom, and it's so warm I shiver.

Zoe strips off the dress in one fluid motion. It cascades to the floor, and she kicks it aside, takes off her panties, and then stands in front of me, completely naked. She's beautiful, and all at once, my throat tightens. My heart beats out of rhythm, and I wish I could blame it on the alcohol, but I know better. It's because of her.

It's always been because of her.

Zoe slips the jacket off my shoulders before loosening my tie and then slowly unbuttoning my shirt.

"I can do it," I say in a voice so hoarse it can't possibly be mine.

"I know."

She gives me a look that's soft and warm, and something inside me clenches painfully. She stands on her toes and kisses me lightly on the cheek. I feel her breasts against my chest, and my skin rises in goose bumps.

She undoes my belt buckle and then my pants, pushing them down my legs along with my underwear. "You can take off your own socks," she says with a smile, pointing at my feet.

I return her smile for a second, and then I remember what a catastrophic evening it's been, and my smile fades. But I take off my socks anyway and let Zoe push me under the shower. The water is so hot it feels like it came straight from hell.

I close my eyes and let the stream hit my body until I feel her arms go around my waist, and Zoe lays her head against my chest. Blinking, I open my eyes again, see her tangled red hair falling down her back, and then look into her eyes as she tilts her face up to me.

"Just hold tight, okay? Only for a few minutes."

I want to argue, but I'm too weak. I don't say a word; I just close my eyes again as I let her hold me. I try to wash Dad's words out of my head. I try not to think about Sam. Because thinking about Sam today feels like inhaling broken glass.

At some point, Zoe turns off the water, dries us both off, and guides me out of the bathroom to her room. She disappears for a moment before returning with sweats and a hoodie that I assume belong to Caleb.

We dress silently, and then she climbs into bed and reaches out to me expectantly. I'm tired, utterly exhausted, and angry, and at the same time, I feel completely empty. I do as she suggests and crawl under the blankets, falling asleep as soon as my head hits the pillow.

CHAPTER 41
Zoe

I went on some dates last year, several, as part of my therapy. But every time, I could only think that it didn't feel right.
—Zoe

I don't know if it's a noise or a feeling that shakes me out of sleep, or just the sense that something is missing. It takes a minute for me to reorient myself and remember that I'm in my room in my parents' house and not in the dorm. And then there's another moment until I notice the emptiness beside me. Jase, who fell asleep exhausted next to me, is gone. I sit up with a start, suddenly wide awake. My heart races, and I panic. He's gone. Where the hell did he go?

My hands shake as I fumble for my phone on my bedside table, only to realize it's not there. I didn't bring a purse when we went to the party, and I gave my phone to my mom. It's probably still in her pocket. Damn it!

It's still dark; he can't have been gone for long. Hopefully. Maybe he went back to school, or . . . my stomach cramps. I jump out of bed and am about to go check if my parents are home when I notice a light shining through the window of my room. I didn't close the curtains properly, which normally isn't a problem until the sun rises. My window looks out over the garden, which is usually completely dark at night.

But not tonight. I look out the window, and my heart leaps as I see a light in my treehouse. Someone turned on the fairy lights. There's only one person it could be.

I don't waste time wondering; I just grab the woolen blanket from the foot of my bed and hurry downstairs. A pair of Mom's boots sits by the back door, and I slip into them and leave the house. I walk through the frost-covered grass, shivering. The rungs of the ladder feel cold and damp under my fingers as I climb up.

I hesitate at the door. Maybe he came here to be alone. But if that were the case, he wouldn't have stayed at our house at all. And he wouldn't have gone to my treehouse, would he? I shake off the doubt and open the door. If he wants to be alone, he can send me away again.

Jase is sitting on the floor in exactly the same place he sat last year, on the night when he came to me for the first time. He's still wearing Caleb's clothes. His hair falls messily over his forehead, covering his face as he looks down. There are blankets next to him, but he hasn't even bothered to pull one over his legs, and no matter how well insulated the treehouse is, it's not warm in here.

"Jase," I say softly. When he looks up, my heart constricts. His eyes are dull and empty, and tears are running down his cheeks.

CHAPTER 42

Jase

I lied to you about two questions you asked me. One of them was my very first answer. I didn't follow you after the dance because I was bored. I followed you because I was worried about you. I lied when you asked me what I saw when I looked at you too. When I look at you, I see everything we could be, and that scares the shit out of me.

—Jase

At the sound of Zoe's voice, I look up and immediately wish I hadn't. There's empathy in her eyes, reflecting the pain in mine. I don't bother to wipe away the tears. They'll just be followed by more anyway.

I had a dream about Sam. That doesn't happen very often. Only on the night of our birthday, and apparently now. The anniversary of his death.

It hurt so much when I woke up because in my dream, he was still alive. He was happy; he was smiling. His heart was still beating. He was *alive*, damn it.

Then I woke up, and reality bowled me over, as though he hadn't been gone for the last five years.

We left him behind, lying in a graveyard in LA. *I* left him behind. The other me. And I blame myself for that even more than I do Mom and Dad.

"Jase." Zoe whispers my name again, her voice stricken.

I don't reply.

Part of me wants to send her away so she doesn't see me like this. I don't want her to see how frail I am, how desperate. I can't bear this horrible weakness, the pain that's tearing me apart. It's always there. That's why I'm trying to block it out. The pain, and all the other things I don't want to feel. But sometimes, like now, I can't do it. It's just too much. And that's why the other part of me, the one that's lonely, sad, angry, and hopelessly lost, wants her to stay.

Zoe comes closer and puts a blanket around my shoulders. Then she stuffs pillows behind our backs and sits down next to me before spreading two other blankets over our legs and snuggling up to me. She leans her head against my chest, her ear directly over my heart.

"You can talk to me if you want," she whispers. I tense immediately. "If not, that's okay too. I'm here. Talk to me or not. But I'm not leaving unless you want me to." She takes my hand and locks her fingers with mine. I'm not able to pull away.

It's a tiny gesture. I've held her hand hundreds of times in the last few weeks, but this feels different somehow. More intimate. More real.

Something inside me breaks with a painful shattering sound. I close my eyes, and my head tilts back until it touches the wall behind me. Silence falls between us, heavy and oppressive. I can't breathe anymore. Zoe squeezes my hand, and again I feel the salty tears running down my cheeks. I hate crying. I hate this weakness and pain. I don't want to feel any of it. I want it to stop. I just want it to stop.

After a while, I break the silence between us. I don't want to talk, not about Sam. But sometimes wanting to and needing to are different things. "Sam was my twin brother."

I feel Zoe tense.

"He was fourteen when he died, a few months before we moved to Boston. His heart just stopped beating. We were at one of his football games; I don't even remember who they were playing. He fell in the middle of the field and didn't get up again. He just died."

Every word cuts my throat like a razor blade. I've never said them aloud. I never told anyone here that Sam died, or how. Not once in five years.

Zoe remains silent but hitches a little closer to me. Her ear is still over my heart, which is beating far too fast. It hurts so much that I want to tear it out of my chest just to make it stop.

"Sam was . . . he was the golden child. Dad's favorite. He played football and always got good grades. He was open and cheerful, and he wanted to be a doctor. He was everything that I'm not, and he was my best friend. Sam was—" I stop, unable to get the words out.

He was the other me.

"We moved because he was everywhere in Los Angeles. We couldn't escape him anywhere. The whole neighborhood knew. Mom couldn't even go shopping at the supermarket without someone mentioning him. She . . . she couldn't take it. Neither could Dad. That's why we moved to Boston. To start again." I laugh bitterly and sniff. "As if it could have been that easy. But they tried. They stopped talking about Sam completely. It felt like they were just canceling him from our lives, just because he was dead." A raw sob escapes me, and I can't hide it. Everything hurts. My body, my heart. Everything.

Zoe raises her head and sits up. There are tears in her eyes to match the ones she wipes from my face. But she still doesn't say a word.

"It never bothered Dad that I was a dancer when Sam was alive. Because he always had Sam. He was the son that Dad always wanted. But after his death . . . I wasn't enough. Not the way I was . . . the way I *am*. And I'm still not enough. I never will be."

"That's not true," Zoe whispers, leaning her forehead against mine. I let her. Her closeness is the only thing keeping me from falling apart completely.

"Mom threw herself into her work," I continue, as if she hadn't spoken. "She pushed every thought of Sam away. She didn't care when Dad complained about my ballet. Or when he tried to force me to go to Harvard. She just . . . stopped being interested in me. Last year, she paid my tuition. Not because she actually wanted to support me, but because she hoped that I would see for myself that ballet wasn't my path. But she cared as little as Dad did about what I really wanted."

"Jase, I . . ." Zoe stops, shakes her head, and expels her breath in a sigh.

"I think it would be different if I didn't look like him," I mumble and squeeze my eyes shut. I see Sam every time I look in a mirror. Maybe that's my punishment for being lucky enough to avoid the same undiagnosed heart problem that cost my brother his life. I see him every day, and he's not here. He's never coming back. And I will never be like him.

"It doesn't matter what you look like. You're you." She kisses me on the temples, and her lips are warm and soft.

"I'm alone." Another secret that I never told her.

"No, you're not." Another kiss. "I'm with you."

I want so badly to believe her. But she rejected me once already, and there's no guarantee she won't do it again. It's not fair to compare this to last year; I get it. Everything is different this time. But that doesn't mean that she'll stay.

"My parents wish I'd died instead of Sam." That's the next secret, but now it's one she already knows.

She says nothing and doesn't argue with me because she knows I won't believe her. Dad was very clear about it tonight. Instead, she holds me so tightly I can barely breathe. I allow myself to lean against her, giving myself permission for this moment of weakness, because it doesn't matter anymore. She knows. She knows everything, and I feel naked and vulnerable.

Zoe pulls away enough that she can see my face. Her eyes are red, but her gaze is clear as she looks at me. She *sees* me. She sees everything that's broken beyond repair.

CHAPTER 43

Jase

I wish I'd told you about Sam before. And
I wish that you could have met him.
—Jase

I wake up to someone gently stroking my temples. My eyes flutter open. Zoe is lying close to me, looking at me with a mixture of concern and warmth. Dim light filters through the curtains, bright enough for me to see the guilty expression on her face when she realizes I'm awake.

"I'm sorry, I didn't mean to wake you up."

I reach for her hand as she tries to pull it back, first kissing it and then returning it to my temple. "That's all right. It's a nice way to wake up." I smile faintly as Zoe strokes my skin again. I'm so exhausted.

"How do you feel?" Her voice is soft and gentle, and my eyes close again of their own accord. I don't want her to ask me any questions. I want her to keep talking and tell me something so I can listen to her without having to think.

"Hungover," I reply as the throbbing starts behind my eyes. My stomach is also pretty numb. "Tired. Empty."

Alone.

But that's bullshit, isn't it? I'm not alone. She's here. She's here, caressing my skin and running her hands through my hair.

"Jase? Look at me."

Reluctantly, I open my eyes. This time, there's something in her gaze that I can't interpret. Something deep and intense.

"I'm here, okay?" she says, as though she can read my mind. I remember she said the same thing last night, and I didn't answer.

"Okay," I reply, because I want her to be here. And I never want her to leave again. This thing between us is the only thing that has made sense in the last few weeks. Fuck, no, in the last year. The only thing that even came close to feeling right. "Don't push me away again." The words come out as a soft whisper, a plea, and I want to take them right back because they're so weak and pathetic. But I am weak, and I'm not strong enough to pretend I'm not.

Her eyes go wide, and a familiar pain flashes in them. "I promise." She slides closer to me, slipping one leg between mine and burying her face against my chest. "I'm sorry I let you down last year," she murmurs into my T-shirt.

"And I'm sorry that someone hurt you," I whisper into her hair.

"I'm sorry that your parents are assholes."

She looks up, gazing at me with wet eyes, and my throat tightens. I swallow heavily. If she starts to cry, I probably will too. But she doesn't. She kisses me gently, and it makes me feel safe.

I pull away to look at her. There's an unspoken question in her eyes. I have one too, and I can't resist it. Not anymore. "What is this thing between us?"

I realize as I ask that I already know the answer. Because it started ages ago. Because even as everything was complicated and awful, it was also real and right.

Zoe smiles, and my heart skips a beat.

"Everything."

CHAPTER 44

Zoe

I knew from the start that you and I were more than just Caleb's little sister and Caleb's best friend. I didn't know what we were, only that we were more. From the very beginning.
—Zoe

"Why do you call me Pixie, anyway?" I ask. I never asked before because it didn't feel right. But now . . . now everything is different.

It's late morning now, and aside from a short visit to the bathroom, we haven't gotten out of bed once.

Jase leans back and pulls me with him until I'm lying on top of him. He tenderly brushes a strand of hair behind my ear. "Do you remember the first time we met?"

I nod. As if I could forget!

"It was the first Friday after summer vacation." His voice is smooth as velvet, and my stomach starts to flutter. "We had just moved here from LA, and I didn't know anyone. But Caleb sat next to me in math, and we hit it off right away. That Friday, he invited me to your house after football practice. We were sitting in the living room when you came home from your ballet lesson."

"I know. You were playing Mario Kart. He was killing you."

Jase sighs and grimaces at the memory. "I was really bad. Anyway, you came back from your lesson, and you were wearing this green dress with narrow straps and a skirt that puffed around your legs. Your hair was down and you were . . ." He takes a deep breath and shrugs a little awkwardly. "Well, you looked like a little fairy."

"Is that why you call me Pixie? Because I reminded you of a fairy?" I have to smile.

He actually blushes, which is pretty cute. "My fourteen-year-old self was obviously not very creative."

"But your fourteen-year-old self was also extremely cute. I always liked it when you called me that," I admit, because I want him to know. I want him to know everything. "It was always kind of . . ." I bite my bottom lip, and Jase stares at my mouth. "Caleb's other friends were always nice to me. They were my friends too. He never excluded me. Still, to the others I was the little sister, first and foremost. It was different with you. You saw me."

He turns us around, gently pressing me into the mattress and kissing me tenderly. "It was impossible to overlook you."

"You too," I say. It's just the truth. I always saw him everywhere. Long before we started sharing our secrets.

Jase gazes at me silently, and it feels like a caress. He waits for me to continue.

"You were the only boy ballet dancer at our school."

"Yes, and I was reminded of that every day." Jase's brow furrows. "Sometimes that kind of sucked."

"Teenagers can be pretty brutal," I reply, and a faint grin crosses his face.

"True words."

"Always." I slide underneath him, and all at once, his hips are right on top of mine. My legs wrap around his backside of their own accord.

"So that's why I was so impossible to overlook? Just because I was the only boy dancer?" Jase asks, tilting his hips a little, just enough to make me catch my breath and send heat rushing through my veins.

"No. You were just different. Quieter than the other boys I knew. Caleb and his friends were all loud and very . . . present. You never talked much, you never made stupid comments, and you barely ever smiled. I wanted you to smile at me. You have a beautiful smile." I tap the corners of his mouth with my fingertips. He smiles, and my heart makes strange flutters in my chest.

"I think you were the only one who made me smile." Jase rolls off me, pulls us both toward the head of the bed, and pulls the covers over us. Everything smells like him—why does he smell so damn good?

"It always felt like a little victory to me when you smiled." I turn onto my side so I can look at him, sliding a little closer.

"Does that mean that every time I smiled at you, I lost?" he asks with a grin.

"No, you didn't . . . I don't know how to explain it."

"That's okay. I think I know what you mean." He wraps a strand of my hair around his finger, and all at once, he looks thoughtful.

"What are you thinking?" I stroke his cheek gently.

I expect it to be about his parents, his sister, or Sam. But I'm wrong.

"Do you think Caleb still has a problem with us?"

I stiffen. Crap. I should have guessed he'd ask me about this sometime.

"No," I answer honestly. "I talked to Caleb a few days ago. After you and I . . ." I can't say it. I blush. "After we slept together," I continue, before I can lose my nerve. "I had a talk with him. Caleb was the only one I could even talk to last year, and I . . . couldn't help it. But no, he doesn't have a problem with it."

"But he had one last year." It's not a question but a statement. There's no point in lying. It was pretty obvious that Caleb didn't like it when Jase and I kissed at the party.

"Yes. But that's all I can say about it."

For a moment, it looks like Jase wants to argue. But then he nods, and a sad smile crosses his face. "I miss him."

"I think he misses you too."

"He always reminded me of Sam."

I push a few strands of blond hair off his forehead, which immediately fall back into place. "In what way?" I ask carefully, because I have the feeling it would do Jase good to talk about Sam.

"He was the same type of person. Sam was a football player, like Caleb. And he had the same kind of self-confidence. The same openness. The same sense of humor." I hear something wistful in his voice, and all at once there's a big lump in my throat. "It might sound strange, but sometimes it seemed like fate put me next to Caleb in math class on purpose. As if the universe knew I needed a friend like him."

I put my hands on either side of his face and pull him down to me for a quick kiss. "Maybe that's what happened."

"Yeah, maybe." This time, his smile is a little less sad. "I'm pretty sure, actually."

He kisses me again, and then we stop talking for a while.

* * *

I'm lying on Jase's bare chest as it rises and falls gently. His breathing is calm, but his heart beats a little faster each time I run my fingers over his skin. I love that I'm the reason for it. Everything feels so simple right now. With his past and mine. There are no more secrets. Only shared truths.

When Jase's stomach growls, I look up with a grin. "I think it's breakfast time."

"What time is it anyway?"

"I have no idea. My phone is still in my mom's purse. But I think it's time to get up." I sit up, but Jase has other plans. His hand slides over the back of my neck, and I'm amazed at how such a simple touch can make my whole body tingle.

Laughing, I pull away from him before he can kiss me. "I know you're hungry. Let's go eat. If we're lucky, Mom will have made pancakes."

"All right." He gives in with a sigh. "But only because your mom makes the best pancakes ever."

I get up and pull him out of bed. I hope Mom really did make pancakes. I get clothes for him from Caleb's room again, and we get dressed and go downstairs. An old ABBA song is playing in the kitchen, and I can hear Dad singing along quietly. I can't help but smile. I stop in the doorway and watch with amusement as he dances around the kitchen. The dishwasher is open, and the smell of coffee fills the air.

Dad stops when he notices us. "Good morning," he says, continuing to load the dishwasher. "Ceara made pancakes." He points to the plate, which is under a lid on the kitchen island.

"Jackpot," Jase whispers in my ear, grinning.

"With blueberries or chocolate chips?" I grab Jase's hand and pull him over to the island.

"What do you think? Chocolate chips, of course." I hear Mom's amused voice from the living room. She's sitting on the sofa, her legs up and a book in her hand.

"That's what I hoped," I say, lifting the lid off the plate. I grab two more plates from the cupboard and distribute the pancakes between them.

"I know which ones you like best." Mom gets up, picks up the cup that's sitting on the table in front of her, and comes over to us. "Is there still enough coffee?"

"When has there ever not been enough coffee?" Dad asks with a theatrical sigh.

Mom kisses him on the cheek. "Never."

I look at Jase, who is observing the whole thing with a mixture of amusement and longing. My heart feels heavy as I remember what he told me about how he lost his home last year. He didn't mean his parents' house.

I nudge him gently and walk over to the dining table, carrying our plates, while Mom and Dad talk about our household's coffee consumption.

"Zoe, can you please tell your mother that drinking too much coffee is unhealthy?" Dad gives me a pleading look, but I shake my head apologetically.

"I can't, because I'd like some too. Can you bring me a cup, Mom?"

She gives me a conspiratorial grin. "Sure thing. You too, Jase?"

He stiffens very slightly before relaxing again, but I notice it anyway. He clears his throat, his voice a little hoarse as he answers. "Yes, thanks."

"Still with milk, no sugar?"

He nods.

"Zoe?"

"Me too."

Humming, Mom takes two cups out of the cupboard and pours coffee for us while Dad watches her, shaking his head. Mom comes over and puts the cups down on the table in front of us.

"Nice to have you back." Smiling, she musses Jase's hair as if it hasn't been a year since she last did it.

Jase looks at me and smiles, and my heart skips a beat. "Nice to be here."

CHAPTER 45
Jase

So much shit has happened in the last few years. My life is a disaster, but sometimes I'm almost grateful for it. Otherwise, we would never have moved to Boston, and I would never have met you.
—Jase

My heart feels strangely light as I lie back in my own bed that evening, Zoe snuggled up in my arms. We've spent practically the whole day in bed, moving from her room in her parents' house back to the dorm. From her bed to mine. Now she's lying next to me, tracing large circles on my chest, and somehow everything's fine.

What is this thing between us?

Everything.

And it really is. It's remarkable how far away Mom's party seems, and the fight with Dad. My breakdown in Zoe's treehouse. But it hasn't even been twenty-four hours, and everything has changed. Because of her.

"Why haven't I ever seen this show?" Zoe asks, snapping me out of my thoughts and reminding me that *Peaky Blinders* is flickering across the screen of my laptop.

"Because you have a weakness for *Gilmore Girls* and all the doctor shows in the world."

She grins. "That's right. I think—" she breaks off as there's a knock at the door.

"That must be Skye. I haven't answered her thousand messages yet."

Groaning, I swing my legs out of bed and go to the door. I open it—and immediately wish that I hadn't. Mom is standing in the hallway, her hair pulled up in a messy bun that I've never seen before. She's wearing jeans and an oversized hoodie. I'm momentarily shocked she'd leave the house dressed this way. She's pale, and her eyes are red like she's been crying.

"Mom, what are you doing here?" I ask.

"Can we talk?"

Fuck no.

"Absolutely not."

The last thing I want to do is talk to my mother now. Not when I'm finally feeling better for the first time in ages. I don't want to hear what she has to say.

"Jase, please."

"No," I snap at her. "I don't want to be with you, Mom. Not with you, not with Dad. You celebrated your birthday on the anniversary of Sam's death, and you didn't care. You didn't care how it was affecting me, or Lia either. You just ignored it. Sam's day isn't yours."

Mom flinches. A look of guilt flashes in her eyes, and my heart constricts. But guilt isn't enough.

"I didn't ignore it," she says, but I silence her with a wave of my hand before she can continue.

"Yes, you did. And you know what? I couldn't care less what you have to say about it. Honestly. It doesn't touch me. Have your parties. Let Dad talk down to you. Live your life. But leave me out of that shit."

"Jase, no. Please, let's talk." She wrings her hand. She looks like she's about to burst into tears at any second. In spite of it all, my stomach cramps painfully. I can't remember the last time I saw Mom cry. But it isn't enough to make me cave.

"I don't want to talk to you. Why can't you ever respect what I want? You've completely ignored me for the last two years. You let Dad kick me out. You cut my tuition money because I didn't do what you wanted. Just do what I ask for once and leave!"

She flinches again at every word I say. I hate this. I just want her to go.

"Jase, please," Mom begs, but I'm done. I'm done with my whole family that isn't really a family and the permanent struggle of trying to make them want me. I'm tired of waiting for them to accept who I am. And who I'm not.

Without another word, I close the door in her face and lean against it, breathing heavily. I close my eyes. Why did she come? Why can't she just leave me alone?

"Jase?" Zoe's soft, unsure voice reminds me that I'm not alone. I open my eyes. She's still sitting on my bed, watching me worriedly. She saw everything, and I'm glad.

"Are you okay?"

I shake my head, and she holds out both hands to me. Exhausted, I climb back into bed with her and let her hold me.

We don't talk anymore. But she's there, and at some point, I fall asleep.

CHAPTER 46

Zoe

Sometimes I wonder if I'll ever be able to be happy again. How can it be possible, after everything I've been through?
—Zoe

Dancers' bodies are pure miracles. We're perceived as delicate, fine, and fragile, but very few people know how much strength is hidden in our slender muscles. Most people don't understand how we can bring our bodies to their limits. They don't understand the forces that impact our knees and ankles when we land hard on the ground after a leap, how we make our bodies perform the most unnatural movements, flexing almost to the point of impossibility.

Dancing isn't just beauty, aesthetics, and art. Dancing is pain, abused feet, and inflamed muscles. It hurts. The audience can't see any of that. They see courage and grace, movements that are inconceivable, dancers smiling through the pain because they're doing what they love. It's what makes us special. What we do best.

Dancing is all of this. Beauty, pain, and burning passion. Sometimes it's bitter disappointment and frustration. But there are also days when everything is right, when you have the right partner and trust yourself.

Today is one of those days.

I'm dancing. I'm dancing with Jase, and it's almost perfect. Every movement, every turn, every lift. His hands on my body, on my waist, my hands, my legs. He's holding me, and I feel safe. Safe and free at the same time. My heart hammers against my ribs, and every muscle is as tense as it can be. It's exhausting in the best possible way. I'm close to my limits, but this time they feel different. They're limits I can exceed. I go deeper in back bends and stretch my legs higher. I ignore the pulling in my muscles and the painful throbbing in my feet. When I catch a glimpse of myself in the mirror, I hardly recognize myself. I am radiant, and I feel beautiful.

For the first time in months, my body isn't working against me. We're in harmony again. I'm in control.

"Excellent, Zoe," Francesca says. She nods appreciatively as Jase and I finally pause, breathing heavily. She smiles at me, a hint of pride glinting in her eyes. I don't think I've ever seen her smile before. "Keep up the good work."

My face glows with exertion and self-consciousness. My skin is covered with a thin film of sweat. I nod and manage to thank her.

"Jessica and Theo, you're next." Francesca beckons them toward the middle of the room while Jase and I retreat to the edge, hand in hand.

It's a bit crazy how fast I've gotten used to holding his hand. Talking to him. Just being with him. Some days it feels as though we've never done anything else.

It's been almost two weeks since Victoria Winslow came to his door. Two weeks during which his parents haven't reached out to him at all. It still hurts when I think about how his parents have treated him. It's just not right.

But in these two weeks, Jase and I have spent every night together. He sleeps in my room, and I sleep in his. We wake up every morning together. Sometimes I wonder how I can suddenly be so happy.

It's strange, isn't it?

Two months ago, everything was different. Jase and I. Our dancing.

How could everything change so fast for the better?

"Stop brooding," Jase whispers, pulling me over toward Mae and Skye.

"I'm not brooding."

"Yes, you are. I can see it. When you're thinking too much, you always raise your eyebrow a little bit."

"Really?" Now I exaggerate it, and Jase smiles. I love his smile. But since the party, there's always been something sad in it. Maybe it was there before, and I just didn't notice because he never showed me the extent of his sadness. Now it's different. I want to chase away the sadness. I'm just not sure if I'll be able to.

"Yes," he replies. He kisses my temple, and Skye makes a gagging sound.

"You're disgusting," she says, but there's a wistful undertone to her voice. And a slight bitterness.

"No, they're not," Mae says and nudges me, grinning. "They're just in love."

"Seems like everyone's in love at the moment." Skye grimaces, and again, I get the feeling there's more to her words than she's letting on. We've spent more time together in the last two weeks. I like her, and I can understand why Jase is friends with her.

"You'll fall in love too," Mae says, trying to cheer her up. But Skye shakes her head with a shudder.

"No need, thanks!"

"But—"

"Hush!" Francesca says, interrupting Mae and looking at us disapprovingly.

A guilty expression crosses Mae's face as she mouths an apology.

We silently watch Jessica and Theo, and then it's Mae and Ches's turn. Each couple performs the choreography that Francesca showed us at the beginning of class.

While I'm watching Mae, I start to get a prickling sensation at the back of my neck. Someone's staring at me. I know who it is by instinct, and my hunch is confirmed when I turn to see Charlotte standing next to Devon on the other side of the room. She seems angry, probably because she heard Francesca compliment me. I return her gaze with more defiance than I actually feel, because I'm tired of her constantly making me feel insecure. I'm tired of it only taking one look from her to make me question myself. It can't go on like this. Not if we're going to be in the same classes together for the next four years.

Part of me wants to talk to her properly. To find some kind of closure. But I don't think I'm quite that courageous yet.

* * *

"Why do you always look up at the balcony when we're in the theater?" Mae asks curiously.

I blush, feeling caught out. "What do you mean?" I ask innocently. But my glowing red face gives me away. It's Saturday, and we're helping the set designers assemble part of the set so they can check if everything fits so far or if any changes need to be made.

Mae points to the upper tiers. "A bunch of empty seats really aren't that exciting."

She's right. But whenever I'm in the theater, I think about how Jase and I kissed on the stage and what we did in the balcony. And then I get lost in daydreams and—

"See? You're doing it again!" She laughs. "So what were you two doing up there, huh?"

"You don't want to know." Jase's voice makes us both jump. He's standing behind us with a cheeky grin on his face, but his eyes are gleaming. "You'll just be jealous."

Mae groans theatrically and takes me by the wrist. "Please, make me jealous!"

"I don't think that would be—" I stop as I see someone walking toward us. It's a blond girl with familiar features and green eyes. Lia.

She stops directly in front of us. Her eyes dart briefly to Mae and me before coming to rest on her brother.

"Can we talk?"

I hold my breath involuntarily, and I can see Jase tense. For a moment, I'm sure he's going to send her away, just like he did with his mom. But he gives me a brief look with an unspoken question. I nod almost imperceptibly. He won't admit it, and maybe he doesn't even know it, but I think he needs his sister. Maybe I'm just trying to convince myself of that because I find it so sad that the two of them are such strangers to each other. We've talked about his parents in the last few weeks, and about Sam, but never about Lia.

There's something going on between them that I don't understand, but I don't want to push Jase to talk about it. I only want him to do it if and when he's ready.

As he turns to face Lia, his face goes blank. "Okay. Let's go outside."

Lia's eyes widen in surprise, like she didn't expect Jase to comply so quickly. But she regains her composure quickly, her face just as expressionless as his. It's crazy how alike they are. They're mirrors for each other, and sometimes I wonder if that's why it's so difficult for them to deal with each other.

Jase said he finds it hard to look in the mirror because he always sees Sam. Maybe Lia has the same problem.

I stroke the back of Jase's hand as he walks past me. He swallows, then follows his sister. I watch them go with a sinking feeling in my stomach.

"Don't worry, Zoe," Mae says. "Whatever it is they have to talk about, they're not going to rip each other's heads off."

"I know."

But I'm still worried, because I'm not totally sure she's right.

CHAPTER 47
Jase

I see Lia every day, and she hasn't asked me even once where I lived over the summer. Okay, we don't really talk to each other, and it's not like I want to. But I wish that she'd at least ask.
—Jase

I follow Lia silently. She doesn't just leave the auditorium but leads me out of the building entirely. It's cold outside, but the sun is shining, and Lia's hair glows golden as the light falls on it. I watch as she pulls her coat tighter around her body. My jacket is still in the auditorium, but I'm not cold. My heart is beating much too fast for that. Adrenaline flows through my veins.

Lia is in a different group for the production, which means she came today just to talk to me. We haven't said a word to each other since Mom's party.

"What do you want?" I ask as the silence between us becomes uncomfortable.

"This thing between you and Zoe is pretty serious, isn't it?"

"You want to talk to me about Zoe?" I stop short. She can forget it. She hasn't shown any interest in me in years; she doesn't need to start now.

She shrugs. "You're a good match."

"How exactly would you know that? You don't know me at all."

"Of course I know you."

"Bullshit," I growl. I hear a rushing sound in my ears. "If you knew me, you would have stopped Mom from having her fucking party on the anniversary of Sam's death. If you knew me, you would have let me know that you were going out to eat on her birthday, or whatever it was you were doing without me."

She flinches like I slapped her, but I'm not done yet.

"You'd have to talk to me to know me, Ophelia. But you don't talk to me. You're like Mom and Dad. You only come to me when you want something. I mean, you only offered me money so I'd behave for Mom and Dad. You don't know me, and I don't think you really want to. So what the hell do you want now?"

"I paid your tuition fees!" she shouts at me. Angry red splotches appear on her neck. She's losing control. Who knows when the last time was that this happened. Or if it ever has.

"So? Do you want an award?"

"A *thank you* would be enough, for starters," she hisses.

"Thank you." The mockery in my voice is unmistakable. I'm such an asshole. I know I should be grateful to her. But I can't. I'm so damn jealous that it hurts. "Thanks for giving me the tuition fee for this semester after not only our parents but also our grandparents refused to support me. Thanks for giving me the money after Dad went out of his way to make sure I couldn't even get a fucking student loan just so he could get his way."

Lia turns pale, like this is totally new information to her. But that's impossible. There's no way she doesn't know.

"God, Jase! They were only trying to protect you. They want the best for you. And yes, maybe their methods aren't ideal, but they care about you."

I burst out laughing in disbelief. Yes, of course. That must be it.

"Do you have any idea how often Mom and Dad argue about you being so emotionally unavailable? They blame each other for you being the way you are. It sucks! Since you've been here, all they talk about is how to get you into Harvard. How they're going to get you to talk to them again. How they want you to be part of the family. Everything is about you."

I stare at her, stunned. "You can't be serious. It's never about me! Ever since Sam died, it's always been about what they want."

I feel like I'm repeating myself over and over again, but no one listens to me. Not Mom and Dad, not Lia.

My sister flinches when I say Sam's name. "They only want what's best for you," she repeats, like a broken record.

"They have no idea what's best for me. And you obviously don't either, otherwise you wouldn't be here spouting this crap. So what do you want from me, Lia? Why did you want to talk to me?"

"Mom has been devastated since you sent her away."

My stomach cramps, but I push down my growing guilty conscience. "So? I was devastated too, when they threw me out last year. I didn't know where to go. You didn't even reach out to me once, if you'll recall. They didn't either. So don't tell me that Mom's upset. I was upset too."

"Please. You were with Caleb and your wonderful extra family all summer. It can't have been that bad." Lia's anger has turned into recalcitrance, but she has no fucking idea what I went through. None.

"I wasn't with Caleb," I whisper. Everything inside of me has gone shockingly silent and cold.

Lia sticks out her chin defiantly and crosses her arms over her chest. She doesn't want to give in, but her eyes have the telltale gleam of tears. "Where were you, then?"

"It doesn't matter." I sigh, and suddenly I'm tired. I'm so sick of these fucking discussions that only turn in circles. I just want peace and quiet. "Why did you want to talk to me, Lia? Did you change your mind? Do you want the money back because I didn't thank you?"

"No." She shakes her head, strands of blond hair falling in her face. "I want . . ." She bites her lower lip, shakes her head again, and laughs joylessly. "Forget it. It was a mistake."

She turns to leave without waiting for an answer. To be honest, I don't have one. I feel empty as I watch her go and wonder how it got this far. I wonder what Sam would say if he saw us like this. He'd probably be very disappointed.

My head hurts. Lia disappears into the dorm, and I turn away.

When I get back to the theater, Zoe is gone.

CHAPTER 48

Zoe

Is it really possible to get over the past? Or does it always catch up with you at one point or another?
—Zoe

Later, I won't be able to remember what I was doing backstage. I think Katie wanted me to get something from one of the prop rooms. In the end, it doesn't really matter why I go there, just that I do.

As I'm turning a corner, I see Reed and Charlotte walking down the corridor. Reed looks angry, and he's holding Charlotte by the arm. He pulls her after him, and she tries to break away, but he's gripping her arm too tightly. I follow them without thinking and suddenly get a bad feeling in my stomach. Charlotte is clearly trying to get away from him, but she doesn't look scared. I walk quietly so they won't hear my footsteps; they haven't noticed me yet. I briefly wonder if I should get help. Whatever is going on between the two of them doesn't seem to be good. But instead, I keep following them and watch Reed pull Charlotte into one of the changing rooms. He slams the door behind them.

But I can still hear their voices clearly when I stop outside the room. There's just a gap of a few inches at the bottom, just wide enough that I can hear every word.

"You're making this more dramatic than it needs to be," Charlotte says.

"*I'm* making this dramatic?" I can hear the incredulity in Reed's voice. "Are you fucking serious?" he says sharply.

I'm about to open the door and ask if everything's okay when I hear my own name and stop dead.

"I can't get Zoe expelled!" Reed hisses.

My body turns to ice. Freezing cold from one second to the next. *What the hell?*

"Of course you can. Just talk to your uncle," Charlotte says condescendingly, and I wonder how I could have been worried for her even for a second.

"I can't! What am I supposed to tell him? That you're a jealous bitch because, unlike you, Zoe has parents who actually love her? Because she's actually liked by her classmates? Should I tell him that you want to get rid of her because she's better than you? I don't know a thing about ballet. Just because I convinced him to accept you here doesn't mean—"

"I got accepted because I'm good!"

He laughs. "You got accepted because you blackmailed me, Charlotte. And then I had to make up some bullshit about your reach on social media being good for the school and how this place means soooo much to you."

His voice sends a shudder down my spine. I should really leave, but I'm paralyzed. Charlotte blackmailed Reed. This is insane. And now she's trying to get me expelled?

"Do I have to remind you why I was able to blackmail you in the first place?" Her voice has become menacingly soft.

"Fuck you, Charlotte!"

"No, thank you. Talk to your uncle, Reed, or I swear to you, I'll tell the whole world that Zoe wasn't lying and that you were the one who raped her."

My heart stops. One second. Two seconds. Then it starts again, much too fast. I'm dizzy. Why am I suddenly so dizzy?

What did she say? My mind is messing with me. This isn't really happening; it can't be.

"Forget it! If I'm going down, you're going down with me, Charlotte! You're just as guilty as I am. You put the roofies in her drink, and you sent me to her room. You told me she wanted it."

I.

Can't.

Breathe.

"And you're a gullible idiot! Make sure she's expelled, and then no one will find out. Now get out of here. If anyone sees you, there will be questions."

The door opens, and I'm still standing there, motionless. Charlotte. Reed. Me.

One night.

Then everything was different.

My chest feels much too narrow. So does my whole body. Everything is so, so wrong.

Charlotte gave me the roofies. My best friend.

Reed raped me. My brother's oldest friend.

I need to run far, far away, and I fight the urge to scream, cry, and call for help. But I can't move.

I'm paralyzed.

Breathe, Zoe.

Reed raped me.

Charlotte helped him.

"Fuck!" Reed's yell snaps me out of my trance, and I whirl around and run. But his legs are longer. He's faster than me, and Charlotte doesn't bother to keep up with him. I want to scream as he grabs me by the wrist and drags me into the next room, but I can't make a sound. My voice doesn't work.

It's so dark in here. So dark. The door closes with a solid click behind us.

PART 5

Coda

Phase Five of the
Pas de Deux

CHAPTER 49
Zoe

For me, the fear of panic is sometimes worse than the panic itself.
—Zoe

"Zoe, it's not what you think," Reed says, swearing as he fumbles around for the light switch. A second later, brightness floods the small room. It doesn't make me feel any better. Definitely not any safer.

This can't be real. It *can't* be.

I must be dreaming, and I'll wake up any second from this nightmare. There's no other possibility.

But it's not a nightmare. It's real.

I'm leaning against the closed door, and it's hard and cold against my back. Reed stands in front of me, too close, trapping me between his body and the door.

I'm captive, and he's here.

He did this to me.

Everything about him is so familiar. His light-brown hair that's always combed back but falling over his forehead anyway. His gray-green eyes with the long black lashes I've always envied him for.

The little scar on his forehead from falling off the ladder of our treehouse when he was twelve. The dimples in his cheeks that are visible even when he's not smiling, like right now.

I've known him for most of my life, and he's the one who broke me.

Shame washes over me.

I feel so dirty.

Abandoned.

Broken.

Alone.

"Really, it's not what you think," he repeats, like maybe I just didn't understand him the first time. I wish that were true. I wish I hadn't overheard them at all.

I want my ignorance back. Immediately.

"Isn't it? What exactly do I think?" My voice sounds thin and suffocated. It's a miracle that I was even able to speak.

My body is numb, apart from where Reed's hand is still touching my arm. That burns like acid.

He's much too close to me. So close that I can smell his scent, sour and masculine.

I'll never be able to forget it again.

I want to get away. I have to. But I can't move. I've lost control over my body. Again.

And again, it's because of him.

You're in shock.

Yes, I am.

Somewhere deep inside, I know I should scream. Call for help. I know I have to do *something*.

"You—"

"Let me go!" I tug on my arm, but his grip gets stronger. I'm bowled over by panic.

No no no. Not again. Please, not again. Please please please.

"You have to listen to me, Zoe!"

"I heard you both. I heard what you said." I sob, and my whole body starts to shake. My stomach is turning, and I think I'm going to throw up. "It was you. You were the one who did that to me." I want to scream, but I can't. My voice isn't doing what I want.

Reed shakes his head, his face twisted in desperation. "It wasn't like that. I . . . Charlotte told me you were waiting for me. That you wanted me. I was drunk. I didn't know . . . I didn't . . ." he stammers, and something inside me snaps. It hurts. It hurts so damn much.

"Charlotte told you that I wanted you to rape me?" I whisper. Tears run over my face, hot and salty.

His gaze follows the tears, then comes to rest on my mouth. I want to vomit and die and kill him, all at the same time.

"She said that you liked me, and you were embarrassed about being the only one of your friends who was still a virgin. She knew that I was into you, and I thought . . . I thought . . ." he breaks off, his voice shaking with agony.

I want to slap him. He has no right to that agony. He took everything from me. And no fucking excuse in the world can make up for it.

My ears are ringing, and my pulse is racing. I feel dizzy. I have to get away.

"Let go of me. Let go of me already!" My voice comes out loud and shrill.

And he does. He puts his hands up, but he doesn't move back. He's far too close to me now. This is all so absurd. So wrong.

"Zoe, please, I'm sorry! Don't tell Caleb, please! It wasn't my fault. Charlotte—"

My hand strikes his face, and then my fingernails catch on his skin and scratch it open. He cries out and takes a few steps backward.

The shock in his eyes shakes me out of my stupor, and so does the blood running down his face. I whirl around, yank the door open, and run down the corridor on shaking legs. Away from Reed and everything he's done. Away from his voice calling my name.

The corridor is far too long. Why is it suddenly so long? I lose my balance and sense of direction. Everything is wrong. *Why why why why?*

I push open another door, and behind it, there's darkness. Warm, safe darkness. I stagger through the room blind and run into something. My fingers meet fabric, many different kinds, and I realize that I must be in the costume workshop.

I feel my way deeper into the room. Maybe it would be better to turn on the light. But then Reed would see the light, and then he would find me. I can't let that happen.

At some point, I bump against what I assume is a wall. My legs won't carry me any farther; they simply collapse. I land hard on my knees and curl up on my side in a little ball.

I cry. I don't remember the last time I cried this hard. Silent sobs shake my body. I have to be quiet so no one hears me.

No one. No one. No one.

Especially not Reed.

I bite my lip until I taste blood.

The rushing sound in my ears gets louder. It hurts. Everything hurts.

He touched me. Again. I've got to take a shower. Wash away his touch. Erase it. I feel so dirty.

I can't breathe. My chest is too narrow; it feels like barbed wire is wrapped around it.

Breathe. Breathe. Breathe, goddamn it.

I need to breathe, but I can't.

Charlotte and Reed did this to me.

Gasping, I roll onto my back. I need to breathe.

Deep breath. Hot tears run over my face.

I can't. Why can't I breathe?

I'm dizzy, and the darkness around me begins to spin.

It's got to stop. It's just got to stop.

Please.

I have no idea how long I sit there until it stops, if it even does at all. But I suddenly feel a light vibration in my back pocket.

My phone.

I have my phone with me. How could I forget that?

Not that it matters now.

Trembling, I sit up and pull it out of my pocket. The screen lights up. Caleb.

Relief floods through me. I swipe the screen and put the phone to my ear.

"Hey, Zoe, I wanted to—" he breaks off when I sob.

History is repeating itself.

"Zoe?" I can hear the panic in his voice. I've heard it before.

"Caleb," I sob. "You have to come. Please."

"What happened?"

"I . . . please. Just come."

"Where are you?"

"In the theater. I . . . don't know where."

It takes twenty minutes and thirty-seven seconds until Caleb finds me and ends the call. He asks me what happened, and I tell him. Then I vomit my guts out. When he pulls me into his arms, I collapse.

Everything goes dark.

* * *

I regain consciousness but still can't find my way back to reality. Caleb helps me to my feet and carries me to the car. History really is repeating itself. He takes me to the hospital even though I say I don't want to go. But he's worried about me, so I go anyway. On the way, he calls our parents and tells them what happened.

Then we're in the hospital, and my parents are there. Caleb kisses my forehead and then disappears, and I know where he's going. To the penthouse, to look for Reed and confront him.

I feel empty. There's nothing left. Only emptiness. A doctor is talking to my parents, but I can't understand what anyone is saying. I'm not listening. I don't care.

Reed was the one who raped me.

He did this to me.

He stole me from myself.

It's his fault that my life shattered into a million little pieces that are impossible to put back together again the way they were.

Mom and Dad bring me home, even though the doctor is against it—I can at least understand that much. I'm glad they don't leave me in the hospital. I hate hospitals. They're so dismal. People die. Sure, some are saved too. But not me.

I just want to go home.

As Mom helps me out of the car, my legs collapse. Dad lifts me and carries me into the house and upstairs to my room. He puts me in my bed and sits down next to me, stroking my hair and saying something that I only perceive as a muffled murmur. I pull the covers up over my head and hide from the world.

The knowledge of what happened is devouring me.

The ignorance was a blessing; I get that now. It protected me from this abyss and kept me from falling. Deeper, deeper, deeper.

There's no bottom. Only falling.

Dad leaves, and Mom stays with me. She's crying. I can hear her, even though she's making a great effort not to make a sound. But she's breathing differently, and that gives it away.

I don't cry. I can't. I don't have any tears left.

After a while, Mom lets go of my hand and stands up, but the mattress sinks again immediately. Another hand slides under the covers and finds mine.

Caleb.

"Hey." His voice is shaking.

I flip back the covers and look up at him. His eyes are wet. His hair is a mess, and he's pale.

"Are you okay?" I ask so softly that I can hardly hear myself. But I can't manage to make my voice any louder.

Caleb lets out a desperate laugh. "Shouldn't I be asking you that?"

"We both know the answer to that question anyway."

He strokes my hair gently. "What can I do to make you feel better?"

I open my mouth, about to say that there's nothing he can do, but then it occurs to me that's not true. "Tell Jase what happened."

"Zoe—" He stops and bites his lower lip, and then tears run down his face. If I weren't already completely shattered, another part of me would break now. Caleb clears his throat and stands up. "Okay. I'll let Jase know."

"Thank you," I whisper, then pull the blanket back over my head and close my eyes.

CHAPTER 50
Jase

Last year, I came to your house a few times, but I couldn't bring myself to knock because I was afraid that you all would send me away.
—Jase

Where is she?

Where the hell is she?

Adrenaline pumps through my veins. Mae doesn't know where Zoe is. No one does. Katie thinks the last time she saw her was when she sent her to get something from the prop room, but she wasn't there. She's not in her room either. Or in the practice studios.

Fuck, Zoe has been missing for hours. She's not answering her phone. Something must have happened or she never would have disappeared without a word. She would have told me.

My heart is racing on the way to my room, as I pull my phone out of my pocket to try calling her again.

"Jase." The familiar voice makes me look up. Fuck, what is Caleb doing here? And why does he look like he wants to burn the whole world to the ground?

I tense as a dark foreboding fills me. There's only one reason that Caleb would be here.

"Where is she?" My voice is hard. Cold. Controlled.

"At home."

"Is she okay?" The question is clearly unnecessary. She's not okay; otherwise, Caleb wouldn't be here. Otherwise, she would have come herself.

"No." His hands clench into fists, and he looks so angry that I almost flinch.

"What happened?"

"It was Reed."

I freeze. I don't understand. And at the same time, I'm afraid I know exactly what he means.

"What?"

"It was Reed," he says again, desperately. His voice is shaking, and the meaning of his words registers. I understand them, but—*Fuck!*

"*What* did Reed do?" Rage boils up, burning in every cell of my body, and swallows me whole. He has to say it very clearly. I need to hear it. Even if I don't want to.

"Reed . . ." Caleb gasps for breath. "Reed was the one who raped Zoe. That's why you have to come with me now and—" he breaks off as I whirl around and run.

Reed raped her.

I'm going to kill that bastard.

* * *

Caleb catches up with me as I'm running across campus. He's faster than me, which is probably unsurprising, considering he's still a football player. He grabs my shoulder and yanks me around so hard I stumble.

"You won't be able to find him," he says. "He ran away. I have no idea where he is."

I pull away from him with a jerk. My heart is pounding so hard against my ribs that it hurts. "I really don't give a shit right now. I don't want to see Reed."

Caleb's shoulders slump. "You want to see Zoe."

I don't bother to respond, because he knows it's true.

"Come on." He puts a hand on my back and leads me toward the parking lot.

His parents' car is parked right at the entrance, diagonally across two parking spaces. But I know Caleb wouldn't give a shit even if there were someone else here to complain.

We get in the car, and he silently leaves the parking lot and guides the car into the Saturday evening Boston traffic.

"How . . . how did you find out?" I say, breaking the silence.

Caleb shrugs, his eyes on the road ahead of us. "It was a dumb coincidence. Zoe heard Reed and Charlotte talking in the theater. They were arguing about it. I don't know any more than that. She . . . she didn't say much, and . . ." he falters, clutching the steering wheel so tightly that his knuckles turn white.

"And what?" I say, because it's clear a piece is missing.

"She was hiding. In the theater. I have no idea how long. I called her about something else, and she was . . . having a panic attack."

This is all so unbelievably wrong. It makes me sick. She was hiding in the theater while I was there. Shit, I was right there, and I didn't find her. I must not have been looking hard enough.

Why didn't I keep searching for her? Why couldn't I have found her?

My head is spinning.

Fuck fuck fuck.

"Fuck!" I blurt out. Caleb is silent and lets me vent.

This can't be real. It can't. But it is. It's fucking reality. Reed raped Zoe. Reed, who has known her for years. Who she grew up with. Reed, that miserable bastard.

"I'll kill him," I hiss, my hands shaking.

A grim smile appears on Caleb's face. "Get in line."

I shake my head. "We can do it together."

Caleb gives me a quick, uninterpretable glance. "This thing between you is serious."

I don't answer, because it's not just serious. It's everything.

* * *

Ceara and Ethan are sitting in the dining room with glasses of whiskey in front of them. I think I need one too. They look up when they hear us, and a weak smile appears on Ethan's face, but it doesn't reach his eyes. Ceara is crying silently. I can't get a word out; I just nod at them.

"She's upstairs," Caleb says.

I hesitate briefly, expecting Zoe's parents to stop me. I wouldn't blame them. But they do nothing of the kind, and finally I start up the stairs. Every step is hard and heavy.

I need to see her. Fuck, I need to see Zoe so much that everything hurts.

At the same time, it scares me shitless.

The door to her room is ajar, but I knock anyway before I go in and then stand there awkwardly, because I don't know what she wants. What she wants me to do.

She's sitting on the bed with her legs drawn up and her arms wrapped around her knees, staring into space. She's white as a ghost, her tangled hair falling around her narrow shoulders. She looks more fragile than I've ever seen her.

"Hey, Pixie," I say softly, letting her know I'm here.

I want to hold her close and never let go again. But I remember how she tensed up when I touched her in the first pas de deux lesson. Even now, after everything that's happened between us, I have no idea how she'll react.

She looks at me silently. Her eyes gleam with tears, but she's not crying. Then she whispers my name, and it sounds like a prayer.

"What can I do?" I ask her. I'm still standing much too far away, even though my instinct urges me to go to her.

But I can't just do that. Not now. This is different. Different from every other time that I touched her or held her.

She rubs her face, wiping away tears that aren't there. "Can you . . . can you just hold me?" Her voice is quiet. Thin and cracked, and my heart angrily skips a beat. I order it to be calm and force my thoughts to remain in the here and now, with Zoe.

I smile. "Anything you want, Pixie."

I kick my shoes off and sit on the bed next to her, pull the quilt up around us, and take her in my arms at last. Her whole body is trembling, and her skin is cold. She lays her head on my chest. I'm sure she can hear my heartbeat, just like I can feel hers at my side. I hold her tight as she begins to cry, and my heart breaks into a thousand pieces.

CHAPTER 51
Zoe

I always thought that nothing bad would ever happen to me. Those things always happen to other people, not to me. Why did it happen? Why?
—Zoe

I have strange dreams about Reed and Charlotte. About the party. Jase. Caleb. Mae and Katie. Tristan and Nick. They're all there, even though it doesn't make sense. I know that even in my dream.

Flickering images. Darkness and light. Panic and burning pain. Total loss of control. My heart pounding against my ribs. A voice shouts, telling me to run. It's my own voice. I try to do it, but I can't move. I can't even scream.

I'm lost.

I'm falling.

"Zoe."

Hands on my skin. Fingers on my cheeks. I know this voice. This time it's not my own.

"Hey, Pixie, wake up."

He sounds worried and afraid. A bit like I feel.

"You have to wake up."

Jase's voice pulls me out of my dream. I open my eyes, blinking against the light. I cry. My mouth is dry, and my throat is closed. I can breathe, but it feels wrong, too hard. It comes out as a gasp.

But I can breathe.

I. Can. Breathe.

"Hey." His voice softens, and he takes his hands away to give me space. My vision clears. Jase is sitting next to me, still sleepy, with dark circles under his eyes and messy hair. He's pale.

"That was just a dream," he says firmly.

I nod. Just a dream. Shaking, I straighten up. I feel sick. When was the last time I ate? I have no idea. I don't care. But I notice that I'm desperately thirsty.

"Could you please get me a glass of water?" I ask, because I doubt my legs will carry me anywhere. As weak as I feel, I certainly won't make it out of bed.

God, I'm so weak.

I hate this.

All of this.

I barely notice that Jase gets up and disappears. A moment later, he comes back and hands me a glass. I drink, and my stomach objects. I really should eat something. But I have absolutely no appetite.

Jase stops in front of my bed, and I know why he's holding himself back, but I don't want him to. I want him to be with me and hold me. So I reach out my hand to him, and he sits down next to me without hesitation. I sigh as I snuggle up to his warm body. My pulse slows. Everything feels calmer. He gently wraps both arms around me. I can feel his heart beating against my back.

"How are you feeling?" he asks quietly after a while. I have no idea how much time has passed.

"Tired." I close my eyes. "And empty. I don't know what to do."

"You don't need to know that yet." But we both realize that's not true.

"I need to talk to the police."

"You don't have to do anything you don't want to," he replies firmly. "If you don't want to go to the police, that's your business. It's your life. And it's your decision."

Tears well up in my eyes, and only now, when he says it, do I realize how much I needed to hear it. It's my decision, and I love him so much for saying it. But I know better.

Reed raped me. I heard what he said. I know what he did, what Charlotte did. I can't ignore that. I have to do something. He has to pay for it.

I want him to pay for it.

I want them both to pay.

* * *

I stay under the shower until I'm red as a lobster. The water is too hot, but I don't care. When I turn it off and step out, I feel a little better. A little more like myself. And above all, clean.

I slowly dry myself and then put on sweatpants and Dad's old Harvard hoodie, which is too big for me. My fingers are still shaking as I weave my damp hair into two thick braids. The girl in the mirror looks young. Much younger than I am. Her eyes are wide, and she's so pale that the freckles stand out against her skin. But the look in her eyes is determined.

I turn away from my reflection and leave the bathroom. Jase is downstairs with my parents and Caleb. I can hear their quiet voices, but I can't understand what they're saying. I don't have to. I know it's about me.

The stairs squeak as I walk down, following the scent of chocolate chip pancakes. My stomach is growling. My family is sitting in the living room, Mom and Dad on the sofa, Caleb in the armchair, and Jase cross-legged on the floor. The sight is so familiar that I start to tear up again, but I bite my lower lip so I don't sob.

Dad notices me first. A gentle smile appears on his face, but it doesn't cover his worry. He looks just as tired as the other three.

"Hey, sweetie," he says. "How are you?"

I just shrug, because I don't have a real answer. I don't know how I am, besides obviously not good. I feel so empty. Mom turns to me. Her eyes are red like she's been crying all night, and now they're wet again, but she manages to smile. "Do you want something to eat?"

I nod, and Mom gets up and guides me to her spot on the couch, and a moment later, there's a plate in front of me on the coffee table. Caleb and Jase watch silently as I choke down a few bites. I can't taste anything, and after three tries, my throat closes, and I can't get any more down. I push the plate away and pull up my legs, biting my lip and tasting blood as the wound from yesterday opens. I hesitate.

I know what I want. I know what I have to do. For myself.

I look up, and my gaze falls on Jase. Of course. Always. He gives me a small, encouraging smile. He knows what I want to say.

I take a deep breath and spit it out.

"Mom, Dad? Will you go with me to the police?"

* * *

But we don't get that far. Dad is upstairs changing, Mom is talking to her lawyer on the phone, and Caleb, Jase, and I are still sitting in the living room when the doorbell rings.

Caleb and Jase exchange an alarmed glance as my stomach cramps up.

Mom and Dad canceled all their meetings and appointments. It's Sunday, so it can't be the mailman. That only leaves . . . I have no idea. I'm not sure if I even want to know.

Caleb heaves himself out of the chair. "I'll get it," he says unnecessarily. I'm certainly not going to go, and Mom is on the phone and didn't notice. I just nod and watch as he disappears into the hall.

"Hey." I turn to Jase when I hear his soft voice. He's sitting next to me on the sofa now; I didn't even notice he was there.

"Hey." I manage a painful smile and reach for his hand, because I need it. I need his touch. I need the feel of his skin. Our fingers intertwine, and his eyes flash with relief. I know what he's thinking because I've thought about it too. He's afraid I might not want to be touched by him anymore. That the panic will come back. The trembling. That everything will start over again from the beginning.

But right now, at least, it's not happening. At this moment, I can breathe better just because he's touching me. Right now, he's keeping me from falling apart.

"Zoe?" Caleb's voice. He sounds different, and I can't quite figure out what it is. Stunned? Incredulous? Maybe both.

Jase and I both turn to him at once. My brother is standing in the doorway, pale and wide-eyed. Behind him are two uniformed police officers with serious expressions on their faces.

I feel cold. My fingers dig into Jase's hand so hard I'm sure I'm hurting him, but he doesn't make a sound, doesn't pull away. Instead, he squeezes my hand tighter. I can feel the tension in his body. It's a reflection of my own. I want to ask why they're here, but I can't make a sound.

Caleb's chest heaves visibly as he takes a breath. "Zoe, the police would like to speak to you. Reed turned himself in."

CHAPTER 52
Jase

Losing Caleb felt almost as bad as losing Sam,
but in a different way—even though it's impossible
to compare. But he was always there for me, and
then from one day to the next, he wasn't.
—Jase

Zoe and her parents went with the police officers to the station, while Caleb and I stayed here. I wanted to go with them, and letting her go without me almost felt like tearing myself in half. I know it's right that just her parents are with her, but it doesn't make me feel any better.

Reed, that bastard, turned himself in. He went to the police and admitted what he'd done. That's why Caleb couldn't find him.

"Here." I look up as Caleb hands me a cup, which I accept. I take a sip without bothering to see what it is and almost choke as the sharp taste of whiskey hits me, mixed with coffee, cream, and sugar.

"What the hell is this?" I raise my eyebrows reproachfully, but he just shrugs, then almost smiles.

"Irish coffee," he explains. "Mom's recipe."

"It's not even lunchtime yet," I say, wondering what I'm even still doing here.

"Sure, but you look like you need it." He sits down in the armchair across from me and raises his own cup. "I think we both need it," he murmurs.

Then we're quiet. Not in an uncomfortable way; we know each other far too well for that. But strangely, things are starting to feel normal between us again, like it hasn't been a whole year since we last talked.

At some point, I break the silence. "How are you?"

Surprised, Caleb looks up, and the next second his face goes blank. "Fine. Everything's okay," he replies. He's lying, I know it. I recognize the mask he's hiding behind.

"Come on, Caleb. How *are* you?"

I take another sip, and this time the taste on my tongue is a little less awful.

His jaw muscles are working. He's clinging to his cup so hard that his knuckles are white. I wait.

"I really want to kill him," he finally manages to get out through clenched teeth.

"Me too." More than that. I want to send Reed to hell without any chance of return. It's what the bastard deserves.

"I just don't understand how he could do it. He was my friend. Zoe is my little sister. He—" Shaking his head, Caleb stops. There's irrepressible fury burning in his eyes. "I'm so angry I want to tear him into pieces. He was my fucking friend, and he raped Zoe. How . . . how can you even get over something like that? It's all such fucking shit. I don't even know what to say anymore, let alone what to do."

"Yeah," I say, because I feel exactly the same way.

How do you go on? Is it even possible? No clue. I don't know if I've ever felt as helpless as I have in these last twenty-four hours. Except for the day when Sam died. And the weeks after. But that was a different kind of helplessness, because there really was nothing I could do. Now I know I can do something to help; I just don't know what it is yet.

To help her. To help Caleb. To help myself. This all just sucks.

This time, Caleb breaks the silence between us.

"I'm sorry," he says.

"For what?"

"For acting like an asshole the past year."

I shrug, because I can't deny it; he did act like an asshole. "We don't have to talk about it," I say, even though I know we should at some point. We can't just sit here and pretend that it didn't happen. I still don't understand why he decided we just weren't friends anymore.

"It wasn't your fault. You didn't do anything wrong."

"I fell in love with your sister." Not that that was wrong; it was totally right. For me, at least. But he obviously doesn't see it that way.

He laughs joylessly. "Yeah, it would have been good to know that. Why didn't you say anything?"

"Because I didn't know . . . I didn't know if she wanted me, and I was afraid it would ruin our friendship." I'm being ruthlessly honest, and it feels good. Too much has happened to be anything else.

"It didn't."

I raise an eyebrow wordlessly. Of course it did.

Caleb rolls his eyes and sighs. "Okay, it did. It ruined our friendship. But not because the two of you fell in love. I didn't have a problem with you getting together. Wait, that's not true. I had a problem with it, but it wasn't your fault." The words stumble out of his mouth, fast and muddled. But there's a missing piece, and I suspect it's something crucial.

"And?" I ask, though part of me would have liked to spare us the answer.

He takes a deep breath, agonized. "I had a problem with it because I was . . . like Zoe. I had . . . feelings for you."

I blink. I can't move. I stare at him. And I understand.

I have to say something, anything, but the only thing that comes out of my mouth is one quiet word. "Fuck."

"Yeah, exactly," Caleb says sarcastically. "Kind sucked seeing the two of you make out."

"Caleb, I'm sorry—"

"Don't," he says and puts his hands over his face, looking exhausted. "You don't have to apologize. You didn't do anything wrong. Basically, I knew that you didn't feel the same way. I was just insanely good at lying to myself. Okay, and I really had no clue that you were into my little sister."

I don't know what to say. My mind is completely blank. My best friend had feelings for me, and I was—am—in love with his sister. What do you even say to that?

"That night when I saw you, I ran away because it broke my heart. Zoe followed me, and we both cried for a long time. And then we got drunk. And then . . . everything got much worse."

"What happened wasn't your fault," I say, hoping he already knows that. But sometimes you just need to hear it.

"Yes, I know." He sighs.

"But?"

"I've been wondering for a year if it could have been different, if I'd taken better care of her. If I'd brought her home instead of leaving her at Charlotte's."

"She'd already spent the night with Charlotte hundreds of times. She slept there after every party. You couldn't have known. And you couldn't have changed anything."

Caleb doesn't look convinced. But after a while, he nods anyway. "Afterward . . . I couldn't talk to you. Not only because I had no clue what to say. I couldn't tell you that I was in love with you. I couldn't say anything. Zoe didn't want anyone to find out what happened. She didn't want to see or talk to anyone. And I couldn't have lied to you. It was easier with the others. They spent the whole summer in Europe and didn't hear a thing. Except for Tristan. He helped me take Zoe to the hospital, but he never asked what happened. With you, it would have been different. You—"

"I would have asked."

Caleb nods. "You did too. It was shitty of me not to answer your calls or messages. And it was shitty that no one answered when you came to the door. It was just . . . easier. As awful as that sounds, it was. It was a clean cut, for all of us."

I stare at my cup and take another sip, but this time it makes my eyes water. Yes, it was easier. For them. And a thousand times more terrible for me. The fact that I understand now doesn't change that. It doesn't make it hurt any less.

"I needed you," I say.

"I know. I'm sorry I wasn't there for you."

Zoe told him everything; I know without him having to say it. Those two don't keep secrets from each other. I'm glad not to have to tell him the whole fucking story.

I look into Caleb's eyes. They're a different color than Zoe's, but I can see a lot of her in him anyway.

"What happens next?"

"I don't know. We wait."

"That's not what I meant. I meant with you and me and Zoe."

Caleb smiles, and it's genuine. "Well, I hope that you make her happy and that you can be there for her. If not, unfortunately, I'll have to kick your ass."

I grin. "Noted."

"And for me . . ." Caleb blushes. "Things won't go back to the way they were. But I'd like to go back to being friends again at some point. And you can get to know Parker too. My boyfriend."

I just nod. My throat feels constricted, and I feel a familiar prickling in my eyes.

"I missed you, man," I say hoarsely, because it's the truth. And because I'm tired of pushing everyone away. Of losing the people who are important to me. I want my best friend back.

A hopeful gleam appears in his eyes.

"Me too."

CHAPTER 53
Zoe

Caleb misses you.
—Zoe

When we get home, Caleb and Jase are sitting on the sofa. There's some show on the TV, but they have their heads together and are focused on talking about something I can't hear.

The sight of them gives me a pang of longing. It's so normal to see them like this. A little like it used to be, if not exactly the same as it was. Jase and Caleb turn around at the same time as they hear my footsteps and Dad closing the door behind us.

I'm overwhelmingly tired as I go to the sofa, collapsing between them with a sigh and ignoring the fact that I'm still wearing my jacket and boots. My whole body feels heavy, just like my head. Like it's packed with cotton balls.

Jase reaches for my hand, and our fingers intertwine. The living room is silent apart from the voices coming from the TV. They're waiting. Patiently. They don't ask how it went or how I'm doing. They don't ask any questions, and that feels good. I take a deep breath.

"It's over," I finally say. And for now, it is. Reed confessed, and I told the police what I heard when he was arguing with Charlotte. I told them everything. About Charlotte and me, about the party, and about how she acted like she didn't believe me, even though she knew what happened. What she did.

She labeled me a liar when she was the biggest liar herself.

There won't be a trial, at least not for Reed. Since he turned himself in, he'll probably get off with a lighter sentence. Which kind of sucks, but I can't do anything to change it. And to be honest, I'm relieved I don't have to tell the whole story again in front of a judge, prosecution, and jury. I don't want an audience.

At least he's getting a punishment, and I know Mom will make sure he doesn't get off as lightly as he hopes. She has damn good lawyers.

"What about Charlotte?" Caleb asks after I've told them everything.

I shrug, exhausted. "No idea. We'll see. Reed also told the police that Charlotte gave me the roofies, but it'll be difficult to prove. She certainly won't admit it. Then it'll be his word against hers."

"But you heard her," Jase says. I can see the anger in his eyes. He's clenching his teeth so hard that his jaw is protruding.

"She'll say that I'm lying." I hate to say it, but unfortunately, it's true.

"But that's bullshit!"

I lean my head on Jase's chest and inhale his scent. Mint and honey. Safe.

I don't answer because there's nothing to say. It's all bullshit, and totally awful, but I did what I could. Now it's out of my hands.

CHAPTER 54

Jase

I want to have a home again.
—Jase

"I can stay here if you want," I tell her for the fourth time, but Zoe just rolls her eyes. It's Wednesday morning. She's still in bed, and I want to crawl under the covers with her and block out the world a little longer, like we've been doing for the last couple of days. We turned off our phones and spent our days in the living room with Zoe's family. We played games and watched cheesy movies. We talked. A lot. And cried too.

"No, I want you to go. Think of your scholarship." There's a reproachful tone in her voice, and I know she's right. I should probably be more focused on it. But I can't. My head is full of thoughts of her, and I almost don't care about the scholarship right now.

"The scholarship doesn't—"

"If you say it doesn't matter right now, I'll throw you out. You've already missed two days, and I still want you as my dance partner next semester. So go!"

I want to tell her that I'm not going back without her, that I only want to be with her. That I need her. But I bite back the words because we haven't talked yet about when she's coming back, or whether she'll come back at all. She's not ready yet.

"Okay. I'll be back after class, then."

"I hope so," she says with a smile.

Then she really kicks me out, and I go.

It's still early when I enter the dorm to get changed for class, but everyone seems to be up and about already. Excited voices echo through the corridors. I feel people's eyes on me as soon as I enter the building. They know what's going on. I can tell.

The news of Reed's arrest spread faster than I thought it would. Half the city knows about it, not just our classmates. Which shouldn't be that surprising, considering Reed is the principal's nephew. Still, I would prefer it if they'd all keep their mouths shut and mind their own business.

"Jase!" I stop when I hear Skye's angry voice. She comes straight at me, dark hair flying like a cloak behind her. Her eyes are flashing with fury. I instinctively back away, but I'm too slow. She pushes my chest so hard that I stumble.

"You're such an ass!" she hisses, continuing before I can ask why. "It would have been nice if you'd contacted me even once. One tiny message would have been enough! Like telling me you were still alive. You dropped off the face of the earth for days! I was imagining the worst!"

"I'm sorry."

"You can't talk your way out of it, you . . . wait, did you just apologize?" Her eyes go wide, and I have to grin.

"Yes. I'm sorry I didn't get in touch. I was with Zoe and . . ." I shrug in a way that somehow encompasses everything I can't say.

Her gaze softens into a look of concern. "How is she?"

I fish my room key out of my pocket and open the door. "All right. She's strong."

She's stronger than any other person I know.

Skye follows me as I walk inside. I toss the key on my desk and grab my dance clothes out of the dresser.

"It's all a fucking mess, isn't it?"

"That just about sums it up."

"Do you want to talk about it?" she asks carefully, and I turn to face her. She's leaning on my desk, her hands gripping the edge, her head tilted.

"No." I can't talk about it. Not now. "But thank you."

"Of course. If you change your mind, let me know. This can't be easy for you."

I clench my teeth and shake my head. No, it's not.

Skye steps away from the desk and comes toward me. Before I can react, she pulls me into a strong hug. "It's okay, Jase."

I want to shake my head again, but she's right. My shoulders relax, and then I return her embrace. For a long time. Until Skye lets go of me.

She smiles gently. "The two of you can do this. It's all going to be fine."

I nod, because I need to believe it. It's all going to be fine.

* * *

The day goes by without me paying much attention to what's going on around me. No one talks to me about Zoe. I can tell I'm still being observed, but no one asks questions. Maybe it's because of

Skye, who doesn't leave my side and gives a dirty look to anyone she sees whispering about me.

During the pas de deux class, it occurs to me that not only is Zoe missing, but Charlotte is too. I ask Skye about her, but she only shrugs. Charlotte hasn't been seen all week, but no one knows anything about it.

I'm just glad I don't run into her. Otherwise, I would probably break her fucking neck.

Late in the afternoon, I'm walking back down the hall to my room, lost in thought. I want to shower and change before I go back to Zoe, and I notice too late that my parents are standing at my door, apparently waiting for me.

Crap.

Dad's leaning against the wall, his arms crossed over his chest. He's wearing a black wool coat over a dark gray suit and looks totally out of place here. Mom is standing slightly apart from him, nervously wringing her hands. I notice that she's lost weight. She's thinner than usual; her face has gotten narrower, and her cheekbones stand out even more than usual. There are dark circles under her eyes.

My instincts tell me just to turn around and leave, but I'm done avoiding them. This has to stop. When they see me, Mom's eyes tear up, and she sighs with relief. "There you are," she says, taking a step toward me. "We were worried. You haven't been in your room for the past few days."

"You were here?" I ask in surprise and open my door.

She nods. "We want to talk to you."

"It can't go on like this," Dad says, but his voice is hard and cold, as usual. Just like his gaze. Everything about him is cold.

"It won't," I say, but I'm pretty sure I mean something different than he does.

He doesn't answer, and his eyes narrow as his gaze bores into me. His eyes remind me of Sam's.

"Can we come in?" Mom asks before either of us can say a word. They don't want to have this conversation in the hallway, of course, and to be honest, I'm not exactly thrilled about the idea either. But I don't want them in my room.

"We want to talk to you, and to apologize," Mom continues. Something in her tone of voice hurts like hell. I laugh and watch as Dad's hands tighten into fists. He probably imagined this differently, but I'm sick of these games. I just want peace and quiet.

"You want to apologize? For what?"

"This is ridiculous. We aren't going to have this conversation in the hall," Dad interjects before Mom can answer my question. He pushes past me into my room.

I see red and suddenly lose control. "Ridiculous? Is that what I am to you? Ridiculous. A joke." I follow him into my room and grab him by the shoulder. I try to turn him around and send him back into the hall, but Mom is standing in the door, blocking the way.

Her eyes are shining with tears. It's clear by looking at her that she expected this to go differently.

Dad doesn't reply, just stands mutely in front of me. His jaw clenches. He's fighting for self-control.

"We can easily shorten this conversation. I'm not going to Harvard, and if it's up to me, we'll never speak another word to each other."

"Jase, please," Mom begs. "We're a family."

"No. We're not a family anymore, not since Sam died. You would have preferred it if I'd died instead, and you know what? Sometimes I wished the same thing!"

I hear Mom gasp, but I'm concentrating on Dad. I see a flash of pain in his eyes that's all too familiar to me.

"That's not true, Jase." Mom comes into the room, and the door closes behind her. The room suddenly feels too small.

I can't breathe, and my heart cramps painfully. This is all too much. I don't want to talk; I need them to leave. But for reasons I don't understand, I continue.

"Ask him what he said when I said the same thing at your party," I demand. My voice sounds hollow, not like myself.

Dad goes pale. "Jase, that wasn't—"

"I don't care," I say. "I'm not Sam. I will never be Sam, and you can't accept that. Not my wishes, not my dreams or who I am." Dad opens his mouth, but I'm not done yet. "It wasn't Sam's death that destroyed our family. It was you! And no apology in the world can undo that. I don't want to hear it. Do you understand? I—"

"Sam died in a football game," Dad says, interrupting me. His voice cracks with anger and pain, and there's a grimace on his face. "He was an athlete, and he died."

"And?" I say between clenched teeth.

"And the same thing could happen to you!"

It takes a few seconds for the words to reach me before I understand what he's trying to say. I laugh in disbelief and push back my hair. "Are you serious? Is that supposed to be an apology? You don't want me to dance because I could die like Sam? That doesn't even make sense!"

Dad glares at me. "Not everything has to make sense."

"For you it does! Always. And that's the worst bullshit I've ever heard."

"It's still the truth."

"Then why are you only telling me this now? In the last five years, you've been treating me like your biggest disappointment. I could never do anything right for you."

"I made mistakes," Dad admits. But it's not enough.

"It's nice that you see that. But it doesn't change anything."

"What do we have to do to make it change something?" Mom holds out her hand to me, but I evade her.

"Shit, Mom! Did you happen to notice that you came here to apologize, and neither of you has actually said you're sorry? You want to bring our family back together . . . but I have no clue why. Honestly."

My parents exchange stricken looks.

"We did everything wrong, didn't we?" Mom's shoulders slump. "We should never have let you believe that—" she breaks off, unable to get the words out.

"But you did."

"I'm sorry." She reaches her hand out to me again, and I avoid it again. Maybe her words should make me feel something, but all I feel is emptiness. A single apology can't undo the last five years.

An uncomfortable silence grows between us. They're waiting for a reply, and I'm waiting for . . . something more. So I can figure out what I'm supposed to do now.

Dad clears his throat and changes the subject. "That girl you were at the party with. That was Zoe Young, wasn't it?"

I stiffen. Is he fucking serious? He wants to talk about Zoe right now? My parents are the last people I expected to be interested in the gossip about Zoe and Reed.

"That's none of your business."

Dad's brow creases in confusion, and then it smooths as he understands. "I'm not talking about what happened to her," he says. "It's about what she said that evening. That I'm the one who's disappointing you."

I tense, and my heart skips a beat again. "And?" I say, because my mind is suddenly blank.

"She was right."

"She usually is."

"I'd like . . . How can we . . . What can we do?" All at once, Dad seems terrifyingly helpless. I've never seen him like this.

Part of me wants to send them away and never speak to them again. They're my parents, but they haven't acted like it in years. It's not my job to save our crappy relationship just because we have the same genes. But another part of me hesitates.

"You should go now," I finally say.

Mom's eyes go wide, and she's about to protest, but I beat her to it.

"I need time to think." A lot of time. "I'll get in touch with you when I'm ready."

The two of them exchange a glance. It's clear that Mom would rather do anything but leave, and Dad doesn't seem entirely thrilled by the idea either.

But for the first time, my parents respect my decision. They leave.

CHAPTER 55
Zoe

I hate therapy. Actually, that's not true. I hate that there's a reason I need it. No, I hate the fact that I need therapy for this reason. And I really need it.
—Zoe

It feels strange to be at home again. Especially without Jase. The last two days felt like a time-out. An involuntary one, sure, but still just a break. School didn't matter, and neither did ballet. Nothing in the outside world mattered.

It was just him and me. Days in bed and on the sofa. Whispered secrets and tears.

Today, it's different. He's back at school, and I can't stop thinking about how much I want to be back with him. Caleb isn't here, and Dad had to go to work, so I'm alone with Mom. The more time that passes, the more restless I become. I don't have anything to do.

My legs are twitchy. Everything is twitchy. I need to move. I need to dance. I want to dance. But I can't just go back to school. Charlotte is there, and the thought of seeing her again makes my stomach turn. I don't know what will happen to her. I don't know if *anything* will happen.

"Zoe, dear?" Mom's concerned voice snaps me out of my thoughts, and I look up. She's standing in front of me, her face so worried that it makes my heart clench. She's holding out a steaming cup to me.

"I'm sorry. I was thinking." I take the cup, and she sits down next to me on the sofa. She looks tired. I'm not used to seeing her like this. She's dressed in leggings and a sweatshirt, with her hair in braids and no makeup. There are dark circles under her eyes, and I know she hasn't slept much in the past few days. Because I haven't slept much either. Every time I woke up in the night and went to the bathroom or to get something to drink, there was still a light on in her study, and I could hear her voice. I think she was on the phone with her lawyer. Because of me. It reminds me of last year, and I hate it. It's all about me and what happened. I want it to stop. I want to turn back time and make everything normal. Why can't I do that?

"How do you feel?" she asks gently and pushes my hair off my forehead.

I shrug and take a sip of tea. Lavender and honey. Calming. I don't know how to answer that question anymore. I feel too much.

"Do you want to talk to Dr. Somers?"

"What good would that do?" I say, sinking deeper into the sofa. "She can't change what happened."

"I know. But she can help you deal with it. She helped you last year too."

I don't answer, because she's right. Dr. Somers helped me convince my parents to let me apply to dance school if I got my panic attacks under control. She worked with me for months. She was patient, even though I behaved terribly sometimes. Deep inside, I know that she can help me now.

But I don't want to talk about it all again. I just want to leave it behind me. If only it were that easy. Nothing about this situation is easy.

"I'm afraid it will start again . . . the stuff about touching," I say quietly. I don't want to say it. I don't want to think about it. In the last few days, I've been refusing to acknowledge it. Because then it might be true. And that would be unbearable.

"Why do you think it might start again?" Mom's voice is soft, and tears well up in my eyes.

"I don't know . . ." I falter, hesitating. I cling to the cup a little more tightly. "It started again the first time I had to dance with Jase. I don't know why. The panic just came back. And now . . . how can it not happen again?" I take a shaky breath and wipe the tears off my cheeks. "Jase can lie next to me in bed, and it feels good. It really does. But I wonder all the time . . . whether it will stay that way. And what will happen if it doesn't."

Mom sighs. When I look at her again, tears are running down her face. She wipes them away and smiles at me lovingly. "I don't think any of this makes sense. As long as it feels good and right to you, it *is* good."

"Since I found out, we haven't . . . you know." I turn red, but now that I've started, I can't stop. Maybe it's strange that I'm talking about this with my mom, of all people. Who wants to talk to their mother about sex? But I have to get this off my chest.

"Do you want to?"

"Yes." The word comes as a soft sigh. "But I don't know. Somehow, I'm afraid that it won't work after everything we've been through. But I want it to."

God, I want so much for it to work. I want to be touched by

him, to lose myself with him. I want his hands on my skin again, to feel his weight on me. I want *him*.

"Have you talked about it with him?"

"Not really."

We haven't talked about it at all. But I know I can. I know I can tell him everything. I just haven't been able to so far, and I don't know why.

"Are you going to talk to him?"

"Yes. But I don't know how. It's all so . . . I don't know. I'm confused."

"I'm sure he feels exactly the same way," Mom says.

"Probably." I sigh. "This is all so damn hard."

"I know, dear. I wish it were different."

"Me too." I lean against her, and Mom puts an arm around my shoulders and kisses the top of my head.

"It's going to be all right. I'm sure of it."

I hope so.

* * *

It's late afternoon when the doorbell rings. I assume it's Jase, even though he should still be in class. It wouldn't surprise me if he skipped theory class to get here earlier. But it's not Jase standing on the porch. It's Mr. Pearson.

"Hello, Zoe." He smiles kindly, but he also looks exhausted. Then I remember that he's Reed's uncle, and I tense.

"Hi, Mr. Pearson," I say, and then don't know how to continue. My heart pounds against my ribs. What is he doing here?

"I'm sorry for turning up unannounced. I should have called," he says. "I'd love to talk to you, if that's okay."

I stand there frozen and can't make a sound. I don't know if it's okay. I don't know anything anymore. What does he want?

"Zoe? Who's there?" Mom comes to the door, and I feel a little better with her standing at my back. "Mr. Pearson. What can we do for you?"

"I'd like to talk to Zoe," he says again. He's talking to my mom, but he's looking at me. His gaze is serious, but unexpectedly warm. "But if it's not the right time—"

"No," I say quickly. "It's okay. Come in." If he leaves, I won't be able to think about anything but the fact that he came here, and I need to know what he wants from me.

Mom and I step aside and let him in. She looks at me carefully, making sure it's really okay with me that my school principal is suddenly here in our house.

"Would you like a drink?" Mom asks politely, inviting Pearson to sit down at our dining table. But he shakes his head.

"No, thank you. This won't take long."

"What's this about?" Mom asks, because my voice still isn't working.

I'm so tense that my shoulders hurt.

"First of all, I want to apologize for what Reed did to you. It's unforgivable, and I know that no apology in the world can make up for it. Still, I'm sorry that you have to go through all of this."

"Thank you," I mumble. My shoulders relax a little. I don't know what I was expecting, but it wasn't this.

"I want you to know that you can take all the time you need. Your place with us is safe. In case you were worried about that." He gives me a tiny, encouraging smile.

"I . . . I don't know if I can go back yet. Charlotte . . ." I break off; my throat is constricted.

Pearson nods as if he had expected this answer.

"As for Charlotte, we also heard about what she did. She was expelled from school. We do not tolerate such behavior. The school is your second home, and we want all our students to feel safe there."

"Charlotte had to leave?" I stare at him in disbelief. I'm sure I misheard him.

But he nods. "I don't know what other consequences her behavior will have, but she is no longer a part of our student body."

I want to say something, say thank you. Anything. But I can't speak. Charlotte is no longer at the same school as me. I don't have to see her in class. I can go back, and she'll be gone. And then I burst into tears again. Tears of relief.

CHAPTER 56
Zoe

You'll probably never read this note, but I have to write it anyway: When you asked me if I had ever been in love, and I answered with yes, I meant I was in love with you.
—Zoe

I go back to bed and am reading when Jase comes in and throws his duffel bag into the corner of my room. It's late, and he looks exhausted.

"Is everything all right?" Worried, I sit up in bed and put my book aside.

He collapses onto my bed with a groan and lies his head on my chest. His arm is heavy across my body. "My parents came today. To talk."

"Seriously?"

"Seriously."

"Both of them?" I ask, stunned that Jase's father actually made the effort to approach him.

"Yes," he says, sighing heavily.

"What happened?"

He shrugs. "It could have been worse."

So it was pretty bad. I brush back a few strands of hair from his forehead. This time, his sigh is soft, and he snuggles up against me. For a long time, we're quiet. I wait until he starts to talk.

"They apologized. Or at least, they pretended to. But . . . it wasn't enough." His voice breaks as he tells me about the conversation with his parents, and my heart aches for him. I hate that it hurts him so much.

"That's so awful," I say when he's done.

"Yeah."

"What do you want to do now?"

"I don't know. I don't have a clue. I need time to think, and then we'll see."

"Then take your time."

He looks up at me, and his eyes are so green. "You told Dad that he was the one who was disappointing me."

"I did." I blush.

He smiles. "Thank you."

I smile back. "Any time."

He takes my hand and kisses my palm. My skin begins to tingle. "How was your day?" he asks, and I know that he wants to ask how I'm doing, but he's not going to, because he also knows that I don't have a real answer to the question.

"Pearson was here." I drop the bombshell, just like that. Jase sits up abruptly.

"What?"

"He came to see me. Charlotte got expelled."

"What?" His eyes go wide, and I have to smile. All at once, I feel much lighter.

"Don't ask me how he found out what she did. But he knows. And there were consequences."

Jase opens his mouth and closes it again. "Fuck." It doesn't sound like a curse. More like an expression of relief.

"Yes."

"She's gone."

"Yes."

"Thank God."

"Yes." I smile.

"How are you?" He puts a hand on my cheek. He strokes my lips with his thumb, and a warm tingling spreads through me.

"Better," I say, and it's the truth. I really do feel better.

He tries to take his hand back, but I hold on to it tightly. Desire is pulsing through my body. It's been days since the last time he kissed me properly—since he *really* kissed me. It feels like an eternity. I think about my talk with Mom, and how I told her that I can talk to Jase. And I know I can. But maybe . . . maybe we don't need to talk just now.

"Don't stop," I whisper.

His eyes widen, and he swallows. He leaves his hand on my cheek. My heart pauses and then beats double time. At the same time, we move closer together. Slowly. A little hesitantly, a little unsure. He caresses the back of my neck, and his touch is gentle and sure. I forget how to breathe for a second as our noses touch. We're still looking searchingly at each other, and neither of us closes our eyes.

I can feel his breath on my face. His lips are so close. So, so close.

The first kiss barely counts. It's a tender touch, so light that for a second I think I must have imagined it. My whole body feels warm and soft, and I want to kiss him. I *need* to kiss him. My lips meet his. So familiar. He sighs, and so do I. And then the tears come again, because he kisses me and I kiss him, and it feels so right.

The thoughts in my head go silent; the voices of doubt fade away. And I know that this time, the panic won't come back. I know that everything between us is really and truly fine.

Because he's Jase.

And I'm Zoe.

Because we're us.

And because he knows my secrets, and I know his.

Jase wipes the tears off my face, but he keeps kissing me, and my lips open. Our tongues meet, and heat shoots through my veins and pools in my middle. I cradle his face in both hands and pull him close, closer and closer, but it's not close enough. He can't be close enough.

His erection is pressing firmly against my belly, and I feel a pulsing between my legs. I tug at his T-shirt. I want to feel his skin against mine. Jase leans back and pulls it off over his head in one fluid motion. His body has become so familiar to me in the last few weeks, but all I can do is stare at him: his defined chest muscles, his flat belly, the muscles that dip into the waistband of his pants. I reach out and trace those muscles, and I have to smile when he gets goose bumps. I take his hands and interlace our fingers briefly before guiding them to my own body. I want him to undress me.

He does it, but agonizingly slowly. First the sweatshirt, then the pants. He hesitates at my underwear, but I raise my hips invitingly, and a second later, the thin garment lands next to the other clothes on the floor. His lips meet mine again, gently and carefully. This is different than before. Less demanding. Less desperate. Somehow deeper. Somehow everything.

Slowly, very slowly, his mouth wanders along my jaw to my neck. He sucks on the delicate skin behind my ear, and I moan softly. Farther and farther downward, over my collarbone, to my breasts. I'm glowing, and I forget everything as his tongue plays with my nipples. He sucks on me, and I arch my back, pushing myself against him, because I want more.

But Jase takes his time, kissing his way farther down my body, then finally spreading my legs. A sound of yearning escapes me as his tongue glides over the center of my desire, and then there's only heat and longing for more.

"Jase," I plead, and I don't even know what I'm asking him for, but he understands me anyway, slipping a finger inside me. I exhale with a tremor. But it's not enough. I want all of him inside me. I reach for him, tugging on his shoulders, and he gives in and raises his head. His lips are wet and shiny and a little swollen. He smiles, and my heart is about to burst, because he's smiling like that for *me*.

"Hey," he whispers, then kisses me gently.

"Hey," I whisper against his lips, returning his kiss.

For a moment, we're both silent. His erection pulses between my legs, and his heart is hammering against my chest. Mine too. We're just tingling, pulsing heat. I move first, raising my hips just a little, and he exhales sharply. My smile gets wider. He reaches between us, and then we both hold our breath as he slides into me.

That feels different now too. Better. More. He starts to move slowly inside me, and I adapt to his tempo, pushing myself against him. I want to cry because it feels so good. So real. So much like us.

"Pixie," he whispers in my ear, and I know what he wants to say.

But he doesn't say it, and neither do I. It's not necessary. I know how he feels; I know what this feeling is between us. He doesn't have to say a word.

"I know," I whisper back. I caress his back and grip his bottom, pulling him even closer. He groans, and the sound resonates through me. I lose control, pushing myself against him, pushing him deeper, deeper, deeper inside me. He changes the angle, and everything around me begins to spin. The world tilts, and I never knew that anything could ever feel this good.

"Fuck, Zoe, I—" Jase breaks off, his body tensing, and then he moans because he can't hold back anymore. And that's okay, because nothing is better than knowing that I'm making him feel this way. But he doesn't stop moving, and the muscles inside me contract. My whole body is in flames, and then his hand slides between us, hitting the point that's pulsing with longing, and I have to bite my lip not to scream, because I can't control myself anymore. Oh God, I can't.

My body arches as I come, moaning his name, and there's nothing in the world but the two of us.

Jase gazes at me. His eyes are gleaming, and I love it. I love him. Everything about him. He smiles, and I know what he's going to say.

"How does that feel?"

I smile, and he knows what my answer will be.

"Like us."

CHAPTER 57
Zoe

I hope that someday you'll read these notes I've written, even though it's insanely unlikely that you'll ever speak to me again.
—Zoe

I return to school two weeks later, even though Pearson said I could take as much time as I need. But I can't wait anymore.

I want to dance.

My parents and Caleb bring me back to campus. It feels a bit like we're in a time machine that took us back to my first day, but at the same time, it's different. Maybe even better, in spite of everything.

My pulse accelerates as my family accompanies me to the dorm. It's not necessary, but I'm happy to have them with me, and I think they might need this closure for themselves too.

It's early Monday morning, and I'll have to hurry to get to my first class on time. The corridors are full, as usual. Students are everywhere. I notice them staring at me as I enter the building, climb the stairs, and finally walk down the hall on the fourth floor to my room.

They've heard what happened. Of course they did. How could they not have? Part of me wants to hunch my shoulders and hide. But I have no reason to.

"Are you sure you're ready?" Mom asks as we reach my room. There's unmistakable concern in her voice.

I smile, and it's genuine. "I am. And Dr. Somers also said she thought it would be good for me to come back."

"I know. It's just—" Sighing, she stops and shakes her head. "It's all right. Forget it. It's just me being worried, that's all. As usual." She laughs, but it sounds nervous.

"I'm fine, Mom," I reassure her, taking my key out of my jacket pocket and unlocking the door.

"That's wonderful. That's really good."

"It is, Mom," Caleb says, putting an arm around her shoulders. "Zoe will be fine, I know she will. She isn't alone here."

"She's really not." I turn around when I hear Jase's familiar voice. My heart flutters when I see him, and a beaming smile appears on my face of its own accord.

He came back yesterday. It was strange to spend the night without him.

"Hey," I say.

"Hey." He smiles. I can't get enough. Of his smile. Of him.

"I guess that's our cue to disappear," Caleb says with a theatrical sigh, but then he grins and gives Jase a quick hug.

I don't know if things will ever be the same between the two of them, but at least they're talking to each other again. And maybe it doesn't have to be like it was before. Maybe they need a fresh start, without secrets. Jase told Caleb about Sam. I think it's good for him to talk about his brother. Every time he mentions him, there's a little less pain in his eyes. It will never go away, it will always be there, but it's a different kind of pain now. Because he's not hiding Sam anymore. He's remembering him. He remembers the way it used to be. And every time we talk about him, he remembers something else. I'm beginning to understand what Jase meant when he said that Caleb reminds him of Sam.

"You have to go back to school anyway," Dad says.

"I might as well skip the first class," Caleb says, making a face. "I hate statistics."

"You go right ahead and do that, but I have to go to class right now. Unlike you, I don't like being late," I say.

"Okay, okay, we're leaving." Caleb messes up my hair, and I wrinkle my nose, struggling to hide a smile.

"Will I see you this weekend?" I ask and hug him.

He hugs me so tightly that I can't breathe for a moment. "Sure. Movie night. I already told Parker."

"Just what I hoped."

I let him go and hug Mom and Dad.

"Let us know if you need us," Mom says, because she can't help it.

"I will," I promise.

They hug Jase and then leave us alone.

He takes a step toward me and kisses me. "Are you ready?"

I take a deep breath. "I think so."

I take a few minutes to change and put my hair up in a neat bun, then I grab my bag, and we leave my room.

We're running late, and Jase should have been at his first class a while ago, but I'm happy that he's with me. We walk over to the practice building together and separate at the second floor.

"See you later," he says, kissing me and going up one more level to his class. I don't want him to leave, but he's got to get to his class, and I have to do this alone now. My legs feel a little shaky as I walk down the corridor. I don't know what to expect. I don't know how the others will react. I don't know anything at all.

Everything will be fine.

When I enter the studio, the others are already doing their warm-up exercises.

Everyone pauses at once. They look at me, and I freeze and turn red, then white as a sheet. I turn to Mr. Conrad for help, but he's also looking at me, with compassion in his eyes.

"Zoe!" Mae's excited squeal gets my attention, and a second later, she's throwing her arms around me. "I'm so glad you're back!"

I hug her, and it feels right. "I am too."

Mr. Conrad claps his hands and gives us a stern look. "There's nothing to see, people. Back to the barre. We have a lot to do."

The others obey, and I give him a grateful look. He smiles at me encouragingly.

Mae grabs my hand and drags me to the barre, where she was just standing. Jessica slides over a bit to make space for me.

I put my hand on the barre, take a deep breath, take the first position, and bend my knees in a plié. I do what I've been doing for most of my life.

I dance.

* * *

As I walk to pas de deux class with Mae, I feel calm. Everything is like it was before, even though everyone knows. No one asks me any questions or makes comments about what happened. I can sometimes feel eyes on me, but there's no gossip. At least not that I can hear.

Jase is sitting with Skye and Ches on the floor as we walk in. His gaze immediately finds mine.

"God, you two are so in love," Mae says in a stage whisper. I think everyone in the room can hear her.

"That's true," I say, because it is.

"I hear we're having a couple's movie night this weekend?"

"Aha, then Tristan already asked you? I wanted to tell you myself, but—"

"That's okay," Mae says gently and squeezes my hand. "I get it. But yeah, Tristan asked me."

"I'm glad you're coming too."

"So am I. Now go to your prince; he's been gazing longingly at you this whole time." Mae gives me a gentle push in Jase's direction.

I suppress the urge to stick my tongue out at her and tow her over to Jase and Skye with me.

"Mae is being stupid," I say.

"That's new," Skye says sarcastically, but her eyes are gleaming mischievously.

"Hey, that's not fair! You're not any better, Skye," Mae says.

"I never claimed to be."

"Good morning, everyone!" The sound of Francesca's voice makes us look around. She walks briskly into the room. Her gaze lands on me, and a smile appears on her face. "Nice that we're all here again."

I swallow, because all at once I have a lump in my throat. Instead of answering, I nod. Francesca goes through the choreography for today's lesson and sends one pair after the other to the center of the room.

"Zoe, Jase, you're next," she says at some point.

Jase holds out his hand to me. I give him mine, and my heart leaps. As usual.

"Ready?" he asks as we take position.

I nod, and he lets me go, putting his hands on my waist. His grasp is firm and secure as we begin to move. Familiar. Just like his steps. And mine.

Our movements are soft and flowing, in harmony. We go through the choreography, and every turn, every jump, and every step is perfect. For the first time.

I smile as Jase lifts me, and I feel incredibly light. Free. I'm dancing, and it's the way it should be, the way it always was. It hurts and it heals. I engage my body and my heart, and I'm sore, but in the best possible way. Because I'm doing what I love. And Jase is all around me: behind, beside, lifting and holding me. He helps me not to lose my balance. We're a single unit, fully in sync, and my heart pounds with joy while my body works. It's hard work, and the steps are difficult. More difficult than usual. But we can do this. I know what he's going to do before he does it. I know when he's going to hold out his hand, when he's going to guide me, when he's going to turn me, and when he's going to let me go.

I don't hesitate as he wraps one arm around my waist and grasps my thigh with his other hand. I reach for his shoulder, bend one leg while I stretch the other upward far behind him. He bends his supporting leg and leans over my arched upper body, and we remain that way for a moment, breathing heavily.

Sweat covers my skin, making the long-sleeved leotard stick to me, and my whole body glows with adrenaline and pure joy. Jase kisses the sensitive skin just below my neck before he straightens us up again, and my feet find the floor. For a moment, I lean against him and return his gaze in the mirror, ignoring the fact that we're not alone, because this moment belongs to us.

He smiles again, and so do I. Right now, everything is totally perfect.

EPILOGUE
Jase

It's the last school day before vacation. We're lying on my bed with my laptop in front of us, a cheesy Christmas movie that Zoe wanted to see flickering across the screen, because tomorrow is Christmas Eve. But I'm not really focused on it.

"Hey," Zoe says, taking my hand. "You don't have to worry about the scholarship, I'm sure of it."

I shrug, because I don't share her optimism, even though she's been trying to convince me for weeks. Because things have been good. Very good. Since Zoe came back, everything has been so much easier and so much better. Especially the pas de deux. We make a damn good pair, but I don't know if it's enough. If everything I've done over the last few months is enough. Maybe I could have done more.

"You *really* don't need to worry." She nods emphatically, looking extremely sure of herself.

I want to believe it too. I really do. But the possibility that I won't get the scholarship still looms over me. "We'll see. Pearson said he'd let me know before the performance."

"Then he'd better hurry. It's in two hours," Zoe says with an eyebrow raised, then gets off the bed. I want her to come back to bed with me because I immediately miss the warmth of her body.

Her closeness. I want to have her with me as often and as close as I can. But before I can ask her, she says, "We should start getting ready now, shouldn't we?"

She holds out her hand, and I let her pull me out of bed. "You don't need two hours to get ready, and I definitely don't."

"I know. But if Peason wants to talk to you first, you should be ready. So come on." She kisses me gently and then pushes me toward the bathroom.

The suit I picked up from my parents' house two days ago is hanging in my closet. It was the first time we saw or spoke to each other in weeks. It was . . . okay. Zoe came with me, and we left quickly. I'm not ready to have a proper conversation with them yet. They don't like it, but they accept it, and that's all I can ask.

"Do you think they'll come?" she asks. Of course she's noticed that I'm staring at the dark suit longer than necessary.

"Maybe. But I don't think so. Lia's not dancing today, and neither am I. There's no reason for them to come."

"Maybe they want to see you. And Lia too."

"Maybe," I say noncommittally, but I don't believe it. I don't know if I *want* them to come either. Seeing Dad would just stress me out.

Zoe sizes me up for a moment, and the look in her brown eyes is hard to interpret. Then she nods and drops the subject.

An hour later, I've been ready for a while, and Zoe is just slipping into her dress when there's a knock on my door. Zoe looks up in surprise. "Is he really coming to your room to tell you about the scholarship?"

"I doubt it," I reply, zipping up Zoe's dress and opening the door.

It's not Pearson waiting in the hallway but Camille. She looks just as stiff as she did on the day she brought me to Pearson so he could tell me that my tuition fees weren't being paid anymore. My heart twitches anxiously.

Fuck.

This is not a good sign.

"Jase, could you please come with me? Mr. Pearson would like to speak to you."

I just nod, because I can't make a sound. My throat suddenly feels constricted, my stomach sinks, and for a second, I have to repress the urge to slam the door and pretend Camille's not there. If I don't get this scholarship, I don't know what the hell I'm going to do.

Yesterday, Mom offered to pay the fees again, and I know it was totally idiotic to say no, but I don't want her money. I don't want to feel like she's only doing it because she has a guilty conscience. And I don't want to worry every day about whether she'll change her mind. It's happened before, after all.

If I don't get the scholarship, then maybe I'll think about it. I need another plan. I'm pretty sure Zoe and her parents would help me, but I don't want that either. Not unless it's absolutely necessary. But it might be, and I'd rather have them help me than my own parents.

"Yes, he will," Zoe answers for me, giving me a gentle shove. I look over my shoulder, giving her a glance that says everything and nothing. She stands on tiptoe and kisses me. She strokes my cheek. "It's going to be okay," she whispers. "I promise."

I want to tell her that she can't promise me anything she has no influence over, but I let it go because I really need to believe her.

"See you." I kiss her again because I can't help it, breathe in her lavender scent, and then follow Camille, who is impatiently tapping her foot at how long I'm taking.

At the end of the hallway, I stop for a moment, turn around, and see Zoe standing outside my room. She's smiling, and she's so damn beautiful it hurts. Her red hair is braided into a crown around her head, with individual strands falling around her face. She's wearing a dark blue dress that I will definitely have to help her take off later.

Get a move on.

Sam's voice echoes in my head, and my heart tightens. But it doesn't hurt as much as it used to. He's not here, but somehow he is. He's always here. Because he will always be a part of me.

I take a deep breath and finally leave the dorm. It's cold and dark outside. Heavy clouds are covering the sky, and it looks like it might snow. Camille doesn't say a word as she leads me to the administration building and up the stairs to Pearson's office. My stomach cramps, and with every step, I get more nervous. But it's going to work out. I'm going to get the scholarship. I have to.

Camille stops in front of Pearson's office, knocks briefly, and then gestures for me to go inside. I open the door and walk in, just as nervous as I was at the start of the semester. This time, he's got to have good news for me.

Please.

Zoe

I think the last time I was this nervous was at an audition, when my future depended on it. Today, it's Jase's future that's at stake. He hasn't come back yet, and I'm trying to convince myself that's a good sign, because why else would they have been talking so long? Camille picked him up forty-five minutes ago. The performance is about to start.

"Don't forget to breathe," Caleb whispers, giving me an encouraging smile. He's here with Parker, Mom, and Dad, even though I'm not on stage today. They wanted to come anyway, and Mom insisted that we all go home with them afterward. Because tradition demands that we spend the last evening before the Christmas holidays together, watching movies and drinking cocoa with marshmallows until we're sick. This year there are six of us, not four, and I think it's going to be wonderful. Jase is spending Christmas with us. He doesn't want to celebrate with his family, and I'm glad that he'll be with me so I won't have to worry whether he's okay.

Like I'm worrying now. I take a deep breath, but it doesn't help. My heart is beating much too fast, and I'm so restless that I can't stand still. He *has to* get the scholarship. He can't lose his place. He belongs here. He needs to dance.

"Look." Parker's excited voice brings me back to the present.

I turn around, and there he is. Finally. I'm already walking straight toward him before I even think about it. Why does he look so serious? Why isn't he smiling?

"How did it go?" I ask when I reach him and take his hands

in mine. We lock fingers automatically, and I immediately feel a little calmer.

Then he smiles. The same smile I fell in love with. "It looks like I'm allowed to stay."

I want to answer, but my voice isn't under my control. My eyes are blurred by tears. They overflow, and Jase gently dries them off my cheeks.

"I hope those are tears of joy and you're not crying because Francesca might make me your dance partner next semester."

I stand on tiptoe and kiss him, which should be a clear enough answer. I'm so relieved my legs are shaking.

"Congratulations, man." Caleb appears next to us and slaps Jase on the shoulder, grinning, as do Parker and Dad. Mom gives him a big hug and tells him how proud she is of him, and he blushes. My heart is about to burst, because for a change, everything has actually turned out well. Everything is the way it should be.

Then Jase takes my hand, and we walk into the auditorium together because the show is about to start.

The Sleeping Beauty.

Emily is the perfect Aurora. She's beautiful and graceful. I watch her, and the thought of standing on that stage myself in three years makes me smile, because I know it will happen. Somehow, I will get there. I will dance, and so will Jase.

The thought makes me absurdly happy.

And hours later, when we make our way to my parents' house, I'm still happy. Caleb, Parker, Mom, and Dad are making cocoa and looking for the perfect Christmas movie while Jase and I go out to the treehouse after I've exchanged my high heels for winter boots.

"What are you doing?" he asks curiously, but I just shake my head and smile as I climb up the ladder to the treehouse in front of him. It's freezing cold, and we won't be able to stay up here for long, but that's not the plan. Maybe I shouldn't give him his Christmas present early, but it feels right.

I switch on the fairy lights, and a warm glow fills the little room. My pillows and blankets are neatly stowed in a corner. Right next to them is the small wooden box where I stored Jase's secrets.

The box I'm about to give him so he can put the notes I've written to him in it. His secrets and mine. Our story. With all the letters I wrote last year but never gave him. I know he did the same thing.

My heart beats wildly as I hand him the box. He opens the lid, and his gaze softens.

"Tell me your secrets, and I'll tell you mine," he murmurs, his voice deep and hoarse and so, so soft. He puts the box to one side and pulls me close. Everything inside me starts to tingle as he takes my face in his hands, and his thumb brushes my lips.

I have to smile; I know what I'm going to do. I tell him my last secret. The one that isn't really a secret and never was. But I have to tell him anyway.

"I love you." The words come so easily. Maybe because Jase knows it anyway. But it's the first time I've ever said it out loud. Here in the treehouse, where it all began. Then he tells me his last secret. And for the first time, it's the same as mine.

AFTERWORD

Visiting the New England School of Ballet with Zoe and Jase and delving deeper into the world of ballet was so much fun, and I'm already looking forward to returning with the other characters.

I did an incredible amount of research on the subject of ballet beforehand, but of course, not all the scenes in this novel are 100% accurate, even though I made it a priority to portray everything as authentically as possible.

I painted a very romantic picture of ballet in *Hold Me* because—let's be honest—Zoe and Jase already had enough problems on their plates and shouldn't have to deal with the pain and pressure of always having to be the best as well.

But there will be three more volumes of the New England School of Ballet series, with Rayne and East, Lia and Phoenix, and Skye and Gabriel. They all have their own dreams and issues when it comes to ballet. Each book will have a different focus, and I hope that in the end, even if I can't do the world of ballet justice, I will at least come close to reality.

For now, however, I hope that you were able to fall in love and dream and that we will meet again next semester.

ACKNOWLEDGMENTS

Writing this is incredibly difficult because it means that Zoe and Jase's story has come to an end, and now I have to let them go. They've been with me for so long—through so many different versions of themselves—that saying goodbye hurts in a way that feels different from parting with the characters in my previous books.

Zoe and Jase have been with me for almost two years, with just a few short breaks along the way, and they've truly pushed me to my limits. I don't think I've ever cried as much as I did while writing this book. They broke my heart in more ways than one and made me doubt myself countless times. But in the end, they also showed me what I'm capable of—and, most importantly, how their story was meant to be told.

Of course, I didn't do this alone. There are so many people who helped bring this book to life, and the truth is, it would never have become what it is without them.

Katharina, thank you for everything. I don't know how I could ever put into words how much you've helped me with this book (and all the others). Thank you for the long—and on my part, often tearful—phone calls, for your constant encouragement, and for always reminding me of what I can do. Thank you for believing in me, for being there whenever I needed you, and for understanding me so deeply, especially as someone who is so easily overwhelmed by self-doubt.

Steffi, we both know I wouldn't have made it through the editing process without you. Thank you for once again bringing out the best in my writing, for letting me bombard you with calls and messages, and for always talking me down from my doubts.

Thank you to Stephanie Bubley and the entire LYX team for your trust, your passion, and your dedication, which shine through in every book. I'm so grateful to be part of Team LYX and for the home you've given me and my stories. A huge thank you as well to the world's best marketing team and to LYX Audio for bringing my stories to life with the most wonderful narrators.

Kathrin, thank you for your support, for always being available, and for simply being there when I need you.

Vivi, thank you—again and again—for everything. For being there for Zoe and Jase from the very beginning, through every version of their story, and for sticking by me through my endless moments of panic. Thank you for lifting me up whenever I felt I couldn't go on, for listening to everything I needed to say, and for being such an incredible friend. I think we've just accepted that we'll always be each other's crying buddies, right?

Becca, Elena, Kara, Maike—thank you for your friendship, for reading and loving Zoe and Jase's story, for answering my endless messages, and for helping me silence my doubts.

To my beta readers—Marie, Kalin, Franka, and Katharina—thank you for your enthusiasm, your thoughtful feedback, and your love for this story. A special thanks to Katharina, as a former ballet dancer, for your careful eye and invaluable guidance on those details.

Sarah, I truly don't know what I would have done without you these past few months. Thank you for always being there, for your unwavering support, and for finding the most beautiful words for *Hold Me*. I'm so lucky to have you as a friend.

Mom, Christina, and Jan—thank you for always being there for me, for your love, and for your never-ending support.

Benedikt, thank you for making it through this past year by my side. You keep saying you don't know anything about writing, but you support me anyway, and I wouldn't be where I am without you. I love you, and I'm so excited for all that's still to come for us.

And finally, thank you to all the booksellers, bloggers, readers, and book people everywhere. Your love and support mean the world to me. I hope I can keep writing stories for you for a very long time.

ABOUT THE AUTHOR

Anna Savas was born in 1993 and cannot imagine a life without books. Ever since her childhood, writing has been like breathing to her, and she always carries a notebook with her just in case a new idea decides to visit her. Anna loves to hear from her readers on Instagram (@annasavass).

CONTENT WARNING

(and spoiler warning!)

This book contains potentially triggering content.
This includes

Rape
Panic attacks
Death
Grief